CRUCIBLE

SETH HADDON

SH BOOKS

CRUCIBLE
Seth Haddon

Book Cover by WendiBones

Internal images by Gaia Smilevska (holographing)

Chapter header illustrations by Seth Haddon

Edited by Drew McBlain

1st edition 2025

GPSR COMPLIANCE

Manufacturer: GuangZhou SeSe Printing Company, Ltd.

301, NO. 233 Pinkang Rd, Shiqiao St, Panyu District

Guangzhou City, Guangdong Province, China, 511401

Product: Hardcover Book

Materials: Eco-friendly paper material with vegetable soy bean ink.

EU GPSR Authorised Representative:

EUREPSTAR GmbH

Schkiterstr. 3

85057 Ingolstadt, Germany

www.eurepstar.com

This book was manufactured using paper and ink products in accordance with commercial standards.

Category (New Adult Fiction)
Genre (Fantasy/ Romance / LGBT)

ALSO BY SETH HADDON

The World of Reforged Series

Reforged

Reborn

Reclaimed

Upcoming

Volatile Memory

CRUCIBLE

SETH HADDON

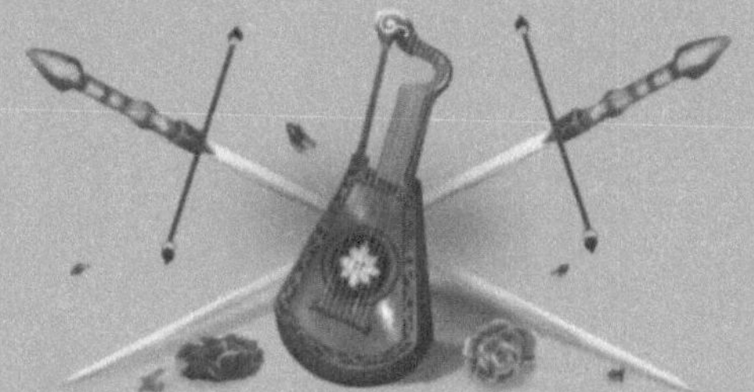

For those who have carried impossible feelings, knowing they could never last.

Palace of Cres Stros

MAP BY SÁMHLAOCH SWORDS

PROLOGUE

"Your father is dead."

Zavrius Dued Vuuthrik was twelve when he heard those words. He was too young to understand the full weight of them, still inexperienced enough that he couldn't see the next tense decade of Uslethian politics unfolding before him. The unruly stain left by the empire was invisible to him, as were the old wounds in both country and people that were splitting open now that the King had been killed.

For Zavrius, all that happened when he learned of his father's demise was a great shuddering relief.

When the rest of his siblings cried out—tearing at their hair, shouting abuse at whichever Rezwyn dog had speared King Sirellius through the neck—Zavrius suppressed a smile. He dug his nails into the palm of his hand, holding onto the biting feeling as his skin broke, lest he slip away somewhere triumphant and happy and give himself away.

Sirellius was dead and with him, a decade-long nightmare. But even at that young age, Zavrius knew when to keep things to himself.

He surveyed the room. Arasne, their mother, addressed them

in the King's private study, an office within the royal family's wing, which held their private library, the music room, and their bedchambers. In retrospect, Zavrius should have known what had happened the instant she called the meeting there.

Whilst alive, Sirellius would have never suffered anyone to enter without his approval and live.

His mother had with her a stringed instrument, which, in all honestly, Zavrius had never seen her without. It sat over the desk, on top of piles of loose papers and surrounded by scrolls left by the King before his journey to the front. Fresh air filled the office, curling in from the windows behind Arasne's head that opened onto a grassy corridor and hedges that ran the palace wall. A faint floral scent wafted inside, and Zavrius smelled the other lingering thing: ichor. Not pulled from the distant gedrok corpse standing eternally in the palace gardens, but still hovering in the air around them.

Arasne had been playing something before she summoned them. *What had she been trying to chase away?* Zavrius wondered. The ghost of her husband? Her own nerves?

Zavrius' siblings were slumped in various states of shock. They had come in and stood waiting for the news in order of their status. Zavrius, the youngest and fifth in line to the throne, thus stood closest to the door. Beside him was Gideonus, fourteen, and a brute. Gideonus had his thick black hair cropped close to the skull. He lacked the characteristic Dued Vuuthrik curl, but instead inherited Sirellius' disdain for Zavrius, who had been 'too soft from birth'. As a result of this ingrained disgust, Gideonus had positioned himself far closer to their next brother, Lysio, as if proximity to Zavrius might effeminize him.

Lysio had not acquired their father's bulky body the way Gideonus and the others had. He shared the slight form of Zavrius and their mother, Arasne, but none of their appreciation for the finer things in life. He had proven himself to their bully of a father—and thus avoided the disdain poured onto Zavrius—by attempting to emulate their eldest brother, Theo. When that had failed, he let himself get bruised and bloody; he trained mainly on speed, learning the rapier, focusing on his footwork to avoid the harsher blows from Sirellius' training.

Next to him stood Avidia, Zavrius' only sister. She was seventeen and frightening. Avidia had shoulder-length hair that curled and frizzed in the heat and deep-set eyes that were always searching. Arasne had once hoped to pass her own unique style of fighting to her daughter, but Avidia had wanted to win Sirellius's approval more than her mother's. She was strong but smart, too, especially with poisons. She was itching for the field of war and had been for as long as Zavrius had been able to comprehend words.

And then there was Theo.

He was nearly Sirellius's shadow. At eighteen, Theo towered over the rest of them. He had thick, ropey muscle in his arms—which he showed off every chance he got—and was the most relentless teaser of Zavrius behind Sirellius himself. With their father dead, the only thing standing between Theo and the throne of Usleth was their mother.

But from the look in Theo's eyes, he wasn't thinking about that. Not yet.

Zavrius had been able to recognize rage for a long while. He knew the way people wore it, the way it pricked at the fine muscles in the face, the way fury gleamed in the eye. Theo buckled with it. He struck the wall, muffling a violent scream with the dull impact of his fist, and for a moment, he turned away from the rest of the room and heaved. His body shook before falling into a terrifying stillness. Zavrius's body reacted the way it always did to this kind of violent display. He went prey-animal still, all the muscles in his body tensing. His eyes flicked to the door, to the promise of safety, and the speed of his heart urged him toward that waiting escape. It took years of practice to keep still, and at the very least, he noticed his siblings reacting similarly: not scared the way he was, but vigilant, standing to attention as if Theo had issued an order.

"We cannot let this go unanswered," Theo hissed finally. He cast a look back over his shoulder, eyes flashing wildly. The sunlight glanced off his high cheekbones and sent his brown skin a striking bronze. One day, he would be an excellent king—at least for Usleth's artists. "What is your order? When do we march?"

One by one, all of them turned to Arasne. She was in her mid-fifties, but ever graceful. Her curly hair was kept in intricate braids away from her face, the strands once a light brown and now the color of bleached starlight. She had her hands clasped together—had dressed and made herself proper as if she were addressing the nobles instead of her own children—and two attendants flanked her, both with their heads lowered. They had been so good at their jobs that Zavrius had forgotten they were there until his mother gave an unseeable signal, and they peeled away from her, shuffling quickly out of the room.

Everyone stood tensely for several seconds after the door closed behind them. Then Arasne shifted minutely, blinking as she inhaled deeply. With the gentle breeze playing in her hair, the sound of summer insects buzzing outside and the scent of flowers filling the air, it all appeared like a scene in a play. No misery could corrupt such beauty.

"In this moment," Arasne murmured quietly, "I am not your mother. I am your Queen."

A stillness settled over everyone once more. Avidia snorted beneath her breath, and Arasne did not hesitate. She struck her hand across the instrument, nails grazing over the gut strings, and with this single chord, she sent the air spinning toward Avidia's cheek. The skin split apart slightly, and Avidia hissed, hand flying to press closed the small wound.

"Do not," Arasne said, and no one moved.

Zavrius was young and didn't quite comprehend what was happening. Years later, when he himself was king and battling the ebb and flow of the Uslethian nobility's death wise, he would look back at this moment and realize Arasne had to secure herself; her children were all violent mongrels, and if she showed a hint of weakness, they would attack. This pivotal moment could have changed the trajectory of Uslethian history, could have meant a foolish, prolonged war and an eventual outcome where their tiny peninsula was absorbed by the Rezwyn Empire.

But as a child, with a body that reacted to nearby shouting and violence as if it was *his* flesh directly suffering, Zavrius could not comprehend anything beyond this moment. What he knew for certain was that his siblings had no respect for their mother. That's what Zavrius feared, that the very reasons they found him intolerable and disappointing would be why they would now choose to undermine the crown.

Arasne wasn't having it. She pulled back the large, throne-like wingback and sat in it. She seemed to fight herself. For half a second, she crumpled forward, head resting in her hand, but she quickly righted herself and sent an assessing look over her five children.

"From now on, I am your Queen first. You disobey me, and you disobey your kingdom. I tell you this as a warning and out of love: if any of you conspire against me, if any of you act on your emotions, I will not hesitate to remove you."

It was a euphemism, that term. All of them, even Zavrius, stiffened at the implication, because it was so unlike what any of them knew of Arasne that, at that moment, it almost seemed like Sirellius's ghost was speaking through her.

Avidia removed her hand from her cheek, which was stained a reddish-pink from the smeared blood. "What have you done?"

Arasne's face remained passive, but her eyes—those eyes! Zavrius knew the tremor in them, the fear for what she was about to say, and so he knew.

"It's the end," he whispered, just quietly enough for Gideonus to hear.

His brother spun. "What did you say?"

"Quiet," Arasne ordered. And then, "The death of King Sirellius and the obliteration of a great number of our forces at the Westgar front have forced me to reconsider Usleth's part in this war."

"Part in this war?" Theo said, objecting. "They threaten our very existence. They mean to kill us all! Destroy our culture, take our power—"

"Thank you, Theo, I am well aware," Arasne spoke sharply and raised a hand to still her son. "That being said, I am not as delusional as your father. If we continue the way we're going, Usleth will die in another way."

She said nothing more for a while, and everyone—save for Gideonus, the dolt—unwound as understanding settled on them.

"I've appealed to Emperor Nio Beumeut for an end to this war."

Outrage. Instant, shouting defiance from everyone in that room except Zavrius.

"There will be a treaty. A treaty!" Arasne repeated, shouting over the clamor, and then more beautiful notes rang out in the study as she began to play, and in playing, summoned a calming arcane melody.

Unwillingly, Zavrius's tension softened. He went slack and puppet-like, and his mind felt easy in that way he knew to be falsely conjured—but where the others were Sirellius's spawn, Zavrius was hers. He knew how to defend against Arasne's attacks, and after finding his resolve, he shook off the worst of the magic and looked his mother in the eye.

He saw the faintest hint of a smile—praise was his reward—and then she softened her playing so they had the mind to listen to her, but not the will to undermine her.

"This is not something I want to make a habit of," she said. "I do not want unwitting slaves for children. I want your support. I know you don't like it. I know you want your father avenged. But I want you to think of it like this: we have not conceded territory. If the emperor accepts my terms, then we remain independent, and we will not suffer so many Uslethian deaths. And whilst I am Queen, it will be this way until I am certain we would win against the empire and its extensive army. Until then—there will be peace."

And one by one, each of Zavrius's siblings broke from the spell as Arasne stopped playing. One by one, they glanced at each other—even Zavrius—and one by one, they all bowed to Usleth's new Queen.

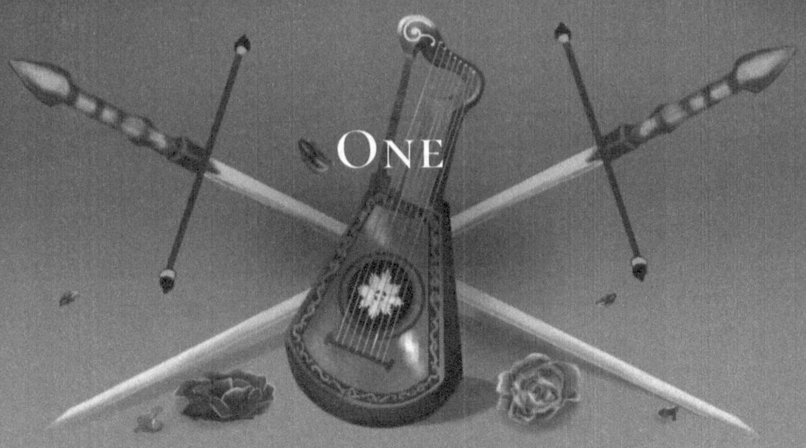

One

Summer in Cres Stros always smelled like jasmine and tasted faintly of floral sweat on the back of Zavrius' tongue. The heat had everyone perspiring and then masking the smell with intense oils, so every part of the palace was overpowered by a cloying aroma.

Which was, Zavrius told himself, the reason he was spending so much of his summer outside.

The palace garden, with its arching, skeletal monstrosity, and its many flowers, was somewhat frequented by the nobles at court, but once Zavrius had carved out a spot for himself and planted himself there as a semi-permanent fixture—forever in performance, always plucking at his lute—he had received fewer and fewer bothersome visitors.

He knew the rumors. He couldn't actually avoid them, no matter how much he tried. He had heard plenty just this summer: *Zavrius was the runt of Sirellius' children. Zavrius was, very possibly, not one of Sirellius' children at all* (though this rumor had been stifled very quickly when the noble responsible for spreading it realized the three-fold treason he was speaking by damning the honor of the Queen, assuming the late king was a cuck, and questioning Zavrius' legitimacy). *Zavrius was little more than a petulant dandy prince—a fair assumption—and lacking in the most basic of manners.*

And the kicker: *should Zavrius ever be let near Uslethian political affairs, he would be solely responsible for its demise.*

Zavrius couldn't quite fault the rumors. He was smart enough to know why they existed and spread, and there certainly was very little in his own actions that might dissuade them.

These had been circling for years, in one way or another, but never had Zavrius overheard so many of them with his own ears. He couldn't account for the shift in the nobility's attitudes; no one told him much of anything. But a great unease sat in Zavrius' gut, and he wished it would go away.

So he had sequestered himself in the garden in hopes of avoiding other people.

The fact of the matter was that Zavrius differed too greatly from his siblings, having inherited much of Arasne's personality. A bad thing, according to both his siblings and the nobles— he had been coddled by her. Empathy, a love for music, and little desire to be stabbed or beaten or humiliated meant he was weak.

So be it.

He sat on the grass, on a blanket he had dragged out here himself. Over his lap lay a beautiful mahogany lute harp, which had been nothing more than a well-made instrument until his mother had allowed him to change the strings in secret. They'd originally been made of gut, but he had restrung the instrument with gedrok tendon, because, despite all the rumors, Zavrius *did* have an ounce of discipline and had wanted to learn his mother's trade. For years, whilst Theo and the others bruised their bodies unnecessarily, Zavrius had been training to draw from the pool of arcane power all Dued Vuuthriks and paladins had access to. A power cultivated in symbiosis with the gedroks.

Zavrius remembered holding Arasne's lute-harp for the first time, feeling the air rush out of him as a tingle of arcane energy ran electric up his arms. Breathless, he'd thought, *nothing will be the same.*

But to be a true Dued Vuuthrik, he would have to reconcile his love of music with the necessity of his country: learning how to kill.

Stop thinking.

He had been doing an awful lot of that lately. Thinking about the past. Thinking about the future, straining to comprehend what might come next. The first morning he had been with Arasne, and she had coughed—coughed so long and hoarsely Zavrius' stomach had grown nauseous—he'd immediately known something was wrong.

Unrest sputtered through his heart, but she wasn't telling him a thing. Petra had said nothing. His Uncle Lestr had said nothing. And it was these small betrayals that had flared Zavrius' petulance. He wanted to be alone, sure, but he also wanted his absence from the palace noticed.

But a week had passed already, and no one had said a thing.

It mattered not. He had spent the week training, turning his fear and his upset into something useful; emotion became a grand resource to pull from.

Today, though, Zavrius simply wanted to play music, without experiencing the fatigue of fueling violent magic with his body's power. He sat and strummed at the lute, sang to himself, and more than once peered through the hedges to watch the paladins train, which was resolutely *not* another reason he had made this his spot.

Zavrius stilled his hand on the lute and closed his eyes. He willed all his worry from his mind and let every thought be muted by the distant clamor, the slam of metal against gedrok bone. Bodies rattled in the paladin armor, and the men and women cried out in raging defiance, pain, victory, defeat. Zavrius kept telling himself he wouldn't look at the damn paladins, but before he'd even had time to finish the thought, he was peering through the hedges.

If Zavrius was being honest with himself, he didn't dislike the smell of sweat. He didn't even hate the sickening overlaps of body oils as much as he claimed. Sure, he'd wanted to avoid rumors, and wanted to sulk conspicuously. He also liked it out here for a myriad of reasons, truly—but namely that he could safely spy on the paladins without adding yet another rumor to his name.

"Is this really how you're spending your summer?"

Zavrius jumped.

Theo Dued Vuuthrik looked down on him with hollow, joyless eyes. He smelled of a floral body oil, and the wine and onions of his most recent meal. Beneath the disdain, his gaze was distant, foggy with tipsiness, and the air between them shivered. Behind him, his retinue stood and whispered in low voices.

With a heavy heart, embarrassment crushed Zavrius' chest. In vain, he hoped to keep the flush from his face. Theo's summer seemed about as productive as Zavrius', though his eldest brother would claim to be winning noble hearts. The nobles in question were guests of the court, gathered in hopes of plumping their own names, or winning Theo's favor.

"I have been practicing," Zavrius managed to say, though his voice came out thick and defensive.

"I had dared to hope you would be doing something useful with your time." Theo stood tall and folded his arms, glancing over his shoulder at the mass of training bodies to his left. Zavrius resolutely did not follow his gaze. "You may be the youngest and without hope for the throne, but I would really expect that by the time I'm king, you'll be more than our little court jester."

Those words caught in Zavrius' mind like a burr. *By the time I'm king. . .*

Zavrius forgot to be offended by his brother's attitude. Did Theo know their mother was sick?

"What do you know?" Zavrius hissed quickly.

Theo's brow buckled, not understanding. He turned away from the paladins and leaned down. Zavrius scrunched his nose up at the scent of his breath and drew back cautiously.

"I know you're out here for perverted reasons, little brother. Do not do something you'll regret. There are courtesans for a reason. Have some pretty boy suck your cock and be done with this fixation."

Silence lingered between them.

Zavrius' chest burned. The child in him wanted this conversation to be over, wanted to look away and wait until Theo grew bored and wandered off. But he knew enough about his eldest brother now to realize Theo reveled in Zavrius' despair. Like an extension of their father, a lingering shade. And so Zavrius would lean into foolishness and brashness and take his own joy in how it upset Theo.

He raised his chin defiantly, cocked his head, raised a brow. "And what of you? Drinking your days away. You went hunting, I presume, but seem to have killed nothing but more of your dignity." Then, for the simple pettiness of it, he added, "You reek of onion."

He pitched that last point very loudly. The looming gedrok skeleton became his ally, echoing his ridicule of Theo's little pawns. It made everything worth it, just to see the way color flamed on Theo's cheeks, burning away the warm olive undertone and leaving him with his shame.

Theo shook. Embarrassment did not come easily to him. Theo

lacked the years of practice that, through his own quips and abuse, had built a dam of resilience in Zavrius.

"You and I couldn't be more different." Theo moved closer, pitched his voice low. "Listen to me. It won't be long before I am king. Do you understand? You *will* have no place at this court except to be my jester. You are already the laughingstock of our family; I will not allow you to wile your life away plucking at your idiotic instruments, taking whichever boy you want to bed, and besmirching our name—not when the rest of us are trying to live in our father's honor."

Zavrius looked past him to the retinue that lingered nearby. Something must have happened on that hunt. A conversation or a joke that hurt Theo's ego—some mention of the multitude of rumors surrounding Zavrius had prompted this lecture.

Was Zavrius meant to go prostrate? Was he meant to beg for Theo's forgiveness right now, stain his beautiful flowing tunic in the grass, and whine until Theo's pity absolved him?

As if.

Zavrius plucked a few strings. He considered showing Theo the extent of what he could do, but something in his gut urged him not to. Part of Zavrius' protection at court was appearing useless.

Instead, he smiled broadly at his brother. "What exactly do you want from me, Theo?"

Nostrils flaring, a grim smile on his mouth, Theo murmured, "I want you to stop feeling sorry for yourself, pick up a fucking sword, and become a man."

"Haven't you heard?" Zavrius said with a shrug. "It's an era of peace."

"You're a fool to think that. You're a fool content to languish his life away."

A tense moment stretched and only grew thickly uncomfortable; whatever Theo wanted from this interaction, Zavrius would not give him. But Zavrius could not let down his guard. With their shared audience, Theo would do much to shame him if it meant saving face.

Yet, he could have laughed. Zavrius spread his arms and shrugged, hoping the casualness of his gesture would communicate the layered emotion; *look at me, I am what you say, I do what you say, and I live happily. Does it enrage you, brother, to see me like this?*

Before he was done with the gesture, Theo had snatched the lute from Zavrius' lap. Time slowed. Shock hit Zavrius hard, and he saw every moment slowly. Theo wrenched it back and turned it over with a mocking laugh. He barely waited for the look of shock and upset to cloud Zavrius' face before he took it by the neck and spun.

Theo whipped the fragile instrument against the femur of the gedrok. A deafening crack rippled up the ancient creature's skeletal leg, echoing back the destruction of the beautiful lute; the supple wood fractured and broke apart. Splinters flew. Nothing but the gedrok-tendon strings were left to hold the thing together; it resembled a crumpled, sharp body, a life snuffed out. Zavrius let out an enraged scream.

It happened in a flash. He wasn't thinking beyond this moment, couldn't possibly be expected to consider the chains of consequence—the incendiary action had made his heart combust. Suddenly, Zavrius was on his feet, and a second later, teary-eyed, shouting, a firebug, he punched Theo in the face.

His brother's head rebounded with a muttered curse. A spritz of blood arced in the air. And for a second—just one, glorious second—Theo looked down at Zavrius with enormous confusion.

Shaking, adrenaline-high, Zavrius bore all his teeth in a wild and happy grin.

Theo wiped his nose free of blood and hissed, "You pathetic little—"

"Boys!"

The call cut across the garden. Suddenly, Zavrius could feel the heat of the day pricking at his neck. His heart thudded and his body jittered with the thrill of violence, but he made himself still.

Petra, their aunt and sister to the late King Sirellius, stood ascetically, body and face devoid of emotion. Her eyes betrayed her coolness, though. Unfettered rage burned in them, and finally, she let the emotion trickle through to the rest of her face. Her lip curled off her teeth, disdainful.

"Out," she hissed without looking away from the brothers. Theo's retinue scattered like rats, and Zavrius felt Theo deflate next to him. He had lost some social game and would pay the price for it later.

This was another reason Zavrius leaned so gladly into the hedonistic image thrust upon him: no one ever expected his brilliance.

"Childlike and disappointing." Petra's voice was clipped. She wore a long, layered dress that hid her wrists; her hands disappeared in the opposite sleeves of the garment, and she held her arms close to her chest. Zavrius imagined her limbs like anchors, like Petra was grounding herself with her posture.

She flashed Zavrius a look. "Ridiculous. You have been out here sulking—"

"—*practicing*," Zavrius cut in.

"—*sulking* for one reason or another. You may do what you wish as a prince, so long as that does not involve embarrassing your mother."

Zavrius' jaw tightened. He had been sitting pretty, minding his own business; he had been training his arcane ability, and occasionally letting his eyes and mind wander when he spied beautiful, glistening men attacking each other. Theo had come to *him* for the sole purpose of disrupting this otherwise innocent activity.

But he could say none of this. Not without inciting Theo's wrath.

Thankfully, Petra then turned her scalding gaze to Theo. "And *you*, who will be our King," –there it was again, like a horrible prophecy, this 'will be', this close inevitability. Arasne was sick. How sick? How close to death? What did they all *know?* The Queen had been coughing. But that was it. Surely that was it. A brief illness, not something that would require political plays.

Petra continued, "You should not need to prove yourself to guests of this court by intimidating your youngest brother, let alone any of your siblings. You are all Dued Vuuthriks."

"And we are measured by the weakest among us," Theo snapped.

The silence carried until Petra sighed. Zavrius' body did not relax. He felt the tide shift, waves carrying him further and further out to sea until he was completely isolated.

Petra asked, "What is your intention, your grace?"

In that moment, Zavrius shivered. He glanced down at the mess of the lute.

Theo spoke. "My intention is to make him stronger. The way Sirellius tried. I love my mother, I love the Queen, and I respect her decisions,"—bullshit—"but she needs counsel regarding my brother, for her love of him blinds her to the truth. He is. . ."

Useless? Pathetic? Weak? Zavrius waited for his descriptor, deciding he would love it like an epithet. However Theo thought of him, the fact it upset him so greatly was a great joy to Zavrius.

Theo cleared his throat and tried again. "It is for the betterment of Usleth that he be trained."

Zavrius waited for something more, but Theo made no quip or judgment of Zavrius' personality or character before Petra.

Their aunt looked between them and sighed once more, tone disdainful and tired. "I will speak to Queen Arasne. This is what I can offer."

"The lute," Zavrius whispered quickly. Petra looked down at it and back to Theo.

"She won't be happy," Petra muttered.

"A misunderstanding," Theo said with a bow.

"You'll be the one to tell her that, then," Petra muttered. "Pick it up."

Flushing and furious, Theo squatted and scraped up the pieces of the lute. Zavrius watched his expression carefully, but if Theo felt the spark of arcane in the destroyed instrument, he gave no indication.

With Theo standing, the corpse of the lute bundled in his arms, Petra bowed before the pair of them. Both Theo and Zavrius dipped their heads politely and watched her turn heel and walk away.

Zavrius bit his tongue and stared after her, refusing to turn even when Theo noticeably shifted to face him. Eventually, when it became clear Zavrius would not budge, Theo leaned forward.

"This is love, brother," Theo said wryly. "I love you as much as our father did."

And on the back of that biting comment, he turned and followed the remnants of his retinue as they retreated into the palace.

In the aftermath, Zavrius stared after them and let his heart race until it became clear his anxiety wasn't going anywhere. He held his breath and pressed his head against part of the gedrok skeleton, wishing he could imbue himself with its size, intimidation, and grace. But all he had was himself. A wiry body with only sinewy muscle. Anxiety with nowhere to go.

Zavrius turned, still breathing heavily, and found himself once more looking out at the paladins, whose training had ended. Free of their armor, most of them were in their underclothes, their skin opulent with sweat, glistening like jewels over their hardened bodies. The rise and fall of their chests matched Zavrius' own, but how different they were. How different their worlds. Zavrius looked upon them as he might a painting: one made of steel, and bone, and sweat.

Even from this distance, most of them wouldn't meet his gaze. They knew who he was and avoided him out of respect, disdain, or a confusing mix of both. But Zavrius only wished for one paladin to look his way.

And he did.

Balen of Westgar. Zavrius had made it a point to learn his name early. For years, that one had caught Zavrius' eye. He'd arrived at, what, ten? A sapling. He'd grown his roots here, broadened that trunk of a torso, and now he was a dashing young man of eighteen, white undershirt near transparent with sweat and clinging to his lean body. He saw Zavrius and smiled, lips quirking at the side, before he bowed, hand over his heart.

That glimpse of a smile held everything Zavrius wanted, and everything he couldn't have.

As if tethered to that motion, Zavrius felt a pull in his own heart, a quickness of it that thrilled him. He almost forgot himself entirely and tipped forward in a bow, too, but managed to stop himself with a nod of acknowledgment. Balen rose still smiling. Zavrius felt hot.

Ah, shit.

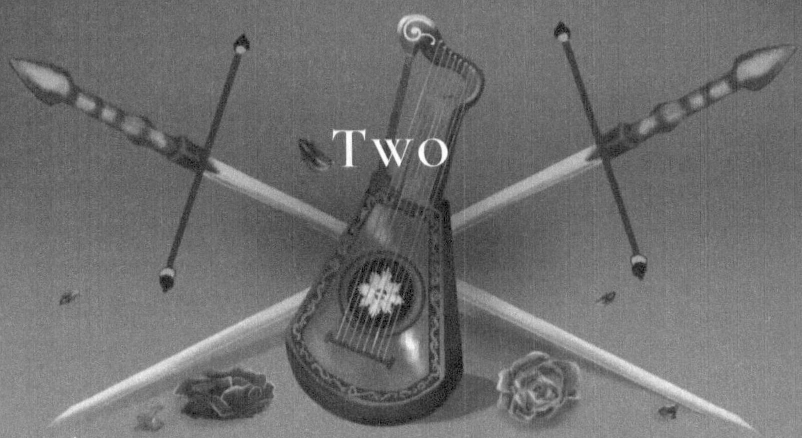

Two

summer storm drove Zavrius inside the next day, and he took more formally to his sulking in the hopes his mother might take the same pity on him as she might a sick cat. But when Queen Arasne finally chose to grace her son with her presence, she had very little sympathy for him.

Zavrius had thrown himself onto his bed some hours ago and had not moved.

Several things were happening. He was being petulant, absolutely. But he also had an emotion he could not name. It had the endless hollowness of grief, and some of the sharpness of self-hatred, but it wasn't quite either of those things. He felt at once outside himself and too much of his body.

When the door opened, he heard a sigh that belonged undoubtedly to the Queen, and all he could think of then was his father's voice. *Get up, you sorry excuse for a man.*

Even that biting tone could not motivate him.

The bed shifted with new weight. A hand came to rest near his spine, so gentle it felt barely there. Zavrius' stomach dropped out from under him—gedroks, she felt like a ghost already.

"What are you doing?"

"Mourning," he said, voice muffled by the pillow. He shifted to look up at her—he really had been crying at some point or another that morning, and now kohl had stained both his face and the pillow.

Queen Arasne tutted and reached out, grabbing Zavrius' chin and shaking it. "The lute was not your fault."

This has nothing to do with the lute. He could have said that. Should have said that, even. But vulnerability was dangerous in court, even in front of his mother. Before he had a chance to really think about it, he was lapsing into that old role; Zavrius the fool arose in his chest and beat down the complicated soup of emotion roiling in his gut.

"Well, I certainly know that!" he sat up, outraged, but quickly deflated. His anger had nowhere to go. It *really* wasn't about the lute, in the end.

Arasne had fawn-colored skin flecked with freckles and a slight, pointed face. Her hair now had the appearance of a splintered almond—brown shot through with white—and it curled thickly around her face, though she braided most of it down her back in complex designs. Fresh, tiny flowers adorned it. Her gown was a simple cream, though up close, the myriad of details overwhelmed Zavrius. The thread shone, imbued with ichor, and tiny medallions gilded the collar and sleeves. A refined look. Zavrius glanced up at her eyes, which were smudged lightly with kohl. Lines pinched at her face, and the skin beneath her eyes was sunken. Thin.

When Zavrius met his mother's gaze, all resolve buckled like kindling crumbling to ash. The Queen had always been very beautiful. She was beautiful now, even as age left its mark on her; thieved warmth from her skin and color from her hair; left her achromatic, a visual reminder of life seeping out of her—it was true, wasn't it? Tears threatened him once more.

Stop it. Stop it; she doesn't need this from you.

"Tell me what's wrong," the Queen said, looking very serious as she rubbed at his shoulder, though her tone betrayed her. Somewhere, deep down, she thought this was funny.

Which only made Zavrius more embarrassed.

"Theo," he said. "I can't do anything right for him. He is acting like—" and cut himself off.

It wasn't about Theo, it wasn't about the lute, it wasn't about his own incompetence or the inevitability of his disappointment to the dynasty whose name he carried.

It was about *her*.

Incognizant to his strife, his mother tilted her head. She smiled at him, cat-like. "Like what?"

Zavrius tightened his jaw. Saying it aloud. . .felt wrong. Dangerous. As if by speaking, he might manifest her an illness, if there wasn't already one there. He shook his head—her hand shot out, not unkindly, and she carefully pulled him back to look at her.

"You know I love all my children," she murmured, "but the others have always kept things from me. You never have. Let's not start now."

Gedroks, what a line. He rolled his eyes and drooped forward until he could rest his forehead against her clavicle. He closed his eyes. Her breathing soothed him, a promise of life.

Very quietly, he spoke as if confessing: "Like your reign will be. . . much shorter than it should be."

To her great credit, Queen Arasne did not react. There was no flinching or balking or surprise, and this gave him comfort until he realized the truth of what that meant.

He opened his eyes. From the angle he'd positioned himself, he was staring down at her lap. Her hand rested there, unmoving.

Had she always been so thin? Green veins shot serpent-like beneath the near translucent skin, and a horde of gedroks stampeded in his imagination, their bodies moving vaporous like smoke from a fire. Both Arasne and those ancient creatures shared the filmy, gossamer appearance to their flesh. He imagined his mother transformed like those eternal beasts. She would look the same, but she'd have all the grace and terrifying power of those ancient beasts. His mother: a permanent fixture, immune to decay.

But it wouldn't be like that at all.

Zavrius suddenly felt very small. Death was not new to him. His father had been skewered in the neck. He had grown up through war. Yet, somehow, he could feel the grand weight of expectation on him, and the crushing limit of his mortality. Eons shadowed him like a yawning chasm at his back. He could slip at any moment into that consuming stretch of time—he was overcome by his own insignificance, his own fragility, a young boy realizing for the third time that day alone that something was wrong.

He pulled away. Considered her. Looked his mother in the eyes.

She was dying. He knew it in his heart.

Zavrius did not move. Queen Arasne could have said so many things to assuage his fears. Zavrius waited, held all the patience in the world in his heart, biting back the nauseous fear infecting his chest; *say something. Tell me he's wrong. Please.*

She didn't say anything.

In the end, Zavrius had to speak, when the quiet became suffocating.

"Please don't go," he whispered.

She flinched and gripped his hand very hard. She said, "It might be a long while. It might not be. It is best not to think on it."

"What?" Zavrius whispered. He wanted more. Every detail. He wanted his mother to look him in the eye and promise she wouldn't leave him in this world.

The Queen shushed him gently and—changed the subject.

Zavrius's heart dropped when she said, "Theo came to me. He confessed to the grievous act of destroying the lute. He shall face the consequences of his actions—"

"—what are they?" Zavrius asked, springing up like a cat.

"—yet I did vow to hear his explanation," the Queen pitched her voice louder. "And so, I did."

Zavrius set his jaw. He felt cornered. "Well? What did the conniving imp say?"

"Your *brother* made good points about the nature of the court and the standing of my queendom. I have brokered a peace that garnered the disdain of half our nobility. Each step I take to neutralize the Rezwyn Empire as a threat incites further animosity from within. Now, I do not expect you to rectify this situation. However, I do expect a certain degree of . . . cooperation. I am aware of your capabilities, even if they are overlooked by your siblings and others. I also understand why you might choose to commit fully to this pretense and, well, darling, achieve nothing of significance with your life." *Ouch.* "But for the sake of *my* image, picking up a sword, waving it about, and demonstrating a semblance of skill might actually do wonders."

Zavrius stared at her.

His body shook, with rage, grief, and surprise. To have his mother side with Theo so openly gave him a brutal taste of what life would be without her. The air in the room tasted dead on his tongue. He looked into his mother's eyes and thought: *I do not recognize her.*

"A month from now, there will be a confirmation ceremony for some young paladins. An intimate thing—I will attend, and your siblings will, too. A handful of court nobles, perhaps, and the paladin themselves, naturally. Why don't you have something prepared? You could spar with your siblings! Or demonstrate with one of the younger paladins. Hm?"

A great fear exploded in his chest. Zavrius liked performance. He actively enjoyed trapping bored nobility in a room and forcing them to listen as he strummed all manner of instruments for hours at a time. But *this?*

The Queen mistook the look on his face, or she must have, for she reached out to cup his shoulder and gifted him a pitying smile. Her voice cracked a little. She coughed the fracture in her expression away. Then, sweetly, she asked, "My boy. Will you do this for me?"

He swallowed every bitter and frightened emotion he had. Even as his hands shook, even as the falls of his bedroom felt dangerously brittle and close to his skin, he stopped himself from shaking and dug his nails into the palm of his hand.

Then he slapped on his most dazzling smile and looked up at his mother.

What could Zavrius say except: *Yes, my Queen.*

He waited until late afternoon before he convinced his body to do it.

Out in the garden, with the sky like a pink bleed and the plants turning black with the loss of light, Zavrius picked up the training sword his father had gifted him at six and swung it about with all the skill he'd had at that age.

The training sword was made of polished wood, but it had been weighted to mimic the real thing. Zavrius had picked up a blade or two in his time—or attempted to. He'd never done any drills with one, though. Nor knew which drills to complete.

So now, with a confidence he most definitely should not have possessed, he thought things like: *the weight of this feels right,* and, *oh, I'm quite good at this actually,* which gave him enough false bravado to move on to the real thing in a matter of minutes.

The real thing was—a broadsword, he thought. Or was it a claymore?—he had filched from the armory and dragged the blade through the courtyard and into the garden. It wasn't that the sword was wildly heavy, but rather, balanced in a way he felt like falling when he picked it up.

The weight seemed to pool around his wrist joint, making them ache as if the pressure might actually snap them in half, but he talked himself into hefting it up anyway. He managed to swing it over his head before he began to tilt. Totally unlike the training sword: it was bottom-heavy, so suddenly Zavrius' whole body was off center and diving down after the gravity-assisted swing of the blade. The sharp edge struck the grass and decapitated two flowers, and Zavrius himself went sprawling after it. He let go of the blade and rolled. Pain pulsed up his shoulder, and a rawer, wetter feeling punched behind his eyes.

Gedroks, you're an idiot.

But at the very least, no one had seen him.

"You'll kill someone like that," a voice called nearby.

Immediately, Zavrius bolted upright. Embarrassment curled hot in his chest, and he bit down hard on his fleshy tongue like the pain could prevent the reddening flush. With the sun slowly setting, everything in the immediate foreground was a dark shadow. But a form stuck out to him. Someone was there.

"Well, kill someone you're not meant to, anyway," the shadow continued as it pushed off the wall. Zavrius' heart seemed to recognize the man's identity before his mind did.

The approaching figure resolved into young Paladin Balen of Westgar, who bowed very sincerely with his hand over his heart. Zavrius used the two seconds of the paladin's averted gaze to spring upright and pat himself down.

"I am Paladin Balen of Westgar," he announced.

A strange liminality collided in Zavrius' chest; officially, this was their first meeting, but Zavrius had been aware of Balen's presence for years. Even at seventeen, Zavrius had never heard a word from Balen's mouth that wasn't his name and title murmured in a chorus with the other paladins. In all this time, he supposed a version of this young man had existed in his mind, nurtured by stolen glances and distant observations. He supposed that was the way many people knew of Zavrius, too: he was made of the assumptions of other people. But now, with the offering of his name, their relationship had forever fundamentally shifted. Zavrius wasn't sure why he could feel it so keenly, but a vulnerability had opened in him like a wound.

He had never before been attracted to someone he shouldn't have been.

That claim sounded false even to his ears. It wasn't exactly true. But now he felt keenly the impossibility of this attraction: a man sworn to protect him and his family could never say no to Zavrius' advances. He had learned the hard way what his title meant when it came to something as dangerous as attraction. It had been another boy entirely whom Zavrius had first kissed: a serving boy, a year or so older.

He remembered it now—all the warnings his body had given him. Everything he had ignored.

The boy standing over him in the dark of the kitchen corridor, breath on his neck, Zavrius looking up at him, gaze lingering on his lips.

The serving boy noticed, and asked: "Is that what you want?"

The reality of the moment seemed stark, the danger obvious, but this was the first bit of interest Zavrius had ever entertained.

He had allowed himself the fantasy, of course, but never the reality. Never the press of his lips against another boy's, never his body flush against another, never the warmth. Desire and anxiety made him rabid. He felt, suddenly, like his body was not his own, and that constant feeling sparked up in him again. *Someone's watching. One of your siblings. Your father's ghost. They'll know, they'll know.*

Something screamed in his mind that the boy had been put there by his father. That insidious little voice saying, *what on earth do you think you're doing? You are a prince to Usleth! You stand here wearing the clothes of royalty, bearing the weight of a country, the blood of the King! What do you think you're doing hiding in this corridor, hoping a serving boy whose name you don't know will risk his hide to kiss you?*

Only wrong doing was done in the dark.

So let me be wrong, he thought. *He wants to kiss you, not the other way around.*

For the first time in his life, it wasn't the other way around.

Zavrius said quietly, "It might be," and his stomach churned, because this was dangerous, wasn't it?

A knowing, smug grin swept over the older boy's lips. He swung the tea towel up and over his shoulder, and it slapped his back heartily. He dusted off his hands on his apron and pressed forward.

Zavrius could step nowhere except closer to the wall. His back hit it, cold stone pressing through his thin tunic, and then the serving boy was crowding him, arms pressing on either side of Zavrius's face.

He was trapped. Giddy with blistering anxiety, his mouth ran dry. Pinpricks of sweat formed at his lower back, and his heart launched itself from his chest, crawling sluggishly up his throat.

All this, and Zavrius could not bring himself to run. He didn't want to run. He wanted–

"What was your name?" he said. He cleared his throat and tried for an ounce of confidence. Or calmness. Or anything resembling nonchalance. "I think I should know your name."

The boy cocked his head. Wisps of brown hair spilled over his cheek. Brown eyes glimmered; Zavrius' nervousness began to make his body ache.

"I'm not sure that's wise, my prince. Not for me, anyway. You understand, don't you?"

The serving boy's breath was warm as it crawled over Zavrius' exposed neck. The prince very quickly decided he didn't really care about the boy's name. He was delaying this out of fear, out of childish worry, and if he kept delaying, then his chance–his one chance!–would disappear.

You'll be back to fantasies. Pressing your own lips to the back of your hand. Pathetic! Just do it, do it. Lean forward and–

In the end, he didn't have to do a thing. The boy grinned at him, smarmy and confident, and leaned down to press their lips together.

Zavrius hadn't seen him since. He had learned his instincts had been correct, and he had been watched. One of Petra's spies had seen the act, and the boy had been sent off. Zavrius had gotten away with a lecture from his aunt and a stern but kind talk from his mother.

Arasne had said: *It doesn't work this way for people like us. There are proper ways to love. I'm sorry, darling, but it matters who you show interest in.*

Zavrius had said, *But you're the Queen.*

Thinking it freedom. Thinking that power is a luxury.

His mother had smiled sweetly. *But love is vulnerability. I won't give any of my enemies the chance again.*

And Zavrius had listened. Had tried to listen. Except a growth spurt took hold of Balen of Westgar that summer, and it became exceptionally difficult to feel absolutely nothing about that.

Still, now, standing before him years later, Zavrius heard his mother's voice and saw the aggravated faces of his siblings, and he knew. Entertaining even the mere thought of this attraction would do no one any good—and certainly not Balen himself, who had been training to be a paladin from ten years old.

Zavrius still felt guilty about the serving boy who had lost his palace position. A paladin curtailed to city guard was the same as clipping a bird's wings; his potential would be snuffed out. It would be heartbreaking.

So, all the more reason to keep this ridiculous crush to yourself.

Resolved, Zavrius cleared his throat. "Zavrius Dued Vuuthrik," he said into the silence. The offering of his name, like Balen didn't know it, earned him a smirk from the otherwise stoic paladin. Balen looked up at him from his bowed position and slowly stood to his full height. His armor shone prismatic and bold. A rainbow bloomed over the sharp cut of Balen's jaw, blazing to life on the back of the dying sunset, *gedroks, do you hear yourself?*

Zavrius cleared his throat, feeling the need to explain. "It's a pretty name, and I've had servants announcing me my entire life. It feels good to introduce myself for once."

Balen dipped his head slightly and said, "The name suits you, my prince," and Zavrius was surely looking too far into that. He'd said it was a pretty name. Did that mean Balen thought. . .?

"You have caught me at an embarrassing moment," Zavrius said. He gestured to the training sword, and to the broadsword he'd floundered with. "I, uh. Well. I clearly need practice."

Balen said nothing, not for a long while. He folded his arms, seemed to think better of that overly-casual position, and turned rigidly still as he replaced his hands by his side. Then, with a conspiratorial glance over his shoulder, he shifted closer to Zavrius.

"My prince. It would. . . be an honor to assist you."

Zavrius' heart flipped. Balen was so close. He smelled of— Zavrius couldn't be sure what. Near natural in his scent, Balen did not drown himself in those pungent oils, and so Zavrius could only draw the vaguest of comparisons. The air around them was sweet with floral vapor, and Zavrius could smell his own sweat, but Balen just smelled of a man, with a tinge of ocean brine, and some unnamable thing that made Zavrius' heart shiver.

Balen breathed steadily as he stepped back and dropped again into a bow. Even with this paladin demonstrating such profound respect for his standing, Zavrius felt incredibly small. Outside of himself.

An interval passed where Zavrius willed himself to speak and finally said, "Please stop that. I never know what to do with myself."

Balen did not shift his body out of the motion, but he did throw up his head. His expression was open shock. Stiltedly, he stretched to his full height and clarified with, "My prince?"

"The bowing. You don't. . . you don't have to do that. And as for the help—"

He stopped talking abruptly. All royal instinct chanted at him to say no. Zavrius might have had no clue as to what he was doing, but there was a safety in failing over and over with only his own ego to see. The thought of tripping up again and again in front of a *paladin?* Such a handsome one, no less? It made Zavrius ill.

Yet, he couldn't bring himself to say no.

The offer was unmistakably kind. Perhaps Balen thought he might gain something from his assistance. A commendation and the like. Only everyone knew Zavrius had about as much sway at the court as one of the two flowers he'd clumsily beheaded. Even a fool could see how poor a political move assisting Zavrius would be.

So it was just that, then. A kindness.

The silence stretched, and Zavrius did not speak. The paladin glanced at him, then away, down at his feet.

"Perhaps I'm overstepping," he mumbled. *So formal*, Zavrius thought. *So refined.* Balen continued, "But no one has ever picked up a blade and known at once what to do with it.

He looked up, and Zavrius felt his own resolve crack when he met those bright blue eyes.

Hastily, Balen added, "My prince."

Zavrius laughed and waved him away. "The formalities are unnecessary. If you bow every time I talk to you, we'll make very little progress. I am Zavrius to you. Besides, Balen. We are two young men in a garden playing with swords. There's nothing particularly refined about that."

Balen—flushed. Ever so slightly. Where redness turned Zavrius' cheeks a warmer brown, it immolated Balen's pale skin. No shame, embarrassment, or nervousness would ever be hidden from his face.

Balen coughed and said, "My p—" Closed his eyes, strained as if struggling to drop the title. "Does that mean you accept the offer?"

Zavrius shrugged. His body fell into its usual, charming choreography; he gestured nonchalance, disinterest, neutrality. But a thrill had sparked through him.

"None of my other teachers knew what to do with me," Zavrius confessed. He added a short laugh, to ensure Balen knew he found the abandonment of his tutors humorous and not remarkably depressing. "I excelled in poetry, music, the arts. My handwriting, I can assure you, is exceptional. But the blade?" He tutted down at the broadsword. "My father was not at all pleased."

"Forgive me for the reminder, but it would be quite difficult to get your father's opinion of you now."

Zavrius stared at him in wonderment.

Balen mistook the expression. His flush only deepened, and he flung himself down into a contrite bow. "My apologies, my prince, I only meant—"

Zavrius stepped forward as if pulled by a rope. "It doesn't matter," he said in a rush.

But it *did* matter. Rebellion thrilled him. His heart raced. No one had ever. . . Sirellius' mark on Usleth was like a wound that never healed. Whether you had loved his reign or despised it, his absence was a reminder of Rezwyn's interference. Few people could ever separate that, and fewer still would ever mention his death in front of the royal family. Balen looked vaguely ill, with a greenish tinge to his pale skin, but Zavrius felt alive. He made a placating gesture to calm the paladin, eyes still wide in amazement. "You're. . . quite right. What's the use in my inaction now for some words said to me years ago? The man is dead. And my Queen has ordered I learn. So."

Balen did not rise, and Zavrius realized he was waiting— waiting for explicit confirmation. "Look at me, Balen of Westgar."

Balen flinched and stood to his full height once more. He blinked rapidly at Zavrius, lips pressed together in a very thin line. Statue-like in his stillness, Zavrius moved closer.

He realized something, then. Balen meant every word he ever said. Which wasn't how court *worked*: how had this young man lasted so many years in a world like the palace at Cres Stros? Honesty and truthfulness only got one so far—and even Zavrius, a prince, had to conceal much of his true self. Balen of Westgar was an incomparable person, and Zavrius felt suddenly worried, infantilizing. *Oh, you poor boy*, he thought. But how enticing that made him.

"Your candidness is welcomed," Zavrius said. "I accept your offer of assistance. But this won't work if you keep things from me. I will be flailing about and embarrassing my family name. It's only fair I learn a thing or two about you." He cocked his head, felt his long, plaited hair shifting over his shoulder. "What do you think of that?"

Balen visibly swallowed and nodded. The air shifted, and all the tension evaporated. "Yes, my prince. It really is an honor."

Back to formalities—but Zavrius could not hope for such dramatic change all at once.

"One day," he said jokingly, "I'll have you calling me by my first name. Maybe even a nickname. Maybe even Zav."

Instinctively, Balen shook his head and laughed. "Oh, no. With respect, my prince, I doubt that."

And with that, Zavrius secured a tutor for swordplay.

THREE

In the amber glow of a bitter morning, at nine years old and remarkably curious, Zavrius Dued Vuuthrik watched his uncle Lestr march a series of children up the terribly long steps to the palace of Cres Stros. It wasn't here that Zavrius first *saw* Balen, per se. He saw only the sheer number of children brought in for paladin training and understood, perhaps for the first time, the distinction between himself and these other young people.

It was another year or so before he realized wholly what he was. Or rather, who he liked. A parade was thrown in honor of the departing Uslethian army, with a great deal of soldiers and paladins marching behind a mounted King Sirellius. Zavrius remembered it vividly because of the color. So much of Usleth was already color; the stained glass, the décor, the fashion. But never before had Zavrius been exposed to so much of it all at once. The crowd buzzed, and no one dressed dully; this was, Zavrius realized with hindsight, a pre-emptive celebration. No one knew that Sirellius would never return.

Zavrius remembered that day for other reasons, though. Here, in amongst drunken revelry, entertainment, sword fights, and demonstrations, he saw Balen of Westgar for the first time. He'd been nothing striking then—a stroppy boy from Westgar, paler than Zavrius and lacking the good warmth to his skin. Perhaps the most remarkable thing about him had been the armor. Most of the other young initiates were slightly older and had more height to them, but not Balen. Clearly reused and not having been reforged to fit Balen's child-like proportions, he swam in each piece. Could barely see his chin past the cuirass.

But then Theo had botched his swordplay sparring in front of a crowd of thousands, and Balen of Westgar—out of all the stony-faced paladins—failed to suppress his laugh. Lightning quick, the young boy managed to disappear the crack in the façade, but not before Zavrius—and Lestr, the paladin commander—had seen it.

To Zavrius, who had spent his young life being compared endlessly to his eldest brother (and then to various degrees the rest of his siblings), to see any kind of dismissal towards Theo felt. . . exhilarating.

Theo's sword demonstration went terribly because, Zavrius later learned, he had just been told he wasn't to accompany their father to battle. But back then, secure in his ignorance, Zavrius had been immediately smitten with Balen of Westgar.

Which was why he was so skittish now.

They were to meet at dawn, just as the yolky sun oozed over the horizon and coated Cres Stros in bubbly morning light. To his own surprise, Zavrius had arrived even earlier than Balen. His sleep had been light and interrupted; nightmares of social blunders had pulled him from his rest, where he'd envisioned each one of his siblings spotting his paltry attempts at training and laughing at him. He felt ill when he woke just thinking about it.

If Theo or any of his cruel siblings spotted him flailing about, he'd never hear the end of it. In all honesty, he'd have preferred them to think him wholly incapable of picking up a sword than to have tried and failed in their line of sight.

The mornings were cool this time of the year, before the sun baked it all to scalding, and so Zavrius wore a long undershirt beneath his ankle-length summer tunic. He expected to sweat, but for now, he shivered, feeling exposed to not only the frigid morning but to the light of day and all the hidden eyes of the court.

The only people up this early were servants and paladins. Zavrius, well known for his languid nature, couldn't recall the last time he'd been up at this hour. His siblings, and even the Queen, rose later than dawn—though usually before mid-morning. By Zavrius' estimate, he should have had hours before any of them would have cause to see him.

Logic, though, did nothing to stop his anxiety, which whipped about snakelike at the base of his spine.

When the grass crunched underfoot, Zavrius threw his training sword behind his back and went rigid. His cheeks flushed pre-emptively, and when Balen came around the corner, Zavrius found his body would not relax. His heart kept pounding like he'd been caught by Theo himself; only the nature of it—the way it raced, the way his body felt—wasn't wholly fearful. A shiver went through his flesh. His cheeks burned to the point he could feel them.

"Cold, are you, my prince?" Balen called as he approached. Slung over his shoulder, he had a sack that rattled and clanged. Weapons, Zavrius guessed, for him to try on for size.

Zavrius said, "I haven't been up this early in years." He sniffed and readjusted his grip on the training sword. "Perhaps my body isn't used to it. It's cool for summer, no?"

"Starts like this but heats up fast." Balen blinked at the horizon, and the morning light hit his face, lit up his skin from the inside. He shone like pearl.

"I suppose your armor keeps you warm," Zavrius said.

"Too warm, sometimes." Balen dropped the sack with a sigh.

The fabric shifted, revealing all manner of swords, both wooden and real. But Zavrius barely glanced at it.

He was thinking about Balen days earlier, panting heavily, the sweat having pooled beneath the gedrokscale plate, the way the white shirt had grown transparent with it, and the way it had clung to his skin, showing off the bulge of muscle on his chest and in his arms.

So now, Zavrius wanted to say, *Why not take it off? You're bound to overheat; why not train without it?*

"My prince?"

Distracted by his own fantasy, Zavrius startled at Balen's prompt. Embarrassed, he cleared his throat to buy time. "Uh. . . are the rumors true about paladins? That you can't survive without your armor?"

Balen smiled and dropped down into a squat. Zavrius watched as the gedrokscale, so well-articulated and formed for the human body, neatly moved with Balen's motions. Zavrius supposed he'd never had much cause to look so closely at the armor his uncle had worked on.

Balen answered his question whilst opening the sack and laying out the weapons. "Not for long, no. We do not have, uh. . .the Dued Vuuthrik resistance to ichor. The way it was explained to me, anyway, is that where your blood has had exposure to ichor for generations naturally, we only get exposed from the moment we drink it. Our bodies can't handle it well, so we rarely take our armor off."

"A shame."

Shit.

Very briefly, Balen's hands stopped working. Then they started up again, straightening each weapon where it lay. Without looking up, Balen said, "Apologies, my prince. What did you say?"

Gedroks, some higher power hated him. First Theo's

nonsense, then the betrayal of his mother—not to mention her illness—and now, here he was, blundering through an otherwise innocent conversation because he thought Balen of Westgar was quite pretty.

He hadn't meant to speak that last hope aloud. But he could hardly renege on it now.

Cursing to himself and shifting his weight awkwardly from foot to foot, Zavrius forced himself to laugh brightly. "I only meant," he said, conjuring bullshit, "that I haven't really had much cause to. . .to ever see the armor up close. Without interrupting a paladin's training, entering the forge—which would be improper, even for someone of my reputation—or making someone uncomfortable, there's no real way for me to inspect the handiwork."

Balen stood and dusted off his hands. Was that a flush on his cheeks, or just pink encouraged by the morning cold? "Then," Balen said, barely glancing his way, "would you like to see it up close?"

Zavrius blinked. Belatedly, Balen added, "My prince."

"Before we train?" Zavrius murmured. "Yes, why not."

This all seemed very silly. A stupid thing to get flustered about. Yet as he walked forward, Zavrius kept talking—he was practically chewing on words, so full of them he was. "Well, I noticed the articulation just now when you bent down. I hadn't realized, which was daft of me. It's such a sturdy material I almost expected the whole thing to be very uncomfortable to wear—"

Before he knew it, he stood before Balen, who was nearly two heads taller than him. As Balen looked down at him from that angle, Zavrius found it difficult to remember his station; by all definitions, Zavrius had the power here. He could leave at any time. He could order Balen to kneel, and the young man would have to do it. Why, then, did Zavrius feel so wholly incapable at that moment? Like a trap had sprung and dug into the flesh of his leg, like he could not move and was at a hunter's mercy?

"Please look at your leisure, my prince," Balen said. He dipped his head again. "When you are satisfied, we'll begin."

So, flushing, Zavrius looked.

He quickly moved around to Balen's back, taking a moment for himself to curse and thrash about in his mind. But then, somewhat eagerly, he thought: *well, I quite like flirting with him.*

No matter if Balen couldn't rightly flirt back, and no matter that, in truth, Zavrius could never be sure if Balen enjoyed the flirtation or if he was doing his duty in allowing Zavrius to have his fun. Zavrius could pretend for a little while that this game was reciprocated.

At the very least, such flirting would be enough to get him through training.

He reached out and trailed his hand over the scales and gedrokbone that made up the armor. At every angle, it shone vibrantly. Multitudes of colors split beneath his fingertips. It smelt faintly of brine, and somehow, through the pads of Zavrius' fingers, he could feel ichor.

His connection to the arcane was, as Balen had said, different from how paladins experienced it. Theirs was a massive pool of power stored in their blood. Balen had confirmed that power to be so potent it would eat at the mind and body of a paladin not mitigating it with gedrok plate. But the Dued Vuuthriks had been long exposed to ichor. After the Mad King Gedrok Ach Meedin, final king of the last dynasty, had lost his mind to the effects of the power, the rulers of the dynasty had been micro-dosed with the stuff. Following that, they had been exposed to it in various other ways; their fashion, their makeup, their instruments. What had started as immunity had now become an affinity—and it was how Zavrius now had a natural magic in his blood.

But the sheer weight of this armor was the thing to strike

Zavrius as impressive. "It seems it takes strength just to wear this," he told Balen and found he meant that two-fold.

Firstly, he could suddenly understand the brawniness of most paladins. Few bodies would emerge under-muscled from paladin training. But secondly, having to wear it always, to contend with the eroding arcane power in one's blood—Zavrius couldn't imagine being locked inside something for eternity.

"Not something for you to worry about, my prince," Balen murmured, glancing over his shoulder to catch Zavrius' eye. Nervously, Zavrius pulled his fingers away from the armor and decided he should stop hiding. He walked back to Balen's front.

"On the contrary. I do not have much strength at all, and I do have to worry about that, given I can barely pick up a sword."

Balen smiled softly. As if on instinct, his head dipped towards the weapons he'd meticulously laid upon the grass. "If I may. . .?"

Zavrius waved his acquiescence and watched as the paladin dropped to his knees. He rose with a broadsword in hand, very similar to the one Zavrius had attempted to train with.

Balen shifted his grip on the hilt and readied his stance. When he swung, it was at once violent and graceful. The air whistled as the blade sliced through, warbling from the force, and Zavrius's vision blurred as he tried to keep track of the movement.

"Gedroks," he mumbled aloud.

"That was the correct way to hold the broadsword," Balen said. "You, my prince," and Balen's grip shifted again so his hand was further up and his wrist unsteady, "were holding it like this."

The blade tilted, and Balen's wrist stretched at an odd angle.

Zavrius flushed. "It's not even that heavy, is it?"

"It's not. But over time, in battle, the fatigue builds. I find there's a particular tendon in my forearm, near the elbow, that really dislikes training with a broadsword for longer than a few minutes."

Balen smiled at him again. Zavrius blinked. Belatedly, he realized the paladin was attempting a kindness, here—finding common ground in Zavrius' dislike of this particular sword.

Balen lowered the blade and approached, shimmying his hand closer to the wrist guard so he could hand the blade to Zavrius.

"We'll need to work on footwork first. But I want to get a sense of your body."

Zavrius froze as he took the sword. He could hear his own rapid heart beat. When Balen let go, a light strain began in his shoulder, and Zavrius found he couldn't look anywhere but the shaking blade in his hand. *Get a sense of your body.* Was there no other way for the paladin to phrase that?

Balen continued his assessment, apparently unaware of his effect on Zavrius, who risked a glance up at the paladin. He moved back with a finger raised to his lips. His brow furrowed, concentration etching lines in his forehead. In the morning light like that, he looked ethereal. The ideal of paladin kind; like honor and goodness naturally existed in his blood. Every muscle of Zavrius's tensed under Balen's gaze. As a prince, Zavrius should not have felt intimidated. Balen's life in Cres Stros belonged entirely to the Dued Vuuthriks; the role of paladin existed to protect the Dued Vuuthriks. Zavrius should have had the power. But Zavrius kept glancing between Balen and the sword, eager to hear the other man's thoughts. Balen's beauty was. . . effortless.

You will fail your dying mother if you keep thinking this way.

Breathing hard, and with his arm beginning to pulse angrily from the position and the weight, he closed his eyes. Birds chirped nearby, and the ambient buzzing of morning insects droned their prophecy of incoming heat.

Then the pain got too much. Roughly, he was yanked back into his body, back to the burning in his arm, which now shook quite violently. With a grunt, Zavrius gave up. He dropped the tip of the sword to the ground.

"Perhaps something lighter, Paladin," Zavrius said. "A rapier."

But Balen shook his head. He approached and reached for the broadsword. Zavrius glanced down, and upon seeing Balen's fingers were free of gauntlets, he went rigid. Barely a second of touch, barely a graze, but his heart skipped as Balen slipped the blade from Zavrius' hand. "A misconception, my prince. Those are barely lighter than a longsword."

Zavrius stayed silent as the paladin returned to the spread of weapons he had brought. With confidence, he replaced the broadsword and picked up another which, to Zavrius' untrained eye, was a rapier.

"A small sword," Balen told him. He got close, handed Zavrius the hilt, and then walked around to Zavrius' back.

"What are—oh."

Zavrius made a small noise of surprise as Balen's arm came around him. From here, he adjusted Zavrius' grip on the hilt.

"There, good. You'll want a lot of your grip to come from the last two fingers. I know it feels odd, but there's more stability there, and flexibility in the rest of your hand means you won't strike so rigidly. Good. How does that feel?"

Zavrius certainly felt something about what was happening, but his mind was unfocused. Barely thinking about the sword or the grip or what this morning was supposed to be dedicated to, Zavrius was thinking about Balen's warm breath on the back of his neck, the exhales that curled beneath his ear with every sentence he spoke. He was thinking about the calloused hand gently shifting the position of his fingers on the hilt. How, if he wanted to, he could take one step back and press his body into Balen's cuirass.

"I'm not sure what I'm feeling," Zavrius said honestly, and Balen laughed. Laughed a bright peal of a sound, and Zavrius turned to the noise, watching the ways the paladin's eyes wrinkled, awed in the way the world burned brighter for a second.

Zavrius pulled his gaze back around.

"Try swinging that around." Balen shifted back into Zavrius' view, backing well out of his range.

Flushing, Zavrius did as suggested, cutting through the air and thrusting. The motion threw both him and the blade forward. It whistled through the air, the thin, balanced point splitting all resistance.

Balen's gaze had shifted minutely, edging towards a soft appreciation. Most likely for the blade rather than Zavrius' handling of it.

"Good!" Balen exclaimed. "That's your blade for certain. Though I think daggers might be even better friends to you."

Balen walked to the bag of weapons, and Zavrius shouted, "Wait. No—not daggers. It. . .has to be a sword."

Here, Balen paused. He half turned, and Zavrius recognized the conflict in his face. Curiosity was getting the better of the paladin, which Zavrius partially reveled in. Would he break? Would he step out of line and ask? Zavrius hoped so--hoped there was more to Paladin Balen than unyielding honor.

Almost immediately, Balen cleared his throat. There it was! A side to Balen Zavrius was sure his uncle would have tried to train out of him. "May I ask. . ."

You can ask me anything.

Zavrius gestured with the sword. "Ask your questions."

Balen dipped his head. "You've never been curious about the blade before. Why now?"

Zavrius paused and thought about this, surprised when a fear rose in his chest. The feeling wasn't wholly legitimate, nor necessary; it was a paranoid anxiety and did not belong in this moment, and yet Zavrius couldn't shake it. To be seen flailing about by the paladin was one thing. To admit that even *this* attempt to better himself was not of his own volition. . .

He felt like a child, suddenly, his path ordained by his mother now as it had been at three before he was wholly sentient. He was a toddler wearing the clothes of a young man; he hoped Balen couldn't see it. Zavrius imagined seeing the twist in Balen's brow, the hint of a despairing pity, gone in seconds. He worried that by admitting the truth, he would ruin something between them that hadn't even yet formed. Yet there was also a buoyancy in his chest: he wanted to speak to Balen. He felt, in an odd way, an urge to say it all.

Because in the end, Balen had watched him make several mistakes and had never laughed.

Long ago, Zavrius decided not to care what others thought of him, but for someone to see him—see the parts too many others had criticized him for—and say nothing badly of him was a novelty. Or a revelation.

"I think you and I live in vastly different worlds, Balen of Westgar."

Balen, of course, could not understand this fragmentary thought on its own. On instinct, he bent at the waist, flinging himself into apology. "Forgive me, I didn't mean—"

"I'm the runt of the litter," Zavrius said, cutting him off. "You don't have to say anything to that. My ego is not a ripe peach; I have survived the court's rumors and jests for most of my life.

The simple fact of the matter is I was not made for swordplay. I was made for songs. For the beauty in music. And as the fifth heir, I have never been expected to be much of anything. But, well, things have changed, and my mother has requested I possess some basic knowledge. She wishes for me to perform next month in the Gedrok Glade when the newest paladins are confirmed."

He laid it all out, stripped back any pretense. "Thank you for your assistance, Balen of Westgar, but if you were hoping to find even an ounce of kinship for our shared love of swordplay, I'm sorry to disappoint you."

A smile cracked through Balen's calm façade. "I may be overstepping, but if you'd told me you were doing this of your own volition, I would have been much more surprised." And then, belatedly, "My prince."

Oh! Oh, is that so?

Zavrius grinned back. Then he laughed, loud and bright. "I do appreciate that honesty."

They both laughed again, and then lapsed into a comfortable silence that quickly became—what? Zavrius couldn't name the feeling. Tension's cousin, but lighter and less strained.

He froze in the way of a prey animal, tendons tight. Every muscle coiled with expectation, and he braced himself for the onslaught of mockery.

It did not come. Balen of Westgar was being serious.

Balen's cheeks bloomed red. Carefully, he stepped over his words. "I can assure you, if you think yourself bad at swordplay, I am far worse at music. I wouldn't know where to start." And then, "But if *you* were to teach *me*, then the pair of us would be even in this matter."

The offer surprised Zavrius. "You would learn from me?"

"I suspect I'll be a poor student," Balen admitted. "But I would always listen if you wanted to perform."

A tightness unwound itself in Zavrius' chest.

Two young men, so alike in duty and yet so separate. Zavrius felt this divide weaken. Understanding broke through and Zavrius dared to hope. After seventeen years of this, positioned so carefully on the outskirts of his family but rendered wholly *royal*, wholly separate from every other class, Zavrius realized how intensely alone he had been. Even nobility could not understand his position, and Zavrius could never really trust the friendships of such an ambitious class.

Balen offered something different. He understood duty and honor. He loved Cres Stros and the Dued Vuuthriks, at least officially. And he seemed—kind.

Zavrius found himself dipping his head, nodding quite eagerly. "Alright. That's our pact, then. Deal."

"Deal," Balen echoed. Again, delayed, he added, "My prince."

So far, it had not been much of a lesson. They stared at one another, and Zavrius refused to pull his eyes away first. A sharp thrill jolted through him when Balen glanced away. Was that a blush on the paladin's cheeks? Zavrius could hope.

Balen cleared his throat and turned back to the sack, picking up the broadsword he'd deposited earlier. "I know I said I wanted to focus on the footwork. But before that, I want to see what you remember from your father's training. I want to see how sharp your instincts are, and where your weaknesses lie."

"My weaknesses? Zavrius laughed. He stabbed forward with the short sword again. "I can assure you it would save us both time to find my strengths. My weaknesses are too many to count."

Balen glanced back at him. "Do you trust me, my prince?"

Zavrius didn't. Not entirely. To stay sane, he couldn't trust anyone he thought to be attractive. Betrayal, lackluster lovers, the sheer incompatibility of his position and theirs—there were simply too many ways to have his heart broken.

But still, Zavrius cocked his head and asked, "What did you have in mind?"

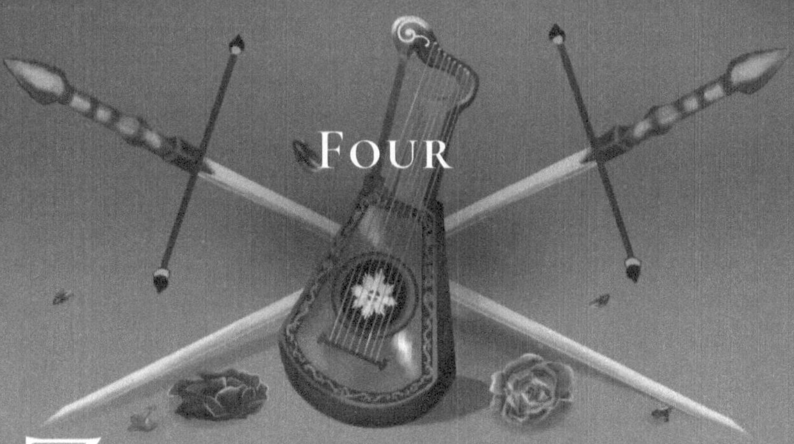

FOUR

Zavrius had not sparred in years, not with swords. The musical engagements he participated in with his mother were not the same, no matter if they were similarly dangerous.

But when Balen said, "You should face me and spar," Zavrius hadn't been thinking about anything else except: *Yes.*

Yes! This was what Zavrius needed: a way to dispel his convoluted emotions. Pre-emptive grief for his mother's demise, the anger of being underestimated all his life, the feral desire he had to lean into every rumor, become the corrupt hedonist they all suggest him to be—now was the time to let it all out.

"Don't hold back," Zavrius commanded. He rotated the short sword in his hand, flexing the last two fingers on the grip like he'd been told. "That's an order."

Balen smirked. "Are you sure about that, my prince? I'll have you on your back in minutes."

Bold. Brash. Delightfully dangerous in how he toed the line. Exhilaration flooded Zavrius as he smiled back, shifting his body into a stance that felt good and comfortable. "Is that a promise, Sir Paladin?"

Now it was Balen's turn to flush, and truly, playing with Balen's mind would be the only to avoid being beaten into the dust too quickly. He knew he would not win. But Balen had all manner of things preventing him from unleashing his full capabilities. Honor and obligation were just the tip. Zavrius half-hoped his order unnerved Balen, whose main oath involved doing no harm to the Dued Vuuthriks at all.

Like this, with only the faintest shadow of memory regarding those early days when Sirellius had trained him, Zavrius launched forward.

He attacked, jabbing at Balen's chest with the short sword. Easily countered, Balen sliced and, with the same motion, moved Zavrius' short sword out of the way. Steel screeched as the blades met. Balen sent the point of his broadsword curving over the short sword's guard; Zavrius had to lurch ungracefully out of the way to save his stomach from a stabbing.

He laughed, panting, and staggered back into a semi-passable pose. He was tripping all over himself. Deep in the recesses of his mind, he heard his father's gruff voice ring out: *Defense, Zavrius! Stop opening yourself up to attack!*

Well, Sirellius' advice had been worth nothing then, and it meant even less now he was dead. Life pumped in Zavrius' chest, and a gleeful, near-manic energy had him moving from foot to foot. Balen, in contrast, seemed calm and still. His feet moved carefully, eyes never straying. Then, lightning quick, he dashed forward.

Zavrius sidestepped the attack, bringing his blade up to block Balen's broadsword from whizzing down towards his neck. He tried to weather the force, but Balen had muscle where Zavrius had none, and his blade shuddered. This—this, he remembered. He had always been the weakest, the smallest, the most unfit. If there was one move he remembered, it was this: abruptly, Zavrius grabbed the short sword with two hands and spun them so the blade turned horizontal. With his knuckles locked against the back of Balen's hand, he punched with all his strength. Balen's hand swung out, pushed away by the force, and Zavrius was able to extricate himself, darting back and away out of Balen's range before the other man could recover.

Balen snapped back to center easily, but a smile toyed at his lips. They circled each other carefully. Sweat began to drip down Zavrius' back. His plait had already begun to fray, with wispy hairs flying free and sticking to his heated skin. A fine sheen of sweat glistened on Balen's face, but his breathing was even where Zavrius' was not.

Balen's attacks were clean and aggressive. At the next blow, Zavrius tried to parry—one-handedly, the way the short sword was meant to be held—and the bones in his forearm shook wildly as the force of Balen's strike traveled through the flesh. He let out a cry of surprise, and Balen's eyes went wide with worry, which Zavrius used to strike back.

It was not an honorable attack. On the back of Balen's dutiful concern, Zavrius spun and stabbed forward. He ended up announcing the attack with a bark of a laugh millimeters before the blade glanced Balen's cuirass. Balen's eyes went wide again as he lunged back and parried.

"You—!" he exclaimed, though his eyes glinted, too.

In Balen, Zavrius saw an echo of Theo, of his siblings, of Sirellius; a training style uniquely Uslethian, a Dued Vuuthrik haunting. He had survived plenty of physical attacks from his siblings. Wrestling, strikes across the dinner table—but Balen reminded him most of Theo. An upsetting comparison. He gave few signs of his next moves. He did not tense his body in antici-pation, did not look where he would strike in advance, all things Zavrius knew he himself was guilty of. Every attack of Balen's seemed inevitable.

So when Balen swept the short sword out of Zavrius' hands

and did as he had first promised, barreling into Zavrius' chest and sending him sprawling onto his back, *that* felt inevitable, too.

Balen stood over him, panting. He was flushed, not from exertion but from shame. Zavrius could tell—Balen's lips kept working over a silent apology, his eyes scanning Zavrius for any sign of injury.

This wasn't over yet.

On the ground, Zavrius spun onto his side and kicked back, sweeping Balen's ankle out from under him. The paladin didn't fall immediately, but he was unbalanced, and with that heavy armor weighing down on him, all Zavrius had to do was kick his shin again.

Balen dropped and rolled, and Zavrius scrambled up to retrieve his fallen short sword. His knees hit the grass, and leaned forward, his fingers almost closing around the hilt before he was wrenched away his feet.

Zavrius yelped. Balen dragged him back over the grass, flipped him. Zavrius started to kick—adrenaline kept him fighting. The option to yield seemed impossible, or dangerous.

"Stop it," Balen said. He dropped the broadsword, took Zavrius' wrists, and pinned him down. "My prince. Zavrius!"

At the sound of his name, Zavrius went limp. Sweat blinded him as it dripped into his eye. Above him, Balen stared down, haloed by the mid-morning sun. His curls dropped low and framed his face. The pair of them looked into each other's eyes.

Zavrius tried to get in control of his breathing, but he had new, growing concerns. Being pinned like this, beneath someone of Balen's caliber—his stomach grew hot. His nethers twitched.

The absurdity of this morning, and the shame he felt, had him blushing in seconds. Still, he couldn't look away. Balen looked like he belonged to the ocean, in a way. The sea had put her claim on him; his hair was always windswept, his cheeks holding a pink tinge as if whipped by the wind. And those eyes—Gedroks! They held dangerous swells, and sea storms, and gentle warms all at once. A boy beautiful enough to inspire poetry, a lifetime muse. Zavrius could imagine making him such.

"You're a natural, my prince."

"A far cry from that." Then: "Please let go of me."

They sprung up together. Both sat in the grass, catching their breaths, glancing at one another and then away.

When the moment stretched too long, Zavrius decided he had to fill it. Nervously, he asked, "What did you learn of me, then, from that demonstration?"

He almost didn't want Balen to reply. The fear that the paladin would see something in him, or realize something fetid in his nature, terrified him. He wanted Balen to—

You want him to like you. But it won't happen. It never happens. And even if it did, so what? You are a prince, and he is obligated to serve you. You can't afford to let that happen. So stop imagining it.

Zavrius looked down at his hands. The logic was sound, of course, if heartbreaking. He disliked managing his attraction, disliked feeling that way at all.

"You fight. . .with vigor."

"Balen," Zavrius said, eyes flicking up to meet the paladin's. "I told you not to hold back. That means with your critiques, also."

Balen made a noise and sighed deeply. "You. . .are brash and reckless when it comes to fighting, my prince. Your instincts are good, though. You know how to get out of the way fast. But you are eager to. . .fight. I think. . ."

He trailed off and swallowed hard, and Zavrius leaned forward with curiosity. "Oh, go on. Don't stop now."

Balen sighed again. "If I did not know who you were, I would never have guessed you were a prince by the way you fight. You put yourself in danger. You seemed to revel in it."

Zavrius' chest glowed with misplaced pride. He knew he should have played it safe. Most of Sirellius' training had recognized the sloppiness in Zavrius' technique. He had been told from a young age to defend himself. Never should he have to fight—not as fifth in line to the throne. Zavrius had been too young to be useful in the war and too far down the hierarchy to ever have to really contend with assassins. For a lowly prince without much ambition, defense should have been his priority.

Yet he couldn't help himself! Just then, with Balen, he couldn't *stop* himself, either. It was like some valve opened in his mind and years of underestimation engulfed all sense, making him inebriated with a childish need to prove himself. To just get in one good jab, to show the shade of his father that he could do it.

Childish. Balen was right: this attitude would get him killed.

"Have I upset you?" Balen asked. Then, unprompted, he added, "During the fight, I did not mean to use your first name without honorific. I—I'm sorry that I—"

No. Zavrius did not want to hear this. It disrupted his fantasy, the gloriousness of a paladin being so brash. He wanted Balen to stop talking. Leaning back, Zavrius stretched an arm out and waved it at the paladin. "Help me up."

Balen shut up quickly and swallowed. He stood, armor creaking as he moved to assist. His hand wrapped gently around Zavrius' wrist and heaved the prince to standing with little effort, like he was a brittle bag of bones, or something equally fragile.

Balen watched him carefully. Their hands were still clasped together, and with sweat rapidly cooling on Zavrius' back, he shivered.

"Cold, my prince?" Balen murmured, echoing his question at the beginning of their session.

"Something like that." Zavrius slipped his hand out of Balen's grasp; the paladin's hand lingered behind, as if holding onto a ghost. "I. . .I think we end this here today, Paladin Balen. I'm in dire need of a bath."

A cold one. Something that could chill him to the bone and urge some sense back into his befuddled head.

The paladin put space between them, backing up so he could drop into a deep bow. "It has been an honor to train you this morning, my prince."

"Call me Zavrius, Paladin."

A pause, a hesitation. Blue eyes glanced up at Zavrius from underneath the brow. "Only if you call me Balen."

Zavrius smiled. "Balen, then. I'll see you at a disgustingly early hour tomorrow morning."

Without waiting for the paladin to acknowledge him, Zavrius spun on his heel, flushed hard, and fled into the palace.

"Thank the gedroks for home is all I'll say," Avidia Dued Vuuthrik muttered between sips of her wine.

Zavrius had received an invitation to family dinner for that evening. These events were rare, but they were, at the best of times, a personal nightmare. The particulars of this invite were as follows: *Your sister returns from her adventures to the east. Come and celebrate.*

The note presumably went to all the Dued Vuuthrik children as a formal summons, though Zavrius' contained the additional postscript: *Zavrius, please.*

As much as Zavrius liked to think himself independent, aloof, and unaffected by what others thought about him, he never could keep the façade up for his mother. Please, she said. Well then, of course he would go.

The Queen had done something she hadn't in many years: organized a meal within the royal wing, at a dinner table that was altogether too intimate for Zavrius' liking. This room's entire purpose was food, and since it was central in the wing, it had no windows. Light abounded anyway: all manner of beautiful glass lanterns hung from the ceiling, and a gaudy chandelier loomed above the large round table where they all sat. Some servants had polished the dark mahogany meticulously, and it shined so much that it gleamed wetly beneath the firelight.

But gedroks, was it *cramped*. The room was no bigger than Zavrius' bedroom, with hidden, seamless doors that allowed servants quick access to the kitchen without needing to traipse through the palace with meals exposed. Fresh flower garlands dangled from the ceiling, but otherwise, years of dust had settled in this space. Even the most meticulous cleaning hadn't been enough to dislodge the stale smell—which wasn't unpleasant, necessarily, but *was* old. Being in here reminded Zavrius of his childhood, where dinners had been tiresome and sometimes terrifying affairs. Sirellius arriving late, sometimes furious for no apparent reason. How easily all his siblings would turn on him the instant Sirellius made a pass, kingly permission granted with his biting words.

Tonight seemed like it would be no better. The roundness of the table made it difficult to establish a hierarchy, which all the Dued Vuuthriks were keen to do. Everyone had sat in a line besides Arasne, with Theo to her left and Avidia, as the honoree, to her right. Lysio took an unnecessarily close seat beside their sister, and Gideonus had sidled close to Theo. This left Zavrius practically opposite his mother, with ample space on either side. Fuck them: he put his feet up on the seat beside him.

Avidia cut a striking figure beside their mother. Out of all his siblings, he knew her wrath the least. Neither did he know her personally. She had long dark hair, a face flecked with freckles, and a long, broad nose that looked like she'd pilfered it directly from their father's face. In many ways, she and Zavrius looked most alike, and both had Arasne's eyes, and the same habit of quirking their lips before smiling. But Avidia lacked any of their mother's warmth.

She was Sirellius' creature, like his brothers.

"The Ashmon Range is pleasantly drab this time of year." Avidia's tone was mocking as she waved her fork about. "Dry sea winds, and rain so forceful it stings your cheeks. And don't get me started on the houses. *Huts*, most of the time. Even the most hospitable of lords could do naught about the fucking cold."

The Queen flinched. "Language."

Avidia rolled her eyes and went to hiss something back, but Gideonus said, "And the food?"

Closest in age to Zavrius, Gideonus was now eighteen. Broad-bodied, he was the physically strongest out of the lot of them— but Zavrius figured his brawn was an overcompensation for everything else about him. Imagine spending one's life picking heavy things up and putting them down, and that being the only thing that made you even slightly interesting.

Avidia looked at him with pitying affection. "Surprisingly edible at times."

"Until you got your hands on it, I'm sure," Theo murmured before innocently burying his face in his goblet. A dig at her aptitude for poisons—something that somehow never managed to incite any rumors, despite it being a very deadly skill.

A smile twitched on Avidia's lips, uncertain. The pair of them were. . .an interesting duo. Zavrius leaned further back in his chair, letting it tip dangerously as he glanced between them. What exactly did Avidia's smile mean? As the two eldest children, Avidia and Theo had been exposed to Sirellius' whims far longer than Zavrius. Most likely a fundamental emotion—maybe empathy—had been permanently corrupted as a result. They circled each other like wild animals, each anticipating the other constantly. Even when they were all smiles, you could feel the tension.

Both wanted the same thing, of course. They had been the loudest opponents to their mother's push towards peace. But perhaps they both wanted the crown—is that what Zavrius sensed now? An animosity that chilled them both to the bone, a political game Zavrius would never play?

Thank gedroks for the order of their birth.

He reached forward and downed his own chalice. The Queen caught his eye and silently chastised him with just a darkening of her gaze. Zavrius pretended not to see it, sitting up properly and summoning a servant to refill his wine.

"I made sure not to poison any of my hosts," Avidia said finally, sipping from her own chalice. "Especially since they let me talk to Paula Kei Gesset."

The way she phrased that sentence struck Zavrius as odd. Avidia was royalty. She would talk to whomever she pleased. But everyone save Zavrius seemed to know who this Kei Gesset figure was, and no one focused on her choice of words. A chorus of excited noises came from the others, most especially Lysio.

"*You*? You had an audience with Kei Gesset?" Lysio folded his arms and laughed loudly. "Why trap that brilliant woman in a room when she has work to do?"

"Who is that?" Zavrius ventured. No one answered.

Avidia scoffed. "Well, she can't work every damn minute, can she?"

The Queen interjected again with, "Language."

"You don't really *care* about her work. I thought you were there for some poisonous plant or another," Lysio said.

Gideonus stood and reached for another slab of meat. "Want to know what I think?"

Lysio's lip twitched. "Not particularly."

He slapped the oozing slice onto his plate and dropped back

into his seat. "I think you're jealous." Quite astute for Gideonus' nature. "You're always going on and on about the Meedins and Rostavia and whatever other ancient monarch gets you all hot and bothered—"

"—it's not so much the lineage as it is the *history*—"

"—and *Avidia*, who doesn't rant on about it half as much as you do, just waltzes into the Ashmons and meets your hero."

A tense silence settled over them. Lysio pursed his lips, and Avidia smiled as she cut into her food. The clink of silver on ceramic only wound the tension tighter. Zavrius chanced a look firstly at his mother, who seemed content to let this run its course, and then to Theo, who had been unusually silent the whole exchange.

So Zavrius made things worse by saying, "Isn't anyone going to tell me who this Gesset woman is?"

Unified in their horror, his siblings all turned their gazes to him.

"You don't know?" Lysio snorted. His tone bordered on scalding.

As the true middle child, Lysio had ended up rather unhinged. Zavrius found him. . .brash. Growing up in the shadow of Avidia and Theo was one thing but needing to *also* stand out against Zavrius' attention-stealing antics (existing in the Cres Strosian court as a dandy music lover) had rendered him combustible.

"You haven't heard about the Crystal Gedrok?" Theo asked.

Zavrius flinched at the sound of Theo's voice. Ah—there he was. The chance to lord over Zavrius had brought his eldest brother back to life. Zavrius flicked his eyes over to Theo, whose grin was wolfish and feral. Unprompted, the vision of Theo destroying the lute came to mind, its beautiful wooden body splintering in the air. Zavrius shifted, gripping the fabric of his tunic beneath the table.

He knew about the Crystal Gedrok. About the legend of it, anyway. But clearly, there was more to learn here.

He sighed deeply. "Do I look like I know?"

Theo's nostrils flared. A shiver of something—disgust?—briefly clouded his eyes. He took a swig from his chalice, and the chair creaked beneath his weight. "Naturally, you've managed to avoid one of our contemporary geniuses, younger brother. The 'Gesset woman', as you put her, is a historian. An archaeologist, to be precise. For, what, five odd years now, she's been trying to find the location of the Crystal Gedrok's cave."

"How have you never heard Lysio go on about it?" Gideonus groaned. Avidia snickered, and so did their mother.

Because he hates me, you fool. He'd rather die than talk to me.

"How strange that I haven't," Zavrius said instead.

"It's a wonderful little story," the Queen murmured. She looked genuinely happy to be there, if a little pale. Zavrius noted belatedly she hadn't really done more than pick at her dinner, and she had dressed simply again, which was the most glaring sign of illness for someone who adored embellishment.

She just wanted her family together, Zavrius realized. His stomach twisted—she didn't deserve this kind of attitude, this apathy. He reached over and drank deeply from his chalice again, welcoming the buzz he would surely regret in the early morning getting stabbed at by Paladin Balen.

"Do tell," their mother said. "Tell us precisely what you learned in this audience with Paula Kei Gesset." She put a loving hand on the back of her daughter's head.

Avidia flushed ruefully. "Well, she said she had a lead. Her and her team, which are, as far as I can tell, a hundred-odd workers she's gathered from the surrounding towns, will move a bit further inland. They've been scouting the shoreline, but she said something about the shoreline having shifted over the centuries. Anyway. I thought. . ."

Here, Avidia paused. She looked to her mother and then to Theo. Zavrius sat up a little straighter. Something about his sister's hesitation made him think she wished she hadn't said that last bit. Or, she was concerned about how to say what she wanted. All of them fell silent as they waited.

She sighed eventually. "I thought it might be wise to invest in her expedition. You know, turn focus from expanding on your treaty with the Rezwyns, mother, and put some coin back into *our* country. Because if she could find one—a crystallized gedrok, I mean—then. . . then our problems would be sorted."

Oh, *shit.*

Avidia had said the quiet part out loud. Her intentions—her *real* intentions—were laid bare. At once, she had challenged the Queen's political decisions and suggested her own direction. She wanted to discover another gedrok corpse. One that, if found, would allow Usleth the necessary resources to bolster the Gifted Paladins and—well.

More arcane warriors meant a better chance of surviving the war. More arcane warriors meant a better chance of *starting* a war, too.

Zavrius could have laughed. Their mother was kind, but if it came down to it, Zavrius suspected she would choose peace over war. No matter the cost.

As it was, a flash of concern blared to life in the Queen's eyes, though it quickly died with expert control. Zavrius looked between Avidia and his mother, and the full realization settled on him. Avidia was not just toeing the line here. Her plans were far more ambitious. Deep discomfort itched at him. If Avidia were queen, or Theo king, they would put a lot of coin into discovering another immortal corpse.

Zavrius shook his head. He let it knock back against the tall wooden chair. "A crystal gedrok? Like the one from legend?" he prodded. Avidia raised a brow, seemingly surprised he knew anything about the topic at all. "Well? You *must* be joking. Or exhausted from the ride back. Sister—that is a legend. That is a centuries-old myth."

Avidia's face soured. "And if it wasn't?"

"What myth?" Gideonus said between mouthfuls.

Lysio rolled his eyes at him. "Are you even paying attention?"

Theo's smile was small and private. He said nothing at all. Odd.

"As legends go, it's old," Queen Arasne called out, answering Gideonus. "Older than Queen Rostavia, so its validity is. . .highly questionable. A cave near the Ashmon Range was said to house a gedrok overrun by crystals. The paladins that took ichor or bone from that creature were said to be different."

The unanswered question—different how?—hung between them all. Theo was the only one who kept eating.

Avidia leveled her brutal gaze at Zavrius and cocked her head. "I'm surprised you have any knowledge of the sort, Zavrius."

Zavrius leaned back into his chair and bounced his leg. "I've read at least one book in my life."

"Really?" Avidia droned.

"Well, most of one," he quipped back. Whatever information she hoped to dig out of him, Zavrius wasn't going to let her get it.

Avidia smiled brightly. "I thought your head was full of nothing but music."

"And a mouth full of cock, if the rumors are to be believed," Lysio grunted.

"*Language*," Arasne hissed.

"Has anyone actually heard from anyone claiming to have been a victim of our brother's oral attacks, or—"

"Enough!" Arasne and Theo shouted together.

The Queen flinched briefly at the unified shout, glancing back at Theo ever so slightly. The man gave her a deferential nod, and ah, Theo played the game differently. Zavrius should have remembered that. Without a doubt, he wanted the crown. He wanted Arasne to bequeath it all to him. What better way than to side with her now, in petty arguments with her children?

The Queen straightened her spine and cleared her throat. "We are not here to squabble over myths or legends, and I am not here to gain counsel from my children. This is for *you*," she hissed to Avidia, who jolted slightly from the force in their mother's voice. "I wanted. . ." A sigh. "Can't we just have *one* dinner where we're all vaguely civil to one another?"

Thick, syrupy tension spread itself over all of them. Zavrius wiggled with discomfort. No one, not even he, dared to continue their squabbling. Part of it was because he respected his mother, and perhaps the others had begrudgingly decided her decade of rule, with its peace and prosperity, deserved a little respect out of them, too. But he also wanted his mother to be happy.

Avidia slid a hand over the table, patting the wood gently to encourage Zavrius to reach out also. Zavrius stared down at the proffered hand like it was poison and folded his arms.

Ignoring his snub, his sister said, "I'm sorry, Zavrius, for assuming you a simpleton."

The best apology he'd received from any of them.

"Thank you, Avidia. I'm ever so sorry I don't believe in your favorite myths and legends."

Arasne huffed beneath her breath, but the matter was settled. Minutes later, Gideonus and Lysio were explaining some new mounted training they intended to involve themselves with.

But for the rest of the night, Zavrius stayed quiet, and for the most part, Theo did too.

He wanted to be the King more than anything. Zavrius could feel it in his bones.

And Zavrius knew if that future played out, he wouldn't last long.

FIVE

ONE WEEK LATER

"See this? How my shoulder is moving? A lot of the force of my swing is coming from the shoulder. But you can see me winding up to that far in advance—I am giving myself away. Flagging what I'm about to do and how I will attack. You don't want to whip your wrist, either. The motion should start with your elbow, and the other joints should move into place. Stay flexible. Do you see?"

Zavrius flushed. He could not, really, see the mechanics of what Balen was doing. This kind of movement was foreign to him. More than that, the bulky paladin armor made it near impossible to understand how the two strikes were different. Zavrius knew that if he were to be on the receiving end of either of those strikes, he'd get struck down either way.

Balen demonstrated further. The pauldrons shifted, plate mail accommodating his wide strike. Zavrius shifted, unsure of himself. His cheeks grew hot, and he thought: *gedroks, this reminds me of my father.*

Altogether, it was not a thought he wanted to be having about someone he found attractive. But in the end, it wasn't that making him flustered—it was the inability to comprehend what was happening and the growing pit of fear and shame that if he couldn't make himself understand quickly, he would be punished for it. Old habits die hard.

So he squinted, hoping to understand Balen's attack more wholly. Was the difference in the force of each attack? A muscle used in one that wasn't in the other? If only he could see how Balen's shoulder rotated! He wanted to ask Balen to remove the cuirass but couldn't—not when he'd fantasized about the armor's removal before, and for entirely different reasons.

Balen slowed, arm dropping as he cocked his head. His eyebrows pinched together as he assessed Zavrius. "My prince, what is it?"

"I—" Zavrius began before biting down on the word. What to say? How best to articulate what he couldn't understand without losing the respect he had garnered? Well, in the end, he would just have to speak the truth. "Your armor," he began with a cough. "It's beautiful, but its pearlescence is its own beacon. Every motion makes it glint; I can't see the specifics, Sir Paladin, of how you're moving your body."

He willed himself to say it smoothly. Nothing untoward should slip through in his tone, nothing to suggest a desire or an attraction. Balen bowed his head, turned around, and made a motion with his hand. The pauldrons unclipped from some unseen place, and Balen carefully removed them, with care and a kind of love in his motions.

Despite Balen's discretion, Zavrius awarded him further privacy by spinning on his heel and facing the rose bushes. Of course, a selfish impetus lay behind that: he thought he might go mad watching the paladin undress in any capacity. With his back turned, Zavrius looked down at the sword in his hand and tried to focus on the paladin's instructions. He gave himself room and exaggerated a strike, flicking at the wrist, and tried again moving from the elbow, though that motion felt too rigid. Briefly, he laughed at himself and put his head back to stare at the sky.

Perhaps he and the sword were incompatible. When he watched Balen move, there was fluidity between paladin and blade. Zavrius recognized it as the same kinship he achieved with the lute. In fact, his affinity for music—and the arcane power he could amass and use with it—could very well be why he was suffering so much here. His body had intrinsic knowledge of a learned skill so practiced it had become like breathing, and the horror of starting over with the blade and feeling incompetent only made things worse.

"My prince?"

Zavrius paused. His body reacted as if he'd been caught doing something salacious: heart rate fast, breath caught in his throat. Half turning, he spied Balen over his shoulder, just a hint of that fair skin and a white shirt.

Don't be a coward.

Zavrius turned fully to face him, saying as he did, "I wasn't sure if you needed privacy," and by the end of that sentence, he faced an armor-free Paladin Balen.

The white undershirt had the shape for billowing, but a fine sweat made it cling in places to Balen's body. It threatened translucence; the material spun in a way where light caught at various junctions and illuminated the seams—Zavrius flushed at the sight. Balen's body was barely hidden. All the strong angles and rounded muscles were hinted at in the folds of the shirt, statuesque, like carved marble.

Balen glanced down at himself. "Please tell me you know I was removing my armor to better demonstrate, and not—"

Not what? Zavrius' anxiety didn't let the paladin finish. "Of course!" he said too loudly. And, in the hopes of avoiding this odd feeling for even a second further, Zavrius turned to the side and swung out with his sword the way Balen had suggested. "It still feels awful using the elbow."

Balen made a noise—was he *laughing* at Zavrius?—and moved around him. Like the first day they'd met, the paladin's hands ghosted over Zavrius' outer arm. Tauntingly, the awareness of Balen's armor-free torso lingered at the back of Zavrius' head. He wanted badly to press back against him, even if that would ruin everything.

"This motion is good," Balen said, palm cupping Zavrius' elbow. His breath rolled in warm waves against Zavrius' cheek; gedroks help him. "But just because you're moving from here, it doesn't mean you must lock up the wrist and the elbow. They can stay flexible. Just start the movement from the elbow and see what happens."

Balen stepped away, allowing Zavrius enough room to spectacularly mess up. Zavrius didn't glance his way, trying to focus on the point of the sword, on feeling his elbow joint, on understanding the way his body moved. After a moment of prolonged delay, he struck forward. His wrist rolled beautifully to accommodate the strike, which came to a natural end at an angle, pointing down at the grass, and for a moment, Zavrius could feel it: how one's body might mold to become one with a weapon.

"That's it," Balen said.

Zavrius turned to find the paladin watching him, unfettered pride glinting in his eyes.

"I said you were a natural," Balen said.

"Hardly natural when I'm being schooled, is it?" Zavrius smiled back. "What you're seeing is a reflection of your teaching."

He straightened and stretched, but his body ached. He had never so consistently exercised before—or at least, never to such intensity. Beautiful late afternoon walks around the garden with his lute hardly worked up this much sweat. But these days of hard work were clearly yielding results. The aches weren't as severe. His grip grew better. Even a slither of definition had appeared in his arms. And Balen was praising him now, wasn't he? He must be doing well.

Balen nodded, touching the back of his head with one hand. "Well—then, I'm liking what I'm seeing."

Zavrius flashed him a look. Was he flirting or being obtuse? He scanned Balen's face, assessing the smile and the flush on the other man's cheeks—though Balen always seemed to be vaguely red, whether it was cold or hot. An adorable quirk of his.

In the end, Zavrius simply egged him on further. He cocked his head back, grinned wide. "Is that right?"

Balen went to retrieve his own blade. "You might be a passable swordsman rather soon, yes."

"And if I lack the skill, I'll at least have beauty."

Balen laughed then. "I don't think it's unheard of to have both." He bent and stood, sword in hand.

Just as he was turning, Zavrius said lowly, "Clearly not. Just look at you."

Balen paused.

If there was anything Zavrius reveled in, it was moments like this, whereby the intersection of his status, his flirtation, and boldness, he could make other men flush. Balen's gaze fixed pointedly on the sword in his hand, but he gained some bravery and looked up.

Whatever grasp Zavrius felt he had on the situation slipped. His heart careened off the cliff of Zavrius' own making; gedroks, he wanted Balen to flirt back. He wanted boldness, brashness.

But Balen was a paladin. It was simply not in his nature.

"An honor to be complimented by you, my prince," Balen murmured with a dip of his head. He hesitated, mouth opening slightly—*say it,* Zavrius begged. *Say what you're thinking, be brave for me*—but training won out, and Balen gently closed his mouth.

Zavrius bit the insides of his cheek and turned his head away. He felt himself reddening for all the wrong reasons, and looking at the paladin only made him feel worse.

Oh, *enough*. He should feel so awful for something so small.

"I think I've had enough of training for the day," he murmured.

Balen's brows pinched, and he lowered himself even further. "My prince, if I have offended you. . ."

Zavrius walked closer to the other man, eyes drifting over his back as he bowed. "Say that you had. How would you remedy it?"

It wasn't a fair thing to say. The paladin had done nothing, but Zavrius watched now as he glanced up, horrified. His eyes widened fractionally. Bewilderment slithered into his features, and he stayed silent for some time, no doubt racking his mind to find the offense.

Balen said eventually, "Whatever my prince desires," and it only made Zavrius' frustration grow. His chest felt odd. This— whatever *this* was—wasn't what he wanted. He was so agitated by Balen's lack of bravado that it felt like his heart lay trapped in a vice of tendon and anxiety, a fleshy prison. He wasn't being fair, and his intuition made his very skin uncomfortable as a warning as if to say: *Zavrius, stop what you are doing.*

"Come play music with me," Zavrius said suddenly. Pathetically, his voice cracked, and he shook his head when Balen looked up, saying, "You've done nothing wrong. Only come if you want to. You have training and all manner of things to be doing, and I know when my uncle scolds, it is fierce. But I want—"

Zavrius swallowed, already anticipating how Balen would reply, and indeed, the paladin said: "If my prince desires—"

"What do *you* desire?" Zavrius said sharply.

Balen shuddered to a stop. He opened his mouth, and after a minute, he laughed. "You know," he said, "I don't think I've been asked that in a long time. I don't think I know the answer. My prince."

"Call me Zavrius. Drop the formality, Balen; you are far too deferential."

"I. . ." Balen paled as he stood up straight. "I find it difficult."

They looked at one another. Zavrius moved first, holding out the short sword for Balen to take and pack away. "I can order you, if you like."

Balen went to his knees to pack the sword just as Zavrius said it; he glanced up from the low position, and the sun lit up the sharp line of his jaw. The paladin's grey-blue eyes glistened bright, an ocean in his stare.

Balen's gaze shifted fractionally lower to Zavrius' mouth as if waiting for the words to pass through his lips. "I. . .do have practice taking orders. Being a paladin, and all."

Zavrius' heart lurched. "Then say my name. Without the honorific."

Balen shifted, turning his body to face Zavrius, though not standing up. Still on one knee, eyes wide and glistening with something akin to fear, he murmured, "Zavrius."

Like a whisper, like a secret, barely spoken. A shared desecration of both their roles—Zavrius' whole body lit up.

He fought the urge to reach out and run a hand through the paladin's hair. "Balen. Come and play music with me, if you like."

Balen's throat visibly bobbed. Beautiful. "Where?"

"The music room, in the Royal Apartments."

But that broke the spell. "Your. . . your private quarters?" Balen's face blossomed a bright red. As if on instinct, his head spasmed in a shake, and he blurted out, "I can't."

"Do you want me to order you on this, too?"

Perhaps a minute passed without anyone speaking, and in the end, Balen didn't ask for Zavrius' order. He packed up the swords, stood, and slung the sack of weapons over his shoulder.

Guilt and doubt rose in Zavrius' chest. "A joke," he said hurriedly. "I won't order you to listen to me play."

Balen looked down at the iridescent bundle of armor at his feet. He didn't look at Zavrius when he spoke next. "I. . .have to return these to the armory. And put my armor back on."

"And then?" Zavrius prompted.

Flushing, embarrassed, but with a tone that belayed his excitement, Balen said, "And then I suppose I am listening to the prince of Usleth play music."

———

Zavrius opened the door to the Royal Apartments and stuck his head in. He heard some chatter from the study, where the Queen was likely in conversation with her advisors, but otherwise, the stretch of rooms seemed conspicuously quiet. It was times like these that Zavrius regretted not memorizing the tedious details of his sibling's lives.

He turned his head back through the door. Balen of Westgar had his back pressed to the carved mahogany, chest rising and falling with such ferocity he could have been about to kill something.

"You can calm down," Zavrius murmured, opening the door wide. "Follow me."

He stepped inside. The vestibule was marble and tile, with paintings, decorations, and bright-colored draperies, all of which slowed Balen down as he stared in awe. Zavrius moved quickly to the music room. "Come," he hissed, and Balen rushed after him and inside. Once the door was closed, he said, "It's not that you can't be in here. I'd just rather my siblings weren't privy to the knowledge. For the rumor mill, you know."

If Balen had questions about that—and no doubt he did—he kept them to himself. Zavrius was grateful, because what would he have said?

Oh, it's just that they'll be able to tell I like you, and I'll never live it down.

The other thought was more selfless: Zavrius did not want to taint Balen's reputation with his own.

"This is. . ." Balen whispered. He took in the room with the same wide-eyed glee he'd just displayed. Zavrius didn't follow his gaze, much preferring to watch the paladin's scanning, inquisitive expressions.

The room itself was not overly large. It had no window on its walls, but it did have an oculus, a beautiful, glass-paned skylight framed by a painted sky. Every wall had been painted a lovely light teal in a gradient wash from this intricate ceiling. Instruments hung everywhere. Every wall, every surface, and all manner of them, from string to wood to brass, Uslethian, Rezwyn, Zvensian, and from even further west. A large wooden desk took up most of the back wall, where tools and several instruments in various states of disrepair sat waiting for Zavrius to fix, tune, or amalgamate into a hybrid creation. This was a pastime he loved, but rarely found motivation for—especially these past few weeks. Cushions and throws were scattered over the floor, treated as various pillowy havens for a musician and his audience to occupy.

Arasne's hands were all over this room. Zavrius had just added his own flair where he could.

"Please, sit."

He didn't wait for Balen to do as he was told, instead walking towards the desk.

There, to his surprise, sat his mother's lute-harp, sitting above a written note.

Zavrius blanched. Behind him, he heard the paladin shuffling but couldn't pull his eyes from the instrument in front of him. His stomach twisted at the sight. Arasne loved this thing, and Zavrius loved it too. Seeing it here as one of the many instruments Zavrius could play and practice with made Zavrius' skin hot and sticky. Another sign—another reminder of his mother's sickness. Another mark of her deterioration, a passing down of her knowledge. Violent nausea shot up his throat, and he hastily tugged the note from beneath the instrument.

It read:

My dear son—

I find myself playing less. Please do not remove the lute-harp from the music room, given the incident with your brother, but do feel free to play and practice with it as much as you wish. It is not yours—not yet. But one day, it will be, and I feel you two should get to know each other.

Remember: she has the blood of the gedroks, the same as us. In a way, she is your sister.

Treat her well.

Your mother

"Everything alright?" Balen called.

Zavrius glanced back to find the paladin perched on a set of cushions. He looked strikingly adorable, legs up underneath his chin and bulky armor widening his torso.

"Just fine," Zavrius said, turning back to the lute-harp. The instrument was a hybrid, possessing the pear-shaped body of a lute and the long, elegant neck and curve of a harp. Twelve gedrok tendon strings ran down its length. It glistened pearlescent because, unlike all the other instruments, it was made entirely from material harvested from gedroks.

He ran his hand over the gedrokbone and felt it sing for him. His very core reacted, and Zavrius shivered. Yes—this instrument had a personality, a life of its own. He picked it up and turned, hefting it at an angle so Balen could see it shimmer. "I want to play this for you."

Balen gestured to the cushions next to him. "Whatever you desire."

Zavrius came and sat next to him, laying the beautiful instrument across his lap. He took a few deep breaths and closed his eyes, though even then, he could feel the intensity of the paladin's stare. Playing for an audience wasn't new to Zavrius, but this eagerness certainly was.

He played without really thinking, plucking at the strings, improvising until a natural melody came to him, and he was swept up in the beauty of the sound and the quality of the music. Every note he could feel rebounding in the hollow body of the lute-harp, resonating out into the world, up through his fingertips, into the cavity of his chest. *This!* This is what he missed when he picked up the sword! This immediate and inevitable coalescence! How easy it became to bare his soul without words, the lute-harp a tool for delivery and expression, and transformative in its own way.

He slowed the melody and splayed his hand against the strings to finish. With his eyes still closed, he thought to the lute-harp: *you and I will be very good friends one day.*

When he looked up, Balen's expression was trancelike. Glazed. Zavrius thought: *how nice*—until he realized what had happened.

Sometimes, he couldn't control it. Sometimes, he would be so swept up in the music that he simply didn't realize he was doing it. But arcane power had leaked from him, the feeling in his gut summoned by the dance of his fingers against the strings, and thus, the music he had performed had been imbued with magic.

Balen was under a spell.

It wore off quickly. Zavrius sat flushed and embarrassed when Balen jolted back into his body.

"That was. . .incredible," Balen said.

Zavrius smiled softly and looked down. "I think I. . ."

Balen raised a brow and sat back. "Mm?"

He wanted to explain to Balen that what he'd experienced wasn't Zavrius' music, but his magic. He wanted to divorce Balen's awe from his playing—he wanted to start again so Balen could hear him play without arcane influence. Above it all, he wanted to tell Balen what he was and what he could do; how good it would feel to trust someone in this world who wasn't his own mother.

But this wasn't something anyone should know about him. It was a secret, an edge he had against the kingdom's underestimation of him. What is he doing, considering telling a crush?

"Nothing," Zavrius shook his head. "Never mind."

"It *was* mesmerizing," Balen said, perhaps not clocking the shift in Zavrius' tone. He shuffled ever so slightly closer, and their knees touched. Zavrius looked down at that connecting point. "You're a wonderful musician, you know."

"You have to say that," Zavrius whispered. He could feel every beat of his heart as he stared at their touching knees. Then he cocked his head; praise never hurt. "But tell me more about how you enjoyed my playing anyway."

Balen grinned, and the grin gave way to a bright laugh. "I. . .I understood the expression on your face. The contentment. I get like that sometimes. Dazed. With the sword, I mean—when I'm training, and I reach some threshold, and I forget I'm training. I forget everything but that moment." He looked down and fiddled with a callous on his bare palm. "You looked like you were experiencing something similar."

Gently, Zavrius shifted the lute-harp off his lap and laid it on an adjacent cushion. He turned back to Balen. Everything in him said: *lean forward right now. Ask to kiss him. Take the risk.* But he lacked the boldness.

Balen's gaze met his. They looked at one another. A lurching feeling unspooled inside Zavrius. He shifted his hand along the ground and laid it gently on that meeting point between their knees so the tips of his fingers were touching Balen's lower thigh.

Balen looked down. His cheeks grew red.

Zavrius could hear his heart. The drum-beat thrum urged him on, begged him to do something.

"Balen," Zavrius whispered.

The paladin looked up. "Yes?"

Zavrius wet his lips and took a deep breath. "Balen, I—"

The door to the music room burst open. Both Balen and Zavrius swung around. In a breath, Balen was halfway to his feet, hand hovering over the hilt of his sword.

It wasn't a threat to be struck down by a blade, but it *was* a threat. In the doorway, half slumped against the frame with his eyebrows raised, stood Theo Dued Vuuthrik.

"Oh, my, brother," Theo said, glancing between them. "What do we have here?"

<h1 style="text-align:center">SIX</h1>

A chill crashed through Zavrius' body. He made an abortive attempt to stand up, but most of his limbs had locked tightly. Beside him, Balen's hand shifted minutely away from the hilt of his sword.

When Theo's eyes grazed over him, the paladin did the inevitable. Balen of Westgar dropped his head and bowed to the heir to the throne. He did his duty, and he kept his honor—and it still hurt like a burn on Zavrius' heart.

Why did this have to happen?

"Ferreting paladins away from their duty?" Theo cooed. He tutted and threw his head over his shoulder, as if to check who else might be around to bear witness to Zavrius' shame.

"That's not—what's happening," Zavrius managed. He said it loud enough that Theo glanced back his way—good. Maybe with Theo alone, Zavrius could manage this. He stood ungracefully, feet tangling in his long tunic, and ignored how all his skin had grown clammy. He put a steadying hand against the wall— gedroks, his own flesh and blood shouldn't have been able to make him feel this way.

Seconds ago, he had been in control. And now. . . .

81

Theo stepped into the room. "Paladin," he called.

Balen went obediently rigid. His fist smacked over his chest. "My prince."

Jealousy roiled in Zavrius' gut. That honorific belonged to him when passed from Paladin Balen's lips. He tried to keep that possessive urge from his face, but Theo's lip quirked at the side. Zavrius could pinpoint the moment his brother knew exactly why Balen of Westgar had been allowed in the royal apartments, and the dread that encompassed him felt deathly. Zavrius stepped forward—to do what? Fight? Yell? Beg for Theo's mercy in this moment?

Theo could have turned and walked away and let him have this. Or he could poison the moment, embarrass Zavrius so completely Balen couldn't risk being seen with him if not to contribute to the rumor that would unfold.

Silently, Zavrius mouthed the word *please.* It felt akin to going down on his knees and begging aloud. Like a dog. *Please.*

But Theo only looked away, gaze dragging over Balen, who remained bent at the waist. The paladin's cheeks were so red that even the shadow cast by his drooping hair could not dull them.

Theo cocked his head. "Why exactly are you here?"

"On Prince Zavrius' orders, sir."

Theo wet his lips and smiled again at Zavrius. "Of course. He led you here like a lamb to the slaughter. I am so very sorry this happened to you."

Balen stiffened, raising himself slightly. From underneath his brow, he glanced back at Zavrius and then up to Theo. Clarifying, voice high, he asked, "Sir?"

"Don't," Zavrius hissed.

Theo took so much from Zavrius already. Theo had hounded Zavrius his entire life and only doubled down on Sirellius' revilement of him following the man's death. Why? Because of the inevitability of his nature? Because he was a dandy, because he wore his hair long, because he played music, because he liked boys? Which was it?

Zavrius wondered if he could ever be perfect in Theo's eyes. Even if he rid himself of everything that made him who he was, would Theo be able to love him then?

Theo seemed to have abandoned his earlier line of questioning, though Zavrius could not relax. As if he had the gift of foresight, he could see how dangerous Balen being here was and how idiotic it had been to bring the young paladin here at all. Zavrius craved one thing for himself, one friendship untainted by rumors of his character. But Theo's eagerness to besmirch Balen by association made him ache. Implicitly, Zavrius understood what Theo was doing now.

Cut Balen lose, stay alone, and maybe I won't drag him down with you.

Zavrius pressed his fingers into the wall as if hoping to grip the flat surface.

Theo moved further into the room, crossing his arms in front of Balen. He gave the young paladin a light tap, and Balen stood to his full height. They looked. . .

Zavrius swallowed tightly as his throat seemed to close. Together, they were nearly of a height. Their strength seemed matched, and though Theo had a handful of years on the paladin, Balen looked like he could hold his own.

"I've seen you before, haven't I, Paladin. . .?"

"Balen, sir. Balen of Westgar."

"That's right. My uncle's little prodigy," Theo smiled broadly. Then he clasped a hand on Balen's shoulder. "You want to be my Prime."

The world stopped. *No,* Zavrius wanted to say, *he would have told me.*

But when? And why? Zavrius had nothing to offer Balen of Westgar, not in the way Theo did. At fifth in the line to the throne, he had so little sway—and coupled with the talk about his character, mere association with Zavrius at all could be enough to subject Balen to poor treatment from others of his ilk. The open association would bring bullying from other paladins. Potentially, he'd be locked out of a position he clearly wanted.

Zavrius' heart raced, and he felt ill when Balen nodded, confirming Theo's thoughts.

Theo regarded him carefully. "You're young. The youngest applicant I think we've had in a long while. Primes tend to be a little more seasoned."

"Tend to be," Balen said, tone edging on defensive. "But not much can compare to the speed and strength of youth."

Theo's brows shot to his head. "You want to fight, then. Brashness and bravado with nowhere to go."

"I will fight," Balen said, "as a means to protect my king."

Theo leaned forward. "I can see in your eyes that you mean that."

A great sundering happened. Zavrius felt it as much as he saw it, the chasm between his body and theirs, the unmendable breakage that was happening now. Theo laid claim with his words and laced a promise in them, and if Balen was just a little bit intelligent, he would see Theo's question for what it was: an offer.

In real-time and with speed, Theo was making Balen an ally.

Zavrius couldn't allow it to happen. He stormed forward and flicked Balen back with nothing more than an irritated gesture. Years of conditioning sparked in the paladin's eyes, and he was backing towards the door in a bow without Zavrius needing to say a single word.

Theo spun towards Balen. "Stop your moving."

Zavrius spat, "Leave us!"

Theo glanced between them and laughed. "Balen of Westgar, if you want any hope of being my Prime, you will listen to me now."

Bastard. *Bastard.*

Zavrius made a noise of upset. He sounded stupid. A dark vortex opened in his gut, and he felt the threat of tears burning behind his eyes. No. He would not cry, not over this, not in front of either of these men. So he made himself laugh. Forced it out until the agitated sound became a genuine peal, head back, shoulders light. Zavrius laughed and laughed and told himself nothing mattered. Not this moment, and not anything that might come after.

"Oh, Theo," he said, wiping at his eyes. "You are a curse I must endure. Our blood makes it such. But it's pathetic to watch you throw yourself on this poor boy to upset me. Stop it. Let him go about his duties."

Pointedly, Zavrius didn't look Balen's way, but he could sense the air in the room shifting. Tension snuck in and though Balen remained half-bowed, he had gone still.

But Theo's breathing grew erratic. Any threat to his authority seemed to send him into a panic, and thus, now he stared at Zavrius, body tense. They stared at one another, at an impasse. Theo's body seemed to be fighting his resolve, and he twitched every so often towards Zavrius, as if intending to strike.

The lute-harp was right there. Zavrius glanced down at it, just for a moment. "Do not make the mistake of underestimating me, brother."

But it seemed *his* mistake was saying that at all. Theo jolted, and the tension erupted immediately with his full-bellied laugh. "*You?*" he spat. "You disgrace this family. You disgrace your title. There is no underestimation happening here, Zavrius, not when your opinion, and you yourself, are worthless. Whatever you think you're doing here will *end.*"

Zavrius breathed deep, puffing out his chest like he could trap the cruel words in his lungs before they burrowed into his stomach. To his great surprise, Balen of Westgar had stood up. He looked at Theo with wide-eyed shock, and Zavrius thought: *Oh. Is this the first time you're seeing who he is?*

Theo continued, saying, "If our mother didn't have such a soft spot for you. . ." but the threat remained unfinished. He jerked back, seemingly remembering their guest. Theo turned and faced the paladin fully. "Balen of Westgar, report to Paladin Commander Lestr at once. Tell him I sent you. I want to see all paladins with their eye on the Prime position at the end of the week. Tell him I'll be watching you train."

Balen dipped low again. "Of course, my prince."

Zavrius watched him eagerly, hoping he might glance up. Zavrius could apologize with his eyes; they might develop some silent understanding. But Balen didn't, and Zavrius's heart felt marooned and alone.

Theo turned back to Zavrius with a twinkle in his eye. "You don't mind, do you, if I ensure he focuses on his training? I'd hate to steal from you a pet."

"What does it matter?" Zavrius laughed. "He's nothing to me. He certainly won't ever be *my* Prime."

As soon as he said it, regret swamped him. First, for the desperation in his voice, the fear that it would betray him, a crack giving way to the larger feeling of isolation, of Theo encroaching on his territory. Secondly, and most intensely, was the fear Balen would believe it. How could the paladin understand the intricacies of Zavrius' relationship with his brother? How obviously caring about anything merely opened him to injury?

If I told Theo you were mine, he would make sure I never spoke to you again. He might find a way to expel you from the palace altogether.

This—Theo's attempt to claim Balen as his own, if just to annoy Zavrius—was a better outcome.

But only if Balen didn't believe Zavrius' words.

Zavrius chanced a look, but Balen stood statuesque. Back

straight and face impassive, he appeared largely unaffected by Zavrius' words. Zavrius felt ill.

Look at me. Look at me, Balen. I don't mean it.

Without another word, Theo dismissed the paladin, who bowed deeper to Zavrius before he straightened, turned, and left without ceremony. Zavrius stared after him until his heart dropped, and then he dragged his gaze back to Theo.

"Are you happy?" Zavrius mumbled.

Theo shrugged at him and cast a bored glance around the music room. "What cause do I have to be happy? I'm merely urging a promising young candidate back onto the path."

Enough of this. The music room was meant to be his and Arasne's space. Theo's mere presence meant rot was leaking into the room, and Zavrius couldn't stand to stay still anymore. He went to push past his brother, but Theo's hand latched onto his shoulder.

"You would ruin him, you know." Theo's voice whispered low. His fingertips dug firmly into the flesh of Zavrius' upper arm, unforgiving with their pressure. "With your ways, he would go from diligent trainee to indulgent loaf."

"It wasn't anything," Zavrius said hurriedly. "It's nothing—a way to pass the time."

"Instead of wasting the paladin's time, consider putting your cock in something as worthless as you."

Theo let go, but Zavrius didn't move. He kept himself level, told himself every cut from Theo didn't hurt. He rolled his eyes and spun back to face his brother. "If only I could fuck your opinions of me." Then, risking looking discomposed, he said, almost pleadingly, "Don't destroy his life to get at me."

Theo's gaze bore a hole into his forehead. Worried he would buckle under that direct and angry expression, Zavrius merely dug his fingers more firmly into his palms.

"I'm just having fun," said Theo, lips twitching upwards at the corner. "Lighten up, would you?"

Theo patted him twice on the back and left, and Zavrius gently closed the door behind him before he sagged against it and sank to the floor, forehead resting against the wood and heart beating so rapidly he could hear it rattling in his skull. *Breathe. Breathe.*

But Zavrius would never be able to breathe freely. Not now, with Theo hounding him. Not with Theo on the throne.

SEVEN

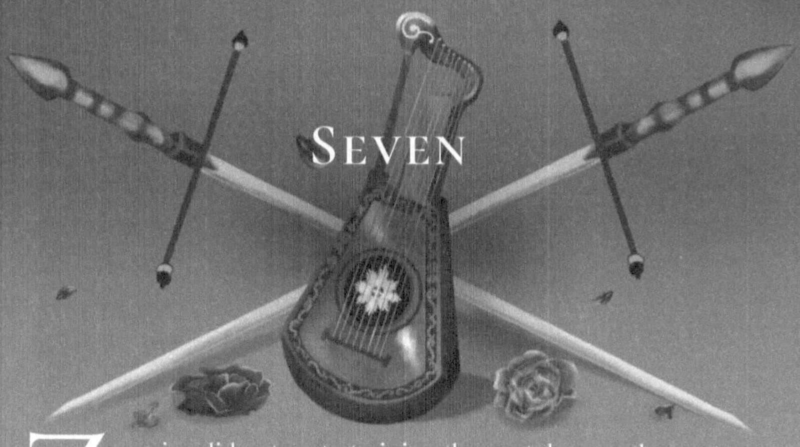

Zavrius did not go to training the next day nor the next.

By the dawn of the third morning, he had convinced himself he was adept enough at the sword to no longer require the paladin's services and that he wasn't concerned about the demonstration in the slightest.

With two weeks left before the ceremony at the Gedrok's Glade, however, he would not be able to pretend for much longer.

For today at least, Zavrius had decided to return to his old habits, except that lounging around now sparked anxiety in his belly. He had grown so keenly aware of his position in court, and the loneliness of it. No young man desires only his mother for company—and the danger of relying so heavily on Arasne became clearer with each passing day as her strength and good health began to fade.

So Zavrius found himself walking. The only bit of armor he had on him was the lute-harp, which, of course, wasn't truly armor, though it had a *known* history that seemed to drip off it— servants recognized it, and a few nobles, too—and hefting it around had the equivalent effect of walking beside the Queen herself. Still, he could wander the halls and have very few people look his way, save for polite bowing, because no one truly wanted to interact with him, and most of the visiting nobles couldn't look at him and keep their dubious sneer completely from their eyes.

He was moving to the kitchen, having missed the morning meal, and intending to pick at the remaining scraps, when he spotted his Aunt Petra. She was nodding to someone, but her eyes were quick, and the instant they landed on Zavrius, she turned bodily away from him. Zavrius waited and, sensing some urgency in the way she spoke to her charge, slipped back behind a wall and carefully watched.

Petra looked up, scanned momentarily, and when apparently satisfied Zavrius had gone, she took her charge and walked away.

With nothing else to do, Zavrius followed.

They crossed back over to the west of the palace, where the administrative wing lay. Zavrius rarely went there, but much of Cres Stros' budgetary and political advisors lingered about behind the double doors. Aunt Petra was no different.

Zavrius watched his aunt walk into the wing. He followed seconds later, opening the large double doors quietly.

He glanced up, taking in the dark tiled floor and the wide corridor. Multiple doors promised offices and storage on both sides of the walls, and muffled chatter could be heard further up the hall. But Zavrius blocked it out, focusing instead on the voice of his aunt, which boomed from the first closed door in the wing.

Zavrius pressed himself close.

"Well?" she was saying. "What have you learned from all this, then?"

"Enough to be concerned, madame."

The voice was unfamiliar, with a resonant quality. Petra spread herself thin throughout the palace, occupying many roles at once, but in that very moment, Zavrius had no doubt the role she played was not *aunt,* but Cres Stros' spymaster.

He heard her disappointed sigh and the sound of a chair taking weight. "Do I need to know names?"

There was a pause, and then shuffling, the sound of paper being dragged across cloth. "I've recorded them, and what they said. But. . ."

Petra clicked her tongue. "But?"

"It is. . .a general sentiment. It would have been easier to write the names of those who have said nothing, agreed with nothing."

Zavrius' heart pounded. He wanted to crouch down and stay there forever, learning slowly how dutifully the court would undermine the peace his mother had fought so hard to restore.

As if reading his mind, Petra grunted, "And of Arasne?"

"It. . .it seems not many want to say outright where they stand about her reign. Though there are rumors. They say she is not well."

Something passed through Petra's lips that Zavrius couldn't quite hear. "She needs to be out more." And then, "Forget you heard that."

"Madame."

"Is it war they want, then?"

A non-committal noise, and then, "The general sentiment is that there is no backbone to this country any longer. That at least twenty years ago, we were fighting for complete independence. This treaty—many think it lets the Rezwyns creep in."

"A slow colonizing," Petra said.

Unprompted and almost too quietly for Zavrius to hear, the spy said, "Prince Theo lends them hope."

Zavrius shifted his weight. He couldn't help it; instinctively, his body tilted forward and pressed against the frame of the office door. The wood betrayed him with a creak, and the conversation in the other room died. *Fuck.* Zavrius breathed deep and squeezed his eyes shut like it would all go away if he didn't move, and by the time he was suffocating, Petra had stood. He heard her footsteps moving toward the door.

Zavrius leapt back and sped out of the administration hallway, nearly running until he was in an empty corridor.

Sweat pricked at the back of Zavrius' neck. He knocked his head against the wall and breathed, breathed, breathed. This—whatever this was—couldn't be ignored the way he would like. Ignoring all his earlier desires for a pleasant day of fuck all, Zavrius turned and pushed back into the central vestibule of the palace.

To be so utterly kept in the dark disturbed him.

Petra, his mother, even Theo—all of them were oddly romantic in their notions of Zavrius' character. He could and would not sit by idly, not especially when failing to secure his position *now* would mean death later. With new purpose, he walked not to the kitchen but to the courtyard.

Warm sunlight struck down in rays, and visiting nobles lounged about, baking in the sun and chatting to one another. He knew he could learn through watchful silence, but even though people found him relatively disinteresting, they rarely let down their guard. When he spotted a group of four noblewomen and one nobleman laughing and smirking, he thought: *there's my mark.*

They were attended to by a courtesan, a pretty, round person with short, curly hair. Though their body was hidden behind layers of chiffon, they wore their draperies with such sensuality that Zavrius felt a spark of jealousy watching them. He stood a little straighter and the instant they were done pouring wine, he beckoned them over with his eyes.

The courtesan walked languidly out of the sun and undercover to where Zavrius had poised himself, pressed up against a pillar.

"My prince." They bowed dutifully and kept their gaze low.

They had about ten years on Zavrius, he guessed. A cloying perfume clung to their glowing skin.

Zavrius cast his eyes over to the nobles. His hands fiddled at his side, fingers running over the fabric of his tunic. He hated feeling like this—all useless and pathetic, scrabbling at the air for purchase he would never find. But he made sure to keep such panic from his face. Zavrius smiled and cocked his head at the courtesan. "Tell me something, and I'll make it worth your while."

"Worth my while?" their voice lilted, broad and dazzling smile splitting their lips apart. "You have a high opinion of yourself, my prince."

Zavrius balked at the cockiness, and then laughed for the same reason. Often, he enjoyed the company of courtesans and the like because of how they treated him. Their jokes amused him, even when they spoke so brashly of his character. After years of being subjected to Theo and the others' cruelty, Zavrius loved this kind of banter.

"Coin," Zavrius snorted. "I'll pay you in coin."

The courtesan smiled and bowed again. "Dove," they said, by way of greeting.

"Dove," Zavrius repeated. "Come by the Royal Apartments later, and I'll pay you."

"For what?"

Zavrius glanced over to the nobles. "Tell me. Have they spoken about my mother at all? Or Theo?"

Dove's smile did not shift from their face, but Zavrius—used to clocking the most minute changes in his family's demeanor—felt when it happened. Not disgust or upset, and not disappointment, either, but a wariness. It crept into Dove's eyes and seemed to corrupt the genuineness of their otherwise warm expression. In response, Zavrius' body shivered. Dove leaned gently against the pillar. Zavrius frowned. Few people were so casual around him that he found himself unsure how to hold himself.

After a moment, Dove told him, "You are not particularly good at this, my prince."

Zavrius flushed.

Perhaps out of pity, Dove leaned forward and whispered, "But I will tell you what I know. The treaty is not well-liked. Rumors abound that Queen Arasne is unwell, and much of the nobility has begun to anticipate what her successor's rule will look like."

Zavrius' heart raced. He didn't know what to ask—or rather, didn't know how to ask his questions well. He said, "They think Theo will be a better ruler?"

"They think their interests align with Theo's more so than they do with your mother's."

A beautiful understatement. He recalled Petra saying, *Is it war they want, then?*

Zavrius almost asked the same question, but he could feel Dove's eagerness to leave. Before they could slip away, he blurted, "Have you heard. . ." he cleared his throat. "Have you ever heard what they say about me?"

Dove met his eyes with new fervor. They clicked their tongue against their teeth, arms folding defensively against their chest. As their whole posture changed, Zavrius found his body shifting to do the same. Petulantly, Zavrius spat, "Oh, go on, tell me. I can take it."

Dove laughed. They said, "I'm sure you can, my prince," in such a sultry tone that Zavrius blushed. "But I. . .think it best I don't repeat everything I've heard. Not to you, at least."

Ah, there it was. The undeniable nature of this court reared its head again. Dove spoke so eloquently and seemed so unbothered by his line of questioning that Zavrius knew instantly he was speaking to one of Petra's spies.

"You're hers, aren't you?"

Dove merely shrugged but pushed themselves off the pillar as if making to leave.

"You're going to go tattle to her now," Zavrius murmured, accusatory.

Dove spread their arms wide. "I'm afraid she pays me more than you will," they said before wandering back into the palace.

Zavrius' heart pounded against his chest. He figured he had a handful of minutes before Petra came to find him—and she would, of course, because asking these kinds of questions was her purview, not his. Zavrius could envision the lecture now, how she would criticize his poor decisions, how she would suggest he would make things worse with his prodding.

But how could she, as an agent of the court, ever understand his unique position? Balanced delicately on a board above a pit of vipers, Zavrius' protection relied almost entirely on Arasne's goodwill. Perhaps Theo wouldn't kill him when he became king, but Zavrius doubted he'd be protected, either. Most certainly, his preferred way of living wouldn't be encouraged.

He glanced around the pillar, resting his cheek against the warm stone. The nobles were well into their drinks. He had some minutes, a lute-harp, and a penchant for arcane manipulation. As if he was going to do nothing.

"Room for one more?"

Zavrius splayed himself quite dramatically against the pillar next to the stone seating the group of nobles had claimed as their own. All their heads whipped around to him. He scanned their faces. Brown skin flushed with red and unfocused eyes: they were deep into their cups.

Seconds passed before they recognized him, and then their eyes went wide. One of them—a noblewoman of a small house—

exclaimed, "Prince Zavrius! How funny! We were just talking about you!"

Zavrius smiled dimly. He thought of Dove and their avoidance of this same question. "Oh? Good things, I hope?"

The laughter that emerged from them was far too genuine for Zavrius' liking. He used this ripple of noise as an excuse to push forward and seat himself beside the single nobleman.

They were all representatives of fairly small houses. Many were from the west, but one of the noblewomen hailed from the Ashmon Range, though the Ashmon nobles had traditionally been very loyal to the Dued Vuuthriks; it wasn't unusual at all for one to be here. Arasne had her advisors live here permanently and otherwise kept her cards close. Visiting nobles were, as far as Zavrius understood it, momentary esteemed guests.

He wondered at the irony of attending the court of a queen whose rule you openly criticized. It made no sense for them to be here, except if—

Zavrius paused.

Except if Arasne wasn't who they were trying to impress. Except if they were hoping for war. Except if they were hoping for plum military appointments when a new power-hungry king took the throne.

He recognized a few of these faces belatedly. Surely, one or two had been at Theo's back when he'd destroyed Zavrius' lute weeks earlier. With that in mind, Zavrius knew exactly what these people thought of him anyway. He could suddenly feel every pore in his skin, a vulnerability that rippled through him. Out of habit, his fingers began to move against the lute-harp. He played softly.

"You don't mind if I play, do you?"

"Oh, not at all," the nobleman beside him said. "Lord Ruseth, my prince. A pleasure to meet you."

"And I you," Zavrius said pleasantly. "How have you all been enjoying court?"

"Oh, it's splendid," one noblewoman exclaimed.

And another, the Lady Giposk "Just wonderful, Prince Zavrius, thank you."

Zavrius kept that inane smile plastered to his face. Swiftly, he conjured a bit of power in his fingertips. He would have liked to work more slowly, but he had such little time; the certainty that Petra would come and admonish him only became stronger with each passing second.

So, in this haze of comfort he created, with each note feeling feather-soft and gentle, he asked, "You all aren't thinking of rising up against my mother, the Queen, now, are you?"

Pleasant laughter rippled around the gathered nobility.

"Rebellion?" Lord Ruseth cried. "Certainly not."

"It's nothing that insidious, my prince," Lady Giposk agreed.

Zavrius kept playing, though softly. He wanted to extricate himself from this situation without any suspicion. They had been drinking for hours, and he hoped that would be enough to explain their openness should any look back at this moment with confusion.

Zavrius feigned a look of surprise. "But you are rather keen for my brother's rule, yes?"

This got them all smiling.

"Well, of course," one of the other noblewomen said. "Prince Theo will make a splendid king."

"Wonderful," Zavrius exclaimed. "Because I, for one, am quite sick of sitting around waiting for the Rezwyns to crush us, aren't you?"

Hilariously, most of them made a noise of surprise, like Zavrius had just gotten up and began to undress. They blinked at him and then at each other, cautious smiles causing their lips to twitch.

"Well. . ." Lord Ruseth began.

The noblewoman from the Ashmon Range said, "Prince

Zavrius, I was unfamiliar with your opinions on the empire. I assumed—"

"A lot of people assume things about me," Zavrius said truthfully. "I project a certain air, and I'm the youngest of my siblings. Perhaps the least well-known among you. Actually, I might ask: what did you think of me before now?"

And without hesitation, without a single thought wasted, she replied, "Oh, that you're a bit of a useless dandy."

Zavrius immediately stopped playing.

As soon as she said it, she paled so horribly and quickly that Zavrius expected her to pass out. He looked at her—stared, really —eyes never moving from her expression.

Internally, Zavrius was laughing. This bit of cruelty was, he believed, well deserved. Externally, though, he maintained an air of princely surprise.

The noblewoman stared back, then away, then to her friends for help—though none of them were giving her much of that, with all their gazes fixed on Zavrius, waiting for his reaction.

"My prince. . ." she began.

Zavrius sucked his teeth. "What was your name, again?"

Pale and unsettled, tears began to prick in her eyes. "My prince, I. . .I am so sorry. I don't know why—"

A sudden interruption: "Prince Zavrius."

The voice came from Zavrius' left. He turned and found a servant waiting in a deep bow. He flicked his wrist, and she stood. She had eyes only for him. "Chancellor Petra has requested your presence in her office."

Ah. There ended his fun.

Zavrius stood and politely dipped his head at the nobles and the carnage he had left them in.

"Lovely chatting with you," he said, and without waiting, he excused himself from the stone circle and began to follow their servant. In his periphery, the lot of them drunkenly scrabbled to standing, and very faintly, Zavrius was positive he heard someone begin to cry.

"You think your mother doesn't know this?" Petra sneered. Her expression crumpled within seconds, and she hid her face behind her hands, rubbing vigorously at the skin. "Gedroks. You can be so like Sirellius sometimes—no, don't get *upset*. It's the brashness. The cockiness."

Zavrius sat stiffly in a creaky wingback chair that had been stuffed into the corner of Petra's office. His aunt stood, though at a defeated angle. Her hands were splayed onto her desk.

Zavrius hadn't bothered to try and defend himself. He saw in Petra the disappointment, the odd resignation, as if his behavior was expected, and more frustrating than anything else.

Petra glared at him. "Your mother has been queen for years. She succeeded your father on the eve of his death, and she has had to wrangle war-hungry nobility for over a decade, all the while maintaining a tenuous relationship with the bloody Rezwyns. You do not need to worry about her rule."

Zavrius imagined giving up, putting his back in the sand, and becoming entirely what everyone already thought of him: a useless dandy without a clue. But *so much* lay between Zavrius and that possibility. He knew too much to live that life and be at peace. For now, he felt as petulant as Petra had assumed him to be. Why should he have to bear this? Why should *he* be the one to endure when it seemed every other of his vicious siblings knew more than him about court machinations, when they had allies, when they weren't in danger of losing everything the instant their mother passed?

Defiantly, Zavrius raised his chin. "It's not her rule that I'm worried about it ."

Petra fell silent. Her face went impassive, and Zavrius bit into his tongue.

Petra occupied a unique position at court. Her loyalty seemed to be more to Cres Stros than whoever sat on the throne, and so she would be loyal to Theo, as she had been loyal to Sirellius, despite the inevitable collapse of their country should they face the Rezwyns on the field once more. Perhaps out of defiance, Zavrius stared unblinking at Petra's expression. In past years, he would have been the first to break. But something in him rose up, and his fear gave way to a frenzied energy—he would not back down. He would not apologize.

To his great surprise, Petra sighed and looked away. Zavrius shifted, unused to being the victor of these silent exchanges. His aunt sank into the chair behind her desk and showed him very obviously what she thought about all this by burying her face in her hands.

"What has Theo said to you?" she whispered.

"You're the spymaster," Zavrius murmured. "Shouldn't you already know?"

She glared at him from between her fingers, eyes dangerous. With a deep inhale, Petra dropped her hands and sat up straight, clearly unimpressed with Zavrius' obvious pettiness.

"Zavrius," she said. "Theo hasn't liked you from the moment it became obvious you were. . ." — a barely subtle pause, a carefully chosen phrase— "who you are." Zavrius snorted. Petra said, "Why are you being so guarded?"

Zavrius made an attempt to stay calm. In his heart, he was at war. Petra was family, but so much of his family hated him, and her duty might mean she couldn't protect him. Might have to actively petition against him if Theo wanted a legitimate reason for Zavrius to die. But he couldn't justify doing nothing. He shifted in discomfort. Anxiety formed a dense knot in his stomach and had him slouching with every taut tug.

"Oh, you know," he said. "Some subtle threats, some overt threats. In general, I suspect I won't live very long in Theo's court."

Petra did not blink at this. Zavrius assumed she had heard far worse during her time as both chancellor and spymaster. But she did, after a long moment, nod—the tiniest confirmation that what Zavrius spoke of was in line with Theo's personality.

"I imagine that was upsetting to hear," she said finally.

How fucking diplomatic. Zavrius rolled his eyes and leaned forward. "I deserve to know what's happening in this court. Theo and the others have years on me. I thought I could lay low; I thought perhaps I could survive by being quiet and unimpressive. But apparently, that has only made me more of a target!"

Zavrius did not say the other thing: that even as he developed his own friendships in court, Theo would swoop in and come to take them away. He was made impotent in every way, an eternal child, and relying on his aunt now only confirmed it. Zavrius flushed and glanced away, hearing how high his voice went and how pathetic he sounded. Fiddling with his fingers, he began to shake his head. "Will you really scold me for trying to stay alive?"

Petra said nothing for a long time. When she finally spoke, it was not what Zavrius had expected her to say.

"Leave it with me, Prince Zavrius."

Which could mean anything. Or nothing.

Zavrius rose without expectation and without having taken any of that scolding to heart.

If he was to survive in this court, he must learn things—and learn them however he could.

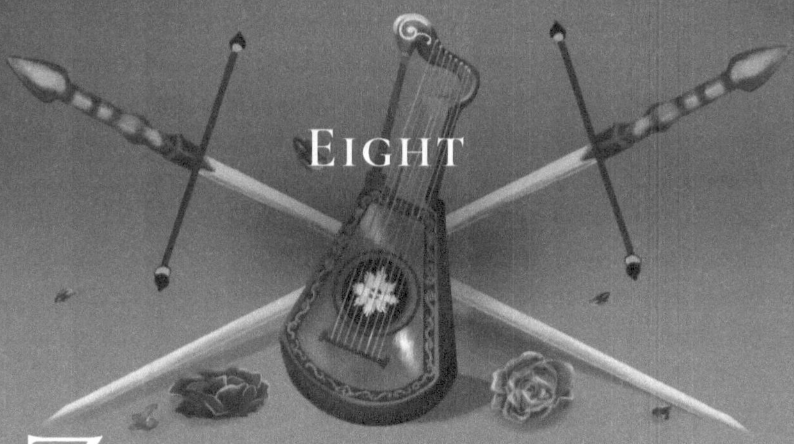

Eight

Zavrius left Petra's office feeling like a small child, all chided and embarrassed and dramatic. He wanted to die, just a little bit, so overcome with the sheer number of things he would have to do to remain alive in a court intent on hating him.

He'd need a better grip on politics. Spies. A deep understanding of the court and the nobles and every alliance that would ever be made, or strained, or changed, or broken. A fucking expanse of complications spanned out before him, and how much time had he wasted thinking he could survive through sheer luck?

It wasn't a waste. You were training your art and your arcane power. Developing a cloak, a lie about your incompetence. You have survived this long through those choices.

But a great grief cracked wide through Zavrius' chest. The horror seemed insurmountable because where in amongst the politics and the spies and the scheming would he find time to *live?*

Was it any wonder that, whilst his mind raced and this sadness soured his blood, that his feet took him out to the back of the palace, passed the courtyard, and squarely to the expanse of green field outside the Forge, where the paladins were training?

Zavrius positioned himself unabashedly in front of the training horde and crossed his arms. With practiced effort, he schooled his face into something impenetrable and pretended he wasn't fixated solely on Balen of Westgar, whom he hadn't seen in a week. Whom he hadn't seen since Theo chased him out, since Zavrius himself said Balen was little more than a way to pass the time—gedroks, he hadn't meant it. He felt overcome with emotion. Too much pressure filled his chest, and it felt—disproportionate. Balen was more than a pastime, sure, but he wasn't a lover. He was barely a friend. And yet, Zavrius could not fight the lump that grew quickly in his throat and the sting of tears in his eyes when he saw him.

Look away, a voice in his mind said, acrid like Sirellius' scolding, or Theo's imitation of their father. Then the voice came again, this time asking: *why are you here?*

Why *was* he here?

He glanced up to watch the training. The paladins fought in pairs, sparring for a time, and then upon Uncle Lestr's signal—a whistle over the fingers—one row would move to the right to attack the next waiting paladin. Balen moved like a force of nature, landing strike after strike on his opponents. He had youth in his favor, but also. . . The paladin pushed himself in every spar like his life depended on the success of that play-fight. As if every moment was *real*. What was that thing driving him? Determination? Or something deeper, like a *need?*

A need to be taken seriously. If it was that, then Zavrius could understand it implicitly.

Zavrius stepped forward for a better look, telling himself he would understand the expression clouding Balen's face with a better view.

He stumbled closer, shifting his gaze every which way to shield his obvious interest. But Balen was a tide pulling him out.

Gedroks, everything about Balen of Westgar reminded Zavrius of the ocean. There was the look of him, of course, with that pale skin flecked with freckles. The way his hair curled as if sprayed with salt, and the color of his eyes, ocean-deep and just as blue. And then, especially since Balen of Westgar should not have been on Zavrius' mind at all, the young prince liked to imagine him blowing in like a sea breeze, unavoidable and crisp.

Now, watching the way the nacreous armor moved over his body, each plate shuddering into place, his movement appeared ocean-like, too. Like Balen himself was a wave crashing over rocks, beautiful and powerful and deadly. Any paladin that Balen faced were like those rocks, and Balen's shoreline destruction over them was inevitable. In part, too, Zavrius felt like rocks, and he knew if he didn't find a way to apologize, to make it known to Balen that everything he had said in Theo's presence was a lie, it would erode at his core for the rest of his life.

Lestr called a , and all the paladins stood up, panting hard. Zavrius must have been boring a hole in the back of Balen's skull, for he jerked up and met Zavrius' eye. A long moment passed. Zavrius let a breath hiss through his teeth, but his body stayed anxious under Balen's icy gaze. *Keep looking at me*, he thought, and at the same moment, *stop looking at me.* Balen must have heard the latter. He blinked rapidly and looked down at his feet.

That look away was the exact opposite of an invitation, but against his better judgment, Zavrius stepped forward onto the field. Several heads rolled towards him, all of them the picture of cautious scrutiny. Paladins, both green and decades into service, stared at him. Zavrius couldn't remember the last time he'd been this close to their training. Before now, he hadn't taken much interest—certainly never enough to warrant him getting so close. He bit down on his tongue and breathed through the pain.

He was a prince. What did it matter what they thought of him?

Reacting to the surprise and speculation on his trainee's faces, Uncle Lestr whirled around. He, too, was unable to keep the shock from his face. He barked a word of order to the paladins, and they broke into small groups for another type of training.

Balen lingered. Just long enough for Zavrius' lips to quirk into a smile. But even this was rejected. Balen turned without a lick of acknowledgment. Zavrius shifted. A headache spawned in his skull and began to throb. What was he *doing?*

"Prince Zavrius," Lestr said over a bow. Zavrius snapped toward his uncle. "An honor. Though. . ." he dropped his voice low as he got close. "What is it? Is it the Queen?"

Concern blistered Lestr's face. Zavrius hadn't seen him by Arasne's side for some time, but he assumed that was part of her ruse—her refusal to admit that anything was the matter with her.

"She's as she has been," Zavrius answered carefully.

Lestr pursed his lips and nodded. "Then your visit. . .?"

"I need to speak to one of your paladins."

Lestr did not hide his disappointment, like he knew the only reason Zavrius Dued Vuuthrik would come to speak to a paladin was because he found said paladin pretty. It might have stung if it wasn't a correct assessment of Zavrius and his motivations. As it was, he shook his hair out and raised his chin, trying for princely defiance or grounded certainty. Lestr remained unmoved.

He said, "My prince," with a heavy tone that straddled pity, "my paladins are busy."

"*Your* paladins, are they?" Zavrius said, and Lestr put his hand over his heart and bowed just so in apology, though it seemed begrudgingly given. His uncle's movements were stiff. Zavrius looked over his uncle's shoulder. Balen was rolling out his shoulders and striking the air as an older paladin murmured to him, gave suggestions, touched his forearm—Zavrius glanced back to Lestr.

His uncle had a comingled look of disappointment and fury on his face, though he at least tried to hide it with a pathetic excuse for a smile. "Prince Zavrius, they are training."

Zavrius rolled his eyes. "I need to—"

"Theo is coming by soon."

Zavrius' heart plummeted. A great wave of fear came over him. He almost cried out, like a scolded child; he let his heart do it instead, making the noise of fury and despair he so badly wanted to scream out. He felt small and feeble as he smiled politely up at his uncle. All he could manage to say was, "Oh?"

"Yes." Lestr gestured towards the paladins with his head. "Theo has requested to be more involved. He has an eye on one or two of the paladins to be his Prime. Which, of course, isn't how it works. It will all depend on how they perform in the tournament. But Theo wants to know how his paladins fight."

Zavrius' fury barely let Lestr finish his awful spiel. "Already planning for my mother's death, is he?" he chirped brightly.

Lestr's face darkened. He dipped his head. "Zavrius. You know that isn't—"

"*Prince* Zavrius," he snapped. He brought his voice low, and before he could think better of it, all the vitriol in his heart seeped between his teeth. "You are the Queen's brother, commander of the paladins, but you are *not* to talk back to me. I do not care what you think of me, though I know it isn't anything good. You should keep an eye on my brother. On *all* of them." He shut up. Stopped talking abruptly, closed his mouth— what was he *thinking?* Lestr's loyalty was about as clear to him as the origins of the gedroks. Zavrius raised his chin. "I am going to take ten seconds of one of your paladin's time. That's all."

He made to move, but Lestr stopped him. Fully put his hands on Zavrius, palm on his shoulder. Zavrius strained his eyes to stare down at it.

Lestr said, "You remind me so much of her sometimes, you know."

Zavrius' heart seized. *Good. Good. So much better her than Sirellius.*

Zavrius reached up and gently removed his uncle's hand. What he wanted to say was unkind. Nothing that had happened was Lestr's fault. Everything that *might* happen wouldn't be Lestr's fault either; he would just be following orders. But Zavrius felt so remarkably empty, then, so fearful, that he held his uncle's hand and asked, "What do you think would have happened to Usleth if Sirellius had never died?"

But it wasn't a question he wanted an answer to. He let go and left Lestr to ponder that violent alternate as he walked towards Balen of Westgar.

Feeling idiotic, Zavrius slowed his pace, approaching Balen and his fellow paladins like a cat stalking prey. The paladin was sparring, though not as he had been. He and another paladin would strike and then pause. The other two paladins were commenting on the form, the power, pointing out openings. As Zavrius approached, Balen's eye darted towards him. Just as their senior paladin called, "*Strike!*"

The paladin opposite Balen barreled forward. Balen flinched back towards the man calling orders. Zavrius heard the sharp intake of breath, and then they collided. They would have gone down together, except the older man righted himself moments before toppling. Balen wasn't so lucky. He landed sprawled on his back, a red flush scalding his face.

"Halt!" the ordering paladin called. "Prince on the field."

The three standing paladins fell into deep bows, leaving Balen to flounder as he struggled to right himself.

"I'm sorry to interrupt," Zavrius said.

"Not at all, my prince," one said. "A pleasure to have you

here. I am Paladin Frenyur. This is Paladin Pei, Paladin Balen, and Gaidis, who will be confirmed in just a week's time."

"Yes," Zavrius said with a short bow. That was right. Less than a week to go before Zavrius was set to demonstrate his new-found swordplay ability in front of numerous young paladins, his siblings, and inevitably, one or two of the nobles Arasne promised wouldn't actually attend. Less than a *week* before he was humiliated in front of too many people. But if he felt anxious about that, he had somehow managed to bury it deep enough to avoid the feeling from surfacing —until that moment. "That's coming up rather soon, isn't it?"

He smiled blankly at everyone and then turned to Balen. "A word?"

The other three turned towards Balen, whose embarrassed flush now only worsened. He opened his mouth. Was he about to protest? Zavrius raised an eyebrow, and Balen almost instantly dropped into a bow. Wordlessly, he began to walk forward.

Zavrius led them away from the training, though he could feel many eyes watching their retreat.

He walked further than strictly necessary, using those precious moments to still his heart—he failed—and *breathe*—also failed. When the distance got ridiculous, Zavrius stopped. He turned.

Balen was upon him immediately. Any defiance had died in the walk. His brows were upturned, his eyes fearful. Balen was scrunching his nose up just before he flung forward into a bow. "My prince."

"Balen," Zavrius said carefully. "How. . .are you?"

Balen paused at that low position and raised himself up slowly. "I'm doing well, thank you. I've. . . been training."

"I haven't," Zavrius said, aiming for humor. The joke fell flat. Balen remained stiff, not even the hint of a smile on his face.

"My brother is set to come by soon," Zavrius said. "I haven't seen much of him since. . .well, since I last saw you."

Balen grimaced. What was that expression? What was he thinking?

"Won't you say something?" Zavrius whispered.

Balen looked down at his hands. His brow furrowed. Again, his lips opened, but no words spilled out.

Fear and rage shivered through him. Zavrius stepped forward. "Why won't you look at me? Balen? *Look* at me."

Balen's eyes shot up. He held an apology in them. Desperately, he glanced back over his shoulder, feet turning to go. He, of course, didn't move, but that he was *forcing himself* to stay felt infinitely worse. "My prince, I—"

"I owe you an apology," Zavrius hissed lowly.

Balen turned fully back to him. Zavrius' eyes were stinging, and he hoped somewhere in his expression Balen could see his sincerity. His desperation. *Please*, Zavrius thought. *Please just hear me out.*

He could have ordered it all away. He could have ordered Balen of Westgar to his bed, and even if it had been frowned upon, who would truly deny him? But Zavrius wanted none of that.

He wanted to reach out and push Balen's hair away from his face. He wanted to wipe the grime off the young man's cheeks, wanted to get closer, wanted too much. Balen deserved better.

Balen deserved the truth.

Zavrius said, "I know you're busy. I know you're. . .I know you're training, and you hope to. . . serve my brother, at the end of it all. But I need to speak to you. To explain myself, and in all honesty, to. . ."

To what?

To tell you the truth of Theo's nature. To beg you to keep training me, beg you to save me from embarrassment next week. To. . .

"I accept your apology," Balen said flatly.

"Oh, come off it." Zavrius rolled his eyes. Balen flinched, but Zavrius didn't care, just stalked forward and jabbed a finger against his plated chest. "You're upset with me, and you don't know how to reconcile that with your loyalty to the crown. Fair enough. But you must let me explain."

He didn't have to let Zavrius do anything, but he would. Zavrius knew it, was banking on it—Balen was too much of a loyalist to turn away from a prince. It was manipulative, yes, about as low as Zavrius could go. But he needed Balen to listen to him. Zavrius would pull rank if it meant

"Meet me at the Royal Apartments this evening," Zavrius said.

Balen visibly bristled, and Zavrius put out a staying hand. "I know it's a lot to ask after. . .after last time. But my aunt Petra is speaking to Theo and Avidia about some administrative tasks this evening, and Gideonus and Lysio are entertaining the nobility. That leaves me. . .alone."

He glanced up at Balen, who had never been more stony-faced. "Please, Balen." He almost said more. Almost confessed that he had missed waking at the crack of dawn to train, that he missed more than that—Balen's hands on him. Balen's smile. Their conversations. And perhaps it wasn't fair to miss those things when Balen was only doing his duty, but miss them, he did. Zavrius said nothing. He could feel their distant audience, whose interest had not waned in the minutes they were standing there.

Balen said, "What do I tell them?" and Zavrius realized the paladin was aware of their watchers, too.

"Tell them the Queen has tasked me with organizing the confirmation affair and that I needed a paladin to talk logistics with. That you'll be talking logistics with me tonight. You came recommended."

"By whom?" Balen said. And then, before Zavrius could answer, "'Talk *logistics*'?"

"The number of paladins to be confirmed, the ichor we will need, how much armor will need to be constructed or reforged. Do actually find that out, though, if you can. Ask Lestr. But in the end, all I want is. . .time. With you. To explain. You should come at sunset."

He said it stilted, unsure when to stop his sentence. When Balen didn't immediately reply, he prompted. "Balen?"

"I'll be there," Balen said over a bow. "My prince."

It felt better than an oath to hear that.

For hours, Zavrius did nothing except wait for Balen, and also make himself look pretty. Kohl lined in perfectly sharp lines over his top eyelid and smudged on his lower, smoking out his under-eye. He chose a mauve tunic that cinched at the waist, and then he played his mother's lute-harp to pass the final hour till sunset. He only managed ten minutes before nerves prevented him from continuing, and he had to sprawl on his bed with his limbs spread. The immobility helped. Kept him grounded. But it also allowed anxiety to settle its roots in his belly, and soon Zavrius was spiraling.

He ran the conversation through his head, imagining each way it could go. He imagined Balen bowing politely but sternly, and Zavrius realizing they would never rekindle what little comfortability they'd had with one another. He imagined Balen turning on his heel and walking out on him—which was unlikely, given their respective statuses, but it still *hurt* to think about. For some reason, Zavrius kept replaying that possibility over and over again, letting his gut feel the stab of stony betrayal, letting his fear bleed everywhere.

When he couldn't take it any longer, he got up, straightened his tunic and his hair (which had started to billow out in a frizz from his horizontal positioning), and then parked himself outside the door to the Royal Apartments with his arms and ankles crossed.

Balen arrived the very minute the sun began to sink. Like a prophecy, he walked out of the colonnaded stretch and into the palace proper, a dark shadow framed by a pinkish starburst of light. Zavrius pushed off the wall to meet him far more eagerly than he'd intended to.

"How was my brother's visit?" he asked brightly. Other greetings would have been better or more proper, but jealousy propelled that out of his mouth.

"Fine, my prince." This version of Balen fell flat. He was reserved. *Wrong.*

Zavrius grimaced. "Give me the details." And then, because he was impatient, "That's an order."

He opened the door into the Royal Apartments, and Balen fell into step behind him.

"Prince Theo is. . .a quiet observer," Balen said carefully. When Zavrius snorted, Balen cleared his throat, adding, "I don't know what to make of his visits."

Because they don't mean anything! They're done to annoy me, not because he wishes to choose a Prime.

"Does he intend to forego the tournament? Choose a Prime based on his wants alone?

"I. . .am not sure the prince is the type to forego tradition."

How polite. Zavrius glanced back over his shoulder. "Know him well, do you?"

It wasn't kind. It wasn't wholly sane, either. What Zavrius wanted was a co-conspirator, for Balen to say: *yes, he's volatile, he's mad, he hates you. I saw it, and I agree with you.*

Balen blushed, but his brow twinged, and Zavrius realized how effortlessly he was screwing this up. He sighed loudly. "Ignore that. Please."

Not quite an apology, but he could only manage one today—and he had to make that one count.

He'd intended at first to lead Balen to the library since the music room had spelled disaster and because the room was beautiful. But part of him worried for their privacy. Theo had never come into Zavrius' personal space unannounced before. . .

So it was that Zavrius first led Balen of Westgar into his bedroom.

Zavrius glanced back in time to catch the dawning comprehension cross the young paladin's face, this look of abject horror and despair and a glint of thrill hiding in his gaze.

"My prince, I—"

"Sit down," Zavrius said, and Balen cast about for somewhere to sit.

The room was not particularly grand, at least by Zavrius' standards. As the youngest, he'd been sequestered into the smallest chamber. It consisted of a four-poster bed, a dazzling rug, and a long, thin stained-glass window depicting a roaring gedrok. The wardrobe, which was large and wooden with double doors, sat stuffed to bursting in the corner. Bits of red and purple fabric crumpled out of the seam between the doors, and tunics were draped over its top. Several more had been laid and over the back of a sitting chair that had become an extension to the wardrobe, but otherwise, that was it.

Poor Balen smiled pleasantly at the clothing-covered chair, and his eyes wandered over to the bed. He kept that pleasant expression unmoving on his face even when the concern began to flare in his eyes. He glanced at Zavrius. "I—"

"You may sit on the bed," Zavrius said as he moved past, sitting first.

Balen did not move.

"Or stand there, moping about; I don't care."

Silence stretched between them. Balen looked comically large standing in his armor in the small, messy room. Zavrius leaned back on the bed and reached for his mother's lute-harp, which he'd left resting against one of the pillows. He plucked at the strings, gaining courage, but he found it awfully difficult to look Balen's way. His chest ached.

"I. . .I wanted to talk. About what happened last week," he said, without looking Balen's way. His leg jittered. He reached out and plucked another chord. Then, because Balen hadn't replied and sitting still was equivalent to torture, he threw himself up and sighed. "Did you hear me?"

"I heard you," Balen snapped. A shiver ran through Zavrius' body. No one spoke to him like that.

As if realizing the same thing, the impropriety of the tone, Balen paled and bowed. "My prince, forgive me. I heard you."

Zavrius got up. "No," he said. "No, I want you to get angry. I want you to speak to me as if we are equals."

Balen frowned and glanced up. He shook his head. "We will never—"

"But it's what I *want*."

Gedroks, he sounded petulant. He couldn't articulate precisely what he meant. He reached out and gingerly touched Balen's upper arm, a motion that had the paladin staring down at where their flesh touched like the point of contact burned him.

Zavrius said, "I owe you an apology. I wanted to say," he took a deep breath and practically choked on the air. "I wanted to say that I'm sorry for how I behaved. For what I said."

He's nothing to me.

And the other thing, which Balen hadn't heard, but Zavrius still regretted: *It wasn't anything. It's nothing—a way to pass the time.*

"It wasn't. . . true." Zavrius spoke carefully.

Balen looked vaguely ill. "I don't understand."

What could Zavrius say? *You mean something to me. . .as my occasional swordplay trainer?* Perhaps Balen had forgotten the words Zavrius had said. Perhaps it—their budding friendship—honestly meant nothing to him. Zavrius fidgeted and said more easily than he felt, "I said things that I regret saying. I regretted saying them the instant they left my mouth. My brother brings out my worst parts, and no, that's no excuse, but I wanted to tell you that I'm sorry for saying what I did. That it isn't true. I like your company. Do you understand?"

It felt like opening up his belly. Every inch of his body froze as he waited for the paladin's response.

Balen, on his part, hesitated. He shifted minutely, and his entire suit of armor creaked with him. Cautiously, he turned his head away and blinked rapidly down at his feet. "I'm not sure that I do."

That enraged Zavrius. Not enough to scream, not enough to shout, but enough that he stepped back from Balen and sat back onto the bed and very nearly told him to leave. He couldn't even be sure *why*. Was he embarrassed? Frightened? Was some Dued Vuuthrik madness settling over him?

It took a long while of controlled breathing and the threat of his canines slicing into his tongue to settle him. By the time he had, Balen was speaking.

"I don't understand many things about you," Balen whispered. He still wasn't meeting Zavrius' gaze. "When Prince Theo came into that room. . .you were different."

He didn't elaborate, though Zavrius expected him to.

"Because my brother is a dick," he spat. "That's the long and short of it: he has never liked me, and he thinks I am a disgrace, and he. . .by association, Balen, he said I would tarnish you. But it isn't about *you*. His interest in you and the paladins is to dissuade *my* interest. I'm sorry, that's probably not what you want to hear, but I want you to know what kind of man you'll be serving should you become Prime." He paused. "And I think you will, you know, when it comes down to it. Win the tournament, I mean."

Balen exhaled so noisily that Zavrius thought something was wrong. He slumped in his armor and began pressing his fingers to it.

"Are you alright?"

"Too much to hear," Balen wheezed. A hiss sounded, and his cuirass clicked away from his body. Balen caught the pieces and laid them down before tearing off his vambraces. He left his gorget and all the armor on his legs and stomped clankingly over to the bed, where he gingerly lowered himself.

His face burned starkly red. Sweat made his undershirt sheer, and it clung to his back. Balen tipped forward and wrung out his hands. For nearly a minute, he sat like that. Zavrius thought about lying down and playing the lute-harp, because he had an itch to do *anything* except sit here. Besides, Balen was dastardly pretty to look at, even upset—and the paladin deserved a kinder observer at that moment.

But just as Zavrius shifted to give him privacy, he reached out —very gently, barely touching, his fingertips pressed against Zavrius' forearm. "Thank you. You didn't have to tell me what happened or why, but I'm grateful you did." They stared at one another. Balen searched Zavrius' face, eyes dipping down as he said, "And I wasn't sure what I'd done. I hated. . ."

Zavrius looked down at where Balen touched him, flushing heavily himself. The paladin misunderstood the expression and jolted away, and Zavrius' hand chased his until he pressed the nail of his forefinger to the underside of Balen's. The paladin dropped his hand to the bed, but neither of them said anything about the contact. Neither of them mentioned how close the other was; indeed, Zavrius hadn't even realized his knee would have to shift very little to press against the tasset protecting Balen's upper thigh. Somehow, Balen wearing only parts of his armor was worse than wearing none of it. It did something to Zavrius, watching him sitting there, half-undressed, half-battle-ready. He found himself breathing heavily.

Balen said hurriedly, "What you said, about the tournament—"

"I mean it." Zavrius wet his lips and nodded emphatically at Balen's shocked expression.

"I. . ." Balen flushed.

"You want it? The role, I mean."

"Badly," Balen admitted. His brow furrowed, and he reached up to scratch the back of his head. "Though part of me wishes I could serve. . .someone else."

Zavrius sighed and thought on this. Paladin Hisud was Arasne's Prime, a woman in her fifties. Though rumors had it that she planned to retire—and that the Queen would allow it. She had been injured years ago protecting the Queen from one of the early assassination attempts following Sirellius' death. It was a wound from which she had never healed. Usually, paladins are protected until death, but Arasne owed Hisud her life. And perhaps, if Arasne's illness was as bad as Zavrius expected, there would be no point in appointing a new Prime.

Perhaps Hisud's departure would be a warning bell. Perhaps when that happened, it would mean Arasne had no time left at all.

Zavrius jerked away from the thought, blurting out, "I doubt my mother will hold another tournament. Hisud will likely serve until my mother passes, and then a new Prime will be chosen. But I could speak to her, if you wish."

"Gedroks, no," Balen said quickly. Then he laughed a little, and the movement rubbed their fingers together. "That wasn't what I meant."

"Not Arasne?" Zavrius clarified.

Balen shook his head.

His stomach—*floated.* Zavrius could have pressed. *Should*

have—the opportunity was *right there*, and more than that, the hope of who Balen meant. But so, too, was the fear of being a fool, and Zavrius found he couldn't overcome that worry. The pair of them lapsed into a comfortable silence, and Zavrius settled into his body. He became aware of every little thing: the ways his muscles tensed, an ache in his upper shoulders, discomfort in his hip. His heart raced. His breathing, though deep, felt shallow. He thought: *all the air in the room is gone*, and when he looked over at Balen, it only got worse.

Balen turned more fully to look at him. His lips parted, but he said nothing. The two of them were perched on the edge of Zavrius' bed, lightly touching.

Zavrius wanted very badly for Balen of Westgar to kiss him. He didn't understand why he wouldn't; why there was that hazy look in the paladin's eyes, but no move forward to close the distance.

You're a prince, his logic reminded him. A prince where Balen was a paladin; their roles were too distinct, and Balen would never risk it.

So Zavrius had to be the one. He had just dragged their flimsy friendship away from the cliff's edge, and here he was about to dive off again. But screw it. Screw it. Balen looked beautiful, and Zavrius felt more like himself when the paladin was around, and they enjoyed each other's company, they *laughed* together. What could be better? What could ever feel better? Zavrius simply had to try.

He glanced down at those parted lips, then back up to Balen's eyes. The paladin blushed—he had seen the movement, but he didn't pull away. He looked down at Zavrius' mouth.

"I want," Zavrius said and then breathed in very deeply.

Balen met his eye. Was there hope in his gaze? "Yes?"

Zavrius shifted forward. Balen let him. He could say, *I want to kiss you*, or he could tip forward and do it.

He slipped his hand away from Balen's and placed it on the young man's cheek, thumbing at the corner of his mouth. Wisps of Balen's breath grazed the pad of his thumb.

Could Balen feel what Zavrius wanted? Did he want it to? Did he crave it; did he find Zavrius as beautiful as the prince found him? There seemed only one way to test Zavrius' hope.

He tipped forward and, at the same time, pulled Balen towards him.

They locked eyes moments before Zavrius' lids fluttered closed. He felt warm breath on his lips, and then the pressure, and the thrill exploding in his chest.

Like that, fingers shaking against Balen's cheek, Zavrius Dued Vuuthrik kissed the paladin.

NINE

The moment lasted for a blissful eternity.

In that immense stretch of time, Zavrius forgot who he was and what was expected of him. He forgot every anxious thought that often kept him trapped in his mind, and instead, he *felt* everything tenfold in his body.

Every nerve in his limbs was alight and tingling. His stomach danced, his breath fluttered. At one point, he was certain his heart would escape the confines of his chest. He shook, too, ever so slightly. The only grounding contact he had was the tentative press of his fingers against Balen's cheek.

The other boy hadn't pulled away. He did not pull away even now. At Zavrius' lower back, he could feel the paladin's bare hand hovering, occasionally grazing the dip over Zavrius' hip.

Do it, you coward, Zavrius wanted to hiss, craved to let the words spill oily through his teeth, like his desire might infect his tepid partner. The urge to growl filled him, and he dropped his hand from Balen's cheek, curling it into a fist around Balen's undershirt. But this proved too much.

The paladin jerked away, his expression foggy. Zavrius

couldn't quite place it; was that delirium? Joy? An apology? He concluded that it was a messy conflation of all three.

"I'm sorry."

Those were the first words out of Balen's mouth. Why?

Zavrius shook his head. "For what?"

Balen took a breath and hesitated, just slightly, gaze flicking up to meet Zavrius' before he flinched away. "I. . .I'm not sure."

This answer made Zavrius irrationally angry. He fought to stay calm and took to balling his fists on his thighs instead. "Well?" he prompted after a tense minute. "Say something, Balen. About the kiss. Because if you don't like it, you're under no obligation to do it again, but—"

"You meant to do it, then?"

Zavrius flushed wildly. "What, you think I fell into you or something?"

Balen had turned a vicious shade of pink. His throat bobbed as he shifted. "I've never—" he cleared his throat, shook his head as if to start again. "I didn't think you—"

"I like men," Zavrius said flatly. "Everyone knows it."

Balen laughed. "I didn't think you liked *me*."

That awful vulnerability flared up in Zavrius' stomach once more. Thus far, Balen hadn't said anything about hating the kiss, but neither had he given any indication he'd liked it, either. It made Zavrius squirm. It made Zavrius want to get up and run.

"I know what you're thinking," Zavrius said, with far more confidence than he actually felt. "I'm a prince. You're a paladin. It. . .might be frowned upon. I'm probably meant for some minor lord somewhere, and you seem the type who'll swear a vow of chastity if it gets you closer to being Prime."

To this, Balen grimaced. "I really want it."

"I know you do." Zavrius' tone softened. He couldn't help it, not when Balen was so sincere with his passions. "I'm not asking for your future. I'm asking for right now. Do you understand,

Balen of Westgar? If you can have me, just for this moment, *will* you?"

Balen's flush only darkened, but he was braver this time. He moved himself forward. The bed sank with the new distribution of weight, and Zavrius' breath caught as his eyes hitched on the oddest of details; part of Balen's upper lip had cracked from the dry wind. He'd started to sweat since the kiss, and new parts of that white shirt betrayed him by turning sheer. He looked simultaneously afraid and ecstatic, and gedroks, this had never happened before. Never like this, never with someone who *knew* him well enough to see the truth of Zavrius Dued Vuuthrik.

Never.

Balen did not answer Zavrius' question with words. He cupped the prince's cheek, calloused hands rough against the fine skin, and he kissed Zavrius again. For a moment, it was only that: light, gentle pecks, a kiss held for many seconds as they breathed each other in. Zavrius couldn't be sure when it changed, only that it did. Somehow, they were suddenly panting, tonguing at one another, hands roaming. Balen's hand tangled in Zavrius' hair and pulled him closer so rapidly they toppled back together onto the bed. Zavrius broke away to laugh but crawled forward a second later to close the gap between them. This felt good. This felt *right*.

Zavrius moved his fingers beneath Balen's shirt and urged it over the paladin's head. When the shirt was free of him, Zavrius did not look right away. He pressed his lips to the side of Balen's neck even as his heart raced and his fingers trembled. Then he pulled back and saw.

Stretched out beside him, Balen looked resplendent. All the muscle in his chest and shoulders were drawn taut and defined. Somewhat greedily, Zavrius ran his hand over Balen's chest, stopping only when the paladin flinched.

"Your hands are *freezing,*" Balen said with a smile. He

propped himself up on one elbow and reached with the other, bringing Zavrius' hand up so he could kiss the back of it.

"Let me get warm, then," Zavrius whispered. He searched Balen's face, testing and shy. Was that alright to say? Was that alright to want?

The paladin's eyes glinted. "Is that an order, my prince?"

It might have been, if Zavrius had wanted to take advantage of that moment, but he was so caught off guard that he could only blush and laugh and throw himself into a messy, misaimed kiss. His lips landed on Balen's nose, and the paladin had to pull him down by the waist for their lips to meet.

Balen's fingers played with the hem of Zavrius' tunic, which the prince encouraged by loosening the tie that kept it closed. Balen deftly opened it and let the beautiful fabric fall just so. It draped itself over Zavrius' thigh and left his torso as exposed as the paladin's own. Balen's hand shook as he thumbed over Zavrius' chest, the touch so smooth and gentle it caused a shiver in Zavrius' flesh, like he was aware of his own body for the first time in his life.

Balen changed positions, hefting himself up and straddling Zavrius, a leg on either side of the prince's hips. The two of them stared at one another, and Balen leaned down for another kiss, which turned slow and sloppy. Something in the fire between them softened somewhat, then, even though Zavrius could feel himself growing hard and was certain Balen was, too—though he'd been too embarrassed to check.

Their kissing slowed, and when Zavrius shifted, Balen dropped to his side. They laid together languidly, moving between kisses to a softer, more vulnerable activity—looking one another in the eyes. Zavrius kept glancing away first.

He wanted to say much. That he hadn't done anything beyond kissing before, and that he wanted to, but his whole body felt brittle. The wrong move, the wrong word, the wrong touch, and he would shatter. "I—"

Balen leaned forward and stole the words from his mouth with another kiss. Very gently, and with an expression so vulnerable and sincere, Zavrius found it almost painful to look at.

Balen stroked Zavrius' cheek. "Let's not worry about any of that right now. It's just this moment, remember?"

Zavrius immediately softened. He nodded against Balen's hand; yes, it was just this moment. That was what they'd agreed upon. His anxiety was misplaced; for now, Prince Zavrius Dued Vuuthrik, with all his worries, did not exist. He was just a boy lying beside another boy and thinking like this allowed something taut to loosen in his body. The knotted panic that had tightened the muscles in his upper back suddenly unraveled. The usual inevitability Zavrius faced—which was a complete inability to ever truly relax, and a brewing frustration with himself for being an uptight prick—went away.

How terrifying. He closed his eyes, knocked his head against Balen's forehead, and felt for the first time in his life utterly at peace.

They must have fallen asleep, for the next thing Zavrius knew, he was being startled awake by a knock at the door. Both young men bolted upright with all the fear as if they'd been caught naked in the act.

Zavrius looked over at Balen. He could see very little. Darkness had settled in the room like an oily mass, the shadows heavy with their judgments. Irrationally, Zavrius' eyes darted to the corners of his room before he adjusted to the low light and returned his gaze to his bedmate. The paladin was disheveled. That crisp undershirt was crumpled and sweat-stained, and his hair sat tousled and scruffy. *The curse of short, straight hair,* Zavrius mused, for he looked down and saw the sleep had given his own locks volume, where Balen now resembled a disgruntled chicken.

"You're drooling," Balen whispered. His eyes had taken on a hard edge. Quickly, he leaned over and wiped a considerable amount of saliva from Zavrius' face—*fuck*—before launching himself off the prince's bed and hurriedly collecting the armor he'd removed hours before.

At the next knock, Zavrius scrabbled up himself.

"Prince Zavrius?" an unrecognizable voice called. "Are you in there?"

"Yes, yes!" he called. He turned and patted down his hair, competing with his own fluster to do something mildly useful. "I was, uh. . . I was dozing!"

He hastily tied his tunic, straightened what he could of his outfit and hair and general self, and gestured wildly for Balen to, for the gedrok's sake, *get out the way.* The paladin stumbled away from the view of the door, and Zavrius cursed as he half-tripped in the dark. He opened the door a slither. Light violently assaulted him, the brightness astounding.

He was greeted by the sight of a bowed back and the top of a young man's head. The person was dressed in a simple but good-quality tunic. A servant, then. "My Prince. My apologies for disturbing your rest, but your mother, the Queen, is calling for you."

"Of course!" Zavrius was surprised his voice came out confident. What could Arasne want? Standing there in the dark, bare feet on the cold floor, Zavrius felt as if he was absorbing something from the heavy gloom infesting the umbral dark of his room. He grew near paranoid, as if spies could see what he had done in here, what he had risked by tipping forward and kissing a paladin. What he intended to do moving forward: keep kissing the paladin. His hands closed around the frame of the door, and he forced himself to smile. "Is that all?"

The servant dipped ever lower. "Unfortunately, she has asked me to accompany you. She has been. . ." a brief pause, an almost imperceptible sound of dismay, ". . .searching for you all afternoon."

Zavrius grimaced at this. "I need a few moments," he said and, without waiting, gently closed the door.

In this instance, his mother could not wait. The urgency of her summons surprised him, and so, too, did her searching. His room should have been the first place to look.

Unless Paladin Balen has also been reported missing.

His stomach sank as he rushed back to Balen, who now resembled a suit of armor. He stood rigid and unmoving in a corner, his breathing shallow. Even as Zavrius got close, he stayed uncomfortably straight.

"I must see my mother," Zavrius said. Balen nodded quietly. "Did you. . .were you supposed to be somewhere this afternoon, by any chance?"

Zavrius hoped to be wrong, but his aunt was a spy. An intelligent man would never assume the best.

"I didn't intend to be this long," Balen whispered, a note of reproach in his voice, though whether it was self-directed or aimed at Zavrius, the prince couldn't be sure. Balen broke suddenly, hand rushing to his forehead. "Gedroks. I. . ."

Don't say it. Zavrius' body tightened instinctively. He could feel Balen edging towards that word—'mistake'—and silently begged him not to speak it aloud. But Balen didn't finish his sentence at all. He sighed.

Zavrius moved forward and kissed him. That should shut him up.

"Stay here," Zavrius said, "if you have nowhere else to be."

He didn't expect the paladin to heed those words, and he deliberately did not make them an order. Putting Balen in this position had already had enough consequences. Zavrius slipped back to the door looking, no more put together than he had a few minutes ago and wrenched it open to greet the servant once more.

***

Behind a desk piled high with mountainous papers, the Queen was seated rather regally in her wingback chair. But the visage faded as Zavrius moved closer. She looked tired.

At least she knew it. Her eyes jerked to him the instant the servant deposited Zavrius into the study—she'd been in the Royal Apartments the *whole time?* Zavrius tried not to panic over that implication—and she did not attempt to hide her scathing once over.

"You may go," she said, dismissing the servant with a wave. Then she shifted forward, chair groaning as it accommodated the change. "You don't look well. Is that why you're in bed so early?"

"A nap that became a sleep," Zavrius murmured. "A mistake, that's all." He glanced to the desk, trying to spy if some of those papers contained the information for her summons of him.

"Zavrius," his mother said, tone curt. He met her eye and withered. "Sit down."

No quips, no resistance. Zavrius knew when to keep his mouth shut. He went to the chair opposite her, bowed for good measure, and seated himself.

For a while, neither one of them spoke. As the moment stretched, Zavrius' anxiety got the better of him. His stomach became a tangle of knots, and he began to play with the hemming of his tunic.

Say something. Say something.

"What day is it?" his mother said suddenly.

He jerked, even if he'd been expecting the sound. "Uh. . ." he fumbled for the date, found it, and then calmed himself as he realized her true meaning. "A week out from my demonstration?"

"Less than that," Arasne said sharply. Zavrius felt relieved that this was a discussion about swordplay and not a discussion about *swordplay* until the sharpness of his mother's tone registered. Why was she distraught? Neither one of them believed he'd do particularly well at this demonstration, did they?

"I don't understand."

She ran a hand over her face. "No, clearly not." The sorrow in her tone, the dismay, all of it told Zavrius he had made a mistake.

"What is it?" he asked. And then, "Who's coming?"

Her eyes met his, finally. Ah, that was it. Someone important was set to attend. Zavrius cocked his head and eyed her down.

"I believe," Arasne spoke carefully, "that several parties I'd have rather never knew about my condition. . .now *know*."

It was a subtle, if convoluted, way of explaining the situation. Arasne had averted her gaze and now sat with her hands clasped in her lap. Zavrius pinched his brows together. "About your . . .?" he gestured over her generally, and she nodded.

Zavrius leaned back into his chair. "Who?"

"Nobility I. . .Nobility who supported your father, and will support Theo."

Zavrius could read between the lines with ease: *nobility who want war and glory and believe, somehow, that the tiny peninsula state of Usleth could survive or defeat the whole gargantuan Rezwyn empire.*

These very reasonable people knew, somehow, of his mother's illness.

"Does Petra know where the breach is?"

Arasne shook her head. Zavrius wanted to prompt further. Why not? How could the spymaster not know these things? Or was it simply not that simple? Was Petra, or even Arasne herself, hesitant to learn who spilled the secret because neither of them believed Theo and the others could be exempt?

Zavrius scoffed, and Arasne read his mind. She tutted. "Don't say it. Don't even think it."

He had a lot he wanted to retort with, but she was in such a state he decided it best not to press.

Arasne said, "Do you know what I need from you?" Zavrius felt that he did, but he waited for her to speak again. "I need a son who is a prince. I need a son who isn't hiding his expertise behind a mask of dandyism and languidness. I need a son who is proficient in swordplay, who is not an easy target; I need all my children to at least *pretend* to be a united front."

It was the last part that urged him to move. He jerked in his seat, and Arasne put her hand up. "I *know*."

"Do you?" Zavrius snapped—a mistake. A childish play. But he could not help it. This was insanity! Why was everyone so convinced that with enough time or exposure to one another, any of Zavrius' siblings would suddenly decide to love him? "They not only hate me, they want me *dead*."

"Oh, don't say that." Arasne's face had turned a sickly color, and she pinched her lips as if nauseous.

It infuriated him. His movements grew agitated as he gestured. "You can't be this blind to it. You may love them, but you know it; they are vicious. They have Sirellius in them, corrupting their blood—they are not like *us!*"

Tears were in her eyes. She snapped, "I am their mother!"

Zavrius stood up. The chair clattered behind him. "And I will be their sacrifice!"

Like that, they stared at one another, Zavrius panting and disheveled and his mother calm and pristine as ever.

What could be done? She knew, and she could hardly leave the throne to Zavrius. She knew what they were like, and she would leave it to Theo anyway.

"Anyone else," he whispered. "Anyone but Theo. Then I might have a chance."

She glanced away. "I still have time."

He wanted her to look at him. She should have had to stare him down, look him in the eye, and understand that even if she could protect him now, she wouldn't be able to do that when she was gone.

He tried again. "Anyone else." His voice cracked. He sounded desperate.

She didn't say anything, and Zavrius felt the pull of obligation in his gut. He had to offer her something, anything in return. "I *am* training. For the demonstration. I have a paladin who has agreed to help me."

"So I've heard."

He scoffed. *Why do you do that?* He did not say this. He wanted to, but he did not say this. His hand flexed and unflexed by his side, and Zavrius sighed deeply. "What is you want from me, then, if not my best?"

"I merely wanted you to be aware of the seriousness of this demonstration."

"I am aware."

Like that, their conversation lapsed towards the awkward, and he could feel the schism opening wider between them. He thought about reaching out; what would she have done for him if he were still a child? Sing? Play a tune for him to calm himself? Would it still work on him, even now, with everything he knew?

Did it matter?

Zavrius took a step back, not recognizing the austere glint in his mother's eye. She was changing, and perhaps she had to change, if she was to survive court obviously unwell. But it meant that every hope Zavrius had ever had about staying who *he* was, with all his quirks and his desires and his interests, were beginning to die. He could feel them gasping for breath in his chest, floundering at the sudden suffocation.

He was going to need to change if he wanted to stay alive.

"I should go," he said, though he had nowhere to be. "I'll train as hard as I can." He shuffled backwards, and bowed low, half expecting Arasne to call out and stop him.

She didn't, not until his hands curled around the frame of the door.

"Zavrius."

He went still, turning as little as necessary to meet her gaze. "With that paladin of yours, do be careful."

He flared his nostrils and tried very hard to unclench his jaw. When he couldn't, he nodded stiffly and left.

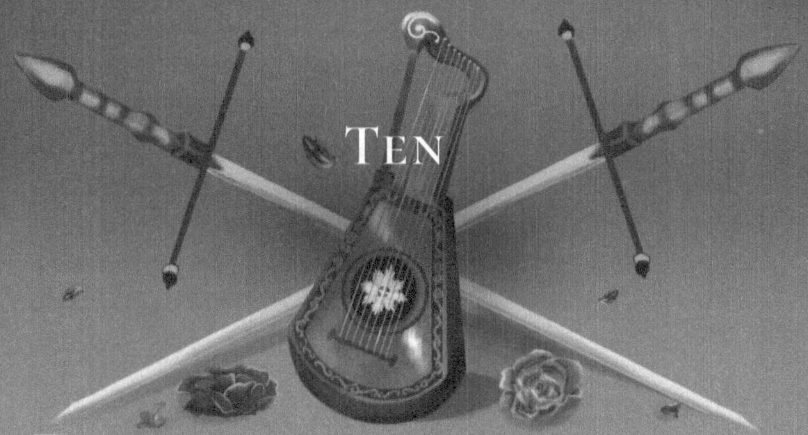

Ten

Balen was not in Zavrius' room when he returned.

Zavrius had expected this, of course, and if he'd wanted the paladin to remain, he could have ordered him to do so. He explicitly hadn't, not wanting to force Balen to do anything under order in the hopes of ensuring some level of equity between them.

So why did the room feel so *empty* when he came back and found the paladin gone?

Zavrius sank onto his bed. Someone—hopefully Balen; Zavrius flinched at the thought of a servant entering his room with the paladin still lurking—had done him the service of lighting his bedside lamp. It cast an inviting warm glow that melted and deformed the shadows into something liquid and malleable. They pulsed softly. When he'd been here with Balen, Zavrius had been sure of eyes watching him from the corners. Now, he felt utterly alone.

There was something precise about that feeling. It cut him right below the heart, a stab into his ribs. The pain throbbed, but the deluge of guilt and shame and fear, like a rush of blood pooling into his stomach, was much worse. Unnamable anxiety pricked his skin, and he curled over himself into a tight ball, hoping to disrupt the roiling in his belly. What was he feeling? Despair? Disgust? Grief? Why was he feeling anything at all— why was this *different* from the many years he'd endured court?

Because you don't have your mother to protect you anymore.

Call it ego, or perhaps the awakening of reluctant maturity in a young adult, but Zavrius bolted upright at that thought. His mind split in two, and the first half revolted. He felt like a child because he had been treated as one for so long. Didn't he have a *right* to feel like this? To want better? To want love?

The other half, a far more stoic part of him, thought: *you have to decide right now if you want to live.*

Zavrius listened to the former and sat up straighter. He'd cried a little, barely been aware of it until gravity took over and tears began to stream down his cheek. He wiped them away with some urgency, sniffled, and slowed his breathing.

He craved the love of his mother, who could not give it to him anymore, not as she had used to. He craved the affections of a paladin, even though they both knew their interest in each other couldn't become anything more. Acting as a no-good dandy had helped him survive thus far, but it would not be enough to survive whatever would happen at the end of Arasne's rule.

Zavrius had to plan, and he had to start that plan now.

"No."

"*Yes.*"

It was bitterly cold that morning. The sun was still stretching across the horizon in its morning excursion, and it had yet to bleed any warmth into Cres Stros. Zavrius stood wrapped in layers before his Uncle Lestr, head craning up with his arms crossed.

The older man was Arasne's brother, but in truth, he'd had little to do with Zavrius in the prince's nearly two decades of life. Lestr possessed the typical fortitude one would expect from a man of his standing. As the brother of the Queen, he had made his loyalty exceptionally clear from the beginning, and as Commander of the paladins, he'd secured himself as a man dedicated to furthering the Dued Vuuthrik line—not as someone who wanted the throne for himself.

He was also the forgemaster. He had acquired immense knowledge of the paladin forge during his youth and now was its sole operator (though there had been talk of training others, a necessity as the man got older). Lestr melted gedrok bone and other material harvested from the gedroks and forged them into armor and weapons for both the Gifted Paladins and the royal family. On occasion, he'd forge the instruments for the Royal Family, too. More often than not, however, he was reforging old armor and weapons. The gedroks were such a rare resource that this had become an inevitable and unquestionable act when a paladin died: If no one could fit the armor, it would need to be remade, or else half of Lestr's forces would lose their minds to ichor poisoning. Or so the story went. No one had been keen to test the theory.

"You may be a prince, but I have full authority over *this*," Lestr gestured roughly towards the entrance to the forge, a round outdoor structure made separate from the keep.

Lestr often spoke to him like this. He occupied that unique realm where nicknames, first names, or the occasional neglect of honorifics were ignored. But the older Zavrius got, the more Lestr's slip-ups seemed intentional.

"I know you don't respect me," Zavrius said flatly.

Lestr bristled. Every muscle went rigid. Perhaps it was a cruel thing to say—paladins were beginning to emerge for training, and Lestr's whole demeanor shifted now that they were being watched. Zavrius took a moment to scan the crowd, hoping to see Balen. They hadn't discussed what to do about his training that morning, or whether Balen would still bother with him. The paladin emerged with two others, laughing and rolling out his shoulders, sheathed sword in hand. He wore all his armor save for the cuirass, which was balanced over his arm. One of the other paladins, a scruffy young woman not much older than Zavrius, spotted the prince first. She flinched briefly and said something, still wearing that smile as if to pretend she wasn't now speaking about the prince's presence. Balen did nothing to aid her attempt. He jerked about, scanning for Zavrius despite his friends' awkward attempts to discourage him.

They met each other's eyes. Zavrius couldn't interpret the meaning behind Balen's expression, but he hoped there was an apology there, or some interest. He wanted Balen to communicate silently, to tell him: I'm glad for yesterday, and sorry it ended so quickly. At that moment, all he wanted was for Balen to *want* to see him again.

"Come on," Lestr grunted. In the silence after Zavrius' quip, he'd opened the door to the forge and presumably checked it for any paladins. Now, he stood at the threshold, eyes fixed on his approaching pupils. Zavrius turned around to stare at him in shock. He had rarely come here. It simply wasn't *done*. The Dued Vuuthriks, in a way, were close to the gedroks—to see gedrok material melted and forged and changed in this way had been an unspoken taboo, as if viewing it would be akin to viewing your own family member melted down and remade. Yet, Lestr had opened his door to his nephew, and the young prince was hardly about to pass up the opportunity. Zavrius made himself not look back, half afraid that Lestr would say something about his interest in Balen. Surely his uncle knew, because Petra knew, and Arasne knew, and all of them conspired with one another. But he hoped he would never have to hear about it.

Zavrius pushed forward into the forge, and Lestr closed the door behind them.

The Forge was ancient. It went back to at least King Gedrok Ach Meedin's time, and Zavrius had learned much about its construction from tutors nearly a decade earlier. With time, though, his knowledge had eroded, and now he could only be certain that ichor had been imbued in the stone to prevent arcane cataclysms. He could feel it, too, throbbing beneath the stone; an old friend calling out to him from afar, the words lost in the wind. Zavrius ignored the feeling and focused on his surroundings. The interior of the room was dark, illuminated only by the firelit sconces running the circumference and the low fire from the hearth that emerged from the center. Zavrius shifted to look at that banquet of craftsmanship and material. The open-mouthed roar of a gedrok preserved forever in stone, with its lower jaw forming the hearth, and the rest of its head reaching to the ceiling, which then vaulted high into a dome. Thick chains secured the hearth, and Zavrius met eyes with the dull sockets of the stone gedrok. When the forge was at work, he knew fire would burn in those empty holes.

Since there was nowhere to sit, Zavrius perched himself on one of the long wooden tables that stretched to the left of the forge. Bits of gedrokscale and bone armor lay scattered at various stages of completion, and many tools were out. That seemed unlike Lestr, whom Zavrius had always assumed to be organized.

"Late night?" he prompted.

"Hmm," Lestr said as a non-answer. Deflection wouldn't work on him. Zavrius needed to convince him of the necessity of this action, and so he stopped his languid sitting and stood.

"I need it for the demonstration."

Lestr rolled his eyes. "The demonstration is a bit of political futility," he spat. Zavrius jerked his head. Surely Lestr was smarter than that. What was on the surface a demonstration had become so much more just since the previous night. Arasne must have told him. Dismissing Zavrius' first chance to reposition himself as a Dued Vuuthrik to be *respected* was integral to him staying alive.

Clearly, Lestr thought differently. He spoke hurriedly, "You are a prince. You shouldn't have to worry too much about self-protection. That's what we're here for."

Zavrius bit his lip. Cold fury blanched him, and a chill ran down his spine. Without looking up, and as coolly as he could manage, he whispered, "You wouldn't say that to any one of my siblings."

Lestr paused for a second before he stumbled over his poor excuse, "Because they enjoy fighting, Prince Zavrius."

What a load of bollocks.

"Lestr." Zavrius raised his head to his uncle.

He wanted to say something heavy. He wanted to say a handful of words and for their weight to ring true in Lestr's body. *Don't you understand what I'm asking you?* Those were his true words, the meaning he tried to imbue in speaking his uncle's name. *Can't you see what I need from you?*

His uncle couldn't, of course, either out of pride or, more likely, because Zavrius had shared very little of his intentions with his uncle.

Lestr narrowed his eyes and then sighed. "Your mother has spoken to me," he said.

Zavrius felt his nostrils flare as he grimaced up at his uncle. "And?"

"And nothing." Lestr shrugged. The way his voice quavered suggested a lie. "There's nothing a new blade could do for you that something tried and true couldn't. This is a *demonstration*. No one is expecting *you* to be brilliant."

Zavrius tried to ignore the emphasis on *you*, as if the expectation of brilliance fell on every other Dued Vuuthrik spawn except for him. But so, too, did his mother's desperation ring hollow in his head, a caterwauling cry:

I believe that several parties I'd have rather never knew about my condition. . .now know.

What did Lestr gain out of pretending the court and all its machinations were perfectly safe?

He stared up at his uncle, suddenly unsure of himself. Arasne and Lestr were close—or Zavrius had always assumed. Had she told Lestr not to worry in the hopes of keeping the truth hidden? Or was Lestr not to be trusted?

"Certain nobility is coming," Zavrius said vaguely.

Lestr nodded in agreement, just as vaguely. "So I've heard."

For the first time, Zavrius felt uncertain.

It had been late when he'd decided to come here in the early morning, and it had been decided on the back of severe emotional upheaval. With a bit of gedrok in a weapon, and with the warbling slice of steel against steel resonating out to their audience, Zavrius could make an instrument of swordplay. He could block attacks, and from the emitting sound, he could imbue the air with his magic. Was it a stupid idea? Perhaps. It certainly held risk. But everything in his body told him to *go*, to *move*, to *do something*, and the thought of rest made his bones ache and his muscles tighten with discomfort.

As if his uncle could read his mind, Lestr crossed his arms over his chest and whispered, "Don't you think it would be worse if what you're planning fails?"

Zavrius grimaced. So Lestr had worked it out. More so, he'd been lying earlier—this demonstration was not as simple as a bit of 'political futility'. Everything their family did now was under the utmost scrutiny from their detractors. It was even worse that their family was divided on most matters, and that Zavrius found himself increasingly alone in his stances. Most of their detractors aligned with most of Zavrius' siblings.

His heart began to race. Which side was Lestr on? He thought about speaking outright to his uncle, but if his plea to his own mother to give the throne to anyone save for Theo went unheard, he couldn't imagine swaying Lestr.

"I am trying to save what little face I can. *Me.* This is all I can do."

"If anyone finds out what you can do, it may be worse for you in the long run."

This sounded harsh, but Lestr's eyes were soft. Zavrius unfurled beneath this advice and found himself leaning once more against the edge of the long table. He wanted to ask questions. A thousand of them flitted through his mind, eager to be aired. Lestr *knew* of his ability—well, when he thought about it, of course he did. Arasne was his sister, and her arcane ability was known to him. Why would she not have taught the only child she'd produced with any interest in music? Moreso, Lestr seemed to understand his predicament, and what his appearance and attitude had afforded him for all these years. Lestr was telling him: *don't risk it.* Don't go out there and risk someone with enough awareness noticing what you're doing to their body and to their awareness.

"I feel. . .impotent," Zavrius murmured. His voice gave out slightly, cracking on the last word, and he screwed up his face against the burn of tears. Lestr's rough hand met his left shoulder, and when Zavrius didn't open his eyes, his uncle's other hand gripped his right and shook him gently.

"You are Prince Zavrius Dued Vuuthrik. You may not be a swordsman, but you are smart. Wily. If anyone is going to survive Theo's rule, it's you."

Survive Theo's rule. "How bad do you think it will be?" he whispered.

Lestr removed his hands and straightened. "There are years until then," he said, and Zavrius raised a brow.

"Years?"

Lestr nodded and did not say more. Thrill raced through Zavrius until his thoughts took a turn. He imagined Arasne thin and frail, living on far longer than she should have had to. He wanted to say: *don't make her do that.*

Zavrius said nothing at all.

"What you can do is your best," Lestr said.

In his mind, Zavrius was brave. Internally, he said, *Do you hear yourself? She wants me to prove I am untouchable, that I am not a rusted link to be beaten away from the Dued Vuuthrik chain. Do not deny me this.*

But a defeated rot took root in his stomach and very quickly infected the rest of his body.

"Yes, Uncle," Zavrius said.

And he felt alone again, with a softness in his flesh he could do nothing to counter.

He would have to get rid of that soft and pliable core of his if he was going to live.

Zavrius waited and watched the paladins train for close to an hour. Their training had shifted, becoming more intense since the last time he had lingered there. Lestr did not hold back on his criticisms. He singled paladins out, called on them for poor form, and threw single paladins against three in skirmish-style spars.

Zavrius, of course, watched Balen for most of it. He had a burning urge to talk to the paladin, but that all fell away the longer he watched the way the young man moved. Every slice, every thrust forward, every dancing step out of the way of a responding blow; Balen's body was as much an instrument as any Zavrius had encountered. He could learn to play it. Learn to master it as he had any of the others that had been gifted to him during his years.

What a performance we could put on.

Lust was a heavy drum, but this beat felt stronger. More compulsive. Zavrius yearned to step forward into that fray if just to dance those steps with Balen of Westgar, if just to see the sweat-sheen on his skin up close, and the way his lip quirked up in barely contained pride for every strike landed. Somehow, in amongst every swing, he saw images interspersed. Balen in an impossible memory Zavrius did not have of him, a concept that felt as religious as a prophecy. The young man's face glowing in the sun. Balen shirtless, in the prince's bed, unafraid to leave, spread out with only a sheet to cover him, streaks of sunlight incisive as they pierced the cracks in Zavrius' curtain and highlighted, knifelike, every divot and shape of the muscles beneath Balen's skin.

Zavrius believed in no gods except music, though the reverence he held for the gedroks skimmed close, but these thoughts of Balen shook him.

His mind shifted to the previous afternoon and the way their lips felt against each other. They'd moved slowly, carefully tiptoeing around each other; Zavrius almost wished they'd done more. He began to imagine it, eyes fixed on Balen's sparring but mind elsewhere. The memories of yesterday began to melt into unformed hope. He didn't know the specifics of what to imagine, and so his mind conjured disjointed images. Their bodies pressed together. Hands roaming. Tongues meeting, a slow lick across his jaw and down his neck. Undefined pleasure from acts he had never encountered before—and Balen was suddenly jogging towards him, having broken away from training.

Rapidly, Zavrius blinked away his thoughts. He stood up straighter and squeezed his arms around his chest, embarrassed by his runaway mind.

Zavrius looked past the approaching paladin to the group of his peers who lingered back, packing up after training, stretching, chatting. Most of them were curious and kept craning to look at the pair of them. Zavrius hoped the assignment he'd given Balen about organizing the logistics of the confirmation ceremony would be enough to cover this moment.

Balen's face burst into a wide and happy grin when he was still several feet away. This hurried eagerness made Zavrius shiver, and he turned in the hopes of downplaying his own flushed smile.

"Hi," Balen said when he got close. Then, with wide eyes, he dropped into a bow. His eyes were sparkling when he met Zavrius' eye next. "My prince," he said, straightening.

Zavrius fought to control his smile, which was threatening to widen and consume his entire face. "Hi."

Balen glanced back over his shoulder and made a quick gesture toward the waiting paladins. Several took the sign to glance away, but plenty more continued their staring. Balen didn't pay them much mind at all, turning back to Zavrius happily. "So," he said, "I asked Lestr about the logistics. He's written up a report, and we can send that over to you, or the Queen, whenever you might require it."

Zavrius' chest seized. "I'm almost disappointed you worked everything out so quickly."

Balen, bless him, faltered. The smile slipped from his face. "I. . ."

Zavrius spoke over him to save him the trouble: "What excuse do I have to see you now?"

Balen exhaled noisily, laughing gently. "Does a prince need a reason?"

Zavrius wanted to say *no* or come up with something witty and charming about Balen being a good enough reason for anything. Instead, he glanced to his right, towards the gargantuan mass of the gedrok in the garden.

"I need your help again," Zavrius said carefully. "As much help as you can give me, right up until the demonstration." He turned back to Balen. The paladin's eyes were wide, his brows upturned, a look of utmost sincerity that frightened Zavrius to see. He swallowed hard. "Can you do that?"

"Let's go right now," Balen said. The paladin began to reach for him but stopped himself. A sad necessity. Zavrius' eyes lingered on his outstretched hand and moved in closer, pressing onto the tips of his toes to whisper against the paladin's ear.

"Kiss me in the garden?" he whispered.

He pulled away before Balen could react and walked to the garden before he lost his nerve.

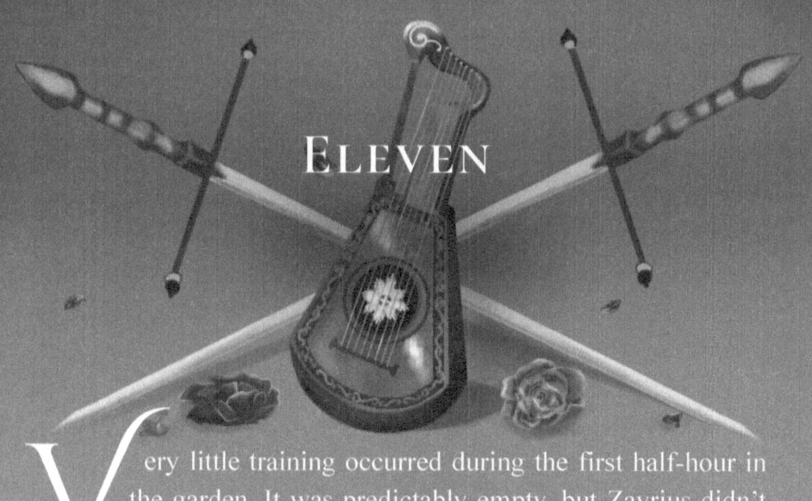

Eleven

Very little training occurred during the first half-hour in the garden. It was predictably empty, but Zavrius didn't want to take chances. He urged the paladin to dump his sword and then took his hand, leading him towards the open carcass of the gedrok.

Most of it was bone, the ribcage thick enough to provide some cover. Zavrius put his back against one of the picked-clean ribs, ignoring the absurdity of this moment, as the unknowable primordial creature was reduced to the confidant of two desperate young men. Balen pushed closer, but not close enough, and all Zavrius wanted was for him to step forward and slip his armored thigh between his legs.

"Kiss me," he hissed, and Balen exhaled. His head laced around the back of Zavrius' head to hold him in place, and he gently pressed his lips against the prince's. Zavrius pushed back with a hunger, shuddering. His hands flew up to grip anything, but there was no purchase along the smooth body of Balen's plate. Zavrius was forced to weave his fingers through Balen's hair, a move that forced their bodies closer, and then Zavrius got what he'd been craving. Something seemed to awaken in Balen, and he drove them both back against the gedrok's rib. Zavrius moaned softly, the sound suddenly loud when Balen broke away, lip grazing across the shell of Zavrius' ear. His breath was warm and shaking, and he seemed nervous. His touches were hesitant.

Zavrius had to show him he wanted this.

"No one's here," Zavrius whispered. Balen nodded, but Zavrius couldn't see his expression from this angle. He gripped the back of Balen's head more firmly and took one of the paladin's free hands in his own. Carefully, he guided that hand down to cup between his legs. Balen's breath caught just as Zavrius murmured again, "No one's here."

Balen let out a sound so sweet and wanting that Zavrius had to pull him closer. His own heart jumped into his throat; he'd never had anyone this close to touching him, and the warm pressure of Balen's palm against his groin made him equal parts hungry and nervous. He pulled Balen back towards his mouth, and they kissed heavily, Balen's hand lazy as it fumbled over Zavrius' erection.

"I wish I could touch you," Zavrius whispered.

Balen took that literally and glanced up and around, hand moving as if he was going to strip himself of his armor right then and there. Zavrius had to stop him, shaking his head. Gedroks, he wanted to push their hips together, and Balen's armor prevented that kind of closeness. But they couldn't go much farther than this in the garden of the palace—and more than that, Zavrius still felt unready.

"Not yet," was all Zavrius ended up saying, and Balen flushed, evidently ashamed.

Balen went to move his hand away, and Zavrius touched his wrist, the other hand cupping Balen's face. "Only stop kissing me now if you want to."

The look on Balen's face was near predatory. "I want. . ."

"What *do* you want, Balen of Westgar?" Zavrius asked teasingly.

Balen shook his head with a breathless smile and crashed his lips against Zavrius'. He moved his hand and laced both instead around the prince's hips, which he bucked against. Firm, impenetrable armor met the tenting rise in Zavrius' trousers, which was not wholly comfortable—but being crowded like this by Balen's work-broadened body thrilled him.

When a gaggle of distant laughter echoed throughout the garden, high-pitched voices reverberating off the skeletal remains of the gedrok, the pair pulled away from one another. They were both breathing hard. Balen wiped a string of saliva off his lips and peered out of their hiding place. He didn't technically *have* to push against Zavrius' body to do this, but that was how Balen chose to look: pressed close so Zavrius could not so much as wriggle, clamped as he was between the rib at his back and the paladin at his front.

Fuck. He chanced a look upwards. Since Balen was taller than him, this angle awarded Zavrius with a view of his outstretched neck, that sharp jawline glistening with reflected prismatic light. Fine stubble turned the paladin's chin a greyish-blue, and unthinkingly, Zavrius found himself reaching up. His thumb ran across the underside of Balen's chin, catching on the scruff.

Balen flinched back and looked down at Zavrius, staring at him in something like wonderment or shock.

Zavrius frowned, hissing out, "What is it?" he craned around, wondering who it was that had shocked Balen so.

"No, no," the paladin said, flushing hard. His hand shook as his thumb came to rest against Zavrius' cheek. "It's nothing. It's no one. They've gone, anyway—just some noble guests on a morning stroll."

Zavrius raised a brow. "Then. . .?"

Balen shook his head again, brows turning upwards. "You're beautiful," he whispered. "You're so very beautiful."

Zavrius, whose first instinct was to laugh, instead made a weak noise. He felt heat rush to his cheeks, accompanied by a thrilling fire in his body.

He glanced away and forced that smile to come. "I've been told," he said.

Balen stayed quiet, though his eyes shone.

Zavrius *had* been told that before. But never like this. Never by someone he wanted to find him beautiful, and never by someone with such incredible sincerity in their eyes.

Strangely uncomfortable, Zavrius said, "Um. We should train, no?"

To his credit, Balen snapped to attention immediately. "Yes. Yes, my prince, we absolutely should."

Like that, they trained for the next week.

Balen would train him an hour after the morning paladin training and another hour close to sunset if they had the energy. It was a grand undertaking, and Zavrius thanked him with stolen kisses whenever he could convince Balen to take a break.

They stuck to the rapier. They focused on footwork. They tried to spar. By the time Zavrius realized he enjoyed getting close to the enemy—that his speed meant he could get close and castrate attacks that required reach—it was too late for him to start training with daggers. Besides, it was a swordplay demonstration.

Zavrius spent most of the day training alone before the demonstration. Balen joined him in the morning for the usual session and made assurances that Zavrius was *good,* that he could *do this,* and other rather sweet attempts to assuage the prince's obvious anxiety. But he couldn't stay all day—hadn't been able to. With the confirmation of his younger colleagues to Paladin status just a day away and Balen's general need to prove himself to Theo and his other paladins that he was a valid choice for Prime, Zavrius knew Balen would inevitably be busy as the months wore on. Technically, if Zavrius were to take on proper princely duties and build rapport with anyone in court, or do anything to assist his mother's rule, he would be less available, too. It felt like their nascent romance was as brittle as Usleth's peace with the empire; contingent on the Queen's health, and on a strange alignment of factors that would see it shatter if one moved out of place.

Zavrius exhaled heavily and stood straight. Sweat pooled at his neck and on his chest, and he was breathing heavily from the exertion. The thought had taken over momentarily, and he'd been lost to it.

So take control of yourself. Breathe.

He tried to center himself. Most of that attempt involved ignoring thoughts of Balen, which swam very easily into focus. Focusing required him to shift his mind to darker things: thoughts of grief, of shame, of embarrassment. How would he recover if he blundered through this demonstration tomorrow? How would he survive a war-minded court who thought him entirely weak? Poor motivation in the long run, and certainly detrimental to his self-image, but it worked in that moment. Zavrius was able to settle into himself and focus on what he needed to perfect.

His footwork was still sloppy. He had speed, but Balen informed him he gave away his next move too early. A stiffening in the shoulders, a glance, a foot pointed in the direction he intended to lunge, and the surprise was ruined. Zavrius practiced darting forward as soon as the thought to move occurred to him. It resulted in jolting, sloppy movements, and swings he couldn't finish for fear of toppling over from his own forward momentum.

Still, he tried. He swung and sliced and stepped until every muscle ached and sweat poured down his back. He trained long after he usually would have stopped, if only because every time he did, anxiety began to claw at his stomach. It was better to stay distracted. It was better to work until the sunset, and he would be too tired to lay awake at night thinking.

"You are going to ruin yourself for tomorrow, you know."

Zavrius was startled so quickly that he dropped his sword. It landed softly, the sound muffled by the soft bed of grass. He spun with his arms still above his head, hands falling slowly as his mind registered the voice's owner, who stood with her arms crossed twenty paces from him.

Avidia.

Zavrius' older sister was not even looking at him as she spoke. Her eyes were fixed on the towering skull of the gedrok with its hollow eye sockets. Her gaze trailed over the primordial form, and Zavrius fought to understand her expression, which oscillated between awe and an almost absurd disgust.

He panted heavily and stood up straight, hoping his exertion would excuse the new rush of red that had emblazoned his cheeks. "Can I help you with something?"

Avidia made a short laughing noise and raised a brow at him. "I highly doubt it." She took a few steps away from the gedrok skeleton and dropped her gaze to him. "I do mean it, though. If you overwork yourself—"

Zavrius sighed rather dramatically and turned away, bending to retrieve his dropped blade. "You don't mind if I ignore you, do you? I'm afraid I don't know how to speak to you when ignoring each other is the only dynamic we've ever had."

Avidia paused a moment before she said stiffly, "Like you've done anything to be memorable."

"I hope you die in a cave-in on one of your expeditions." And then, into the stiff silence, he chanced a look over his shoulder. "What? Did I hurt your feelings? Are you going to tell mother?"

Avidia gnawed at her lip. Her eyes took on a soft, pitying glaze that made Zavrius' insides revolt. He whipped his head back around and began to half-heartedly slice at the air. What was he doing? He was a petty person, certainly, but this? These quips had a bite to them. It took him a moment to understand that what he was feeling at that moment was fear.

He was frightened of her. To him, she was another Theo, but at least she tended to avoid Zavrius altogether. Where Theo seemed to revel in twisting the knife in Zavrius' proverbial wounds, Avidia preferred pretending Zavrius did not exist. Or was not related to them. To have her here, seeing him training, seeing the effort, how much he *cared*. . .

His heart raced in his chest. The urge to speak danced on the tip of his tongue. *Don't tell Theo. Please don't tell Theo.*

Avidia scoffed suddenly, unprompted. She said, "You know what? I might tell Theo we should take a little trip tomorrow. To the Gedrok's Glade. We were planning on skipping the whole affair. It's. . .well, it's a confirmation ceremony. It's not particularly exciting. But if we're supporting our baby brother's long-awaited first foray into swordplay, well. . ."

Zavrius lowered his blade and looked up at the sky. "What do you want, Avidia?"

But when he turned back to look at her, she was shrugging. "I don't particularly *want* anything. I just saw you. And you never. . .it surprised me to see you doing much of anything, really."

Zavrius blinked at her. Her lip curled away from her teeth in a grimace. A fly buzzed around her face, and she waved it away, instinctively taking a step closer to him. "Listen," she said, resuming her crossed-armed defensiveness. "I know you've heard the rumors about Mother. I. . ."

Zavrius bit his tongue. He held himself impossibly still. *What? Why are you talking to* me *about this?*

Avidia wasn't looking at him anymore. Her gaze had slipped away. "Our brother has a vision for his court. I'm sure you know that too because, despite what the others think, I reckon you're rather smart." That caught Zavrius by surprise. She chanced a look at him and scrunched her features up. "Don't get the wrong idea, Zavrius. I don't like you. I just wanted to say that it's good. It's good to see you trying to stay alive."

She left a lot unsaid, but Zavrius implicitly understood. Whatever Avidia thought about Theo's plans, she could at least recognize what was motivating Zavrius now.

When he didn't speak, too dumbstruck by this almost-niceness, she gestured vaguely to him. "Means you've got a bit of our father in you after all."

Which felt at once like a compliment and a targeted attack. She squinted up at the sun. "You should finish up. Take a bath, rest, all that." Without another word, she turned and began to stalk out of the garden, through the rosebushes, of course, rather than along the designated path.

He didn't thank her; he couldn't even begin to think about opening his mouth, let alone forming any words. Instead, Zavrius watched his sister go and wondered for a moment what it might have been like if she'd been born first or him a little earlier. If Arasne had had more influence over her. Perhaps they might have been friends—or at the very least, better siblings.

No matter now. He sniffed, shaking the thought away.

The minutes of stillness had already taken effect on his body. Now that the sweat had cooled off, a chill tickled down his limbs with the late afternoon breeze. His muscles ached, too; a sudden exhaustion burning in his forearms and calves, and a bright burning in his lungs that felt wonderful and terrible concurrently.

He looked down at the blade in his hand, where callouses had begun to form over the joint between his palm and his fingers. The skin there now matched the thickened skin that covered his fingertips, formed from all the strings he plucked. A sudden, deep pang of longing filled him. He hadn't played the entire week.

You won't have to wait much longer.

Zavrius packed up and decided on Avidia's suggestion of a long, relaxing bath before bed.

A long day awaited him, and she was right. He needed both his mind and his body to cooperate with him tomorrow.

Twelve

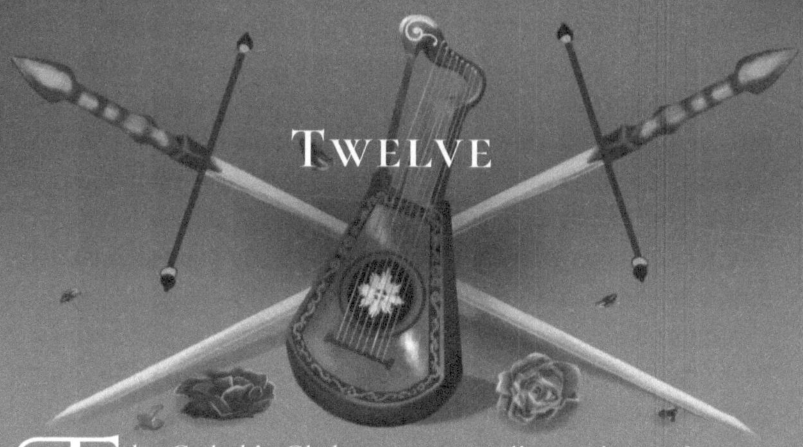

The Gedrok's Glade was a sprawling majesty of green life, and if Zavrius had ever been inclined towards moments of faith, it was here in amongst the trees and standing before the eternal body that he felt most in awe.

The gedrok here loomed like part of the scenery. Where the palace gedrok had been inevitably stripped to sustain the Gifted Paladin's constant need for armor and weaponry, this one still had much of its flesh and scale attached to it. It served a multitude of purposes. At once, it was rendered a reserve, a fallback when the other gedrok was over harvested—and yet also something venerated. Revered. Its location conferred a sacrality upon it. The natural clearing surrounded by trees and woodland, and in the center, the resting body of a primordial creature preserved by forces beyond human understanding. The gedrok itself slumped into the ground. Most of it remained intact. Its head, perfectly preserved, reminded Zavrius of a calcified cat head. The skin had shrunk against the bone and pulled at the eye socket, turning the expression reptilian. That glassy eye stared out at them as the paladins set up their demonstrations and rituals.

Zavrius, whose anxiety had been running rampant all morning, found peace staring at the creature. Green had eaten through its shell or made root in the ageless flesh, and in entropy-defying brotherhood, fungal masses dotted along its body. Rope vines loped over its exposed ribs and tangled with the bone, moss and green plants dangling like entrails down into its cavity. Beneath this natural artistry, the Queen and her children were separated from the growing crowd of onlookers and paladins. They stood on a dais that had been constructed beneath the gedrok, save for Zavrius, who was viewing all this from afar. He pointedly did not look at his family for very long.

Momentarily, Zavrius' attention shifted to the growing crowd. More had attended than he'd been expecting. The nobility were gathered towards the center-back of the glade, well out of the way of a field of flat grass in front of the dais, where the ceremony would take place. There were about fifty attending nobles, accompanied by their various attendants and servants. This number alone surprised him, given the nature of this ceremony. It bordered on religious formality—not particularly something nobility often signed up to attend. And yet.

They had at least done him the service of standing in provincial order so that he might have some clue who everyone was. From right to left, he saw nobles from Westgar, Shoi Prya, Cres Stros, and the Ashmons. Vaguely, he wondered which ones among them hated his mother. Who amongst those pristine figures were lying in wait for Theo's succession?

Zavrius bit his tongue and looked away. The paladins took up their own space on the field. Many were seasoned, but the new recruits were obvious in their stance and the way they stared at the gedrok's majesty. They were given away, too, by how they wore their armor—or how it wore them. The young-faced few swam with each step, their cuirasses bobbing up towards their chins. Several elder paladins were attempting to readjust what they could on a few of them. After their confirmation, they'd have their armor fitted to their bodies, but for now, they had to contend with looking rather foolish.

Zavrius looked next to the wandering troupe of musicians setting up in front of the dais. Their presence had been his suggestion. Every event worth attending needed music—and Zavrius knew his own gut would rumble less if he had the familiarity of his own art in the air around him. He would need to go and introduce himself soon.

But first. He found his attention had returned to the gedrok and its ever-lasting, all-seeing eye. He stared at the glassy orb, half expecting it to roll towards him. Zavrius couldn't help the feeling of kinship that sprang up inside him from a deep well. In a way, coming before this beast was like meeting an old ancestor, the progenitor of a dynasty in which every royal had in their blood the same sparks of ichor that had fueled the gedrok itself. When he thought about it, or when he concentrated, he could sometimes feel that power spinning through his blood. Energy, willpower, a thrumming vitality he could distinguish easily from the natural energy of his youth. He crossed his arms and swallowed hard, almost ashamed to be feeling this way before something that was little more than a husk.

The paladins gave the gedroks a reverential treatment, almost placating the creatures—which Zavrius could respect, even if he would never mirror the behavior. It fell too close towards faith and religion for his liking, which in turn made his mind conjure the Rezwyns and all their idiosyncrasies. Their faith empowered them to war, to conquering and colonizing. For the Uslethians in their tiny peninsula, only the presence of the gedroks and the fear generated by their confusing nature (and, naturally, their relationship with the paladins) had prevented a full-blown absorption. Though the empire had tried. In part, the Rezwyn's own faith had hamstrung their assault, and Zavrius had learned he could not devote himself to other forces, no matter how mystical. So now, he pulled his eyes away from the gedrok.

Your magic is your own. Your ability is your own. A glance to the crowd, where a few noble eyes darted quickly away. *Prove all the bastards wrong.*

"Do you really think it's appropriate to perform for this event?"

Zavrius let the words rush through him, happy to find he gave no jolt of surprise at the interruption. The voice was gruff, annoyed, and familiar. He glanced back over his shoulder, and there Lysio Dued Vuuthrik stood, arms crossed and black hair scruffy as if it had just been violently ruffled.

Resting on the ground before Zavrius' shins and protected by a walnut-wooden case was Arasne's lute-harp. Zavrius shifted in place and raised a brow at Lysio. "When am I usually *appropriate?*"

Lysio snorted, a smile twitching at his lips despite himself. He flung his head around behind him. Zavrius followed his gaze past the growing crowd and to the sight of Theo watching their inter-action carefully from the vantage of the dais.

Avidia's idle threat turned out to be not idle at all. All of his siblings had done him the service of attending.

"What does he want you to do?" Zavrius murmured. "Bestow great abuse upon me? Tell me how awful I am?"

Lysio flinched and turned back around. His warm-brown face burned, deep and ruddy, but he made no replying quip. Curious. Zavrius stiffened instinctively. He didn't like this. Not one bit.

Lysio, seemingly ignoring Zavrius' earlier question, said, "What makes you think anyone here *wants* to listen to your bloody lute playing anyway?"

Zavrius smiled. "I'm under no illusions. I love a captive audi-ence." He made a dismissive gesture out at the crowd before turning back to his brother.

Lysio raised a brow. "At least you're self-aware."

"It'll help soothe my nerves. Now tell me: Did Theo make you come?"

Lysio stared at him. Zavrius stared back.

Enough of this. It was like none of his siblings even *knew* him; years of belittling and insults and exclusion, and Lysio was here now to do what? Throw him off before his demonstration?

Do they know they're only hurting themselves?

Unless that was exactly the point. They wanted to further discredit Arasne's rule and emphasize Zavrius as a weakness. A liability.

Zavrius steeled himself, trying for easy confidence as he said, "Listen. I'm already likely to embarrass our family, so there's no need for you to waste your breath on whatever clever insults you have prepared." Zavrius turned and began to walk towards the dais. Lysio wouldn't get to him today.

The wet grass forced him to step tentatively, lest he fall, and he was making steady progress until Lysio took his arm and wrenched him roughly back.

"Bastard!" Zavrius said immediately.

Lysio let go. "No, I—"

Zavrius felt himself flushing, half from fear and half from shame—*damn it, Zav, do not let him shake you.*

Lysio glanced back at the dais, "When I heard you were sparring, I couldn't miss it. None of us could."

"Yes, I'm aware it will be very amusing for you."

Lysio looked back. "I came to wish you luck. I don't think. . .I think it's unfair."

Zavrius baulked. A wash of shock shredded through his stomach, but he didn't dare let himself hope Lysio meant what he'd said.

He waited, and Lysio took the cue, adding, "You'll embarrass us for certain."

There it is.

"Alright," Zavrius said, meaning to leave, but Lysio stepped forward again.

"For what it's worth, it. . .it's strange to see you so. . ." and this time, Lysio gestured to the sword strapped at Zavrius' side. Zavrius looked down too, eyes lingering on the pommel. Suddenly, he could feel the blade against his thigh and where the guard dug into his hip. A curious sense of unease washed over him. *Another life*, he thought, and it was that thought that allowed him to make sense of Lysio's babbling.

"Oh," Zavrius murmured, fighting the urge to hiss out his next words. He failed. "Do you see me as human, now? Worth your time since I've picked up a blade?"

Lysio's features twisted, but Zavrius struggled to feel guilt. That *was* what Lysio had meant, wasn't it?

As if to confirm, Lysio said, "I only. . .If you'd been like this —if you'd tried like this earlier, and if you hadn't been coddled, we could have been—"

He bit off the word, but Zavrius heard it. *Brothers*. He scoffed and nodded to himself.

Their love is conditional. Never forget it.

"Right," Zavrius spoke as brightly as he could, smiling pleasantly at his brother. He put out his hand which Lysio clasped with a frown bonding his eyebrows together. "Enjoy the demonstration."

"I will," Lysio said, though his tone sounded uncertain.

Zavrius picked up their mother's lute-harp and gave the case a little wave. "I bet you're glad to be present for my performance, too.

Lysio gave a tight-lipped smile. "How did you convince Mother to let you do that?"

"She loves me the most," Zavrius said immediately. He

believed that, but Lysio gave a derisive snort that suggested he did not. Zavrius continued with, "And she feels bad for me."

Zavrius did not have to communicate the *why* behind his last point, and he didn't wait to see how it affected Lysio. He walked the thirty-odd paces to the front of the dais, stiff-lipped and jaw clenched to the point of pain. He glanced over at his mother unthinkingly. Arasne had donned a long flowing dress in a pale blue, with loose fitting sleeves and her hair in tight braids above her head. Free stands fell like wisps to frame her face. Rouge had warmed her cheeks to a lively pinky-brown, and her kohl-lined eyes turned the look more serious, more regal. She looked healthier than she had in a while. All her energy seemed to have been funneled into this moment; a demonstration of Arasne's own.

Something happened to Zavrius around his family. He became different, like a younger version of himself surfaced—a version that was perpetually in pain, and reckless, and fearful. Leaving Lysio now, adrenaline doused his mind and went shaking through his limbs. He felt another bolt of concern when he looked up at his mother. There was no danger. No threat. And *yet*.

"Prince Zavrius?"

Zavrius' body had deposited him exactly where he'd intended to go. Blinking back to awareness, he found he now stood before the troupe of musicians. There were five of them, of varying ages and genders, and all with the ashy brown undertone of Usleth—though the depth of their color ranged. One was as pale as Balen, sporting that Westgar-paleness like the ocean wind had wicked all their color away. This person looked close to thirty and had a wooden flute in hand. Two were percussionists, wearing big drums around their necks. The first of this unusual pair was a man in his fifties, white steaks coiling through his dark hair, which curled like Zavrius'. He'd pulled it behind his head; a mistake, Zavrius thought, since it exposed a very large forehead that led down to a bulbous nose. Not a particularly handsome fellow, but even Zavrius' vanity had nothing but good thoughts about the man's eyes, which shone with —was that *respect?*—when they fell over Zavrius. Beside him stood a woman perhaps ten years his junior. Lean muscle rippled over her arms. She had an athletic body, strong and well-defined, if lithe.

She whispered, "Prince Zavrius," bowing when his eyes found hers. She was unmistakably from the Ashmon Range. Her accent proved it; her words stiff and clipped, voice loud—a defense against the province's windy conditions, where yelling proved necessary to be heard.

The other two were much younger, closer to Zavrius' age. The first, a beautiful young man, had his black curly hair cropped close to the scalp. Unable to resist beauty, Zavrius' eyes wandered over him. His shoulders were perfectly rounded, and though he was not a lean man, he was undoubtedly strong. Zavrius felt rather small standing before him and enjoyed the way that feeling sparked something in his stomach, but for the gedrok's sake, he reined in that wandering eye of his and focused. The young man must have seen his expression; a small twitch of a prideful smile edged at the corner of his mouth. He, like Zavrius, was a lutenist.

Beside him was a rotund woman with long reddish-brown hair and the dark skin of Shoi Prya locals. She had with her the most fascinating instrument. Its bowed body resembled a dissected lute, though its strings—few as they were—appeared more in line with a violin. Wooden keys were somehow also incorporated; they emerged like misshapen teeth from the raised wooden deck in the instrument's center. The player of this enchanting contraption wore it horizontally across her body, large hand resting on a hand-crank that jutted from the instruments side.

"Now that," Zavrius said, chin nodding towards it, "looks absolutely fascinating."

The woman flushed and grinned wide. Zavrius spotted a

nervous energy in her, but there was thrill, too, at the recognition. Her hand hovered over the hand-crank.

"Play some for me," Zavrius said, knowing she wanted to.

Without even a word of acquiescence, she turned the wheel. The sound that emerged caught Zavrius entirely off guard. He'd expected the strings to sound as they did when plucked or when a bow was drawn over them. This sound emerged deep, layered, and striking—a steady, unwavering droning. She pressed those unshapely keys, and the pitch of the droning changed; a yowling, ancient cry that made Zavrius shiver.

When she stopped, he was grinning. "Brilliant," he said, and she curtsied.

"A pleasure, Prince Zavrius."

The others bowed, too, and looked up expectedly for Zavrius to clarify his engagement of them. Cautiously, Zavrius brought his case forward, and all eyes dropped to it.

"I don't intend to step on any toes," Zavrius said, fingers straining as they gripped the edge of the wooden case, "but I do hope you'll allow me the honor of opening this ceremony myself. Just one song, I promise, and then I will gladly acquiesce to you."

He felt himself flushing and admonished himself for it. In truth, of course, he had no need to explain himself. Even less of a need to feel any shame for this seemingly egotistical act. He was a prince, firstly, and he was Zavrius, secondly; rumors had done enough to explain what sort of person he was. This band of musicians might have even expected he'd pull something like this.

Except Zavrius *wanted* to explain himself. If anyone would understand, it would be fellow artists, and to emphasize that point, he cast a look out at the growing crowd.

"I'm not a swordsman, but I am set to spar, today. It's the kind of performance I've never partaken in." Here, he glanced back, hoping some spark of empathy would flare to life in their eyes.

"I'd like to prime myself with the kind of performance I'm used to."

"Of course, Prince Zavrius." The flutiest, and presumably the troupe leader, threw themselves into a deep bow quickly mirrored by the other musicians.

In him stirred the urge to press. *Are you sure? Do you understand why?*

The questions pushed at the front of his forehead, urging his tongue to move. Stiffly, he pressed his lips into a smile. No need to overexplain

"Thank you," he said, hoping he could imbue his words with true gratitude. "Do feel free to join in, if you like."

He left it at that and nodded in acknowledgment when they bowed once more. A sapling of guilt tried to take root, but Zavrius shifted his thoughts towards practicality.

Do this, and everything will work out.

The bustling did not stop as Zavrius approached the dais, but he felt eyes on him, now, boring into the back of his head and scrutinizing his appearance. Zavrius felt he and his strange interests had been inevitably diluted by the athleticism required by this demonstration, but he'd be damned if he made himself *too* palatable. He had only thinly lined his eyes with kohl and put his hair into a low bun at the back of his head to keep it out of his face. This alone felt remarkably wrong; the lack of sophistication to the up style made him feel vaguely unwell. And so he'd had to compensate. He wore layers, as was his inclination. Arm coverings that stopped at the wrist and went to his upper arm. A tunic with a dramatic cut at the shoulders and a neckline that plummeted to his mid-chest. Over that, a short, rectangular tunic that opened on either side, pinned with gold brooches to the tunic beneath it and held closed by a girdle at his waist. All of these clothes were various shades of dark maroon, save for his hose, which was colored cream. He wore sturdy boots with only a few embellishments, which were colored white to not clash with the hose. Damn the inevitable critiques; if Zavrius was to be beaten, he wanted at least to look good, and looking more like himself was worth any scrutiny. More than that, he almost wanted to be underestimated. It would make what he was about to do that much easier.

He took the stairs in twos, eyes flicking up to the watchful audience of his family. Arasne gave him a quiet, near doleful smile, apologetic in its own way. Seeing it caused something upsetting to happen in Zavrius' stomach. He grimaced, thought: *not now, it's not her fault, I hate this, gedroks, I want to die*, all at once in a flurry of thought and feeling. He looked away from her to the others.

Theo's smile was altogether different. For the outside observer, it might have even appeared genuine. Zavrius glanced away from the others, not needing much to ascertain the meaning behind their expressions. Lysio came up behind him and sidled into place. Immediately, Theo leaned down to whisper in his ear —no doubt an attempt to extract information. What had Lysio said to Zavrius? What had Zavrius said in return? So on and so forth—weren't they all *tired* of this game?

Zavrius stopped in the center of the dais without so much as an acknowledgment and gently placed the case on the floor. He bent down and unpacked it, spending longer than was strictly necessary running his fingers over it, inspecting it as if expecting damage, and finally tuning it. All this took five minutes, though he could have easily done it in half that time. With his eyes fixed on the instrument, Zavrius could at least pretend he was alone.

He loved performing. Loved it. He loved the thrill of the eyes on him and the way some people *saw* him, if only briefly, like the mask of the insipid and vain prince lifted with every note played. But this situation upset him in a core way. His gut churned, nerves pricked at him, his heart tangled in knots.

If this performance did not go well, then his next—what everyone was here to watch—would be that much more difficult.

"The paladins are ready, my prince. What shall I tell them?"

Zavrius glanced up. A royal attendant was bowing before him, the boy's hair falling flat like hay over his face. Zavrius pushed to standing, lute-harp clutched at his side. Time to put these nerves to rest.

"Tell them I'm ready," he said.

For three minutes, Zavrius stood in the center of the dais with his eyes downcast. Around him, attendants came to move the wooden instrument case aside and relay to the rest of the Dued Vuuthriks that the ceremony was about to begin. Uncle Lestr approached the dais and bowed before climbing it and positioning himself to Zavrius' right, on the opposite side of Arasne and her children.

Zavrius did not meet the man's eye. He wasn't sure how his uncle felt about this little performance—but it wouldn't matter soon how anyone felt.

Slowly, almost reluctantly, the chatter and bustle in the glade came to an uneasy silence. Zavrius waited until he could hear the wind, the distant whisper of birds, and the occasional creaking of the thick vines covering the gedrok above him before he breathed deep and glanced at his uncle.

Lestr stared back, unblinking. Disapproval burned in his eyes, though he kept his face placid. Zavrius cocked his head. No introduction, then? No announcement? So be it: he would introduce himself.

With a deep breath in his lungs to propel him forward, Zavrius positioned himself near the edge of the stage.

"I am Zavrius Dued Vuuthrik," he said, pitching his voice as loud as he could. The cavity of the gedrok's chest amplified his voice, pushing it out to the far edges of the glade. With it over his head, he could again imagine himself to be its descendent, its fledgling. He tried to take power from that. "It gives me great honor to play for you to open this ceremony, where will we confer the title of Paladin upon a deserving few."

There was a spatter of polite applause, accompanied too by whispers—no doubt from those itching at the bit to hear him play. Zavrius cleared his throat, briefly anxious. He looked out at the paladins, spent a moment scanning the crowd, trying to find Balen in amongst them all—couldn't—and then said, "I wish you all luck."

Then, there was nothing else to do. Zavrius closed his eyes, put the tips of his fingers against the strings, and played.

A hush went over the crowd as the music began, soft plucking echoed by the gedrok's body and reverberated back by the thick press of trees around the glade's perimeter. The tune built and built until music emerged and with it, a nascent, yawning emotion in Zavrius' chest.

It took barely a minute before the other musicians joined in. That was a testament to their skill: this was one of Zavrius' own compositions and not one he had played before. As much as he appreciated the accompaniment, which seemed to lend his performance credence and resulted in several of the nobles leaning forward with renewed interest, Zavrius tuned them out.

His performance was not only needed to calm his nerves but everyone else's. It was a necessity. Because of this, it required all his focus. He let the feeling in him fill up his body. He focused on his fingers, the skin, the way the tendon strings felt against the calloused tips. Each note sparked in him, rippling through the gedrokbone body of the lute-harp, and then amplifying something within Zavrius' blood. Those flecks of ichor, a foreign body in his flesh, warmed inside him, and he went dizzy with the power. The arcane flooded through him. Eyes closed, Zavrius focused on every note like it was its own creation. In each one of these, he stitched his intention, imbued the sound with ease, with calm, with interest, until the melody became hypnotic. This he did slowly. He extended the song to nearly four minutes, and as each second passed, he pushed the audience a little more. The air around him changed, and the relaxation that fell over the crowd thrilled him.

It was nothing as serious as control. That was far too difficult for Zavrius—too difficult when your opponent was a hundred unique personalities and minds fighting your intrusion. But a subtle, suggestive shift in attitude towards a prince such as he? All Zavrius needed was a kind, less volatile collective. An audience less inclined to find him pathetic when he inevitably failed to win his fight. But of course, several of those minds required more work than others.

Zavrius spotted them in the crowd. The nobility who had attended was more than he'd expected, and he knew none of their names. But his mother's voice rang in his mind:

I believe that several parties I'd have rather not known, know.

Zavrius looked out at them and focused his mind there. All of them, all fifty of them—he could do it. He began to play for them and them alone, satisfied with the calm he had thrown over everyone else. This last minute of play was intended not to *control* the nobles, per se, but to sway them. He needed the nobility united if just for a moment—and he needed it to last at least until the end of his demonstration.

For this, he added lyrics:

In Gedrok's Glade where twilight clings,
A creature rests, the past it sings,

Beneath its form where shadows fall,
Pearlescent scales, a tale it brings.

In nature's hush, the secrets laid,
Of ancient times and mystic kings,
Its silent form, a legend's call,
Eternal peace in Gedrok's Glade.

Untested conjecture, but Zavrius had often wondered about the use of his voice. If his own body had ichor burning through it, then surely the same arcane power he funneled through his instruments could enroot in the warbling of his voice. Another layer to the spell: that's what he was aiming for. Zavrius had no way of knowing the truth to this, but he played with false bravado, and in his mind's eye he conjured the thought of a blanketing power coming to rest like a veil over the horde of nobility, a shroud through which their comprehension of the events to come would tilt towards Zavrius' favor.

With the lyrics finished, Zavrius began to end the song—though he knew better than to cut it off abruptly. Some people, though few, could feel the distinction in their minds with a severed end to the magic, a dizzying realization as their senses returned to their control. He couldn't let that happen. So he played the tune softly, more sparsely, easing off with precise care. The troupe of musicians, skilled as they were, understood the cue. They eased off until they fell into silence, and once again, it was only the dulcet plucks of the lute-harp sounding, and then not even that. Zavrius stilled his fingers. The echo pulsed in the gedrok's cavity.

Eventually, even that quietened, and Zavrius was left standing before a crowd of eerily quiet people.

The first applause that occurred came directly to his left, and the sound jarred him so viciously that he snapped around. Zavrius started. His siblings blinked rapidly, falling into polite applause, though their expressions suggested a distinct lack of clarity. Did they know why they were clapping? Had he gone too far? Though as Zavrius looked, a begrudging admiration flickered over Avidia's face; her lip curled downwards, eyes wide as she spotted him as if to say, *Zavrius, you did well, for once.* Zavrius scanned his brother's faces, though none of them were meeting his eye. A frown burrowed into Theo's brows. Best not to interrogate that expression too closely.

All his family appeared vaguely pleased with him. All except his mother, whose stare bordered on violent.

Of course, she knew what he'd done. If anything, this power belonged to Arasne's school of the arcane—she had perfected it. Zavrius was little more than her student. Her claps were severe, sharp, loud, and it took Zavrius a moment to understand she had been the one to clap first, disrupting the latent daze of the lingering spell.

Flushing, Zavrius pulled his gaze from her, unable and unwilling to meet that expression. Yes, there were risks—but surely she understood the greater risk of letting him perform without aid? This was a group determined to undermine the Queen's rule, and if even one of her children lacked skill in this area, it reflected poorly on her. But more than that: how could she assume he would allow himself to be so thoroughly embarrassed like this?

I will not let myself be thrashed to oblivion by a paladin.

Arasne might have only been thinking about her own rule, but Zavrius, cursed by youth, would have to live on when she died. He could not appear weak. Not in front of his siblings, not in front of the nobles, not in front of the paladins.

Cautiously, Zavrius looked out at the crowd. They all

applauded him with a fervor—more than he'd been expecting. Zavrius dipped his head in polite appreciation before he dropped low in a sweeping bow. He threw his arms out towards the troupe of musicians who had accompanied him, and the crowd redoubled their efforts. But Zavrius knew when to call it. He took no further bows, as much as his gut longed to soak in the praise, and instead moved quickly to join his family. He avoided all eye contact, though he could feel the tension wafting off them all—his siblings, for the sheer horror of having *enjoyed* one of his performances, and his mother, for her knowledge of what he'd done. Bodies shifted behind him, but Zavrius refused to react, even when his mother's hand clenched his shoulder and she whispered, "We'll discuss this later."

Defiant, nostrils flaring, Zavrius tried for nonplussed ease. "What's there to discuss?"

Pointedly, he did not turn around, even when Arasne's grip became an uncomfortable pressure boring into his shoulder. Zavrius clutched the lute-harp to anchor himself, like the connection to the gedrokbone would somehow center him, remind his flesh and his blood of its arcane origin.

Calm down. Stop being anxious. But of course, he couldn't. It was never that simple.

"Prince Zavrius, the youngest of the Dued Vuuthrik dynasty, we thank you for your performance!" Uncle Lestr shouted as he strode back to center-stage with sudden energy and bluster.

From there, the ceremony shifted. Lestr explained what would happen. The young people who would have the rank of Paladin conferred upon them would line up and perform a series of drills. This was entirely for show, as Zavrius understood it; none would be turned away. Following this, the process of extracting ichor would take place—it would be freshly and directly tapped from the gedrok, placed into a chalice, and the ritual would begin. Then, new and old paladins would begin to spar. This was usually the entertainment portion of the event, though for Zavrius, it was the source of his great anxiety, as he would be thrown into the mix. The musicians began to play a soft tune, the drumming sparse, though with distinct beats for which the new paladins could pace themselves to. Everyone on the dais turned to the left as the crowd turned to the right, a sea of bodies in flux, a swelling tide. On cue, the line of young trainees stepped forward.

All of them were dressed in mismatched gedrok plates. Most of the senior paladins had armor crafted from gedrokscale, which was more malleable and sturdier, but some were bone through and through. Zavrius could tell because they shined just that little bit less. Much of this younger cohort were in mismatched assemblages, taking whatever spare pieces they were given. All the recruits were without helmets. Their young faces were stern and serious, and even though some had tremors, Zavrius felt a kinship with them. He could *feel* the severity of the want, the desire to become something more than they were. He clenched his fist unwittingly by his side, thinking, *I see you. Good luck.*

It didn't matter that this was a formality. He wanted them all to do well. As he watched them draw their blades in sacrosanct synchronicity, swords held aloft as they bowed first to the Dued Vuuthriks and then to the gedrok, emotion welled behind Zavrius' eyes. Fever and the urge to move buzzed in him. All these young people were dedicating themselves to a life of service—to him, to his family. Something akin to guilt, or perhaps shame, clouded Zavrius' vision.

In perfect cohesion, they moved to demonstrate, raising their blades, and slicing forward, retreating in a controlled line, calling out with spirited cries to mimic battle. Their more senior counterparts waited behind them, all still with distant expressions. At some unseen command, the new recruits formed a single-file line and began marching towards Lestr, who had descended the dais and now stood straight, arms held behind his back. Attendants had moved towards the gedroks' lower left leg, where a square of scale and plate had been removed. The hole was precise, with just enough room on either side for the apparatus to be placed.

One of the attendants bowed with his hands outstretched to Lestr, displaying the device in the joint cushion of his two palms. From this vantage, Zavrius could barely see it, but he still found himself craning for more detail. He needn't have done any of that. He knew what it was. Extracting ichor required the bones of the gedrok to be tapped. Ichor, commonly mistaken for the *blood* of the gedroks, was actually harvested from within the bones themselves like the very skeleton of those primordial beasts required a pool of arcane power to function.

A hole had been burrowed into the bone prior to this act of ceremony with paladin power, angled upwards to encourage the flow of ichor downwards. Now, Uncle Lestr turned steadily towards the attendant whose arms remained outstretched, and from the bed of his hands, Lestr picked up the spile.

It was made of gedrokscale and much larger than any spile used in the extraction of sap from trees. This, highly detailed and about as old as the Dued Vuuthrik dynasty, was about half a forearm in length and deceptively light. That last part Zavrius was only guessing, of course, as he watched Lestr pluck it up one-handedly and place it in the pre-prepared hole. A small ceremonial mallet appeared next, brought by the attendant to Lestr's left. This Lestr raised above his head, earning a loud huff of sound from the gathered paladins.

With the mallet, he hit the spile once, twice, three times, each swing of the hammer accompanied by the collective cheer of paladin voices. Then the chalice came. It was made from silver and decorated with pearl, though no gedrok material had been used in its creation. Lestr placed it against the gedrok, opened the spile, and ichor flowed free.

Zavrius didn't want to think about it, since too much bodily awareness unnerved him, but he could feel the ichor in the air. The instant it flowed, he knew. He sensed it, understood its movements as it gathered in the welcome bottom of the chalice. The spile was forcibly stopped just moments later, the amount of extracted ichor carefully measured against notches within, ensuring the paladin would not be overconsuming. One at a time, they walked up and were given the ichor, and they would walk the length of the dais to bow before the royal family. Arasne had already stepped forward to the center. From here, she thanked them and blessed them, and the paladins were politely escorted to the back of the gedrok, where they'd presumably writhe about for a few minutes as the ichor took effect. Zavrius wasn't sure; he'd never seen that part.

In any case, it went like that, paladin after paladin confirmed into the order, and when it was over, a cheer rippled through the crowd at the same time Zavrius' heart sank to the depths of his stomach.

Because it was *his* time now, and that ceremony had taken close to an hour. Would his spell hold up? Would he manage to not make a fool of himself, of his family?

In the end, there were greater things to worry about, since by the time the sparring began, he was pulled aside by Lestr and given the bad news.

He would not be sparring with a new recruit.

He would be sparring with a paladin named Balen of Westgar.

Thirteen

"*Because it makes no sense!*"

Zavrius' voice went high. He was already halfway shouting when he pulled back, but the gedrok caught the outraged tones and doubled them. Flushing, Zavrius ducked his head. He'd have to hope no one in the gathered crowd heard that.

Lestr had pulled him towards the back of the gedrok to prepare. Recovering newly appointed paladins were sprawled around him in various states, battling nausea, excitability, and all the other glorious side effects of ichor consumption. It made Zavrius' exasperation appear absurd.

Lestr wasn't looking at him. He had turned his head away. For a moment, Zavrius' anger and fear were overwhelmed by the sheer disrespect.

"You will look me in the eye," he said.

Lestr turned, a brief, unhappy glare sparking in his eye. "It's not up to me."

Zavrius faltered, mind running wild with the possibilities—though they were few. How many had control over the decisions of Commander Lestr?

Zavrius squeezed his arms closer. "Theo, then?" When Lestr didn't immediately reply, he scoffed loudly. "Of course you'd listen to fucking *Theo.*"

The few new paladins still conscious in the vicinity winced at that. Zavrius saw one attempting to crawl further away in his periphery. Lestr waited for a moment and then mirrored the prince's posture, folding his arms defensively.

Zavrius refused to break first. Why should he have to? Lestr had blindsided him with this news.

It wasn't about fighting Balen. Or rather, it wasn't *just* about his opponent being the young man he fancied.

It was about shame.

As Zavrius saw it, there were two reasons this had worked out: Theo had realized another way to cause Zavrius shame was to strongarm their uncle into changing opponents, or it was sheer coincidence.

"He's a good fighter," Lestr said.

"I'm well aware."

"What I mean is that he'll know to hold off. A newer paladin might not have the foresight to—"

"To go easy on me?" Zavrius struggled to contain his voice. He'd dropped his arms to his sides and stepped forward, but his whole body trembled. His nails dug into the palms of his hands, but he only clenched tighter—he could feel the familiar burn of heat behind his eyes, but he would control his body as he knew he could.

Straightening, Zavrius recovered his calm and pursed his lips, falsely inspecting his nails to stall further. Then, finally, he stepped forward and lowered his voice to a fierce whisper.

"I want you to understand, Uncle, the position this puts me in. We are all on the same page, yes? That my demonstration is intended to shore up my mother's rule? Ensure our wayward nobility do not see the cracks in the façade, so to say?" He gestured to himself. "You put me up against a fresh paladin, and maybe I could hold my own. But against this new opponent— established, and skilled, and devoted to our lineage, devoted to the point he wishes to serve my brother as his Prime—there are only two things that can happen. Either he beats me, and I am proved a dandy, or I beat him, by his goodwill, and our entire paladin force looks weak. So what will it be?"

Lestr flushed and glanced away, but as Zavrius finished speaking, the pieces clicked into place. He laughed and spun on his heel, staring out at the cluster of trees and that dense green. Perhaps he should walk into it. Walk and walk until he got himself lost forever.

"You know I tried," Lestr said. He walked slowly to Zavrius' back and placed a hand on his shoulder. "I said you were untrained."

Not quite the comfort Lestr thought it was, but no matter.

"Confirm it for me," Zavrius whispered, closing his eyes. "Or better yet, tell me I'm wrong."

"You're not wrong," Lestr said, and Zavrius' stomach twisted into a knot. "The Queen made the call."

Fuck. Fuck, fuck—gedroks, of course she did. He stepped away from his uncle's touch, mind a flurry of activity and fear and betrayal. Was this punishment for his spell? Undoubtedly, that had played a part. But Arasne had never been *vindictive!* Surely, she wouldn't have done this without good reason?

"The excuse she gave you was. . .?"

"Not that she needs one," Lestr warned, before adding, "That you two have been training together. That you should be able to. . .do this subtly."

Zavrius turned to meet his uncle's eyes. He scanned them, saw the conviction in them. Then, that was it.

"She wants a performance." Zavrius clicked his tongue. "A balancing act between paladin prowess and the youngest Dued Vuuthrik's ability." He didn't wait for Lestr to confirm—the truth sat like a stone in his gut. His mother wanted to showcase *both* these strengths of her rule at once.

Zavrius' mind raced. Why? That question plagued him—*why?* If she had known this to be necessary, he was certain she'd have said something. So what could have possibly happened in the hour of the ceremony for this to be necessary?

Unless. . .

Zavrius turned around. "Is she hurt?"

Lestr's lip curled. He glanced up to the sky. "Sometimes, I do forget how quick you are, my prince."

A small, tired smile crept up Zavrius' lip, though it didn't last long. He folded his arms again, walking forward to his uncle. With his anger ebbing away, Zavrius could see the exhaustion writ plain on the older man's face. Those lines were etched deep, shadows of old carved eternally into his forehead and lower eyes.

Zavrius waited, and the expression in Lestr's eyes shifted minutely, hardening into that of an adept commander rugged from duty.

"When you performed, something happened. Or rather, didn't happen. We'd. . .we had expected *something*. There was a single archer posted in the trees."

Zavrius frowned. "An archer? But they fired no shot! They had an hour. More, even. All of us were standing there."

Zavrius shut his mouth when he finished the sentence, recalling how he'd felt in the forge with his uncle just a few days before. Lestr had been nonchalant. Dismissive, even. He clenched his jaw and asked, as carefully as he could, "You said. . .it was a demonstration. That no one expected me to be brilliant. But I'm sure you understand *why* she wants me to do well if an assassin was lying in wait."

Lestr didn't respond to that. Zavrius hoped that pride stopped him, and not some deeper machination, like familial betrayal.

His uncle continued slowly, "He. . .well, it happened when you began to play. You played so well, young Zavrius, that he. . .climbed down the tree and handed himself in. Blubbering. Claims to be a free agent, but his weapon was of too fine a make for that to be true. And in all honesty, he's not particularly smart. Drunk, too, or he's taken something. My guess is a noble paid him at the last minute, and he panicked. Needed something to quell his nerves. In any case, Petra will find out the truth."

Lestr's eyes were knowing, but Zavrius felt frozen in sincere shock. He had played, and a would-be assassin had *turned himself in?* It seemed impossible.

Forced to consider the possibility, though, Zavrius paused. His own mother had trained him to sway people, to have that power. Why *wouldn't* it be possible to do more? The man's level of intelligence might have assisted. The altered state of his mind, brought about by the alcohol, most certainly had. But Zavrius had never been able to conjure such effects from anyone, and this news was both terrifying and liberating all at once. He'd demonstrated a power that allowed him to influence another person's actions and not just their emotions. Quickly, he controlled his expression, softening his eyes and his jaw into indifferent composure. If Lestr clocked the shift, he said nothing. Now, it was Zavrius' turn to inspect his uncle's expression.

When you began to play. . .

What Lestr knew or did not know about his ability, Zavrius opted to pretend he hadn't heard that part. Surely, Lestr *knew* what his sister could do, but the fewer people who comprehended Zavrius' own talents, the better.

"How many people know about this?"

Lestr said, "You, me, the Queen, Petra, and the four paladins who apprehended the man."

Not his siblings, then. Good.

"The four paladins. Do they understand what happened?"

Now, it was Lestr's turn to purse his lips. "They believe it was the guilt, my prince. That his profound shame inspired him to hand himself in."

Zavrius gnawed at his lips and folded his arms. In all honesty, a drunk would-be assassin handing himself in out of guilt was a more fathomable reality than what Lestr was suggesting. In any case, this lack of understanding of his abilities was what he wanted. "I want you to keep it that way."

"The Queen has asked us to do something similar, my prince. As few people as possible will know."

"Good. That's good."

Which left, well, not much. Zavrius swallowed and tested his voice with a cough. "Where is Paladin Balen?"

Lestr's eyes softened in that knowing way, like he could feel the burden of his request settling into place on Zavrius' shoulders as the young prince accepted the load. He sighed, just slightly, his relief palpable. But Zavrius gave him nothing more—no soft smile of understanding, no nod of acquiescence. This was duty and self-protection all in one.

But he had to wonder: what did Balen think of all this?

Lestr led Zavrius to the right towards the back of the gedrok. Its serpentine tail slumped and curled, the tip licking up against its own haunches. On the opposite side, Zavrius could hear the ongoing demonstrations of green paladins sparring. Somehow, in the stinging song of clashing metal, he could sense they were close to the end.

Soon, Zavrius and Balen would be announced.

The paladin in question sat on the ground, knees up to his

chest. The gedrok plate articulated beautifully, allowing him the full range of motion, and each part of the armor sat layered like scales. At the first sound of footsteps, Balen's head snapped up. It took less than a moment for him to register Zavrius, and he shot up to rigid attention, bowing gracefully as they got close.

"At ease," Lestr commanded after a confirming look at Zavrius. "I've explained the situation to the prince. He understands the necessity of this, as I am sure you do." The way Lestr delivered that line suggested Balen had had his own biting remarks to share, but now the paladin made no move at all. He took Lestr's words with silent, stoic obedience.

Lestr continued, "I will leave you two to discuss. You have, at best, ten minutes. Closer to five."

They both watched as Lestr turned and left, and then continued staring after him for much longer than was necessary, as if trying to delay the inevitable conversation.

Zavrius moved first, spinning to face Balen. "Thank you for saving my mother."

The words caused an awful rippling to conquer Balen's features. He scrunched up his nose and eyes, disgust and pain evident in the motion. "That was. . .only luck."

Clearly, he regretted not magically knowing a drunken archer sat somewhere in the trees. "Hardly your fault."

Balen opened his mouth, breath sharp—he hadn't liked that, hadn't agreed with it, and Zavrius could sense what he wanted to say. That it was his *job*, his *duty*, or any number of honor-bound statements he might fish out at that moment. Instead, Balen stopped himself. A flush had burned across his cheeks.

"It doesn't matter now," Balen said softly. "Though I am sorry it's come to this."

"Don't be," Zavrius said. He glanced around, quickly lacing his pinky finger around Balen's own, just for a second. He pulled away and knew a flush threatened his composure, too. "It's done, and I won't mind being beaten by you the way I'd have minded with a green paladin. Though we must. . .figure out the logistics."

Balen visibly swallowed. "The politics, you mean."

Zavrius dipped his head. "Sounds like you understand the struggle. Here's what I think, anyway: we are a bit fucked."

Balen barked a laugh, then smothered his own mouth as the sound reverberated through the gedrok. A tense moment passed as he waited to hear the ongoing sounds of sparring; Zavrius watched with a low smile, thinking him rather adorable despite all that muscle.

Zavrius said, "It will be a hard balance. I think. . .I need to hold my own, at least for a while."

"Can we manufacture a draw?"

Zavrius doubted this very much. Who would call it? How long would be an acceptable spar to prevent suspicion? He pressed his palms into his eyes, frustration quickly rising. *Breathe. Breathe.*

Balen stepped closer. The paladin made no move to touch him, but Zavrius felt his presence as surely as his own. The urge to turn, to pull the other man into a kiss, was fierce. Zavrius glanced over at Balen, down at his lips, which parted softly when the paladin noticed his stare. Then Zavrius cleared his throat and turned his body to face Balen fully.

"It's a dance," he said softly. "And you'll have to lead because I barely know the steps. I'm fast, at least. If you signal your moves, I should be able to get out of the way. Let me land one, and then you can show off. We can end with a struggle that you ultimately win." Zavrius paused and nodded to himself. "It's believable. More believable than a draw. But it should. . .serve the purpose. I'm not a complete pushover, and the paladins are a strong force."

Balen nodded. Neither of them said what was on their minds. Zavrius thought: *if the nobles hate Arasne, nothing will be enough to stop that.* But he shook that thought free and let it drift into the ether. If he could only control the 'now', then this was what he would do.

What seemed only a blink of an eye later, the two of them were alone on the green stretch of field in the Gedrok's Glade with a hundred pairs of eyes on them.

Zavrius' anxiety was sharp, angled like glass shards piercing at his skin. It was a manifold emotion; before him stood Balen of Westgar, labor-broadened body filling out his armor and cool, focused expression boring into the prince. Attraction burned hot and heavy in Zavrius' chest, but the unease of being perceived corrupted it, made the feeling rancid like an itch in Zavrius' gut. Under this many eyes, and with enough rumors already tainting his image, Zavrius' attraction to the paladin was as dangerous as any blade. He felt, then, more concerned that a noble would somehow guess at the nature of their relationship than see through the ruse they were about to perform.

Don't be ridiculous.

Zavrius straightened, nostrils flaring reflexively as his body adjusted in place. In his hand, the hilt of the small sword pressed uncomfortably into the flesh. He felt surveyed, seen, flustered by the eyes, that noble crowd pressing at the edges of his vision, a horde blocking him in. His anxiety veered violently to claustrophobia until he bit down on his tongue, using the pain as an anchor.

Focus on Balen. Everyone else is a border, a wall to help keep your eyes on him.

And in the end, it was an easy thing to look at Balen of Westgar. Balen met his eye and nodded just so. Zavrius nodded back. Like that, they stayed staring at one another, a bond just as tangible as a hand on his shoulder. Together, they found a pocket of stolen intimacy carved into a moment of superb vulnerability.

Zavrius did not flinch when his uncle walked out and called for the crowd's attention, though he felt his breathing grow rapid and heard that rabid racing of his heart echoing in his ears.

Keep looking at Balen. Keep looking at Balen.

"The Gifted Paladins are an order devoted to the protection and posterity of the royal family. We dedicate our lives to uphold the lives of our rulers; the dynasty responsible for Usleth's continued peace, protection, and prosperity."

A polite cheer went up when Lestr paused, though he spoke over it quickly. Zavrius wondered if he was worried about it petering out. Worried about what the silence might represent.

"Today, we have the pleasure of the entire Dued Vuuthrik family joining us to witness the confirmation of our new paladins to the order. And now we have a further great honor. We will be witnessing a spar between rising star Paladin Balen of Westgar and the youngest Dued Vuuthrik, Prince Zavrius. Welcome to the field!"

Now the cheer went up, and Zavrius tore his eyes away from Balen's face. Magnified by the gedrok's hollow body, the sound echoed out throughout the Glade in a thunderous wave. All those eyes on him, all those faces—and not one reproving, not one anything except the picture of excitement. It jolted Zavrius. He couldn't remember the last time he'd ever been celebrated like this by a crowd. Electric, nearly better than any performance, he allowed himself the luxury of believing them.

In this moment, they love you.

And even if he couldn't afford to forget himself entirely—for this dance with Balen required concentration—he let his ego inflate just enough to lift his head above the water.

Lestr left the field, their silent signal to begin, and Zavrius turned bodily to face Balen. He shifted the short sword into position just as Balen rolled his shoulders back, his own great sword tilted at an angle, tip facing towards the earth. An imposing sight he was. Emboldened by the prismatic scale and with the hulking form of the armor's progenitor slumped in eternal sleep behind them, Balen looked divine. In contrast, Zavrius was armorless, a necessary evil he now partially regretted. He had spent so long training to hold a sword properly that he and Balen hadn't even covered how to hold it properly *whilst wearing armor*. The shift in weight confused Zavrius' balance so much that it simply wasn't possible, and perhaps the lack delegitimized their display since Balen would not be allowed to harm Zavrius in any way—*stop thinking.*

He heard that in Balen's voice, his own subconscious generating what it knew would silence his mind. Zavrius took several steadying.

Everything in him went into watching Balen move. Zavrius had to anticipate everything. The young paladin stepped slowly to the side. Zavrius responded, stepping in the opposite way. They fell into an easy rhythm, circling the other in a careful assessment. Zavrius found himself wishing he'd worn different shoes. The boots he'd chosen were of fine make but their grip was questionable, and each soft sidestep on the wet grass unnerved him when he felt his weight give. Balen rolled out his wrist next, stretching that great sword as if it was an extension of his own arm, and when he placed his other hand around the hilt, Zavrius' body knew to brace.

He feinted forward, and Zavrius fell for it, jerking back to a chorus of poorly controlled tittering. How quick they were to turn —that brief reprise from the collective reproach of the nobility made this response all the worse. Zavrius buckled. What ought to have happened was polite silence from the watching crowd, and this shameful sound caused Zavrius to bite down on the fleshy part of his tongue until the burn of shame behind his eyes became a sting of tears. Damn. *Damn!*

Balen made a soft motion with his head, almost placating. He raised no hand nor did much of anything with his body to signal, but Zavrius *felt* it. Balen's eyes weren't full of pity or anger or even sympathy. Yet Zavrius felt drawn. In the paladin's gaze, Zavrius could see himself reflected, body far too tense, and whether he imagined that sight or not, his body settled in the connection of their gazes. Balen was like an island in a storm, that solid rock foundation upon which Zavrius felt confident enough to stand. On the one hand, this demonstration was a performance, and on the other, something much more meaningful.

With more focus, with less emotion, Zavrius realized, too, that the response of the crowd was his own doing. If he had softened their perception towards him, increased their expectation of his performance, then this was a *good* thing.

You want them worried for you. You want them excited when you land a blow. You did this—so use it.

Balen gestured with his head as if to say, *Dance with me.* In response, Zavrius flicked his short sword up, relaxed his posture, and nodded.

Zavrius charged. Balen reacted just as fast. Their swords met in a sharp sting of sound, scraping off one another as they moved apart. They circled, approached, met in the middle with their blades against each other—foreplay, it was, and just as teasing. The earlier disrespect of the nobility decayed into adolescent avidity; like fickle children, they changed their minds again, and now this display was worth their interest. But when Balen and he met again in the middle, Balen whispered tersely over their swords, "Watch out."

A tiny warning. It was too late. By the time the words had registered, Balen had extricated himself from the blade lock. He jockeyed the great sword around, spinning it horizontally so his fist was against Zavrius' hand. Launching forward, Balen punched both Zavrius and his short sword aside. The force was so strong that Zavrius had no recourse—no way he could shift, no speed that would allow him to block. Balen whipped his blade down towards Zavrius' shoulder. There was an incoherent yell from somewhere in the crowd—or perhaps Zavrius himself—but Balen flipped the blade at the last moment, slapping the flat of the sword on his mark. Just as quickly, Balen lifted the sword deftly, giving Zavrius an opportunity to skitter back. Zavrius did, just enough that he could lunge forward again with ease. In this moment, they were training again, and Zavrius was *trying*. No game, no performance—he lunged and struck, and Balen deftly parried every attempt, his gaze calm and collected. There was not even a bead of sweat on his brow.

In contrast, a dampness clung to Zavrius' neck. His throat felt raw, burned from exertion. But he refused to let it stop him. *Couldn't*, actually, let it stop him—he needed to at least try and fight. Not all of this could be faked. So he dove forward again and again, and Balen landed another blow by simply stepping out of the way. Zavrius' momentum carried him forward, and before he had a chance to turn, the flat of his blade slapped at Balen's back.

Which *frustrated* Zavrius, given the effort he was putting in. If he had an instrument, if he could just *show what he could do*— he killed that thought with a series of quick forward jabs, one after the other, hounding forward until Balen was slightly off balance. A flare of surprise burned in Balen's eye. *That's it*, Zavrius thought, *there I am.*

Then, before his own ego could sabotage this play, he clenched his jaw and charged; the next move overtly signaled. Balen began to raise his sword to deflect before Zavrius had even struck forward, and it was perfect—the perfect chance. Balen anticipated him to strike high, and so instead of stabbing towards Balen's shoulder, he sliced down. Since Balen wore armor there was no need for Zavrius to pull back. He followed through, slashing down over the plate. From the minute blow came a cacophony of sound, a shrill scream of metal against bone that echoed out into the field, and Balen jumped back, offering both Zavrius and the crowd a deferential nod. They came together several more times, and they had learned each other's movements now. Balen landed a blow, and then Zavrius blocked his next attack, perfectly anticipating the strike before it happened. Balen blocked one of his, and then Zavrius broke through to strike into his shoulder. When it became clear neither was going to win—though Balen without a doubt could—they locked their blades together in a faux struggle.

"Well *done,*" Balen whispered. Zavrius fought to hide his smile. "On three."

Balen waited for three breaths and shoved. They both pushed back with great force, stepping back out of each other's range until only their sword tips were touching. Panting, they stared at one another. This was it. This was the end. A cheer went up, happy surprise spilling through the gathered people like a flooded lake. And though they could have, perhaps *should* have, kept going, they lowered their swords at the same time.

Balen walked forward, bowed low before him, and then slipped his hand around Zavrius' wrist. Momentarily shaken by the sudden closeness, Zavrius did nothing but gawk. Then his arm was being lifted high over his head, and the people who had despised him all his life were cheering.

His heart seized. Looking out at all of them made him dizzy. Looking at Balen was even worse. But he embraced the inevitable vertigo given to him by the sheer beauty of the other man and stared. Balen's smile was contained but strong. His lips stretched wide across his face, lips flaring at the corner. Pride, Zavrius thought, was wafting off him. Zavrius' heart raced at that thought;

something about Balen seeing him, about not finding him wanting, drove him insane.

Lestr's voice cut through the crowd, and Zavrius heard only
bits of it. His name, then Balen's, then something about the
unique prowess of Usleth as a nation. But Zavrius didn't look
away from Balen. Not once.

At that moment, he thought: *I don't ever want to look away
from you again.*

Fourteen

His mother said nothing to him in words, but she kissed him on the cheek a few seconds too long, and that communicated more than enough for Zavrius.

The ceremony had concluded, and plenty of the nobles had left in carriages, preferring to return to Cres Stros early. But all the paladins remained, and the royal family, too, and the nature of the event shifted with the setting of the sun as if without that bright orb watching they could lose the strictness of the ritual. In that orange haze cast by the sunset, fires were lit, and the band switched to jauntier tunes. Barrels of ale had been rolled out, though they were low in alcohol content to maintain at least the pretense of respect to this site.

Cres Stros loved its parties. Uslethian parties tended to be excessive, with costumes and escorts and animals, with music that went on, and guests that never seemed to leave, and it had been that way since Zavrius was young. His memories of those events were a blur, a jumbled mess of light, sound, and general revelry. By the time he developed sentience and a smidgen of personality, he was ten, and his father was dead. The months following were an odd time. Peace with the empire was becoming an option, and the general emotion in Usleth straddled grief and triumph. At the first party to celebrate the treaty, feeling keenly the absence of his father now he could be unstoppered and free, Zavrius Dued Vuuthrik had realized what he was. Realized how much he liked the way that serving boy looked at him, realized what his father had seen in him and disliked, realized all of it all at once like a reckoning.

Now, in a similar way, as all others danced and drank around him, an all-consuming emotion filled him up. He stared at Balen from afar as he talked to the newly confirmed paladins. Zavrius' longing was apparently obvious—Arasne came and looped her arm through his, pulling him close.

"My son," she whispered.

Zavrius frowned a little as the intensity of emotion in his chest shifted towards something nostalgic. He leaned into her touch, fighting to drag his eyes from Balen. He glanced over his shoulder at Arasne. Arasne's Prime, Hisud, stood at a respectful distance by her side like a dark and vaguely angry shadow.

Hisud was a woman in her fifties. She had the characteristic dark, ashy tones of someone born towards the south-west of Usleth. Her hair, a thick mane of curls, had long ago been sapped of its color. A few black strands remained in thin streaks, and she had wrenched the whole lot of them away from her face. It exploded out over her shoulders anyway. She looked—haggard. Standing at attention for this many hours had very clearly taken its toll on her, and her old injury was bothering her by the way her stance swayed.

Zavrius leaned over Arasne's gentle hold of him and said just loud enough for Hisud to hear, "Thank you for your assistance today."

Hisud flushed slightly, grunting out, "It is my duty, Prince Zavrius."

Arasne's lips pinched together, and Zavrius let Hisud be, slinking back to face his mother.

Arasne glanced at him. "She's upset," his mother whispered. "Thinks she can't leave now. We had just had a conversation about it, you see. About her retirement."

Zavrius fought to keep his reaction small. "Well, it's not been done, has it?" His voice came out strangely defensive. Of course, all paladins were meant to protect the royal family, but the duty of the Prime was in their sacrifice and devotion to the monarch. Never once had a paladin left the service in any way other than death. And after today, where an assassin had very almost taken the shot. . .

"Zavrius," Arasne whispered softly. Her voice was equal parts admonishing and. . .sad. "You already know I'm dying."

He went stiff. He didn't look at her, didn't look at anyone, briefly saw nothing except a blinding white that suppressed his vision. His body shook for a moment until he regained control.

"I know," he said softly. And he had known, in the quiet way a child can sense when something is wrong with a parent. An insidious *wrongness* in his belly. She was alright now, but like some awful prophecy, Zavrius could feel how it would eat at her until she wasted away. She would keep ruling until she couldn't, and she would hide it from almost everyone, and the illness would claim her anyway.

Arasne stared out at the revelry. Her breathing was even. Nothing in her posture suggested unease at the thought of her death. How long had she known?

Paladin Hisud, on the other hand, looked upset. Shaken. More shaken than perhaps she should have been at her age, with her experience. Though Arasne had left it mostly unsaid, Zavrius could guess. Prime Paladin Hisud was old herself, nursing a decades-old injury, and perhaps—by the way she held herself now, the way shame wafted off her—had been upstaged by the younger paladins during that afternoon's assassination attempt. Now her Queen was relaxed, blasé about her upcoming death—it must have hurt. It would call into question those decades of sacrifice.

"She's given so much of her life for you," Zavrius murmured.

"Yes. I don't want her to give *all* of it."

"It hasn't been done. Primes serve for life."

"Well, I am Queen," Arasne said, petulantly. "I'm allowed to make changes."

It wasn't a conversation that would be particularly productive. Zavrius had no energy to test his mother's limits in that moment, knowing far too well he would reach his own before he reached hers. Besides, did it really matter, in the end, if a Prime left the service? He relaxed a little into her embrace, letting their cheeks rest against one another.

It felt good to be her child. Hers and hers alone, with no Sirellius corrupting him.

"Did I do well?" he whispered. How childish he felt, then. He wanted his mother, and he wanted her praise.

"Thank you," she whispered, squeezing him. It was an answer, and yet not one.

For a moment, they stood in silence. Zavrius closed his eyes and breathed deep. Later, she might have words with him about his spell, but for now, she seemed content to let him be. The breeze was warm, and the sounds of joviality thrummed in his chest.

"Why don't you dance?" Arasne asked him.

Zavrius opened his mouth, then closed it. He wanted more from her. The urge to ask about the assassin sat on the tip of his tongue, and he swallowed it, knowing she would step away—that this brief access he had to his *mother* rather than his *Queen* would disappear like a shadow in direct light. So he thought about her question. Instinctively, his eyes darted to Balen. Their dance had just finished. Who else could compare?

"I don't think I want to dance."

His mother made a low noise beneath her breath. With her free hand, she patted his forearm and then took her arm away. She turned Zavrius towards her, and though her eyes were very serious, a gentle smile lay upon her lips.

"Go on," she whispered.

His heart thudded against his ribcage, barely contained. "I—"

Words failed him. To convey the vulnerability, the exposure, the violence of emotion he felt—it all seemed too much.

"You're fifth in line," she said, not to dismay him but to encourage him. "I can't promise you won't need to make some sacrifices later, but for now, you should enjoy it."

"It?" Zavrius said slowly, fumbling with the nebulous term.

Arasne shrugged. "Him."

From the Queen's side, she pulled her lute-harp into view. The pearlescent body shimmered with the movement like dappled light on waves. She proffered it to him.

"For what?" Zavrius asked, hand outstretched to take it. His mother only shrugged again. Devious.

She left him like that, flushing, ashamed, and excited all at once. The weight of an instrument in his hand felt good, and with the distractive power of music at his fingertips, Zavrius at least felt less anxious about the overwhelming task ahead of him: *conversation*. He stared over at Balen, who had just thrown his head back in a laugh. The strong jawline flexed, his throat bobbed; he was beautiful. He liked Zavrius in return. So what was he waiting for?

Go on, coward.

Zavrius turned and stalked towards one of the ale barrels. "Pour me something, would you?" he asked the attendant, and with some liquid courage in his stomach, he approached the paladins.

Some other young man saw him first. His eyes went bulbous in his head, wide as he registered Zavrius' approach, and tactlessly, he muttered and gestured to the others, who began to move apart before seeing who it was. Zavrius kept his gaze fixed on Balen. He watched every minute movement, the way his hair bobbed as he turned, the first glimpse of his nose, and then the glisten in his eyes as he registered Zavrius' presence.

All of them dropped into a low bow the same instant that gravity got a vice grip on Zavrius' heart.

Zavrius fixed his gaze on the sea of hair. "Rise."

Balen was the slowest to raise himself out of that sweeping posture, and when he did, his eyes were fixed on Zavrius'. His lips twitched up in a small smile, almost like a reflexive movement, though he didn't try to hide it. From that low angle, with Balen looking up at him like that, devious little grin pricking at the corners of his mouth—*gedroks*, it sparked something inside Zavrius' body. He couldn't help it. Any solid grip he'd had on his thoughts got away from him, gathered weight until he could imagine Balen naked on his knees, looking up at Zavrius with that same small smile, the same upward strain to his eyes, sparkling with want.

"You did very well, my prince."

It wasn't easy to stop his wayward thoughts. They wanted free rein—were gnashing at the bit to keep running wild—but Zavrius could not afford that. Not here, not anywhere except behind closed doors. Zavrius snapped his attention towards the new voice. A man fifteen or so years older than him smiled pleasantly. Genuinely, even. He was broad and tall, every part a paladin, like Lestr himself had forged the man. There was a softness in his eyes that relaxed Zavrius, who so usually had to defend himself against all kinds of comments. Vaguely, recognition prodded at Zavrius' mind, but so rarely had he had cause to know the names of every paladin in the order. Now, though, it was best he knew—not just to mask his closeness to Balen of Westgar, but out of *respect.*

"Thank you, uh, paladin . . .?"

"Duart, my prince." The paladin bowed slightly again, then threw his arm out towards two young people watching the exchange warily. Both new recruits were marked by mismatched armor and an expression of general fear characterized by eyebrows plastered in upturned dismay.

"I'd like to introduce you to our newest recruits, Vekus and Silvana."

Both bobbed their head in another bow, which Zavrius returned.

"Congratulations," Zavrius said politely before he turned to Balen. "And you. You are formidable."

"Am I?" Balen said with a smile far too wide. "It was a pleasure to spar with you."

It was a secret moment, that little smile they shared then. A bit of transience and stolen privacy. Certainly, there would come a time when their interest in one another was a known secret—something Zavrius had to make sure Balen understood. But for now, they had the fleeting luxury of it being truly *theirs.*

Zavrius seized the lull in conversation, uncaring if his eagerness would give him away. "I actually had some questions about your form, if you don't mind. I know it's a time for revelry, and I would hate to take you from your friends, but—"

"It would be my pleasure." Balen stepped forward far too eagerly. He forgot himself, bowed as he walked, and barely spared a glance back at Duart and the new recruits. His zealousness meant Zavrius had to follow suit, and the young prince quickly turned away and began to lead Paladin Balen away from the intensity.

Not that there were many places to go.

He just wanted a quiet moment. He wished he might turn and ask for Balen's hand and dance around with some of the other nobles, but it was too much of a risk—too much blurring of the lines he had just fought to maintain. So he walked quickly and quietly around the sprawled body of the giant gedrok, and peered cautiously around the back, where Lestr had spoken to him earlier.

Thankfully, it was now free of paladins. Any recruits who had been made nauseous by ichor consumption had vacated. Zavrius kept walking until he found a spot, and then he gestured for Balen to sit.

Out of sight, they sat with their backs against the gedrok's back haunches. Mud and earth, dredged up by the paladin's earlier marshaling, now soiled Zavrius' fine tunic. He was probably humiliating himself. Most certainly, Theo would say so if he saw —but then Zavrius looked over and saw *him.*

Balen had his hands in the grass. He'd picked a weed flower free and was spinning the thin stem between his fingers. Petals blurred into the shape of a white bulb, and Balen's soft gaze watched the dancing flower with ease.

Looking at Balen felt difficult. They kept sharing small glances, flitting looks, small smiles: a thrumming grew in Zavrius' body as intense as ichor. For a good minute, they said nothing and did nothing. Zavrius fought the urge to start strumming at the lute-harp, a magical crutch, and only when it all became too much—when Balen's smiles made his heart lurch and his body thrum, did he push himself forward into a kiss.

Balen inhaled sharply as their lips met. Zavrius breathed him in, too. Upturned earth and that mossy brine scent of the gedrok's body filled his nostrils, and under that, the smell of Balen himself. Sweat and his natural smell made Zavrius want to crawl forward, but instead he strained at an awkward angle, unwilling to commit fully by turning and putting his knees in the dirt. Balen's hands caressed his face. One came to rest so that the palm cupped his cheek and his fingers pressed firmly at the back of Zavrius' head. The touch felt hungry. Purposeful. But Balen's honor seemed to prevent him from doing anything more. His hands did not wander far, even if part of Zavrius wanted him to.

Together, they leaned back, still locked in the kiss. Their heads met the firm fleshy shell of the gedrok, and like that, in a trilateral connection, Zavrius felt three points of ichor thrumming through his core.

He pulled away with tears in his eyes, tears dredged from that ancient source in his blood, a feeling that was not wholly his. Connection and attraction and the thrill of reciprocation, all underlined by a feeling of wonderment and power. If Balen was disturbed by the glistening in Zavrius' eyes, he made no comment save for pressing his lips to Zavrius' brow.

When they met each other's eyes, Zavrius laughed. Giddy joy filled him, and he couldn't meet Balen's eyes without feeling thrilled. Balen began to laugh, too, and both turned away from each other, settling so their backs pressed against the gedrok. Their fingers sat beside one another on the ground. For the first time, Balen made the move. He reached over and held Zavrius' hand, squeezing once.

"You were brilliant," Balen said, which made Zavrius laugh again. Balen turned. "No, I mean it. That was the best you've ever performed."

"In swordplay, maybe," Zavrius said. "Though if I'd been *fighting* anyone else. . ." He looked down. "Anyway, I must thank you. I would have embarrassed myself, my family, and my country if you hadn't trained me."

Balen looked like he wanted to say something to that, but his only response ended up being another squeeze of Zavrius' hand. Something shifted. A chill went through the air, and as the cheering revelry picked up on the other side of the gedrok, a hollow feeling opened in Zavrius' gut.

"I'm sorry to steal you away," Zavrius said. He pulled his hand away and pretended to smooth out his tunic. "I just wanted a moment."

"I wanted a moment too," Balen admitted. Then he flushed fiercely and rubbed the back of his neck. "I, uh. I want a lot of moments. With you."

Zavrius was glad Balen wasn't looking at him as he said it. His chest seized violently, and the urge to yell manifested in him biting down hard on his tongue. He made a little noise of pain in his throat. Balen didn't react to it; he had turned to the right to stare out at the trees.

What Zavrius wanted to say was: *I want that with you, too. I want to look at you openly. I want to smile at you and kiss you, and I want to be unafraid of that openness.*

Instead, he said, "I don't know if you know what that means."

Balen said, "I know."

"You're a paladin. Your duty will come first."

Now, Balen turned. "You're a prince. Your duty will come first."

Zavrius had to give him that. He sighed loudly and pursed his lips together. Balen frowned almost gently, the brows lowering fractionally below his wispy fringe.

Zavrius wished there was a single word that might communicate the complexity of their dynamic. He wished he would tell Balen how vulnerable it made him, how terrified—how burdened he was by his lineage and his future. Balen would understand some of it. Maybe all of it. But more than anything, Zavrius did not wish to hurt.

I'm frightened.

He thought about saying that but didn't. Couldn't. He squeezed Balen's hand back.

"I don't know what it means," Zavrius said slowly, "and I can't promise you anything. But I want. . ."

To kiss you often. To do more than kiss you—often. To be held by you and hold you in return. Can we do that?

Balen leaned forward like he could hear the unsaid words, both hands coming to cup Zavrius' cheeks.

"My prince."

"Call me Zavrius," he whispered, reaching up to touch the back of Balen's hand. "You're not allowed to kiss me again until you learn to call me by my name."

Balen's eyes dropped to Zavrius' lips, where they lingered, unashamed and full of desire. "Zavrius," he whispered. "Zavrius. Zavrius."

His name like a hymn, spoken with reverence and longing. Zavrius exhaled, and Balen caught his breath, swallowed it whole. The paladin leaned forward and kissed him with gentle sweetness.

"You'll be my lover, then?" Zavrius whispered. A sense of danger filled him. He pulled his eyes away from Balen, briefly ashamed by his desire. He wanted to say: *'lover' however you want it to mean,* almost desperate to make it clear to Balen: *I have done nothing before with another man except kissing. Do you understand what you're saying yes to?*

Saying yes to all of Zavrius. To his relative innocence, his inexperience, his hope, his desire, his position, and all the complexity that came with it.

But Balen apparently did not need those details to respond. "I'll be your lover," he whispered, "if you will be mine."

Zavrius kissed him again, again and again. He thought: *I am fifth in line and nobody, but I could be somebody to you.* And: *you could be my paladin. Out of all of them, you could be* mine.

And Zavrius Dued Vuuthrik was, in that moment, truly happy.

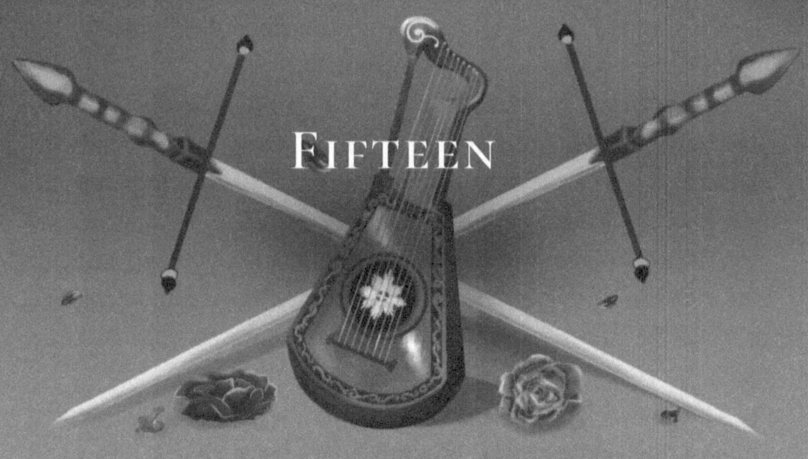

Fifteen

A week later

When the news came from the Ashmon Range, Zavrius' heart dropped.

Like some awful foresight, he knew intrinsically how it would all unfold, and before he was even told that Balen would be leaving the court, he'd already cried about it.

"It's outrageous," Avidia was saying. She had called them into the dining hall in the Royal Apartments—had invited three of her siblings she could at least tolerate, and Zavrius had slinked inside of his own accord. Arasne was in bed. 'Over-fatigued', she'd said, though she'd taken to her bed more and more in the week since the attempt on her life.

"Outrageous and. . .*gedroks*," Avidia sighed. She moved her hand to cover her face.

The dining room felt suffocating with his siblings spread out as they were. Avidia turned and faced the wall across from them. Theo was the only one of them sitting. He'd pulled a chair out and laid himself back languidly, and though his posture suggested ease, his eyes betrayed him. They were distant; he was plotting something. Lysio and Gideonus had barely moved beyond the threshold of the door, and Zavrius, stuck behind them, had to peer between their bodies to scout the room.

Sprawled on the dining table was a message hastily scrawled and brought with great urgency from a town in the Ashmons called Tergosti. Zavrius knew his history; it had been an ancient port town long ago, though the land had shifted and pushed the town further inland, with the shoreline a few minutes ride away. It had a paladin statue but no regularly stationed paladin to activate it. Thus the news had come by rider and straight into Avidia's hands.

The others were silent, tense as they watched the unnerving stillness of Avidia's form. Zavrius squeezed between Lysio and Gideonus and reached out for the discarded message, dragging it towards himself to get a better read. The script was scrawled. Ink blotches had smeared in the corners like the bottle had spilled.

Instantly, he knew it was a request for aid.

GEDROK SITE AT TERGOSTI ATTACKED.
GOVERNOR IS INJURED. PAULA KEI GESSET IS DEAD.
PALADINS REQUESTED.

A quick message and lacking in detail, but Zavrius' imagination took care of the rest. Paula Kei Gesset, whom Avidia had visited in the Ashmon Range, was an archaeologist directing the excavation of several sites in the Ashmons. They were following leads, however mythic, to uncover a new gedrok body. If she succeeded, the Dued Vuuthriks would benefit greatly—the forever dwindling resource of the gedroks eternally unnerved Zavrius if he thought too long about those consequences.

But Paula Kei Gesset had been killed.

The *why* was less important than *what next?* As far as Zavrius could tell, if the site had been attacked, it had been a deliberate thing. A murder. Either someone had hoped to take the site for themselves, or otherwise overestimated the value of what Kei Gesset had already uncovered. Zavrius had heard nothing about any find; Kei Gesset had likely only uncovered more dirt. But the *potential* of finding a gedrok had been enough to earn her death.

He glanced at Avidia. He knew instantly she wanted to go.

Because she'd wanted to *invest* in the dig site. Potentially, she had already pulled from some personal coffer to fund it. Uncovering a gedrok and gaining control of it would not only shore up the Dued Vuuthriks but make it far easier to start a war with the Rezwyns and *win*. But without Paula Kei Gesset, the potential of finding the site was greatly diminished. For too long that crystal gedrok had been a myth, and Zavrius doubted it would ever be found, let alone in his lifetime.

"You're going, then?" he said.

Lysio flinched in his periphery, surprised Zavrius had spoken up. Avidia did not react. Theo watched her carefully, jaw working minutely as he mulled it over himself. When another moment passed in silence, Theo stood from the chair with a heavy sigh.

"I'll speak to Commander Lestr," he said. Avidia gave a stiff nod and turned to follow. She said nothing more; both her and Theo left without another word, abandoning Zavrius with his two brothers.

Zavrius put the letter back on the table. "Murder?" he asked, forgetting how much Lysio had loved Kei Gesset's work. He flashed Lysio a look, saw the puffy wide-eye stare of abject horror, and said, "Lysio. I'm sorry."

His brother scrunched up his face. "Fuck off," he muttered. He was aiming for severity, or some sort of hardness, but Zavrius knew well how to hide strong emotion. Lysio didn't. Tears glistened in his eyes and his cheeks deepened to the color of rusty brown.

Zavrius crossed his arms and turned to Gideonus, who stared at Lysio impotently. "Will you two go?" Zavrius asked.

"Might be overkill," Gideonus said softly. His words made Lysio tense, and he added, "Theo and Avidia and the paladins will be enough. It's probably chaos over there, anyway."

"Coward." Lysio rubbed at his eyes. "Shit. This is shit."

"Has anyone told the Queen?" Zavrius glanced between them, but neither met his gaze. The letter had gone to Avidia first. What a breach of protocol. "No? Alright, I'll do it."

He pushed off the table, grabbing the request for aid as he went, and squeezed between the two of them.

Lysio's hand snapped out onto his shoulder, his grip firm. "Wait."

Zavrius tensed. Instinct had him looking at the door rather than glancing at his brother, counting the steps to that handle, mind calculating how fast he could be if Lysio and Gideonus grew violent. But when Zavrius stopped moving, Lysio let go of him.

"Maybe she should. . ."

The hesitation in Lysio's voice made Zavrius snap around. "Maybe she should what? Not know about this?" He looked between his brothers. Gideonus grew sheepish and glanced away, but Lysio held firm even if his brow trembled. Slowly and carefully, Zavrius said, "She is the Queen."

"She's unwell," Gideonus whispered. He screwed up his face and drew his hand over his mouth. With a wild gesture, he added, "Stress will make it worse."

"Oh, yes, I'm sure the stress of her children *undermining* her authority will be the solution!" Zavrius barked with an unhappy laugh. Cowards, the both of them—either worried about how this news would affect Arasne, or because they didn't want to be exposed to her wrath. Worse was the thought that Lysio was consciously supporting Theo. Undermining Arasne deliberately had a much sourer taste than childish wishful thinking.

"Shall I tell her neither of you wanted her to know, or. . .?" Zavrius glided towards the door, feigning complete calm. Neither of his brothers spoke. He glanced back at them when his hand curled safely around the handle and found them both staring. Nothing about their expressions felt good to Zavrius. He pursed his lips, turned away, and left them behind.

Queen Arasne had her back to Zavrius when he entered her chambers. Curled up on her side, with the blinds drawn and the room stuffy, Zavrius felt unwell himself the instant he walked inside. He looked at her. Lying like that, with the faint pale ruffles of her shift peeking out from beneath the sheets, made the Queen seem small. Smaller than her title, and smaller than his mother— his mind split around the memory of her and this newer, wasting version.

Zavrius approached slowly. The air, stagnant in feeling, crawled down Zavrius' throat like a warm-scaled beast; his lungs grew muggy. He watched the consistent rise and fall of Arasne's chest and decided she was sleeping. Better to crack a window and wait for her to rise normally than for him to suffocate in this sickly haze of still air.

At the first creak of the window being pushed open, a sharp intake of breath hissed behind him.

"No, don't."

Zavrius paused and looked back at her. Her hair was a mane of black and grey curls strewn haphazardly over the pillow and around her face. A single wide eye stared out at him, bloodshot and straining. The skin beneath her eyes seemed thinner, the circles darker, and her overall complexion looked sapped of something vital. He clenched his teeth at the sight of her and balled his fist at his side, taking a sick pleasure in the blunt pain that danced through his flesh when he dug his nails into his palm.

"You need fresh air," he said, continuing to push.

In the smallest voice he had ever heard emerge from her throat, she said, "It's cold."

Zavrius let go of the window and spun to her. She'd never been like this. Never. He rushed to her side and went onto his knees, taking her pallid hand between his. She hadn't been lying —her fingers chilled even him.

Zavrius searched her face. A fine layer of sweat beaded on her brow. "What has the physician said?"

She closed her eyes like the question pained her. Her hand shifted in his like she wanted to pull away, but Zavrius pressed down firmly. No. She would not pull away from him. She would not leave him like this.

"Mother," he said firmly.

"They are not sure what it is. I don't know what else to say to you. They don't know, so they do what they can, and some days will just be like this from now on. Alright?"

No, of course it wasn't *alright*, but the rage had reinvigorated her. She'd half sat up to shove the mess of curls out of her face. How girlish she seemed, then. How young. Zavrius felt his chest clench, and his face must have shown it, for she softened suddenly. The Queen's eyes went wide, and she sat up fully, burying her face in her hands. A big sigh escaped her, and Zavrius stood and scooted onto the bed.

"I'm sorry," she said. "I don't feel well."

"I know."

She sniffed, and then something happened on her face: she refused to be this version of herself, so she neatly packed away all the mess, and stepped back towards her usual self. "It is but one day in my whole life. I'll be alright."

Zavrius found he could say nothing to that, nothing to support or question her. He shifted and rolled so he could rest on her shoulder, seeking a comfort that wouldn't come. His mind had seen his mother small, and now that image seeped like a poison into everything. Nothing he could do would shift this new understanding: Queen Arasne was human, and she was dying, and one day, much sooner than Zavrius hoped, she would be gone. So lying as he was, with his head beneath her, briefly safe from her gaze, he closed his eyes and squeezed against the hot sting of tears brewing there.

He held his body still, refusing to let the sobs rack through him, and he tried his best to let no tears fall.

"Something's on your mind?" Arasne asked, her touch gentle as she stroked Zavrius' hair.

He didn't wait. Zavrius pulled the request for aid from his tunic and handed it to her.

"The rider brought it right to Avidia," he said, hoping she would hear his disapproval and the immense upset he felt at the breach in command.

All he felt from her was the minute tensing as Arasne registered the letter. She plucked it from him, opened it with a greedy speed, and read just as quickly. Her body did not shift out of that tense position and if Zavrius listened closely enough, he would have sworn he could hear the tendons creaking in her arms.

After a moment, she put the letter down on her lap and closed her eyes. Zavrius said nothing, didn't move; he was frightened of her reaction, worried he had made things worse by doing this. Lysio's words assaulted him. Maybe his brother had been right— maybe this was the last thing she needed.

"I'm sorry," Zavrius said quickly. "You're not well, and I—"

"Shh," she murmured. Her body stilled so Zavrius stilled with her, listening to her even breathing and the slowing of her heart. When that organ had returned to its usual rhythm, Arasne said, "I needed to know." Her hand appeared on Zavrius' shoulder, and she squeezed. "Where are Theo and Avidia?"

"They've gone straight to Lestr. They. . ." he sat up and looked at her. "You can see the truth of this, can't you? That they're worried their gedrok-based plan for war is now compromised? The greatest motivation here is their own hides."

Arasne's face shifted only slightly, like she'd bitten into something disgusting and was now attempting to be polite to her host. "Theo is taking the initiative. If he's going to be king, it will be good for him to lead something like this."

"You're *taking his side?*" Zavrius asked. Incredulity sizzled in his tone. He couldn't help it; the sting of betrayal split open his gut. He stood up and backed away from her. What could he say to make her understand? How could she hear this and let it slide when something as seemingly innocuous as a paladin ritual required *weeks* of his own blood, sweat, and tears to be passable?

"Zavrius," she said softly.

He wouldn't relent. He bit down on the inside of his cheek and gnawed until the pain became too much, and it still wasn't enough to stop his rebellious voice from speaking its mind. "If you let him walk all over you, your legacy will be in shambles before you're even gone."

He wanted to leave, then. Storm out and slam the door. But he stayed and waited for his reckoning, chest prideful and posture straight.

Go on. Let her shout at me. I know that I'm right.

For a long moment, neither of them spoke. Then, when it seemed she would finally say something, there was a knock at the door.

Arasne muttered something too soft for Zavrius to hear. She

gathered her strength and swung her legs over the side of the bed. "Who is it?"

"Commander Lestr, Your Majesty," a wan voice called out.

Arasne hesitated, drawing her gown more tightly around herself. "Admit him."

The door clicked open and swung wide. A small servant was in a low bow, their eyes downcast, and behind them, Lestr loomed like a shadow. He caught sight of the Queen and blanched, though he waited for the servant to close the door behind him to say, "My Queen, I'm sorry to—"

He cut off abruptly when he spotted the discarded letter on the bed and Zavrius standing beneath the windows.

He reset his jaw. "Right. Prince Zavrius. I'm glad to see. . .you *have* explained the situation to the Queen, then?" When he nodded, Lestr visibly relaxed. He cast a glance at Arasne, rather pleadingly, and Arasne sighed.

She looked over at Zavrius. "Would you leave us?"

Zavrius nodded and did as he was asked, even when his own complicated feelings were left unresolved. They swam in his stomach with gut-churning speed. He wrenched the door open and was greeted by the fleeing back of the servant who had clearly lingered to eavesdrop—something Zavrius couldn't fault, since the instant he closed the door behind him, he also pressed his own ear against the wood of the Queen's chamber door.

His mother and Lestr waited for nearly a minute before they spoke. Zavrius heard the wood creak as Lestr began to pace. Finally, he stopped and said, "I'm sorry to. . .gedroks, Arasne, but you look like shit."

A laugh from the Queen, bright and surprised, and then Lestr's furious backtracking, "No, I shouldn't have said that. I should *not* have—"

"I do, don't I?" the Queen's voice sounded high and muffled through the wood. "Whatever this is, I hate it. I—"

If she said anything more, Zavrius couldn't hear it. Someone sniffled.

"You're beautiful," Lestr murmured. "You're my sister, always." He said something else, but his voice dipped too low for Zavrius to hear.

"Let's not," Arasne said. "We have other things to worry about."

Another beat stretched. Lestr eventually said, "I want to be clear that I didn't know about this until Princess Avidia and Prince Theo came to see me."

With her tone entirely different, Arasne said, "The letter was brought straight to my daughter."

"Hm," Lestr acknowledged. "You're worried she's tried to win the Ashmons? That the letter is evidence of that?"

"Someone over there favors her. No matter that all the Ashmon nobles have been loyal up until now," Arasne concluded. And then, all in a rush, "I'm worried Zavrius is right and that Theo will be a bad king. That the pair of them are sabotaging me now, milking my absences, feigning ignorance."

"What would you have me do?"

More silence. Then, the creaking of the boards as new weight joined Lestr; presumably, Arasne had stood up. "Send twenty paladins—not Hisud, I need her here—and a contingent of the city guard. Avidia leads. You go as well. I want you to report on her performance and on anything suspicious. Get the names of her contacts if you can. I want to know if she's plotting against me."

"Of course. And Theo, my Queen?"

Then, music to Zavrius' ears: "Theo stays here."

It happened fast after that. Zavrius sped away from the Royal Apartment and moved out into the palace, heading for the barracks where Balen—and the other paladins—would be. The air was sticky and warm that day, and he felt instantly suffocated. His lungs grew heavy, the back of his neck beneath his hair clammy, and discomfort grew in his chest where he suddenly wanted to be outside of his body. Nausea, fear, upset—a conglomerate of emotions roiling in his chest, heavy like a whole new world had grown in there like a tumor, heavy enough to make his skeleton crumble.

"Zavrius. Zavrius!"

He jerked around. Petra, who seemed to permanently lurk about in the palace halls, waved at him. Her own eyes were wide with concern, and Zavrius had no doubt she'd already found out. What could she want from him this instant?

He ignored her, breaking into a run. His beautiful sandals slapped across the marble, the heavy impact reverberating up his shins, and his brittleness was made manifest like that.

Everything in him might fall apart.

Through the palace, Zavrius pushed past the muggy, oppressive air made worse by perfumes and incense, and dashed into the eastern wing. Servants buzzed about, and one or two armor-free paladins dropped into a bow at the sight of him, but he couldn't spare even a glance. He knew in his heart of hearts that Balen would be selected to go. It was a good chance to prove himself; probably any of the paladins who had put their names forward hoping to be Prime would go as well.

But Zavrius didn't *want* Balen to go. At the core of this great, suffocating emotion was that childish thought. He deserved to enjoy time with Balen, to explore this budding relationship. He deserved it, and he would not get it; as always, everything in his life came after duty to the throne.

The barracks buzzed with sound and activity. Was it a normal amount of noise, or a room full of people discussing an excursion to the Ashmon Range? Zavrius knew he should have waited outside or approached the barracks in any kind of reserved way. With the right positioning, he could understand what they were discussing and use that information to calm himself or refocus. He wasn't stupid. He eavesdropped all the time.

So why was he unable to stop himself this time?

Mindlessly, body spurred on by emotion and desperation, Zavrius found he had bolted into the barracks.

Though the land the Cres Strosian palace occupied was technically large enough to accommodate a separate building for the soldiers' barracks, the paladin barracks were connected directly to the main keep. Further down in the city proper sprawled a garrison for the city guards and other military personnel. But up here, this space had been dedicated entirely to the Gifted Paladins. The connection to the palace only emphasized their importance—and made accessibility to the royal family all the easier.

This was a place Zavrius had never entered. He'd walked past and seen the open door and the bustle of activity inside. Nothing more than that. Now, his first impression of this space was *mess*—an ironic thought since it was clearly the barrack's mess hall he'd stumbled into. To his left lay the connecting door to the armory, and the door on the opposite side of this room opened into the living quarters and beyond them, a small bathhouse—he at least knew the layout of his own home—but the room he stood in now had long wooden tables for eating, small tables set aside for games and chatting. A communal gathering point where paladins might relax after training.

Zavrius was not meant to be here for a variety of reasons, but he was a Dued Vuuthrik, and he wanted to see Balen of Westgar. Even when a moment of fear flashed bright in his chest, he made himself stand tall to face the sea of faces that had turned to him. He counted nearly fifteen paladins milling about, all of whom had snapped to rigid attention in place. Most of them were without their armor or wearing very little of it, taking a momentary break.

Bits of gedrokbone and scale lay abandoned across the room. Torchlight flickered off the pale pearlescent forms, planting nacreous rainbows along the walls.

Zavrius raised his chin. "Balen of Westgar," he said very simply.

One or two of the paladins exchanged a glance, but an older man—Frenyur, was it?—dipped his head and said, "I believe he's in the bath house, my prince."

So Balen hadn't been told yet. None of them seemed to know. Zavrius tried to smother his giddiness. "Take me to him."

SIXTEEN

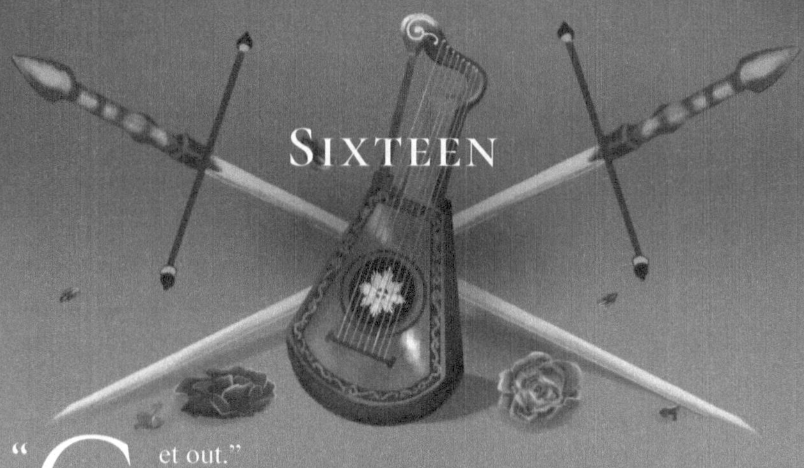

"Get out."

Steam blurred the edges of his vision, the heat from the baths fogging the tiny room. Zavrius could see bunched bodies turning to stare at him; his fist shook at his side, because this was ridiculous, and he was overreacting, and yet he couldn't help it.

"Balen of Westgar. Either all of you get out, or he does."

A murmur started up. Belatedly, Zavrius realized what he was doing. Balen's reputation was about to be smothered by the black mark of Zavrius' own. He couldn't do that.

"It's a matter of national emergency," he said. "On behalf of Queen Arasne, I order you—"

"My prince. I'm here." The voice called out from the back of the bathhouse, and it was *his* voice, lilting as it echoed off the tiled wall. The bathhouse consisted of maybe three baths for paladins to soak in. Through the fog, Zavrius saw the broad form of Balen rise from the water, all detail obscured by the steam. He wrapped a towel around himself, and then Zavrius heard no sound save for the wet footfalls approaching him. Despite the steam, he felt eyes on him.

"Thank you, paladin. I apologize for interrupting your leisure. Please follow me."

Zavrius turned on his heel and left, aiming for detached politeness, but his palms had grown clammy, and he had an unnecessary amount of anxiety burning in his chest.

They moved back into the hallway towards the sleeping quarters. It took everything in Zavrius not to look back. "I'll let you get dressed."

He failed immediately after that, though, unable to help the desire that tugged his eyes behind him. His heart jumped. Balen's broad form took up everything, with only a bit of cloth hiding the part of his body that Zavrius had begun to think about at night. Zavrius lingered too long and jerked to meet Balen's eyes with a flush. He turned around to face the paladin, and in a hushed voice, he said, "I am sorry to do this to you."

"What is it?" Balen asked, a slight frown lowering over his beautiful eyes. "Is everything alright?" No hint of reproach in his voice, nothing to suggest he was mad at Zavrius for barging in as he had. But Zavrius couldn't have this conversation in a hallway where anyone might overhear, and he certainly couldn't have it when Balen was barely clothed.

"Come and meet me by the gedrok," Zavrius said.

It was late afternoon by the time Balen made it to the garden. Zavrius had been leaning against one of the massive, stripped ribs, eyes closed like a cat as he soaked up the last rays of the sun. Being outside grounded him enough that he got a handle on his racing heart, but when Balen arrived and announced himself by slipping his hands around Zavrius' waist, a new anxiety exploded in him.

Zavrius jumped with a small sound.

"Shh. It's only me."

It was hard to look at him that day. A contradiction, a paradox: Zavrius longed for nothing more than to be held by Balen, to be seen and not found wanting, but meeting Balen's eyes made him vulnerable. The paladin was smart, and Zavrius was not good at hiding his emotions around the other man. Too long with a view of Zavrius' eyes, and Balen would be able to tell how infatuated Zavrius had become of him, how much desire he had, how much he wanted to reach out now and have Balen kiss him.

"Only you," Zavrius said instead. He risked a glance up. Balen had put on trousers and an undershirt, nothing more. He had come without question. Gedroks, he was a good man. Zavrius reached up, the tip of his finger grazing over Balen's jaw, and in response the other man stepped forward, his hands slipping from his waist to around Zavrius' back. Balen fell into him like that, tipped forward at the hips knowing Zavrius' mouth would catch his. A lazy, intimate kiss. Zavrius moved his hand from Balen's face to his shoulder, where he squeezed with vigor. Balen responded with a deeper embrace, and Zavrius thought, *why does he have to leave?*

He pushed on Balen gently, and the kiss broke apart. Balen's expression shifted minutely towards disappointment. "It *is* serious, then?"

His sincerity made Zavrius grin. "Did you think I barged into the barracks for a kiss?"

"I wouldn't put it past you."

Zavrius cocked his head, smile spreading wide. "I'll admit, when I saw you in that towel, I almost forgot why I was there."

Now it was Balen's turn to smile. His eyes grew heavy—it was his presence, Zavrius hoped, that was tugging the paladin away from sensibility down towards desire. They both let the moment stretch. Balen stole a quick kiss, lips lingering when he pulled away. Zavrius felt every nerve light up. He wished that moment would last forever.

"But you *haven't* forgotten why you're here, have you?" Balen said finally. When he had pulled away, he resumed his honor-filled posture. The paladin had returned.

In response, Zavrius found his own body straightening, too. He relayed the letter and what he had learned from Arasne quickly.

"I think it's obvious you'll be called to go," Zavrius said. Then, correcting himself, "I think you probably *should* go. It will be good for your career to volunteer to protect the crown's interests."

Balen took this news as well as one might expect. He did not flinch; he only frowned here and there at various details. Finally, he said, "Is that why you came to the barracks?"

Zavrius flushed severely. His skin burned prickly hot, and since it was accompanied by shame, he could imagine in grave detail how ruddy his face had grown.

"I—" His voice came out in a shameful squeak. He cleared his throat and gnawed at his tongue. Balen waited patiently, but Zavrius' body felt as if he were on trial.

The truth was better than this silence. Wasn't it? He puffed his chest and raised his chin, pursing his lips in that nonchalant way he always aimed for.

"It's very simple, actually. I am selfish. I don't want you to go." It all seemed so small and so silly in that moment. All of Zavrius' selfishness became stark: people had died, and Balen had a duty, and here Zavrius stood wishing he wouldn't have to go. But he felt the need to say it, to own up to his longing. "I know that you *will* go, and I am not trying to derail your career. You have your honor and your devotion and all that. It's only that I. . .couldn't bear to let you go without saying how much I'm looking forward to your return."

How wonderful it was for Balen's skin to be so pale. His flush grew like a fever over his cheeks, painting them a bright scarlet.

Balen stuttered, "My prince. Zavrius, I—"

"Take care of yourself," Zavrius said loudly, as if speaking with volume might save Balen from anything other than a good fate. "Don't do anything stupid. Don't die. And make sure you make it back uninjured, because I've hardly gotten a chance to know you, and I wish to keep doing that."

He spoke quickly because it was easier, but he hoped Balen could hear the sincerity in his words.

Very quietly, Balen whispered, "You wish to keep doing that."

Zavrius flashed him a look, then dropped his gaze to his mouth. "And other things."

This was a whole different conversation, one they'd barely touched on, but one Zavrius hoped to have again soon.

"That's why I called you out here," Zavrius said. A solemn realization settled on him: he cared very much about Balen of Westgar. "I know you will be fine. I know it's nothing like a war. But if you get hurt, I'll be unhappy. Actually, I might order you to stay uninjured."

When Balen said nothing, Zavrius repeated, "I order it. Stay uninjured."

"Alright, alright," Balen said, breaking into a smile. He laughed, but his eyes were wide with emotion. His eyes dropped to Zavrius' hands, which he took gently between his own. "What will you be doing? Whilst I'm gone."

"Pining, I suppose."

Balen raised a bemused brow. "Missing me already?"

Zavrius found the quip easily and knew he could reply with his usual tone, but he found himself on the tips of his toes pushing against Balen's body. A giddy energy ran through him, and both his hands came up to grip the front of Balen's shirt. He decided it was better not to speak. They kissed with a languid, exploratory pace. Zavrius' breathing grew ragged as something in him shifted, tilting away from the demure farewell to a heated desire. His hands roamed, gripped at skin and hair and cotton, his grip firm but inconsistent—he tugged and pressed and pulled, wanting Balen closer. The paladin pushed forward and pressed Zavrius against the gedrok's rib, and with Zavrius stable, he moved the young prince's legs apart with his knee and *pressed*.

Zavrius made a surprised noise at the touch. Friction was good, was needed—he felt the answering flood of warmth rush between his legs, and Balen must have felt it, for he moaned into Zavrius' mouth. Zavrius clung on to him. Nerves sparked through his body, mixing with desire. It confused him, how much he wanted more from this man and how terrified the thought made him. Balen moved his knee away and gently pressed their hips together. Testing, Zavrius thought, since Balen pulled away from the kiss and searched Zavrius' eyes.

"Is this okay?"

Zavrius paused, thinking. Balen had palmed him over his clothes before, but something about this moment felt different. "Yes. I'm nervous, but—yes."

Balen cocked his head. "Nervous?"

"I—" Zavrius started. He what, exactly? He knew he felt that giddy excitement, the nerves of being touched like that for the first time and by someone he found dazzlingly attractive. But the weight in his chest was a different fear. Yes, he worried something might happen to Balen in the Ashmons, but more than that, perhaps selfishly, Zavrius realized how much it would hurt. How vulnerable he was. How much want and desire had the same effect on his body as a sharp blade would: a slow vivisection, opening his neck to groin. Zavrius wanted a closeness, and that would require Balen to see everything of him, every part, even those parts that were dark and rotting and nothing like how a prince should be.

"Zav?"

"I want to touch you," he said, flushing suddenly. His heart leaped into his throat as if trying to wrangle those words back into his mouth. It was all too late. He flushed fiercely.

Balen's thumb stroked Zavrius' cheek. The look in his eyes was gentle. Amusement and heat pulsed warmly. "You're allowed."

Zavrius didn't know what to say to that. Of course he knew this desire was reciprocated. Or at least, he knew that *logically*. But he felt stupid standing there. Unknowledgeable. He lacked the confidence he could at the very least usually fake, and no matter how much he willed himself, he couldn't summon that bravado.

"Help me," he whispered instead. He pressed his lips into Balen's again.

Balen didn't question it. He reached up slowly and intertwined their fingers, just for a moment. Then he wrapped his hand over Zavrius', calloused fingers grazing over the smooth back of the prince's hand, and Balen gently pulled until their hands disappeared from Zavrius' view.

The prince fought the urge to look down. He wanted to see; longed for the confirmation of Balen's desire to be shown so plainly to him. The tenting of the paladin's trousers, the bulge in his own. The way they pressed together. But Balen's gaze was like a heavy tide, and Zavrius lacked the strength to swim away. He let himself be pulled into Balen, and when his palm felt the cotton trousers and the warm bulge beneath, he struggled not to moan. His heart raced. He couldn't move his hand. Balen pushed his hips into Zavrius' palm whilst pressing the back of the prince's hand forward, locking himself in a firm grip. They kissed over this. Experimentally, Zavrius squeezed his hand; the answering open-mouthed gasp made him shiver.

He could do this forever, he decided. Time slowed. Practically stopped altogether. They might have been there like that for seconds or hours, and he wouldn't have minded.

I don't want you to go, he didn't say. But suddenly he whispered, "You're going to miss my birthday.

Balen looked up. A haze of flush burned along his face. Gently, he extricated himself from Zavrius' grip, binging both his hands to cup the prince's cheeks. "Then I'll have to make it up to you when I return," he said, and he kissed Zavrius once more.

Zavrius watched twenty paladins, his uncle, and Avidia Dued Vuuthrik ride out of Cres Stros that afternoon. Avidia had argued there was no time to wait for dawn—that the two, maybe three hours they could gain before sunset that evening might make all the difference. So it was settled. They would ride to one of the towns or hamlets to the west, sleep, and then continue in the morning.

Zavrius wasn't the only one to see them off. The steps at the front of the palace were occupied by the Queen, dressed beautifully as she always was, Lysio and Gideonus, dressed dully, and Petra, who wore an expression of reserved concern with more zeal than her clothing. Theo was conspicuously absent.

As Zavrius watched, he tried to stand divorced from his own body. If he remained present, if he allowed himself to be fully there as Balen rode away, he knew he would not be able to withstand the suffering. In truth, Zavrius wasn't sure if everything he felt was justified. He had not known Balen that long. Nor had their relationship been anything except nascent desire for longer than a held breath. But the way his body felt in that moment, the way his heart tugged as he gazed over the Sea of paladins, suggested a bond as integral as his own flesh and blood. It was as if a piece of his own heart was riding away from him, every step tugging on the gaping wound left behind, and Zavrius could not stand it. He stopped searching the helmeted heads of the departing army and stopped looking for the idiosyncrasies that would mark Balen from the rest of them. Only then did he find it bearable to watch as Balen of the Gifted Paladins galloped away from him. In a way, this apathy was Zavrius' own sort of armor. His mother might have known how he felt but if his brothers had known, Zavrius would not survive their amused reactions. Still, even when Lysio and Gideonus grew bored and wandered up the stairs, even when Arasne herself had finished watching the small army depart, Zavrius stayed. He stayed until the pearlescent sheen of paladin armor stopped glinting on the horizon. He stayed until he couldn't see anything at all, and even then, closed his eyes and tried to imagine Balen on that gelding, riding fast, his armor clanking. How his breath would sound, how fast his heart would be beating, how sweat would gather on his skin beneath the helmet.

After that, Zavrius told himself he was being ridiculous. That this—this feeling, the enormity of it—wasn't rational. Balen was a young man, and that was all. Theirs was not some great love; they barely knew one another.

But what if it *could* be? Balen had seen him vulnerable. All the parts of Zavrius that were scorned in this court Balen hadn't blinked twice at. *That* fact alone raised him up above all others, and Zavrius could imagine loving him. Could imagine it with ease.

When the hot sting of tears began behind his eyes, Zavrius tugged himself away and hurried inside to embrace the first of many excruciatingly long nights as he waited for news.

It would take a week or so to ride to the Ashmons at a high speed. A day to understand the situation, and then however long —a week? Two? *Longer*?—to intervene. The paladins would likely stay until some form of justice was rendered and perhaps linger until the governor could reclaim his position.

At a minimum, Balen would be gone a month.

A month. But what was a month in the context of his life? A blip. A blink of an eye. He could do it.

The first few days were the easiest. After those, he threw himself into training with a new vigor. On occasion, he trained with his short sword—and then with daggers—but more and more, he felt the pull towards Arasne's lute-harp, which she still had not plucked from his grasp.

Music grounded him and inspired him. It was an easy distraction and one that did not frustrate him half as much as swordplay did. In the early hours of the morning, Zavrius would go to the far reaches of the palace grounds, where trees sat precariously on the edge of the raised hill, and he would practice. If the would-be assassin at the paladin ceremony was anything to go by, Zavrius already had the skill for compulsion. Instead, he focused on sharper attacks. Things he might use amid battle, things with real bite to them, spells with sharp teeth that would flay flesh from bone. He had played around with this power before, of course—Arasne had taught him. But he hadn't been focused, convinced that his position as fifth in line made him somehow exempt from the machinations of the court.

He knew better now.

Every day that month, he stood barefoot in the dewy grass, moisture clinging to his ankles, and he would play. A pluck of the strings would send an arc of arcane power slicing through the air. His attacks were sloppy at first. Wounds would open on the bark in jagged stripes. But with time and focus, they became deeper, more deadly, until one day, he struck with almost casual grace and severed a branch from a tree. The wood split so fast the wooden limb had no time to even groan before it crashed down into the underbrush. Birds wheeled away shrieking, and Zavrius laughed.

His birthday wasn't particularly spectacular. He could have—if he'd wanted—asked his mother to host some lavish event. But when the day rolled around and Zavrius blinked blearily into the morning of his eighteenth birthday, all he wanted was for Balen to be sleeping next to him. Nothing else could compare—and nothing else did. He had a quiet dinner with his mother, and his gift was having her all to himself. None of his wretched siblings were invited.

And then, just like that, a month had passed.

Balen was not back yet.

Zavrius had thought of the month as a crutch of sorts. He could handle the exhaustive passage of time by believing it would end. A week, into a week, into a week, until the final dawn; manageable swaths of time. But when that final evening rolled around and there was no answering gleam of armor on the horizon, all the fear and worry and obsessive need he had managed to bottle down the day of the small army's departure came rushing back into his lungs. Zavrius nearly drowned in it.

He had waited on the steps, feigning interest in how Cres Stros looked lit up at night, but as the sun withered behind the horizon, Zavrius felt nothing but a low broiling fear. He stood in a long-flowing tunic. The wind whipped at the thin fabric, and the chill rushed through his core. Zavrius tightened his grip to keep it closed at his front and tried to ignore the sting in his eyes; the breeze cut against the tears already forming. He stood alone out there, thankfully. Even in the dark, he worried about the hot burn of shame visible on his cheeks. How pathetic he was. How desperate. He turned tail and pushed into the palace, stomping towards the administration ward.

"What's happened to you?" Gideonus called out, spotting Zavrius' retreat into the palace. Zavrius ignored him, even when Gideonus' snickers were echoed in the tittering of several young noblemen at his brothers' side. Zavrius had no time to worry about them. His heart hurt. Something felt *wrong*.

He pushed into the administration ward and lurched to a stop outside Petra's door. Compelled, almost, his limbs felt laden. The shame of his worry, and what his worry signified, almost prevented him from lifting an arm.

Do it. You are a prince worried for the order dedicated to protecting you. You are allowed to ask.

He knocked once against the wood. The greeting, "Yes?" was muffled. His aunt sounded tired. As he pushed inside, she pressed her fingers against her temples and shook out her hair. Papers were scattered haphazardly across her desk, and nothing illuminated the room save for a small dying candle.

"You'll go blind like that," Zavrius murmured.

She snorted and leaned back in her chair. The flame pulsed softly over her cheek, casting shadows in the troughs of her skin. "It's my timepiece," she said. "With better lighting, I'll work forever."

Zavrius made a noise of understanding and nothing more. Lingering like that by the doorframe made him recall his childhood. A young boy hovering, waiting to be let in—waiting to be allowed comfort from his eternally busy parents. Petra noticed the look on his face and tilted forward.

"What is it?"

"I wanted. . ." Zavrius cleared his throat. He stepped inside and closed the door behind him.

Petra took one look at him and sighed. "I haven't heard anything."

Zavrius deflated. He glanced away from her, hoping to hide the rush of heat bubbling behind his eyes. This was a mistake. He shouldn't have—

"You're worried for your uncle?"

Zavrius shot her a look. As *if* she didn't know. "Please. I know who you are."

Petra opened her hands in a shrug. "I was giving you a chance to save face."

Zavrius stalked forward and dropped into the waiting chair. He drew his legs up under his chin, feeling stupid and heavy. Petra wasn't particularly soft. If he wanted comfort, he should have gone to Arasne. But this problem—the ache that came with waiting, the wound in his cavernous chest that wouldn't heal until Balen returned—seemed too much to put on her or perhaps too small when compared with her illness. He buried his face into his knees.

"I know I'm an idiot," he said.

"I never said—"

"Shouldn't they be back by now?" he whispered. Testing, he peeked out at her, glancing sideways from the fort of his limbs.

Petra's lips pursed together in an unreadable expression. She shuffled through a few papers and began to sort them, clearing space on her desk. "We heard that they made it there, and that there were several. . .layers to the situation. These things can take time."

I know. I know this. But I don't—I wish—

Even the thoughts sounded childish in his head. He sat up straighter, sniffling. Petra had given him a non-answer. It wasn't good enough.

"Tell me this, at least. Did this seem like a dangerous expedition to you? Are they in any danger?"

Petra looked at him like he was stupid, and Zavrius conceded with a heavy sigh. Stronger men than Zavrius could not have pretended to be unaffected by her stare. He sat up from his posture of defeat and pushed back his hair. "I need you to tell me if there's something I don't know."

This was the wrong thing to say. The air went tense as Petra's gaze darkened. "I don't need to tell you anything," she said, tone disbelieving. Belatedly, she added, "My prince."

They stared at one another. Here was demonstrated the fine line their relationship would always walk. Petra's position elevated her from much of Zavrius' power by rank. She had been ordered to her secrecy by the Queen. Zavrius knew she would not tell him anything.

He got up, put himself into a pace with a deliberately anxious rhythm to it. Scanning the room, he cast about on her shelves for anything he might use—and spotted something of his own creation. A little guiltily, Zavrius stepped towards it.

He'd always enjoyed tinkering with instruments, even going so far as to make his own. This—a long, reedy strip of wood with three strings—had been one of his first attempts as a young boy. Petra had kept it, like a token, and since she wasn't much of a sentimental woman, seeing it here shocked Zavrius to the core.

"You kept it?"

Petra mumbled something and sighed. "Of course, I kept it." She gestured in a general way towards his person. "You trusted me to have it. It meant a lot to you as a child, and you know in my role, trust is everything."

Trust is everything. But in this court, Zavrius doubted very much that Petra trusted much of anything, including him. That was what he told himself anyway when he reached out to pluck at those strings. He closed his eyes, breathed deep, and with that intrinsic power in him, sang out his compulsion sweetly.

"Tell me. Have there been any more reports from the Ashmons you haven't disclosed to me?"

The instrument was not made with gedrok material. Simple gut strings thrummed beneath his touch. He knew it wouldn't last long, if he even managed to persuade her. Most likely, she would realize what he was doing, and he'd land himself in a lot of trouble. But

Zavrius hated feeling impotent. Too many people underestimated him, and he would not fall into that honey trap of underestimating himself. It would be too easy to sit around waiting, but he would never forgive himself if, in a week or two or three, a message came from the Ashmons revealing there had been trouble. Casualties.

Call it nascent, amorous obsession—if Balen of Westgar didn't make it back, Zavrius would lose his mind.

Petra let out a heavy sigh, which Zavrius translated as disappointed acquiescence. Then she was saying, "My prince, I didn't want. . .Commander Lestr sent word of an attack. A small contingent. They came at night, slipped past the watch, and attacked the paladin camp."

Zavrius' heart dropped. He was flooded with a dizzying fear that, when coupled with his over-active imagination, showed him violent images of Balen's demise. He saw in his mind's eye the blood, the gore, the viscera—Balen with his stomach opened, Balen choking on his own blood, the light leaving his eyes. Zavrius' stomach lurched into his throat. He was expected to sit around and wait. How could he sit around and *wait?*

Petra continued, "Most likely, the paladin presence confirmed the attackers' misconception that that damned foolish woman had actually uncovered a gedrok. I think—"

She bit off that last word. A hardness flooded into her eyes, replacing the far-away glint of something lost in their train of thought. Zavrius' fingers hovered over the strings. He stared at her.

She knew. Her nostrils flared, and a minute tightening occurred in her body. An ever so slight expression of rage began to spark to life in her eyes.

Zavrius figured it was a good time to leave. He stepped back from the instrument and dipped his head politely. "Have a good evening, Aunt Petra."

A pause stretched long until it became tensely brittle. Eventually, Petra's terse voice said, "And to you, Prince Zavrius."

Released without a scolding, Zavrius replaced the makeshift instrument, turned tail and fled out of Petra's office. This would undoubtedly come back to bite him in the coming days, but for now, he had his answer.

So, too, did Zavrius have his course of action. It hadn't been long, and yet Balen had become a bit of a fixture in Zavrius' mind. They had grown up near one another, in each other's periphery, and now there was something tentative between them, something *more*.

A prince would wait. A prince would ask the Queen for a dull administrative assignment to while away his time, or focus on his training, or do any number of more suitable princely activities than what Zavrius' heart longed to do. But Zavrius already had a reputation for being a rather lousy prince. What was one more mark against his name?

Thus, Zavrius snuck into the kitchen, grabbed cheese and bread and dried meat and bundled them all up. He dressed in the sleek form-fitting outfit he had donned for the paladin ritual, slipped the lute-harp onto his back, and walked casually to the front of the palace, where he informed the palace guard on watch that he was going for a walk. He fulfilled this promise by walking directly to the stables, where he requested a horse.

Then he trotted that horse down the slope and out the gate, allowed out with the simple, "Queen's orders."

That night, he rode to the edge of Cres Stros, grabbed a lit torch from the massive gates, and did the very dangerous thing of riding vaguely into the night. Damn it all.

He would not wait to find out if Balen of Westgar was injured. Prince Zavrius would go to the Ashmons himself and drag that young man back alive.

SEVENTEEN

The roads out of Cres Stros were aglow with fire lamps burning coronas into the dark night. By this orange haze, Zavrius sped his gelding into a gallop. The moon was already waning, and Zavrius guessed he had only a handful of hours before dawn came about and someone realized what he'd done.

That was, of course, if Petra hadn't already realized.

Zavrius refused to be dragged back in shame to the palace—not before he unearthed the fate of the paladins.

So he rode. Head low and eyes focused, straining against the thick fog of night and the whipping winds, horse and young man galloped down that road at full speed. It was thankfully empty this time of night, and this strip of cobbled road was well managed enough that Zavrius was afraid of neither bandits nor potholes. At least for an hour or two, he could ride at this breakneck speed without risking his own death.

But he hadn't been in a saddle for this long in years. Bumpy carriage rides were his domain and though he considered himself a rather proficient rider, enduring the days of travel would prove difficult. He should have worn leathers. Should have considered the chafing ache that would turn his inner thighs raw.

Forget it. Ignore it. Salve can fix that. But if Balen is dead—

If Balen was dead, nothing would mend the hole in Zavrius' heart.

His grip tightened around the reins, and he steeled himself, focused on the ride, and only slowed nearly two hours in when the lamps had petered out. By that time, he had come along the Gedrok's Glade and now took the left-diverting path away from the green haven, trotting more cautiously down into the dark expanse. Now, he had only his own torchlight to go by. The night slipped into that uncanny time before dawn; the froth of silver light dimmed, and the dark became a waning purple. The torchlight only added a muggy fog to Zavrius' vision so that everything looked fuzzy, as if the land had been painted by someone with poor eyesight. It meant he had to move carefully.

"Woah!"

The horse whinnied beneath him, half-rearing up at the sudden stop. Zavrius carefully pressed against the animal's flanks, urging it out of a gallop and into a steady rhythm by which he could consistently ride. His stomach was already grumbling, that royally treated body of his beginning to ache. But Zavrius wanted to push through—he intended to ride until exhaustion got too much for him. A small town or village somewhere along the Royal Highway could house him. He would plait his hair into a bun and rub some dirt on his face. It wasn't like Zavrius was particularly *known* in person; rumors about his personage were far more popular than him. It would be fine. He would be fine. He would make it to the Ashmons without issue.

Another hour in, he stopped to eat and stretch his legs, letting the gelding graze and drink from his own waterskin. Then he got in the saddle again. All the tiredness in his body lessened when he saw the sunrise bursting through the foliage. The tightly packed trees made the sun look jailed, made every stretching ray appear like a desperate outstretched hand reaching for him, yearning to warm his skin. By the time the sun rose high enough to escape the tree line, Zavrius was nearly falling asleep in his saddle.

Which was when he heard it.

The clop of hooves against the ground. A steady rumble of them. More than one horse. Without a doubt, there were riders on the road.

Zavrius quickly dismounted and threw himself into the tree line, coaxing the patient gelding in behind him and tying the beast to a tree. He ran back closer to the road and pressed his body against a trunk, peering around to spot whoever approached. Then, several smudges appeared from around a bend. They slowly resolved into bodies atop horses, and then it was another minute before Zavrius could make out anything of use. The figures were cowled and caped. Bandits? They would have to be brazen to hold up the Royal Highway.

Then one of their capes slipped, or the sun hit them just right —a prismatic glint, a rainbow of color dazzling the road for half a second before their horse plowed through the sunbeam. Paladins.

Zavrius stepped out into the road.

The effect was immediate. Three sets of horses whinnied, their distress echoing out into the forest beyond. Three cries went up. One of the riders dismounted with great speed and drew their weapon, and the sound of scraping steel repeated twice more when the other two dismounted.

"Halt!" one of the riders called. They kept their hood up, but Zavrius could see the shape of their armor beneath the fine fabric. The other two presumable paladins began to fan out to flank him. "Who goes there?"

Zavrius didn't answer right away, worried they might whisk him back to the palace. But this delay only caused the paladins to advance with their weapons raised.

"That's not necessary!" he called out. "I am Prince Zavrius Dued Vuuthrik. I come seeking news of my sister's expedition. Are you deserters? Or messengers?"

An uneasy silence spread out, and none of the three paladins lowered their weapons. Zavrius might have felt perturbed by that if he wasn't dressed down so much and alone on the Royal Highway.

"If you are who you say you are," the paladin to his right said slowly, "then you must understand I will need to verify your identity."

"Do you know what Prince Zavrius looks like, Sir Paladin?"

"I do."

"Then come forward and inspect me."

The other two paladins advanced with the third until he raised a hand to halt them. They rocked to a stop but kept their bodies so tense even Zavrius could tell they were poised to lunge at a moment's notice. The third paladin lowered his blade though conspicuously did not sheathe it. A shiver went through Zavrius' spine as he watched the man's grip grow firmer on the hilt. Slowly, the first paladin reached up to his hood and peeled it away from his face.

Zavrius exhaled shakily.

He recognized him. Balen had introduced them. Dwane, was it? Something like that.

"We met in the Gedrok's Glade," Zavrius said, and the man nodded. He was close enough now to inspect Zavrius up close, and within moments, he had sheathed his sword and dropped into a low bow.

"Duart, my prince."

Without any verbal command, the other two paladins followed suit. Duart did not look back to confirm and instead glanced up at Zavrius. His expression bordered on confusion. Deep-set circles had appeared beneath his eyes, and a cut ran across his temple, blazing red with infection. He looked otherwise unharmed, but the sight of him only made Zavrius' stomach churn.

Too many questions vied for priority, and Zavrius found he could say nothing at all. His heart leaped in his chest, and he awkwardly wet his lip, glancing between the three of them.

Finally, he said, "You did not answer my question."

Paladin Duart jumped a little. He shook his head. "Not deserters, Your Highness. Messengers. Calling ahead for the royal physician in Cres Stros. We need to set up the infirmary."

Zavrius blanched. That did not bode well. He resented the way his stomach flipped because he knew he feared for one person alone. How fucking *evil* of him.

"There have been casualties," Zavrius said carefully. To this, Duart nodded. Zavrius worried at his lip and asked, "Any. . . fatalities?"

Duart looked stricken. "Not. . .yet."

Someone—or, more likely, a great number of people—had been injured. Gravely. Enough to warrant this rush ahead, like mere minutes might save a life. He couldn't ask after Balen. He couldn't single out his concern like that, not when people who had dedicated their lives to his family name were hurt and dying.

He had only a moment to decide. Within the span of one breath, Zavrius turned heel and dashed back into the forest where he untied his gelding and led the poor thing back onto the road. He mounted as Duart called out, perplexed. "My prince? What are you doing? Your sister is fine, my prince. So is your uncle."

That's not who—

Zavrius paused, realizing to his shock that he had not *thought* those words. Gedroks, had he said that aloud? The look on Duart's face and the tense silence of the other two told him *yes*. He clenched every muscle in his body and stared at Duart, crushing the tip of his tongue between his teeth.

"You know I must advise you to return home, Prince Zavrius."

"Advise me all you like," he seethed. "I will ride to meet them. I care not if you have orders from the Queen herself—you *will* let me pass."

He instinctively reached up to his shoulder, where his fingers grazed against the long neck of the lute-harp. If it came to it, he would compel them. If that failed, he would have to reveal what he could do—his new, more violent tricks. Zavrius' heart thundered at the thought. What was the alternative? Run home with his tail between his legs?

He would not remain that dandy.

In the end, he needed to do neither. Duart finally spoke, gaze fixed on Zavrius' quivering hand. "They're a few hours behind, slowed down by the wagons." Then he turned back to face the waiting paladins. "Silvana, go with the prince. Yehda and I will continue to the palace."

Zavrius did not fight this. So long as they weren't returning him, he didn't mind an escort.

The two younger paladins saluted, and the woman assigned to him dropped her hood. Silvana was a tall young woman about Zavrius' age, body lean and strong. She had dark coloring, wavy black hair reminiscent of Zavrius' own, and she had pulled it roughly into a low ponytail. She didn't say a word to him but bowed low. Silence was welcome in that moment. Zavrius couldn't muster the energy to talk.

After briefly considering the condition of his horse and deeming the gelding still fit to push hard for the next few hours, they said their farewells. Paladins Duart and Yehda sped on to alert the palace, and Zavrius and Paladin Silvana began the gallop to the ambling army.

Fear had made a nest in Zavrius' throat, and this new certainty that death lay in wait like a predator only sent that worried bird fluttering manic in Zavrius' mouth. He bit down hard like he was trying to sever the fear's wings and leaned forward closer to the gelding's mane, like the angle might speed it along. They were silent. They rode for hours in that tense condition, with only the blare of wind in their ears and hoofbeats on the ground to pass the time. At least the wind was so loud that Zavrius couldn't form a single thought. Everything melted into the rhythm of the ride, an arrhythmic heartbeat his own organ matched. *Get to Balen. Get to Balen. Get to Balen*—or the other mantra, more of a command to the universe, sent up in a desperate prayer: *keep him alive.*

Zavrius became so focused on this that time slipped through his fingers, and before long, the army appeared on the horizon, a shambling mass of dark bodies. Even from this distance, Zavrius could tell they had been attacked. Within three hundred paces he could hear them, some mumbling and shouting at their approach, and others crying out. The screams of the wounded hatched another chick of fear in Zavrius' body, this one low and large, hopping around in his belly. Another hundred paces closer, and he could smell them. A mass of unwashed bodies, though sweat and the natural odor of humans after extraneous activity, turned out to be the least offensive of the scents pervading Zavrius' skull. Blood, tangy in the air. Urine. Feces. The general fog of malaise that made Zavrius' skin crawl, an inherent urge to run waking up in his body.

He did not run.

At the front of the army, Avidia and Commander Lestr sat abreast atop their horses. Zavrius had gotten close enough now to watch the bulge of shock widen Avidia's eyes. She, frozen in her disbelief, said nothing. It was Lestr who swung back in his saddle and bellowed, "Halt!"

The army obeyed slowly. Lestr's order rippled through the bodies. Zavrius craned his neck. There had been twenty paladins sent with a contingent of the city guard. Fifty or sixty, Zavrius guessed. Only the paladins had been mounted. But several of the horses had been repurposed. Wagons draped with wounded paladins trailed behind single horses. Five wagons, with one or two people in each. Some were sitting up and silent. Others hissed in pain, moaning in delirium. At least one was entirely unconscious. A paladin, their armor still on.

Zavrius' heart dropped.

The wagons were flanked by the healthier soldiers. Three mounted paladins rode behind Avidia and the rest brought up the rear, with city guards peppered everywhere to protect the weak core.

When Zavrius had finished this quick assessment, he glanced back at Avidia, then Lestr. He knew he was flushing. Both of them had flat, accusatory expressions etched onto their stone-cold faces—but Zavrius wouldn't be deterred. They might disapprove of his joining them but turning him away would only be silly now. They were all going to the same place.

"Uncle," Zavrius called out, before turning to his sister. "Avidia. I came as soon as I heard."

"To do what?" Avidia growled. Her voice rasped in her throat. A black-blue bruise blossomed from beneath her cuirass, and Zavrius guessed she'd been hit in the jugular.

Zavrius cocked his head at her. "To check on you. What else could I mean?"

Lestr said, "Petra didn't send anyone?"

Without registering the full extent of what he meant, Zavrius replied, "She did not." He paused after he'd spoken. Lestr's face hardened. Either Petra had been confident of their return or had decided not to send the resources—a decision she could not have made without the Queen's approval.

Not wanting to feed any bad image of his mother, Zavrius hastily added, "She assured me you would be fine. But you know me. Anxious, erratic, impulsive. And so I came."

Avidia snorted, apparently amused by his self-description. Zavrius waited for her to say anything more, but his sister was haggard. Exhaustion had planted itself clear as day onto her body, and she sagged with the weight of it and with the weight of her wounded army.

"I met Paladin Duart on the road," Zavrius said, happily surprised by how steady he sounded. "Both he and the other paladin will alert the physician."

His body longed to move. Balen was there—right there, in amongst the wounded—and here Zavrius sat, pretending he had come for such vague reasons. As if sensing his rider's anxiety, the gelding stamped impatiently underfoot. Zavrius hesitated and then dismounted.

"We can't stop. We can't afford to!" Avidia barked.

Zavrius made eye contact with a soldier, a young woman clinging to her comrade for support as she limped along and passed the reins to her. Her eyes went wide.

"Take them. I'll walk with the men."

The injured soldier slipped the reins from Zavrius' hand gingerly, eyes flitting up to Avidia for approval.

Avidia gave a flick of her wrist to allow the young woman to mount but said nothing. Her face twisted in Zavrius' periphery as he walked past her. Lestr's, too, was sourer than Zavrius liked to see. He refused to meet his uncle's eyes; however, Lestr knew how he felt about Balen and had no doubt solved the great mystery of why Zavrius was here at all. Avidia most likely knew, too. He wanted to lose himself in the crowd and seek out Balen, but he had to at least *pretend* he hadn't been spurred here by desperation and fear.

"What happened?" he asked.

Avidia's face hardened, and Lestr glanced at her. He did not wait for her, in the end, saying, "We sent a report of the attack back to the palace."

"Yes, I know that much. But what *happened*?"

Lestr sighed. "A group attacked us. We had camped at

Gesset's dig site, and we'd thought we'd quelled the issue. Fifty or so people had driven the workers from the camp and set up their own. They were continuing the work, thinking they'd find that damned crystal gedrok. They didn't, of course. We cleared them out—or thought we had. A week later, the governor was on the mend, and we were preparing to leave. Then, a smaller group attacked us in the night—ten or so who must have escaped the initial purge. We let our guard down."

Zavrius watched for Avidia's reaction to this and was only mildly satisfied when his sister pursed her lips even further. Her stare was distant. Something more had happened. Negligence, perhaps? A terrible part of Zavrius' brain hoped she had been responsible.

Lestr continued, "We fought. We won. The governor has since regained control, and they are publicly closing the site. Without Gesset, there's not much confidence in finding the thing." He sounded angry or displeased. A new gedrok would be miraculous for the paladins. The crystal gedrok is something out of *legend*.

Avidia said, "They were fools. We crushed them." But her voice lacked conviction.

What had she wanted to get out of this, exactly? Zavrius had assumed she'd wanted to find the gedrok, wanted to use its mythical power against their mother in her fight for the throne. Now that the site had been closed, Avidia was made impotent. Unless. . .

"*Publicly* closed," Zavrius clarified, glancing between the two of them. "But. . .?"

"No," Avidia said sharply. Her mouth drooped. "No, we can't afford to leave any of our men there. Besides, it's delusional to think the creature will be found. Especially now."

If she was lying, Zavrius couldn't tell. A genuine depression laced into her words—Avidia had bet on a losing race. He thought about saying something, biting into the already bleeding wound since the opportunity to hurt her came about so rarely. But an insistent pull in Zavrius' gut tugged at him, urging him away from this mess. He turned to look at the hollow, tired faces of the army and said as loud as he could, "I am glad to see you all. Thank you for your service to my sister." Then, he glanced back at Avidia. "I am glad you're well."

He found he meant it, at that moment. She stared at him like he'd grown two heads, and Zavrius began to position himself to slip into the middle of the army.

"I can play for everyone. Soothe their minds."

"You will do no such thing," Avidia snapped, but Zavrius had already slid the lute-harp's strap the correct way so the round body of the instrument sat snugly against the crook of his arms. He strummed a simple chord. The sound thrummed out around them, buoyed by the encasement of trees. The birds answered the sound, chirping and chittering, and for a moment, Zavrius forgot where he was, closing his eyes to breathe it all in. He used that moment with his eyes closed to will his anxiety away. How could he support Balen when he himself was terrified? But closing his eyes only conjured the image he had seen on horseback. That body lying in the wagon, paladin armor glinting. The body looked to be about Balen's size. About Balen's build. The longer Zavrius had his eyes closed, the more convinced he became that it *was* Balen—unconscious, injured, barely clinging to life—and, shaking, his hand strummed a discordant cord that made himself and several others visibly wince.

"Or I could ruin everyone's day a little more," he said to cover the slip, aiming for brevity. The joke did not land. He met Avidia's glare (she had turned in her saddle to give it to him) and awkwardly cleared his throat. Then, without waiting any more, he played. The army began its slow amble towards Cres Stros as Zavrius played the song. He imbued each note with as much power as he could muster, thinking: *willpower, calm, energy.*

Whatever state of mind he could muster in these people, he wanted them to feel good. Healthy. They needed to pull from what little energy they had to make it back to Cres Stros in time for their injured fellows to get help.

For Balen to get help.

He only played one song, and by the end of it, he had positioned himself perfectly in the center with the injured atop their wagons. He said hello to a few of them, shuffling awkwardly to the wagon with the unconscious paladin, and without thinking—or rather, without giving a single shit what anyone around him thought—he strung the lute-harp back into place and swung himself into the wagon too.

A few titters went out, conversation starting up. He was sure he heard his name, and a few jolts of surprise as people further back caught sight of him. He ignored them all.

His hands were shaking. Quickly, he inspected the figure, eyes seeking the wound. He could not find it, which meant it was beneath the armor or that the paladin's clothing had been changed after the wound had been treated.

He put his hand on the cuirass. Its engraved solar center was stained a muddy red. Flecks of dried blood were crusted in the crannies. When his fingertips touched the gedrok bone, his own flesh danced with power. Very faintly, the person's chest rose and fell. He looked up and cast about, hoping to see Balen's head poking out somewhere he simply had not looked. But this was a small contingent. Even calling it an army seemed laughable now that he was among them.

Gedroks, but if Balen was in another wagon, Zavrius would have seen him by now. If Balen was conscious, surely he would have called out. Zavrius could almost hear his voice.

"*Prince Zavrius?*" Balen would say, voice tilting high at the end as if asking a question. He would have muscled his way between two other soldiers, mouth parted in surprise to see the young prince there.

"Yes," Zavrius would reply. *"Yes, I came. I had to, you see—I was going mad."*

He might have truly been going mad now that he thought about. He took his hands away from the cuirass and placed them on either side of the unconscious soldier's helmet. "Balen?" Zavrius whispered. No answer.

Well, he could sit and fester in this awful waiting, or he could be sure.

Carefully, he pulled the helmet free.

Zavrius' breath caught. For a moment, Zavrius had the dizzying relief of not recognizing the face beneath the helmet. A bruise spread from the man's jaw and nearly swallowed his round cheek. *It couldn't be Balen,* some illogical voice said. *It's not Balen.*

But as Zavrius' teeth lowered onto the flat plane of his tongue and a clarifying spark of pain thrilled through him, he saw the sweat-sheen skin, the rose-color blooming beneath his fair cheeks, the smear of dark hair made flat by the helmet and *recognized* him.

Balen of Westgar was unconscious.

EIGHTEEN

Zavrius' stomach flipped. He moved his whole body to accommodate the chilling, nauseating feeling, lurching over Balen as if shielding the young man from a danger long past. He squeezed his eyes, hiding from the feeling but blocking his sight only exacerbated every other emotion in his body. The wild fluttering of his heart increased tenfold. Zavrius grimaced as fear made his body shake. If he didn't calm down soon, he would vomit.

Carefully, Zavrius lowered himself back onto his knees. The chill of his fear, whilst overwhelming, had made his body glacial in its processing. As the nausea ebbed away, his heart slowed, and a new disbelief settled on him, just short of a compensating apathy.

All of Zavrius' logic said this: that Balen was in the best place possible. They were traveling back to the city, and a physician would be informed and at the ready for his return. He would be fine. He would live.

It might have been entirely convincing if Zavrius knew what injury Balen had sustained, but the only thing stronger than his fear in that moment was his shame. He was already pushing the limits of appropriate; in fact, he was entirely banking on his youth, his known nature, and everyone else's utter exhaustion, hoping they would accept his interest in this unconscious soldier as a kind prince worried for his protectors.

Gedroks, he felt impotent in that moment. All the bravado of charging out of the palace to rescue Balen had fallen short, and now he sat with his knees underneath him and the man he— certainly didn't *love*, but absolutely *appreciated*—suffering beneath him. He put his hands on Balen's cheeks as if he might feel the young man's inner workings. If he could do it with gedrok material, surely he could do it for Balen. They shared ichor, didn't they?

Zavrius closed his eyes and steadied himself to the persistent clopping of hooves and the ambient rumble of wagons along the ground. He listened until the sound became droning and sent all his focus to the man before him. Zavrius felt the spark beneath his fingertips, the tiniest spark of something in his blood reacting to the same something in Balen's.

What's wrong with him? Show me.

But if this was a skill he could actually conquer, he wouldn't conquer it now. Nothing happened, and in truth, beyond the mere presence of the ichor he could only feel that Balen was slightly feverish.

He glanced to his left, where an infantry soldier marched steadily along. Much of her face was covered by a half helm, though her lower face was left exposed. It gave Zavrius a direct line of sight to the unhappy twist to her mouth, like gravity had taken both corners of her lips and pulled.

"Soldier," Zavrius called.

She and three others around her jolted to a stop.

"Y-yes, my prince?"

"What happened to this paladin?"

Her eyes flicked down to Balen, who laid corpse-still. "Infection, my prince."

"Wound on his thigh turned bad, my prince," another added with a sweeping bow.

"Thank you," Zavrius nodded, releasing them both. He waited until they had walked a few meters ahead before he turned to look down at Balen. He cupped the other man's cheek. Balen had a beauty to him that made him glow. Even with such sickness, even with his skin pallid and cheeks flushed, the sweat made him look like he was covered in morning dew, misted by the world waking up. Zavrius tried to pretend that's all it was.

No one had ever—

Zavrius swallowed hard. He didn't know what to do with all the fear, with the weight of the emotion. He existed in liminality at that moment; where Balen lay between life and death, Zavrius had been marooned between lover and prince. He looked down at Balen and did not understand his emotions, for never had his position and Balen's been in such stark contrast.

If Balen died, he'd have died for the crown. It didn't feel right, even if it was. If anything happened to Balen, if he left for good, if he died *like this*—

A tear fell onto Balen's face. Quickly, Zavrius wiped both his and the paladin's cheeks with the edge of his tunic before rolling and hunching himself into a ball of limbs. People would be looking, inevitably. He didn't have the willpower to lie about why he shed tears for a dying paladin.

Some time must have passed, for when Zavrius looked up, he could see the palace of Cres Stros in the distance. The mid-morning sun burned hot, scalding his scalp, and he blinked his fatigue rapidly away. He rolled towards Balen, whose condition seemed not to have changed. A hand to his forehead, a quick check of his fever—it hadn't broken yet, and Zavrius had no skill in medicine to be sure if the paladin had improved at all. He found himself squeezing at Balen's armor anyway, willing the gedrok material to *do* something, wishing it might heal him.

"Don't you dare," Zavrius muttered. "Don't even think about it. I order you to wake up. Hear me, paladin? I *order it.*"

Balen did not wake up. He didn't even stir. But briefly, Zavrius felt better for saying it; what little authority he had in this world often came down to those three words: *I order it.* Like this, he had at least done what he could do.

The rest would be up to Balen's body and whatever work the physician could manage.

The streets of Cres Stros were thick with people that morning. Zavrius sat up and closed his eyes as warm wind gusted through the thin vestibules. Home had a smell to it. Scented oils and stone that had been warmed by the sun. Hot, spiced meats on racks to dry and roasting sweet nuts whose smell wicked toward Zavrius from the markets. They passed a warehouse of artisan furniture, and the scent of freshly primed wood filled Zavrius' lungs, reminding him of a dying forest. The movement of the wagon, too, felt as familiar as breathing. The slight jostle over cobble-stones. The pauses for the traffic, or the great shadow that fell over them passing beneath the gate. The smell of mountain water wafting from thin aqueducts. Flowers blooming on trailing vines. It smelled of summer. It sounded like summer, too—joyous, like life had been restored.

Without opening his eyes, Zavrius reached down and squeezed Balen's gauntlet-free hand.

"Hail!"

"Princess Avidia. Commander Lestr!" The voice carried.

Zavrius' eyes snapped open, and he craned forward. They'd arrived at the base of the palace. Queen Arasne's seat sprouted from the hillside like a primordial plant, so well rooted it appeared in places to spring naturally from the ground, a chthonic creation.

Zavrius spotted Duart rushing down the steps to the palace, taking the steps in twos. A thin, bird-like woman matched his pace—the physician. A line of paladins were standing at the top of the stairs.

Lestr called out, "We'll need stretchers. Paladins!"

Every one of the paladins on the stairs saluted and turned tail. Whomever of the returning paladins could stand rushed forward. The infantry parted until Zavrius and the wounded soldiers were exposed. The horses pulling the wagons were urged ever closer to the stairs and positioned for ease of access. As the stretchers were brought down, the wounded were raised onto them and taken back up.

Zavrius leaped out of the wagon. "This man is unconscious!" he called, calling a stretcher to him. "Infection and fever!"

He fought the urge to scream, to add a desperate *please!* onto the end. Paladins came to move Balen. Someone whom Zavrius didn't know made a low noise at the sight of Balen's exposed face.

"Balen," she hissed. Then, "Quickly!"

Zavrius watched helplessly as Balen's limp body was hefted from the wagon and laid onto a linen stretcher. From what Zavrius could see, they only had three. As the wounded were ferried up into the palace, he turned his attention to the physician, who was in furious conversation with Lestr. She looked—ashen. In shock, probably. He was about to storm forward and demand how a single woman was expected to handle all these cases when a flurry of activity occurred at the top of the stairs. Several people dressed in linen aprons rushed down to assist the paladins. One went straight to the physician, presumably for his orders.

Now that Zavrius watched, he couldn't recall such a number of medical personnel flittering about the palace. No official royal infirmary existed; the Cres Strosian infirmary was a public building. But it appeared an exception had been made. Zavrius walked closer to the discussion and heard Lestr say, "I will speak to the Queen now."

"Yes, yes, of course," the physician was saying. A worried look made her brows crease. She turned to the waiting man and told him, "Start making a salve for the paladin's infection. Make extra—we should assume others are at risk. This is your priority. For Churid's team, assess those with more minor injuries. Go."

The man left with only a curt bow to suggest he'd heard her, and Zavrius turned to see Lestr already hauling himself up the stairs. Avidia, too, had already disappeared. This lower level was now chaos as servants dashed about to grab the horses and clean the wagons. The city guard took stock of themselves and the healthy in their ranks began the march back to their garrison. Zavrius stepped away and set his sights on the top of the stairs— where the shadows poorly concealed Petra from view.

Well, he had expected that, hadn't he? There was no point in fearing her wrath now. He had accepted the certainty of a verbal lashing the moment he left her office. So, head proud and blasé attitude bleeding out of his pores, Zavrius began his ascent.

He took his time. The sun hurt now, making the back of his neck prickle and sting with overexposure, but he kept his climb slow. Strummed the lute harp a bit. Thanked paladins for their dedication as they rushed past him. But soon enough, the stairs were empty, and Zavrius could no longer linger.

Zavrius clutched the reedy neck of the lute-harp. "Give me strength, would you?" he murmured, playing a chord with intention as if he might imbue himself with his own power. Maybe it worked, maybe it didn't; he pretended that it had, that now his bravado was anything but false. It made it easier for him to smile widely at Petra, haunting the shadows like a black cat. Her eyes were fierce. Disappointed.

"Aunt," Zavrius said lightly.

"Prince Zavrius," she said. For a moment, Zavrius doubted

she was going to do anything at all—the silence stretched out between them until it grew brittle and sharp. She smashed it apart with an angry flick of her wrist. "We need to talk."

He could have caused a scene but decided against it. Zavrius followed Petra inside wordlessly, trailing behind her the entire walk to the administrative wing and into her office. There, she held the door open for him but refused to meet his eye.

"Sit down," she said as she closed the door.

Zavrius refused.

Petra said nothing, sulking past him to stand ominously at her desk, an attempt at intimidation that fell largely short because Zavrius didn't care about her opinion then. He wasn't sorry for what he'd done.

"Go on, then," Zavrius murmured, inspecting his nails. Dirt and blood had crusted beneath them; he needed to bathe. "Say it."

In his periphery, Petra's mouth upturned. Her breathing became so heavy that he could note the rise and fall of her shoulders without turning his head. He did, though, eventually, and it was when he finally met her eye that she exploded.

"You," she said, "did something very stupid."

"Yes."

"Do you think yourself immune to all the dangers of this world? Or do you think yourself smarter than the entire royal administration *and* the Queen herself? If we thought they were in danger, we would have sent someone."

"You said you didn't know!" Zavrius snapped. "So either you lied to me, or—"

"And what if I did lie?"

Zavrius' teeth clattered together, and he seethed at her. Perhaps the smart thing would be to walk out of this room and beg his mother's forgiveness, for no doubt Arasne wanted a word or ten with him. But Zavrius found himself rooted to the spot, melted to it, really, by the heat of his anger. He flexed his hands, hating how young he felt, how weak. Carefully, every word was spoken as if brittle, "You think me so entirely useless that I can't comprehend the risks of a prince alone on the road? *If* I had been recognized, *if* I was completely unable to defend myself, *if, if, if.* But you decided you could protect me from the truth, or you thought I didn't need to know this or that about what was happening to people who have dedicated their lives to mine. My eldest sister can lead the small militia to the Ashmons, but I'm not allowed to even know their *fate?* I know what you think of me—what you've always thought of me—and I am sure I can't do anything to alter that. So what is the point in me asking nicely? What is the point of anything if I am confined to these walls and can't even follow after the man I—" He bit off that word, flushing deeply. Zavrius raised his chin, steadying his breath. "Nothing is ever expected of me, and yet everything is. Both you and my mother are inconsistent in how you treat me. I deserve better than this. You should have told me."

"She didn't tell you because she correctly presumed you would be a fool."

Horror washed over him. Zavrius snapped around. Lurking in the shadows of the office stood Theo, practically a ghost to Zavrius, who had seen so little of his brother in the recent weeks he'd thought he'd been blessed by a higher power.

Zavrius thought about saying nothing, waiting for Theo to deliver another biting quip, but he could feel his cheeks burning and already wanted to scream. "It seems our reputations precede us both, brother," Zavrius snapped. "As I recall, you weren't allowed to go either." Theo's lips pinched together like a cat's puckered arse. Good. Let him suck on that sour knowledge. "What do you want, Theo?"

"I want to remind you that this behavior won't be acceptable in my court."

"This behavior?" Zavrius said, incredulous. "Riding out to meet a returning party? Oh, the *scandal* of it all."

"Stop it," Petra snapped. Her dark eyes flashed between the pair of them and, as usual, her expression made Zavrius feel very young. "I asked Theo to be here. Not—" she said sharply, finger raised to quieten Zavrius' opened-mouth betrayal, "—to scold you, but to. . ."

She looked helplessly over at Theo, and when Zavrius turned, he looked—different. Not because of any great transformation or mutation, but due to the slightest glint in his eye, a light betraying the darkness of his expression.

Was that. . .a tear?

Zavrius frowned. At once, the realization hit him. Queen Arasne had not summoned him. Queen Arasne would have called him immediately, wouldn't she, as both a mother and a ruler?

He narrowed his eyes at Theo. "What news have you come to deliver me, then?"

He said flatly, his voice already heavy with pre-emptive mourning like the palace bells, their giant brass bodies undulating with their droning elegies. The resounding *gong, gong, gong*, a death knoll announcing loss to the city.

"She had a turn," Theo said stiffly. "Collapsed." Zavrius wasn't sure what his face did, but it made Theo clarify rather quickly: "She's still alive. And she's awake now. She's asked after you."

Several things happened. Firstly, he noticed the change in his body, a great tightening of every muscle, and a constricting in his lungs. Then, the wave of unnatural calm descended upon him like a god rain. Zavrius shivered and thought: *okay*.

Logically, it wasn't okay. Distress clawed at the recesses of his mind, but the fog of a necessary apathy kept it at bay. Calmly, Zavrius assessed his brother. Of all his siblings, Zavrius had to wonder why Theo had been selected to deliver this news. Petra knew better than most how tenuous their interactions could be. Their only bond was one forced by blood and proximity—little love lay between them. If any. The way the pair of them stood there, side by side and staring at him, made Zavrius feel ill.

What *was* this?

"Are you blaming me for it?" Zavrius whispered tensely. He glanced to Petra, then back to his brother. "Is that what this is? You want to parade me before the consequences of my actions? Are you to be my council? To say: look at what your recklessness does to your ailing mother?"

Petra flinched. The movement looked strange on her, so unlike her usual demeanor. "I thought—"

"You thought what?" Zavrius stepped forward to the pair of them and showed his teeth. "How much Theo would love to tell me this news? How much joy he might take in making me question my role in our mother's suffering? Gedroks, what is wrong with you?"

Petra's eyes were wide and glistening, but she had too much determination to let herself cry. They breathed hard together, heaving. Zavrius bit into his tongue.

"Leave her. Zavrius—leave her. Look at me."

Zavrius tore his gaze over to Theo. The other man wore a furiously dark expression. Strangely, he looked as if he took no pleasure from this interaction. Which was bullshit.

"She will not tell it to you plainly, but I will. I have no qualms in doing so. You think, and you have always thought, that because you are a prince, you can shirk things like duty, responsibility, and honor. You look at the encroaching threat of the Rezwyn pests, and I swear you would thank them if they brought a traveling band and whores for you to lie with. You have no integrity. You are fickle. Weak. Our father knew it, and I know it, and Petra knows it, too. Whatever sad attempt at glory you were aiming for by gallivanting about at night, it has failed. You will *stop* your nonsense. You will pick up an administrative duty. You will stop with your instruments and whatever else you do to while away your life. You will live up to the greatness of our name. Do you understand?"

Zavrius stared up at him. Theo was very much a man in his twenties. He had the bravado and the broadness to his body, a barrel of a man. Why, then, could Zavrius not see anything except their father when he looked into Theo's eyes? He was just Sirellius in a different skin. It was Zavrius' childhood all over again.

Zavrius opened his mouth to speak. Somewhere in his mind existed an archive of carefully constructed conversations he had mulled over for nearly a decade. What would he have said to Sirellius if he'd been the person he was today? Zavrius had thought he'd stand up for himself or, at the very least, generate some biting quip to sting his father's over-inflated pride.

But apparently, all he would do was stare. It was all he could do now. Impotence and fear worked like shackles, weighing his tongue down, so all he could do was stare up at his eldest brother in abject shock. His chest fluttered, and that slow-rising burn of shame moved up his throat, a bile to ablate his bravery.

Don't cry. Don't you dare. The longer he stood beneath Theo's scrutiny, the more difficult it became to keep his tears to himself. He didn't dare look at Petra, either, worried for the pity that no doubt had consumed her expression.

He didn't have to let them see, though. With his last bit of effort, he tore himself from the pair of them and turned on his heel. Theo scoffed immediately. "Off to Mother, are you?"

Tears did bubble up, then, chased to the corners of Zavrius' eyes by a push of shame. "Why, yes," he hissed. His voice, at least, was steady. "She called for me, after all."

He strode out of the room quietly, and pretended he wasn't crying as he pushed his way out of the administrative corridors and down towards the Royal Apartments, where he dismissed two palace guards from afar before they could see his blotchy complexion up close. Once inside the Royal Apartments, he took a few shuddering breaths and craned to hear. Very gently, he took the lute-harp from his shoulder and laid its neck against the wall. Still no sound of other people.

The worst thing that could happen now would be for Lysio or Gideonus to appear—Zavrius would not survive another interaction. Thus, he crept slowly towards the Queen's chambers, careful to distribute his weight along the wood so it did not creak, and when he grew close enough, he strained to hear again. And good that he did, for he heard voices inside. Arasne's was noticeable not for the usual mellifluous nature of her voice but for the intermittent coughing that punctuated her sentences. Zavrius cringed and ground his teeth. The other voice was modulated, calm, and feminine. Avidia.

Zavrius pressed his ear closer to the door, hoping to hear even one clear word, but they were speaking too quietly. Nothing but muffled conversation came through until the sudden involvement of footsteps which grew ever closer. Zavrius pushed himself away from the door and moved languidly to the left where he positioned himself against the wall. He didn't much care if Avidia saw him, and the shameful cry Theo had engendered in him had drained his will to hide. When the door opened, Zavrius glanced up. Sure enough, Avidia caught sight of him. She worked her mouth silently, assessing him from the top of his braided head to his feet. Then she called back over her shoulder, "Zavrius is here for you."

"Oh!" Arasne exclaimed. Fabric shifted as she moved in her bed. "Good. Send him in."

Zavrius stepped forward and half expected Avidia to use the opportunity to say something foul to him. But she said nothing at all. Even held the door open for him. Zavrius glanced back at her, frowning at her inscrutable expression before he turned to their mother.

Arasne sat upright beneath the covers. Though she was dressed in a nightgown, the white linen sleeves were ridiculously large, giving her the appearance of a cloud struggling out from beneath the duvet. She looked as she had the past few months: unwell, but not obviously so. Her eyes were bright, like she was happy to see him.

Zavrius' stomach twisted. Something felt wrong.

"Come." She patted the bed beside her, but Zavrius refused her summons.

He crossed his arms defensively and planted himself in the center of the room.

"What is it?" Arasne asked, voice faltering.

"I'd prefer to stand for my scolding."

Arasne's shoulders slouched, and she glanced away at him, feigning interest in the far edges of a room she had no doubt scoured for hours before now. "You know I must speak to you."

"Then speak to me as an adult. None of the patronizing. But know this: Petra and Theo have already told me what a disappointment I am to the family, and I am aware no one trusts me to do anything useful. My reputation is too tainted. All I wanted—"

He stopped talking, realizing he was whining and ashamed by the childishness of it all. It didn't matter what he wanted, nor his intentions. What mattered was what the Queen made of his adventure.

Without turning, Arasne said, "It reflects poorly on me if you gallivant about."

Gallivant about. Theo's words. He had a strange sense of doubling, the fear that perhaps Theo's words were not Sirellius' at all but their mother's.

He stiffened. She still wasn't looking at him when he next spoke. "Whether or not any of you approve of who I am, you need to trust me as part of this family. I need information—not only if I am going to survive at court when you're gone, but if I am to stop myself from bringing shame upon the throne."

Now she moved, head dipping as if in apology as she turned to face him. "What did Theo suggest?"

"As punishment? An administrative position." Zavrius thought. He gnawed at his lower lip. Perhaps he needed to do something that might edge his reputation toward something more favorable in the long run. He looked at his mother. "Which I wouldn't mind."

Her brows shot up her forehead. "Oh?"

"Something to the west, maybe." He stepped towards her, dropping his arms. "I could speak to lords and ladies. I could play for them. Check in on taxes or what have you."

"You want to get out of the palace?"

Zavrius didn't meet her gaze, hearing the hurt in her words. He lowered himself onto the bed, and she scooted over to allow him more room. "I want to be trusted. Though. . .maybe I do want to be away from here."

Without the threat of his siblings judging him for this or for that. Without the threat of a grand political blunder. But then he thought of Balen and went cold at the thought of leaving. How difficult a month had been. He didn't want to imagine the rest of his life mapped out in stints of time away from a lover.

"Though perhaps I wouldn't want to be away for too long," he said finally, looking down at his hands. He picked at the callouses forming on his upper palm. "I don't like being useless," he said sharply.

"Yes, I'm well aware."

"I won't apologize, either."

In his periphery, he watched as the comforting hand Arasne had raised to pat his shoulder hovered awkwardly in the air. She drew back and sighed deeply. Zavrius could hear the rattle of air in her lungs, a raspy malaise. His nostrils flared. It sounded—wrong.

"Theo is going to take on some of my duties," said the Queen. Zavrius went cold.

"Avidia will take on some of his, and down the chain it will go. So yes. I think it might be good for you to start something in the way of diplomacy. Letter writing is a good place to start. There are some southern lords we could check in with. Lord Oren Radek, for example. He's only a bit older than you, and he's fresh to the role. You could start some correspondence. Eventually, visiting Shoi Prya and Westgar for tax collection would be ideal."

"Alright," Zavrius said. He meant it and didn't. Everything felt unsteady beneath his feet. Very suddenly, he didn't want to be next to her anymore, for there was no comfort in this woman. He stood abruptly. "I hope you're feeling better. Let me know if I can do anything to help."

He went to go and heard the catch in Arasne's throat.

"Would you. . .play me a song?"

He turned back. The way she had said that. . .

"Play you a song?" Zavrius said, turning. "Or. . .play you a *song*?"

She nodded at the second. "Put my mind at rest."

"I doubt I'm strong enough," Zavrius murmured because he didn't know what else to say. Never before had Arasne asked for Zavrius to work his power on her. She had always been stronger, too obviously resistant for him to both. Besides, it was—improper.

"Try."

He didn't ask if it was an order and instead quickly dashed out to retrieve the instrument he'd left standing by the apartments' door. When she saw the bell-shape body of the instrument, the bone streaking rainbows into the candlelit room, Arasne laughed softly.

"You've grown to like that one."

He gripped the feeble wooden neck firmly. "It's my favorite." Zavrius meant to say it lightly, but it came out stern and serious. He lifted the strap over his body and played without thinking, letting some tune form in his mind. It lilted, drifted away from a sweet, honeyed tune into something melancholy. The power he put into it was cautious, which simply wouldn't do for someone like Arasne, whose blood was his own. With every deep breath he took, he urged more of his power into the notes, thinking: *let her rest. Let her be calm. Let her body not hurt.* Minutes passed, and Arasne let the music wash over her until her eyes were drooping and sleep claimed her.

Zavrius played for another minute before a sob broke through his wordless song. He stopped abruptly, but his mother didn't stir. Drowning in her big-sleeved gown, skin ashen, sleep claiming her like death would—he hated this.

Zavrius turned, uncaring about everything they had discussed. It all could wait.

Balen could not.

Nineteen

By the time Zavrius had found the makeshift infirmary and convinced the physicians to let him in—that it didn't matter to him how improper his being there was, nor how much the sight might upset him—night was beginning to fall.

Queen Arasne had given up the main hall for this purpose. It was such an imposing room, with or without guests, that Zavrius didn't even blink as he stepped inside to the chaos.

The injured lay on cots on the floor, spaced out across the stretch of marble. Medical workers fluttered between them, though only a few wounded received intense attention. As far as Zavrius could see, no one had died; no white shroud covered anybody.

Many of the soldiers were sleeping, even though the sun was only now setting. Sharp rays marked the marble floor, and the far part of the room had already been plunged into darkness. The empty thrones were shadowed, sitting empty, but with the stark contrast of the sunlight, they almost appeared as if part of a different world. Two thrones occupied by ghosts, eternal sentinels overlooking the wounded and dying of their dynasty. Zavrius had been told that Balen had been placed in that part of the room, and that his treatment had been completed for the time being.

Zavrius carefully picked his way through the corridor of free space, nodding down at workers or soldiers who caught his eye. Many tried to bow or dip their heads somehow lower than their horizontal form, which made Zavrius feel at once proud and upset as he continued his walk. Any true prince might have stayed and comforted the wounded. Someone doing his best to conceal his attraction to one soldier in particular *certainly* would have lingered. But Zavrius was over pretending. In that moment, all he wanted was to see Balen of Westgar alive and well, and damn whoever saw; damn whatever they thought.

Balen was easy to spot. They had only removed the cuisses and greaves of his right leg. The rest of his body remained cocooned in the prismatic paladin armor. He had been positioned right near the thrones, which Zavrius was thankful for. A voice in the back of his mind suggested someone had mentioned it might be best—Petra, perhaps, with intimate knowledge of Zavrius' interest in the paladin. Better to have him slightly separated than for Zavrius to loudly proclaim his feelings in the middle of the room. Whatever the reason, whether it be good fortune or for his benefit, he could not complain. Zavrius watched from afar, staring at the steady rise and fall of Balen's chest, and then he slipped quickly over and went down onto his knees by the paladin's side.

Zavrius put his hands on Balen's thigh. Part of the pant leg beneath had been cut away to expose the raw puss-filled flesh of the wound beneath. A foul-smelling salve had been smeared over the leg and seemed to be sucking all that fester from Balen's flesh. Zavrius ignored it, ignored the unpleasantness of the sight and the stench. He pressed his fingers into Balen's thigh. The touch felt good. Needed. The warmth of Balen's feverish body made Zavrius feel selfishly happy. He was here! He was here, in the flesh, *alive*. Zavrius didn't realize how tightly he was squeezing Balen's leg until the young man groaned. Zavrius whipped his head around, watching at the paladin's face contorted, brows crashing together. Seeing him in pain made Zavrius feel strangely electric. What better display of life than a body fighting a wound, reacting to pain. Balen would be fine, Zavrius decided suddenly. Everything would be fine.

He shifted so he could cross his legs and, because he didn't want to leave and figured no one would really bother him, he tilted forward until he could rest his cheek on the cuirass. He hadn't planned to sleep. Honestly, the grooves of the gedrokbone were deeply uncomfortable, with all the patterns and embossed details digging into his skin. He figured the discomfort would keep him awake. But something unlocked in him being back in Balen's presence. Every time he breathed in, he could smell Balen. The salve and the sickness, too, sure, but the *scent* of Balen—his sweat and whatever natural odor his body made. Breathing in made Zavrius feel at home, but at the same time it made his heart race, a tepid, teenaged fear at being close to someone he fancied.

He slept. One moment, he was resting his eyes, and the next, he was waking to a voice and a hand in his hair.

Zavrius jolted awake not in a panic but with a rush of glee. His body knew before his mind did, rocking him awake with the thrill. He felt the weight of Balen's hand in his hair, let himself lay there for a minute as Balen stroked his scalp, and listened to Balen murmur words so softly Zavrius couldn't distinguish them even from such a close difference. When he shifted, Balen's voice stopped. So, too, did his languid petting. Zavrius sat up, and Balen's hand drooped, sliding from Zavrius' head to his cheek, where he cupped it. Zavrius pressed his face into the warm palm, using his own hands to drag Balen somehow ever closer. They stared at one another, stared until the eye contact became somehow unbearable, every second flaying another layer of skin and flesh away from Zavrius' core. He was seen, and it was more vulnerable than nakedness. Swallowing hard, Zavrius glanced away.

"You're beautiful," Balen whispered.

"You're feverish," Zavrius replied, though he felt himself flush. He wanted to bury his face in Balen's hand. Or better yet, the crook of his neck. He wanted some unnamable thing, wanted to fold Balen up and slot him between his ribs like a memento.

Then, as if realizing their position for the first time, Balen said, "You are lying on me. In front of everyone."

So what? Zavrius glanced over his shoulder. No one looked their way. Most of the people here were wounded and sleeping. He said, "I would do more than lie on you in front if I thought it would help you heal."

Balen's breath caught. He stopped breathing. "It might."

Zavrius turned back to face him, eyes dropping to the other man's lips. They were dry and cracked and Zavrius wanted to reach down and kiss them, lick over those cracks with his tongue. Stupidly, his core grew hot. Zavrius swallowed hard and dragged himself further up Balen's body, resting his palms down onto the cuirass and his chin on his hands. Balen's hand came to rest once more in Zavrius' hair.

"I came to get you," Zavrius said, "and you were rudely unconscious."

"You came to get me?" Balen's eyes flashed wide in shock and fear. "What do you mean?"

"What I said." Zavrius searched Balen's eyes. "Whatever is happening right now, I want you to stop it. I've had plenty of lectures about my actions already. I couldn't—"

Again, heat burned behind his eyes. How embarrassing.

Zavrius spoke carefully, picking his away around the words. "I'm not done with you. I rather like you. Going off and dying in the Ashmon Range didn't really align with the plans I had for you."

There might have been a lot Balen could have said to that. If Zavrius were in his position, he'd be asking things like: *Done with me? Whatever do you mean?* or *I wasn't exactly trying to die.* But the paladin just stroked Zavrius' hair and murmured, "What did you have in mind, Zav?"

Zav. Gedroks, his heart leaped up like a dog for a treat at the way Balen said his name. Stripped of his title, stripped of even his full name, the nickname made Zavrius' body relax and grow hot at the same time. He wanted to put his hands beneath Balen's armor and feel over his heart. He longed for some closeness, some intimacy. Attraction mingled with an innocent desire for closeness, and he tilted forward, parting his lips to take Balen's between his own. It was a long, chaste kiss, until it wasn't. Balen grunted, either from pain or something more, and Zavrius found himself letting out a small, excited moan. The excitement was manifold; Balen was back, Balen was going to be okay, and, gedroks, Zavrius longed to be touched by him.

They pulled away from one another. Zavrius stole a glance over his shoulder, and either luck or politeness meant no one was looking their way.

"Dangerous," Balen said, though his smile was broad. He looked at Zavrius like he was something truly beautiful, something precious, and Zavrius withered under the intensity of Balen's gaze. The paladin reached out and tilted Zavrius' head back to him. "Happy Birthday, Prince Zavrius."

A grin split Zavrius' lips apart. "Thank you, Paladin Balen."

"I have a gift for you," Balen said, casting about for his possessions.

"Lestr most likely has them. Don't—just. . .give it to me when you're better."

Zavrius didn't say what was really on his mind: that if Balen kept kissing him, or if Balen pressed his lips against the inside of Zavrius' neck, he would think that the most wonderful of birthday gifts.

"I should let you rest," Zavrius said quietly, if only because he could not trust his own body. As much as he wanted to stay with Balen, he would be pushing his luck to sleep on the marble floor beside him. "I'm. . .I'm very happy you're back, Balen."

Balen stared at him for a while, eyes soft and a smile blooming on his lips. "I'm happy I'm back, too." His voice came out honeyed, the words dripping sweetness.

Zavrius left the hall feeling like he had a great well of enormous depth inside of him. Every sweet expression Balen gifted him, every flirtation, every kind word, plunged the well deeper. From this, Zavrius could draw sustenance. Balen liked him. He *liked* him and had missed him just as fiercely. The comfort of their shared attraction bolstered him until he was practically skipping through the palace halls.

Everything felt good in that moment. Zavrius was sure the future was bright.

As Balen recovered, Zavrius began writing letters. It wasn't a terrible assignment, and it meant he could familiarize himself with the Dued Vuuthrik's vassals and their various interests and concerns. In the fortnight it took Balen's infection to subside, and for him to resume light training, Zavrius received four letters in response to his own. On that same tray that was delivered to Arasne's office—which she had kindly lent him for this purpose

—came another letter. More of a note, really, tucked neatly underneath the letters marked with official seals.

Zavrius glanced at the servant who deposited the tray on the desk, a stony-faced woman who didn't so much as smile as she put it down.

Zavrius slipped the interloper from the tray, holding it aloft for the servant to see. "What's this?"

"I'm not sure what you mean, my prince," she said, and Zavrius did not press further, even as a ruddy brown tinge made its way onto her cheeks.

Someone had put it there, and Zavrius' heart raced at the thought of that. It was not a great conspiracy. He knew before he opened it who it was from and greatly enjoyed the idea of all the bargaining and favors called upon to deliver the letter just so.

It was, Zavrius thought, rather romantic.

The note was written on very thin parchment—not a full sheet, but a salvaged scrap that had been folded meticulously to hide the obvious tears around its edge. When Zavrius unfolded it, he was met with a stilted and messy script, as if its author was unused to holding a quill.

Zav,

I've returned and somehow haven't returned.

It won't feel like I am home until I see you in the garden again.

Come tonight, at twilight, near the fourth and fifth ribs of the gedrok.

Yours,

Balen

Zavrius fought the urge to crumple the letter out of sheer emotion. One word had done enough to jolt through him like lightning in a storm. *Yours. Yours. Yours.*

What to make of that? They hadn't said anything explicitly. Zavrius had never said the words: "I want to be yours. I want you to be mine," even though he felt in his heart that it was true. Seeing the word *yours* thrilled him to no end, firstly for its implications, and secondly for how it made him feel.

Zavrius had such a spirit that often rebelled at the thought of entrapment. Duty and his title and avoiding music and avoiding all his passions were all ways others had tried to ensnare Zavrius in the past. Now that he had seen the word *'yours'*, he became aware of a part of himself that had feared this very moment, worried that *'yours'* might mean 'belonging to' or 'owned by'. But if Zavrius closed his eyes and let that word flit around in his heart, he felt it meant something else entirely. Balen was his not to keep, but to nurture. His to love and encourage and grow beside. And Zavrius wished to be Balen's, too, in that way. He wanted someone who would look past his title and be *his*; Zavrius, the young man, not Zavrius, the prince.

He jerked his head up and called out, "Fahsi?"

Distantly, the sound of footsteps returned to the room, and as the servant approached, Zavrius furiously scribbled his own reply.

"Yes, my prince?"

"If you happen to remember how this note appeared on my tray, would you kindly return this reply?" He held the note aloft.

"Of course, my prince," said Fahsi, sounding exhausted and bored by the request. But as she took the note and left the room, Zavrius saw a small smile appear on her lips.

He looked down at Balen's note and pressed it to his nose,

breathing in the ink and the scent of the paper, hoping he might catch a note of Balen's scent pressed into the grooves of the parchment. He couldn't, but it didn't matter. This bit of paper felt about as important to him as his own royal title. Like a talisman, he folded it back up and put it in his pocket.

Night could not come soon enough.

TWENTY

Zavrius found himself too excited to eat his dinner. He used the excuse of exhaustion and slipped away, claiming he'd be retiring early. A silly farce and not needed—he could wander into the gardens if he pleased. But since his expedition, he knew both Arasne and his siblings were interested in his comings and goings, and he wanted this moment with Balen—whatever it was—to be perfect.

In his chamber, Zavrius dressed in a wine-colored tunic and watched as the light outside morphed from a blistering sunset to a deep purple, the slit of his window acting as a sliver of the outside world. Then, when he was confident he couldn't hear the comings and goings of his siblings, he opened the door a crack and slipped out of the Royal Apartments.

A crisp night air greeted him. The scent of orange blossom and jasmine chased the chill away; the stone colonnade still pulsed with trapped heat, and the smell of summer flowers made Zavrius feel warmer, even if the breeze raised goosebumps on his flesh. Laughter bubbled up from his right, and he heard Lysio's grating voice running excitedly through the night as he regaled some poor trapped nobles with some tale. Zavrius turned his attention ahead, where the gardens had submerged beneath a cool, blue-black shadow.

His heart skipped a beat as he walked, and as the light from the palace muted, the swathe of black night smothering it, both joy and calm settled over Zavrius' heart. He approached the gedrok, eyes straining as they adjusted to the night. Camouflaged by both his armor and the low light, Balen waited exactly where he had said he would be.

Zavrius stepped uncaringly and let his feet crush the grass beneath. Balen did not startle but turned, his smile wide and bright even in shadow. The moonlight shone down on him and made his teeth dazzle. Though night was a veil muffling Balen's beauty, Zavrius could still perceive the other man through it, and knew he wished to press himself close to the murk of evening to better see him.

"You came," Balen said brightly. Zavrius was reminded of Balen repeating his words in the great hall. *You came to get me?* All surprised, inflection high. Now, those words again, said differently. Resonant, certain—not surprised Zavrius had shown up, but glad for it.

How could I stay away? Zavrius wanted to say. *Don't you feel it in your blood the same as me? The pull of ichor tugging my heart towards yours?*

"Fourth and fifth." Zavrius pointed to the ribs on either side of him. "You were very specific."

"It's where the heart would be," Balen said as Zavrius jolted to a stop beside him. "Where you now stand."

You're my heart, he thought. He did not say, out of fear of sounding stupid—of being too hasty with excessive sentimentality or romance.

He ended up saying those words, he supposed, in a different way. He walked close to Balen, stood on the tips of his toes, and raised a hand to gently guide Balen's face closer so he could press their lips together. Zavrius aimed for a chaste greeting, but as per usual, he misaimed rather terribly. He was off-balance, ungraceful. Three seconds on the tips of his toes and he was tilting far too forward, and then crashing into Balen's chest. They staggered back together, Balen laughing over Zavrius' lips but not pulling away. The gedrok's ribs supported them, and Balen kissed him feverishly, hands roaming—hands *searching*, without any of the paladin's usual restraint. One palm went down Zavrius' back and cupped the firm rise of his arse, and that was what made Zavrius pull away with a huff of surprise. He panted, out of breath, and laughed a little.

"I missed you," he said unthinkingly.

Balen dragged that same wandering palm up to rest on Zavrius' cheek. "I've missed you, too."

Zavrius had the strange urge to cry out at the way Balen looked at him. It was as if his body hadn't been made to contain this kind of emotion. The strength of it—a vibrating force of excitement, desire, attraction, and *joy*—threatened to split the very seams of Zavrius' skin. It felt at once violent and delicate, a thriving tree with tiny, frail flowers sprouting from its many limbs, with roots far too deep to be contained by Zavrius' lithe form. He dug his fingers into the paladin's pauldrons and tried to keep a giddy smile from his face.

Come to my bedchamber tonight, Zavrius almost blurted out. Sense made him stop, made him consider. Balen stroked his face and leaned down, planting a soft kiss on Zavrius' forehead.

"Sit and talk with me for a while," Balen said. He took Zavrius' hand and guided him to the central grassy plane protected by the gedrok's ribcage. They sat together on the cool grass, facing one another, Zavrius' knees pressed against Balen's greaves.

"You're delaying giving me my gift," Zavrius said, "which, to be clear, is the only reason I'm here."

Balen snorted. "I am delaying giving you your gift," he said, "because I know it's the only reason you're here."

"Ah. So this is entrapment."

"You trapped me first."

"In sword lessons?" Zavrius rolled his eyes.

"In something else," Balen said, sounding cagey. He leaned back onto his hands and waved vaguely in the air. "Talk to me, my prince."

So Zavrius did. They caught each other up on their weeks, and Zavrius craned forward with interest even when Balen's tales were slow, about his recovery or his training or the strange dreams that the salve had given him. By the end of their chat, nearly an hour had passed, and Zavrius had shifted so his legs were slung over the tops of Balen's thighs, their bodies close. If not for the damned armor, Zavrius might have been bold enough to press a hand to Balen's chest. To feel the race of that man's heart, the warmth of his flesh. Perhaps he would even skim his hand lower, feel the small bump of a nipple, slip a daring hand around Balen's waist.

Zavrius cleared his throat, prompting Balen to glance down at him; a simple ruse that made it easy for Zavrius to reach up and kiss him. Balen's hands laced in Zavrius' hair, and he had no qualms about wrapping his arm around Zavrius' waist, shifting them until they were lying back in the grass.

But Balen's forearm, clearly meant to keep Zavrius close as he went horizontal, was unfortunately caged in armor. "Ow," Zavrius grunted as one of those bony extrusions stabbed his lower back. He rolled awkwardly so Balen could free the offending arm and then lay back onto the cool grass, raising his arms to cushion his head. "Now that you've stabbed me, I definitely deserve my gift."

Balen laughed, hand disappearing to his hip where he fished

something free. "I suppose that much is true. In fact, I have something that might assist in future."

Zavrius' mind went wild at that, courting several stabbing euphemisms with his excitable youthful brain. But Balen only pulled away and sat up, holding out his hand to lift Zavrius upright, too. Zavrius wordlessly took it.

"Close your eyes. Put out your hands."

Zavrius did. He waited eagerly. Promptly, something cold and well-weighted pressed into his palm.

"Now open."

Zavrius blinked his eyes open but didn't know what he was looking at. It looked almost like a dagger. The hilt certainly followed Zavrius' expectations for a dagger, with a hilt and a guard, though that was where similarities shifted. The blade was made of a thick steel, and deep serrations ran evenly up one side, like the barbed teeth of some animal.

"I don't understand," Zavrius murmured, raising the thing high and turning it over in his hands.

Balen shifted, placing his hand on Zavrius' forearm. "Swap hands," he directed, and Zavrius shifted the thing to his left.

"It's called a swordbreaker," Balen said. "Imagine a weapon is coming towards you." He pulled at Zavrius' arm until the prince's wrist naturally flexed inward to the left, which sent the swordbreaker at an angle. Zavrius imagined a blade coming towards him, the thin point directed at his face. "You catch it," Balen said, jerking Zavrius' arm upright. Zavrius saw what would happen in his mind's eye, the thin blade slotting between one of those serrated grooves. "And then you've broken his attack. If you turn the sword towards yourself," and Zavrius rolled his wrist back to his body until the swordbreaker's serrated edges were facing back towards him, "any caught blade would be pulled forward. Very few swordsmen would let go, too."

"So I can drag them closer. Get in with a short sword or a dagger."

"Yes," Balen said. His breath warmed the side of Zavrius' neck.

"It's beautiful," Zavrius said. "Beautifully deadly."

"Like yourself."

Zavrius snorted and flashed him a look from beneath his brows, though his snort wasn't wholly derivative. That compliment had landed well. Balen's tongue was its own kind of blade, though Zavrius doubted there was little he could do that would break the paladin's attacks.

"Why this, though?

"Well, you're a good fighter, Zav. You have all the right instincts. I don't understand why you never pursued it."

"Because that's what I was told. All my life. I'm the family disappointment, remember?"

Silence swallowed all sound. Zavrius realized slowly he'd never quite explained the mess of his childhood to Balen of Westgar. The other man looked curious, though he quickly stifled that interest. Zavrius could see the question resting on his lips, Balen's body stiff as he fought ingrained lessons and a curious urge. He wanted to know.

Zavrius sighed and ran his thumb over the swordbreaker. What had Balen said to him all those weeks ago? *It would be quite difficult to get your father's opinion of you now.*

"I know you've heard the rumors about me. Where do you think they all started?" When Balen didn't reply, Zavrius filled in the quiet. "I was not good at swordplay as a child. I wasn't *good* at any physical display, and for my father, that made me about as useful as a dead mouse. You knew that much already, but maybe I. . .I don't know, I'm not conveying the extent of it particularly well. His fury was. . ." A memory reared up, and Zavrius flinched away in horror, his body remembering a blow and the resulting pain. Swallowing hard, Zavrius pushed through. "It became easier to lean into everything he hated than to try to impress him. So I stopped trying. My mother, at least, embraced me, even if it meant I was flamboyant, and musical, and wasteful with my days."

Briefly, he imagined if he'd been born in any other position. If he had been in Theo's place, born first—nothing would have stopped Sirellius' fury or his rancor. Any chance of joy or happiness or love would have been squandered. *It's the only thing I'm grateful to Theo for.* Being born last had been a great boon to Zavrius.

"Easier to fail," Balen surmised. The paladin tilted his head. "I know the feeling well."

He could have been talking about anything. Zavrius heard those words and thought: *I'd rather you never love me than for you to one day leave me.*

A thought that seemed to come from nowhere.

"But you don't believe any of that now, do you?" Balen asked, edging closer. He brushed the hair away from Zavrius' cheek, and Zavrius leaned in instinctively to the kiss moments before Balen pressed his lips against the skin. "You know you're brilliant."

"I do know that," Zavrius said and meant it. "I am witty, and pretty, and the greatest musician to ever live"—because sometimes hyperbole was the best armor—"but I also know that I am eccentric, that rumors abound, that my life at court—or my life in general—may be subject to people who have spent all their lives hating me."

"What? What do you mean?"

Balen's stare bore a hole in the side of Zavrius' head. He shouldn't have said anything. He shouldn't have said what he did, at least. Zavrius wet his lips and tried for a laugh. "Oh, well. I'm merely musing about the future, dear Balen. What might happen when Theo takes the throne."

He didn't say the quiet part out loud, but Balen heard it anyway.

The paladin drew back, his eyes wide. "I won't let that happen to you."

"When you're Theo's lapdog?" Zavrius asked. "By the bones, he's cruel enough that he'd probably order you to do the job."

A new tension wafted between them. Shit. Zavrius didn't want to be speaking about this. He wanted to go back moments earlier and kiss Balen once more.

"Let's. . .let's speak about something lighter," Zavrius murmured.

But Balen would not be swayed. He reached out, thumb and forefinger firm on Zavrius' chin, and dragged the prince's face towards his own. Despite the dark, Zavrius could see the severity of Balen's gaze.

"I won't let that happen to you," Balen said again, "because I love you."

A breath. A sharp snap of cold air rushing over Zavrius' body. He briefly heard nothing but a sharp ringing tone in his ears, and then the dull echo of his heartbeat racing and his own shuddering breaths. Distantly, he heard a crack of laughter echo out through the garden, and he snapped around to stare off in the direction of the sound and the palace lights. Balen's hand drew away.

Then he turned back to Balen. "What?"

If Balen was disturbed by how long it had taken Zavrius to reply, he didn't show it. Granted, Zavrius could see only the vague smudge of expression on the paladin's face, and likely, a lot of nuances were lost in the dark. But overall, Balen had a pleasant, if expectant, look on his face, like a well-trained puppy waiting for its treat.

"You love me?" Zavrius said again. Everything awful they'd just been speaking about vanished.

What was the emotion he felt? He couldn't name it, couldn't

pin it down to comprehend it. Fear? Joy? His own burning love for the man before him? He found it too difficult to keep searching Balen's face and stared down at the grass instead.

Gedroks, he *did* love Balen, didn't he? There was a horror in that realization, a great shuddering vulnerability as if his stomach was splitting open. What had love ever done for him except hurt? Or worse: who had ever loved Zavrius unconditionally? He found himself wondering what the extent of Balen's love would be, and a bit of prophecy came to him then, or a warning dredged from the depths of his experience: *this is going to hurt.*

Trusting a lover not to harm him felt about as silly as trusting his siblings not to mock him. Or Theo not to end his life as soon as he had the power to. But what else could Zavrius do with this emotion growing tumorous in his chest? He could cut it out, or he could nurture it, accepting the likelihood it would hurt him in the end and choosing it anyway.

He looked up at Balen. That calm exterior had cracked slightly. Fear glinted in Balen's eye, illuminated by a ray of moonlight hitting his face and gorget just so. The paladin leaned forward and slipped his finger through Zavrius' on the grass. "You don't have to. . .repeat it. You don't even have to feel it. Perhaps I shouldn't have. . .*said* anything. But I—"

"I love you, too."

It came out a small and broken thing, a baby bird with a wounded wing. Zavrius wanted to cry when he said it, terrified of whatever covenant he had just made. But then he met Balen's eye and was met with a wide, beaming smile—and that joy was infectious.

Zavrius laughed. His hands rushed out and grabbed at Balen's hair. The other man knocked their foreheads together, his breath rushing out in a great gale of an exhale, relief and happiness lifting them both off their feet and onto their backs. Balen kissed him, and Zavrius let the swordbreaker slip from his grasp, tangling his fingers through Balen's hair and tugging on the strands. Balen returned the touch with more force. A spark of slight pain teased at Zavrius' scalp, the roots straining.

"Ah," he said, open-mouthed, panting hard. He craned his neck high. Balen's gaze flickered to the exposed line of his neck and moved there immediately. He kissed Zavrius' neck, grip softening in Zavrius' hair, and warmth began to twitch throughout the prince's body. Nothing else mattered, suddenly—or rather, the intensity of his desire shoved all his concerns away.

At the end of the day, beneath his nerves and his worries, there was this moment between them. After it passed, perhaps there would be dozens, hundreds, *thousands* of moments they could share together. But Zavrius would not hope for it. He would take what was offered to him.

"Come to my chamber," he whispered.

Balen pulled away abruptly, head jerking up to scan Zavrius' face.

"I don't know what I'm doing," Zavrius said. "I've never. . .*done* this."

He didn't elaborate, too embarrassed to speak plainly. Balen, though, was bolder.

"Never," he began, hand sliding down Zavrius' tunic, then lower, then— Zavrius gasped sharply as Balen said, "Done this?"

Zavrius shook his head in a rush as heat traveled to his groin. He could feel the pressure of Balen's hand on him, and that much connection was enough to stir him.

Zavrius shook his head. Would Balen mind that he was inexperienced? Was it a burden to bestow such knowledge upon a prince? When Zavrius strained, he could see surprise writ on Balen's face.

"You thought I had?"

Balen said nothing; Zavrius had trapped him unkindly. He could lie and say no, or he could say yes—yes, he believed

Zavrius to engage freely in trysts and tumbles, as the rumors said. So Zavrius saved him, "I hope there is no pressure. Regarding my title, I mean; I don't—"

"Any other man would think it a point of pride to be a prince's first."

Zavrius paused. "And you?"

"A privilege. To be *Zavrius'* first." He said it softly as if embarrassed by the sentiment. Balen glanced away. "I want to—if you want me to."

He did, very much so, even as his stomach burned with nerves and a pre-emptive shame; he had never loved like this and never shown anyone his body.

"H-have you?" Zavrius whispered. It was a bid for connection. Part of him hoped Balen said no, just so Zavrius could take comfort in the knowledge of their shared floundering.

Balen paused, a stiffness settling over his face and limbs. "I. . .have," he whispered carefully, almost apologetically. "Is that—"

"At least one of us knows what to do, then," Zavrius said quickly. He didn't want to linger on that knowledge. A ball of jealousy had appeared in his throat, even as his logic tried to swallow it. How could he be jealous, in the end, when Balen wanted *him* now?

Balen sat him and dragged Zavrius with him. He kissed Zavrius' cheek, then his lips whispering "We don't have to. . .do everything. We can take it slow."

Zavrius flushed despite himself, angry that he didn't understand what 'everything' entailed or what 'taking it slow' meant. He said, "All I know is that I'd rather you had fewer clothes on right now," and meant it.

Balen laughed, the sound sweet and high. His fingers slipped beneath Zavrius' chin and made their eyes meet. "You are so good at giving orders, my prince. Are you good at taking them?"

If Zavrius had been blushing before, he practically combusted then. A giddy thrill filled him: how wondrous it would be to be told what to do, not from the Queen or his elder siblings, but by someone meant to be beneath him on the hierarchy. Even if Zavrius felt Balen to be on his level, his body shivered with the impermissible nature of their tryst. Would it be wrong for a prince to stand naked and embarrassed before a paladin? Would it be improper to go down on his knees, to take the other man in his mouth; to service him, as he had seen whores do at the wildest Uslethian parties, as he himself had dreamt about doing, but never dared practice?

He pressed himself closer, opening his mouth against the paladin's lips, and said, "Shall we find out?"

Twenty-One

They ran together hand in hand, laughing until they reached the sobering light of the palace and broke apart. Zavrius led the way, heart racing, and Balen trailed behind. Two guards stood by the Royal Apartments but gladly slinked away when Zavrius relieved them. A quick canvas inside, and then he reached out for Balen's hand, dragging him into the wing and down the hall to his chambers before anyone saw.

A servant had been in at some point to light the lamps. A great pile of clothing that had previously been strewn across the floor now sat neatly folded on the corner chair. Zavrius turned and bolted his door, his breathing coming in short, and he had to dig deep for the courage to turn and face Balen in the center of his room.

"We should at least be on equal footing," Zavrius said. "Remove your armor."

Balen dipped his head, a small smile pulling at his lips. He raised a hand to the hidden seams of his cuirass and whispered, "As you wish."

One by one, those beautiful pieces of armor clattered to the floor. Zavrius watched transfixed as Balen lost his manufactured bulk; it was like a flower losing its petals until only the bud remained, except Zavrius found the armor-free sight of Balen of Westgar far more beautiful.

"There." Zavrius sounded more confident than he felt. He took Balen in. The other man stood tall and broad, and he wore that white undershirt again, sporting dangerously translucent patches where sweat had thinned it. His breeches were a deep olive green, cinched around his hips and tight in the thighs—and, well, another place—and Zavrius flushed deeply at how fitting they were. He slipped out of his shoes and stood barefooted on the carpet, and Balen followed suit, small smile never leaving his lips.

Now what?

All the ease that came with self-pleasure, the familiarity, and the promise of release twisted away from Zavrius now. Shame and nerves curled up into his mind in its place and made his motions uncertain. He knew he wanted to defile Balen, to be defiled by him. He knew he wanted to look up into the young man's eyes and *see* him, to whisper *I love you* as Balen touched him for the first time.

Balen saw the question on his face and stepped forward. Wordlessly, he led them both to the bed, guiding Zavrius to lay down—though he did not clamber on top, instead sliding his body next to Zavrius. He leaned forward, and Zavrius' mouth opened under his. Each kiss stole thoughts and sense from Zavrius' mind; he could not think, and instinct moved his body closer to Balen's until they were pressed close and sharing in each other's warmth. Balen grew firm, swelling with the kiss, and pulled Zavrius to him, barely leaving room for the prince to slip his hand down to cup over Balen's breeches. Slowly, Balen lifted his hips toward Zavrius' touch. His breath came in short. The lamp glowed across his skin, revealing the pink flush to his cheeks and the upturned curve to his eyebrows that betrayed his pleasure. Then Balen surged forward so Zavrius went flat on his back, and his fingers moved deftly beneath the prince's soft tunic, hand loosening the tie until it spilled open and revealed Zavrius' chest.

Zavrius' body grew taut like a bowstring. He couldn't understand how easily Balen disarmed him: how, under his gaze, that bowstring tied around Zavrius' lungs and was pulled back. He didn't dare to breathe; or rather, found that he couldn't. He was immobilized beneath Balen's broad body and completely forgot himself. Forgot how grateful he was for the cover of night and the privacy of a locked door forgot to feel nervous, or shame, or any kind of fear. Zavrius, splayed and vulnerable beneath another man, felt *seen*. And how wonderful the feeling was.

Zavrius looked down at himself, unable to stop the quickened pace of his breathing. Balen's callous hand dragged down the supple skin, thumb grazing a nipple, appreciative moan airy as it left his throat.

"I love you," Balen whispered. "You're beautiful, Zavrius. I love you."

Zavrius' breath caught, the flush intense as it raced up his chest and burned onto his cheeks. He reached, and Balen tilted down so Zavrius' hand could skim through his hair. The paladin pushed into the palm of the prince's hand like an eager cat, and all the thrill in Zavrius' body became a quiet desire.

"I love you, too," he whispered. Excitement came, a dull roar in his ears. "Touch me."

Balen's eyes flared to life, and then Zavrius could hear his own heart pounding in his chest. He knew what words the paladin would speak before he said them. Balen's mouth cracked open, voice purring as he asked, "Is that an order?"

"Yes." Zavrius didn't hesitate, nor did he elaborate. But Balen needed no further prompting.

Zavrius' belly trembled as Balen's hand moved over it and then lower, disappearing beneath the band of his trousers. When

Balen's warm fingers found him and squeezed, Zavrius gasped. He had been aching badly; the touch was like a poultice, cool water on a burn. He raised his hips. Balen used the opportunity, taking his other hand and pulling Zavrius' trousers down over his thighs. Wordlessly, Zavrius nodded to Balen, and the paladin followed suit, sitting upright to strip himself free. They were naked together, breathing fast, eyes wandering over the other's body. Fiery embarrassment tried to take control, but when Balen leaned down and kissed him, when Balen said, "You really are so beautiful," when he searched Zavrius' eyes for permission and moved his head back to the crook of Zavrius' neck, kissing there as his hand stroked gently down to that burning part of Zavrius' body, every anxious thought vanished. A great love of life filled him, vicious in its strength. This moment could have lasted forever, and Zavrius would have been grateful.

Balen twisted them so they were lying side by side, their hands wrapped around the place of each other's pleasure. With silent signals, they worked each other and never looked away. Zavrius watched Balen keenly, searching his face, studying him, until the rhythm and pressure he enjoyed became obvious things. Quickly, though, did Zavrius' own pleasure build. He had never had another hand on him like this; he had to fight his body, desperate to stretch the moment out as long as he could manage. Balen's relentless pace gave him no rest, and Zavrius matched it, over-eager. He heard the catch in Balen's breath, saw the jump of the other man's brows. A distant knowledge settled on him: Balen was close, as close as he was, but Zavrius's awareness drifted as pleasure consumed his body, the heat burning shame away, scalding him down to his purest form.

"Look at me," Zavrius found himself saying as Balen's eyes rolled close. And when their eyes met, Zavrius could hold on no longer. The intensity of the paladin's gaze ripped through him, and the feeling gathered and gathered in Zavrius' belly until he cried out. He arched as the feeling flowered in him, moan drifting to a faint whine. He must have stopped moving because he opened his eyes to find Balen finishing himself, eyes squeezed shut and flush sunset-red over the hills of his cheeks. Balen's mouth opened, and Zavrius leaned forward to steal the sound from his tongue. He swallowed the moan and felt the warmth spurt onto his belly and then lay together, panting in a tangle of limbs.

Drowsiness overtook Zavrius, but he fought the urge to fade. He wanted to look at Balen forever, to speak to him, to sing, to grip him hard, and make sure he never left.

Balen's eyes were still closed. He shifted, rolling onto his back. His brows had crashed together into a frown that reawakened Zavrius' fear. Was that regret? Fear? Now the fog of orgasm had cleared, did Balen wish he'd never done that? Sweat rapidly cooled on the small of Zavrius' back and chilled him.

Tentatively, he placed a hand on Balen's chest, and almost instantly the other man snatched it up with both of his like the prince was some great treasure. He still hadn't opened his eyes but he tugged Zavrius close. Zavrius rolled into him like a pill bug, letting Balen's arms form a protective shell. The paladin panted above him. Their bodies met, warm and sweaty, and Zavrius only wriggled closer. Balen kissed his forehead, then pulled back just enough to cup his face and look at him. The paladin's eyes were only slightly parted; Zavrius recognized the expression as that heavy, pleasured exhaustion his fear had chased away.

"You," he said, and nothing more. *You* like an exaltation, said hopefully. Said with wonder. *You.* A bashful smile erupted on Zavrius' face, and he pressed closer, running his fingers up and down Balen's back.

"You," he said back, and with that quiet understanding, they kissed gently and fell almost immediately into a deep sleep.

Zavrius awoke the next morning feeling warm, sated, whole. Sunlight split through those high windows and cast sharp planes of light across the room. Half of Balen's back had gone white with the glow, and Zavrius grew transfixed on the other man's nakedness, which felt deliciously taboo to see now in the light. It was like opening a clamshell and finding a pearl inside; Balen's pale body the pearl, so usually encased by the armor. He reached out and touched a hand to Balen's back. The other man immediately stirred—no doubt light sleeping was trained in the paladins, and Balen more so given the injury he'd received in the Ashmons —and turned to face him, one eye cracked as if to check it was really Zavrius. Seemingly satisfied, Balen exhaled and closed his eyes again, swinging one heavy arm over Zavrius' waist. The pressure there was good. For what might have been an hour or might have been mere minutes, Zavrius breathed against the crook of Balen's neck, relishing the warmth of the embrace.

"Turn over," Balen mumbled eventually, and Zavrius did, relishing the feeling of being held so intimately, safe in the paladin's arms. Balen moved close enough that Zavrius could barely feel the seam between their two forms, and that closeness meant he could feel that Balen was hard, as he was; this new position meant Balen could raise his hips and touch his erection against Zavrius' skin, one experimental rub between the cleft of Zavrius' ass. He stiffened, waiting—but Balen made no further move, and Zavrius found he liked that: liked Balen's bid for lazy intimacy over a repeat of last night. A giddiness rumbled in Zavrius' chest: Balen was taking his time, and it allowed Zavrius the ability to fantasize about many mornings like this; it allowed him to muse on how this might mean Balen intended to touch him again and often. Perhaps so often, the paladin need not rush to touch Zavrius now.

Encased and safe, they fell in and out of a dozing sleep until Balen bolted upright in a panic and stared out the window, trying to gauge the height of the sun. Zavrius jolted beside him and craned back to stare at the man's tense jaw. But Balen squinted and sighed with great relief. His whole body was unwound, his lean body revealing every tensed muscle relaxing before he collapsed back beside Zavrius.

"It's early," he said, rubbing at his face. "By the bones, I'm so well rested that I thought I'd slept in."

Zavrius made a happy noise at that. *My work has paid off*, or, *there are benefits to sleeping with a prince*—two quips he didn't voice. He slipped close and kissed Balen gently. "I'm glad you slept well."

"Your doing."

Ah—despite his best attempts, Zavrius' ego swelled up at the indirect praise. He knocked his head close to Balen, hiding his smile and tinge of a flush on his cheeks. "*Our* doing, I think. There were two hands at work last night."

"Well, a handy hand you have," Balen said. He spoke over Zavrius' groan, hand lacing in the prince's hair. "A natural, I'd say."

Zavrius waved the accused hand in Balen's face. "That hand has had a whole lot of practice, I'm afraid."

"Then try your left next time."

"Perhaps I'll use more than hands, " Zavrius said, swelling with glee at the glint that stirred in Balen's eyes.

The paladin surged up to take Zavrius in a kiss, twisting their bodies with ease and flipping the pair of them. Zavrius crashed back into the pillow with a nervous, excited laugh, and Balen's hands laced through his. The paladin dragged both their arms above Zavrius' head. Stretched out like that, Balen had little leverage; he laid on top of Zavrius, the velvet smooth skin of his inner thigh warm against Zavrius' upper thigh.

"Stay," Zavrius said as the kiss began to slow. He could sense the shift. Balen's body had grown taut. Obligation was an invisible thread tugging Balen out of the prince's bed, and Balen would have to follow sooner or later. Zavrius tried his luck, anyway, reaching up to tuck a strand of stray hair behind Balen's ear. "Stay."

"You know I want to." The apology was obvious in those words, and before Zavrius could think of some excuse to keep Balen beside him, the paladin had grunted and stood. Zavrius sat up and let the sheet pool just beneath his navel. Balen stole a look, eyes hungry when they reached Zavrius' face. But he did not turn around, just set about retrieving both clothes and armor from where they'd been discarded the previous night.

Zavrius savored his naked form, enjoying how he could stare openly as the other man dressed. He ate the scene up with desire. The muscles in Balen's back rolled and stretched with every movement, the flesh there lean enough to reveal all to Zavrius. When he bent over, Balen's spine popped up, knobby heads revealing themselves like fish in coral—the ocean making itself known in Balen's body once more. The mundanity of the activity did nothing to dispel the beauty Zavrius saw in it. Balen drew those tight breeches over himself, and Zavrius could see the firm glute and thick thigh somehow accentuated. The seams of Balen's undershirt replaced the well-defined serratus, but Zavrius fancied he could still see the fan-shaped reach of muscle beneath it. Even as Balen began to replace his armor, encasing himself again in that hard shell, covering the pearl of his naked beauty, Zavrius' opinion didn't change. He could have been sweat-covered, dirt-covered, gore-covered. He could dress only in sacks. None of it would matter. Balen's beauty somehow went beyond the physical.

"When can I see you next?" Balen asked, not turning around.

Now. This afternoon. Every day for the rest of our lives. Eagerness leaped to the forefront of Zavrius' mind, but he showed none of his obsession. He leaned back against the pillow. "How busy are you in this coming week?"

Balen clicked his tongue. For a moment that, and the rustling of fabric as he dressed were the only sounds. "Hard to say."

Something in his voice caught as if on a burr in Zavrius' mind. He sat up straight again, peering at Balen as if staring long enough might reveal the truth to him. "You aren't telling me something."

Balen glanced back now, feigning confusion. He was a poor liar. Caution was writ all over his face. "No, I—"

"You were just in my bed," Zavrius said quietly and hoped those words said enough.

Balen deflated. When he sealed the final clasp of his cuirass, he turned around. The armor transformed him, but Zavrius felt a sudden distance between them. It wasn't just this impenetrable suit that made him feel this way.

Zavrius stood. He didn't care that he was naked. The way Balen's eyes dropped down his form and lingered low made Zavrius feel as if he were wearing his own suit of armor, too.

"Balen," he said, voice tense.

Balen visibly swallowed. "It's. . .your brother." He couldn't keep his eyes on Zavrius. They kept drifting away on a sea of guilt. "Prince Theo's interest is stronger than ever."

"In you?" It would be one thing if Theo merely wanted to graze through the offerings of the Gifted Paladins, but if he'd taken an interest. . .

"In me." Balen looked sheepish. He met Zavrius' gaze slowly. "Please don't think the worst of me if I try to prove myself to him. I believe you, about his nature. I do. But I—"

"But you were ten years old when you were brought here, and you believe in my family, and you want your own honor. I'm not so stone-hearted not to realize that," Zavrius said. He clutched his arm, feeling the idiocy of his nakedness now.

Balen closed the distance and pulled him closer. The cool of the armor wafted off the plate. "You are the only one I love," Balen said.

Zavrius longed for him to say more; he wanted the safety of a thousand words, Balen's intentions written plainly out before him. He wanted Balen to prophesize their future, to say: *us? Oh, we last forever. There is no end to us*. Instead, Zavrius floundered for a security he intrinsically doubted was there. Theirs was not a safe love; it couldn't be by its very nature, and he had known that going into it. So why was he so shaken now?

"Don't fall in love with Theo," Zavrius said. He was only half joking. Balen laughed loud, and Zavrius smiled at the sound, but his gut churned.

"How could I when I'm looking at you?"

Balen leaned down, and they kissed. He pulled away and looked at Zavrius with soft eyes. "I do not regret last night," he said.

Zavrius' heart jolted. He'd been unaware that had even been a worry of his until relief relaxed him. "Neither do I."

Balen's hands wrapped around Zavrius' waist. He felt small standing there with Balen's armored form twice the width of his body, but it was not an unwelcome feeling.

"Kiss me again," Zavrius whispered, and Balen did, both hands gentle as they stroked his hips and his waist. Zavrius wanted to pull him back to bed, and Balen knew this—knew this because Zavrius' nakedness exposed so much of him. Teasingly, the paladin leaned down and cupped between Zavrius' thighs— just briefly, just enough pressure for Zavrius to open his mouth in a gentle gasp.

Balen made a low, amused noise and kissed his cheek. When they pulled away, the paladin slipped his hand from Zavrius first and then his body out of the door.

"I love you," he whispered, poised on the edge of the threshold.

"I love you, too," Zavrius said, and he wished he could paint the moments in his mind so he might forever keep the image of Balen of Westgar grinning at him like that at the edge of his bedroom.

Zavrius stood in the center of the room, staring after him, feeling foolish for a good minute before he wrenched a throw from the bed and wrapped himself in it. He sat back on the bed and curled over himself. He had two emotions in him: joy at the previous night and fear that he'd just begun to play a very dangerous game.

Talk of his brother had soured the morning. Falling in love with Theo didn't have to mean romance. But the allure of power, the promise of being raised up beyond one's station—Zavrius could only imagine how thrilling that desire would be. If Theo told Balen he would be Prime and the only thing he had to do was never speak to Zavrius again, would he do it?

Don't be ridiculous.

Logic scrambled up from the precipice in Zavrius' mind and helped to beat back this manifestation of his insecurity. He could not cast judgment on a version of Balen that existed only in his mind. Nor should he let his worry cloud what had transpired last night: The first bit of desire consummated so wholly in his life.

So Zavrius lay there another half hour or more, merely ruminating on how Balen had touched him.

Twenty-Two

Zavrius' fears went unanswered. Instead, every passing day served as proof of a growing devotion; all the nerves in Zavrius were slowly put to rest, and his body learned to love openly. He had grown so used to loving in silence, to having crushes grow, bloom, and decay in secret, that he transformed noticeably over the next few months.

Arasne noticed first, as mothers often do. Zavrius had the skin of a man in love, warmth that made him glow from the inside. It put him in stark contrast to her own complexion, which grew more pallid the longer her sickness consumed her. But soon, it was noticeable to all others, too. Petra raised a brow; Lestr commented that Zavrius looked *'stronger'*. His siblings appeared somewhat more wary of him, like for years Zavrius had been translucent, or a shadow, and only now had become corporeal.

He didn't like to put too much stock in that thought—that someone else could bolster him so noticeably. But the truth was, there were mornings he woke up and looked at himself and realized all the work of his training had paid off, and muscle had begun to harden his soft edges. He noticed his eyes sparkled, that he had the energy to wake willingly in the early morning; it wasn't so much *Balen* as what loving Balen meant. That Zavrius could be himself and be happy. Zavrius could be himself and *thrive*.

They did not have as much time as he would have liked. Sometimes, it was as little as once a week, a stolen kiss in the dead of night. Other weeks were filled with hours of languid kissing, of Zavrius sneaking Balen into his quarters, or joining him in the gardens for dangerous rendezvous. Every time they went to each other, enjoyed each other, it felt like the first time. No matter the nature of the touch, nor what part of the body, Zavrius' heart would leap at the thrill of it, of the joy, a pre-emptive ecstasy coursing through his blood. Balen would say, "You are beautiful," and Zavrius would open for him, blossoming like a flower coaxed out of hiding by the weather.

So, in this way, Zavrius began to watch Balen train, even though it felt at times like he watched his own end in the making. The never-ending ache of love was this: loving Balen felt inevitable, and Theo's influence felt inevitable, too. For months, Zavrius had managed to skirt Theo's ire, and briefly, Zavrius had thought that Theo had noticed his strength, too, that seeing the browned skin bulge over slight muscle had put his brother's fears at rest. Finally, Zavrius was becoming someone worthy of the Dued Vuuthrik name.

Oh, to be so naïve.

Zavrius should have known. Perhaps he did know, and his mind hid the truth from him. Theo Dued Vuuthrik did not hate Zavrius entirely because of what he looked like. It was who he was that offended him. Indulging in love, courting a paladin, playing his music, idling in his free time—all of it was a great offense to the thrill of a country at war, the vision Sirellius had been preparing his children for. Zavrius represented the great antithesis of their father's hopes and dreams for his children, and Theo's punishment would be grand.

Zavrius knew this. He had known it his whole life. Why, then, did it come as a surprise?

The day was tepid, but the wind was sharp. Zavrius leaned up against the Forge, trying to warm himself on the stone before the afternoon breeze sapped it all away. He drew his cloak tightly around himself, but it whipped wildly about his legs anyway, threatening to blow him away completely. He doubted he would last out here for long. Already, the cold had struck his ears, and a low headache began to pulse in his temples.

Watching Balen made things easier, of course. It was the only reason he was here.

Balen's training had taken on a new form—or rather, a more precise form. There were more skirmishes, more group fighting, one against many as if they were competing in a tournament or surviving the odds in a real battle. But Zavrius knew the select few paladins who spent hours every week attacking each other's bodies with wooden sticks were doing it to harden both their flesh and their mind in the pursuit of a larger goal.

This was made all the clearer by the presence of Prime Paladin Hisud. She lurked to the side and said very little, reporting her observations to Lestr entirely, but her being there at all equaled a large sign that read: *Train here for a chance at being Prime Paladin. Train here to take my place.*

Zavrius didn't like seeing her. She unnerved him; first for her looks and her strength, and then because of *how* she lurked. She had a shadow quality about her, as if she wasn't quite meant to be seen in daylight. Zavrius supposed he hadn't seen much of her lately at all. Namely, though, part of Zavrius felt that her indulging in this training meant she thought the Queen's reign was close to its end.

That Arasne was close to death.

In the grand context of a dynasty, 'close to death' could mean anything from a single breath to several years. Zavrius had to hope it was years—if not for the love of his mother, then for his own hide. No matter where Arasne stood on the precipice to death, he couldn't fault anyone here for their interest in what came next. But he could marinate in his bitterness alone.

Theo's presence left a sour taste in his mouth.

"Good, good," Theo was saying, clapping wildly as he walked beside Balen and two other paladins locked in a three-way fight. Balen's opponents bore down on him, driving him back. One tried to lock Balen's sword with her own; Balen's other opponent dove forward, reaching for Balen's wrist. A flurry of motion blurred, and Theo darted across Zavrius' vision, but in a second, Balen kicked one of his opponents down and danced away from the remaining standing paladin. His colleagues were calling out, occasionally clapping. Only Lestr, Hisud, and Zavrius were silent.

He loved Balen. Just watching him put his strained heart at ease.

When Arasne died, Zavrius would take the time to mourn. But he would go gleefully to the Prime Paladin tournament, and he would put aside his fear, and he would cheer for Balen of Westgar to win until his voice cracked from overuse.

Quicker than Zavrius thought possible, Balen threw the wooden blade of his sword over his shoulder so the pommel was raised and jammed the end into his opponent's head, stepping back to gain range and then jabbing forward into the exposed flesh above the gorget. His opponent dropped his weapon in a yield.

Zavrius pushed himself upright in thunderous applause. Pride swelled in his chest, and Balen heard him, perking up at the sound. The fierce look of joy on Balen's face surprised him—the force of that smile, the look in his eyes, put them both on a different plane of understanding.

"Break," Lestr called.

Balen dropped the wooden parry sword and extended his hand to his fallen comrade. The bested paladin took it, and only the smallest flicker of annoyance betrayed his otherwise smiling demeanor. Balen patted him on the back as he passed.

Zavrius waited with his arms crossed. Usually, Balen attracted a small crowd. The younger, greener paladins admired him and often wanted to tell him so, and some of the older ones could appreciate his raw skill. Many of the older paladins grouped together, Zavrius noticed, and if they could acknowledge Balen had something worth forging, they wouldn't admit it to his face. From afar, Zavrius watched Balen smile and chat with his fellows. He was breathing hard, still trying to catch his breath from the fight. Eventually, Balen found a way to excuse himself. At the smallest signal—a foot turned towards Zavrius or an obviously apologetic gesture—Zavrius would move. They did this often, and today was no different.

Zavrius walked out of the exposed field and back towards the palace to the right, where the colonnades stretched towards the outer wall. The left path led back towards the central atrium and the garden and was far more popular for visiting nobility or other Dued Vuuthrik spawn to lounge about. Zavrius had laid claim to this area. The gardens made him too vulnerable this time of day; the sun would betray them, Balen's armor a glinting beacon. But for a few stolen minutes, this always proved safe.

Zavrius weaved his way through the colonnades and turned again so he would be hidden from anyone looking from the field. He knocked his head back against the wall and closed his eyes, trying to convince his body to relax and soak up the sun before the cold night chased it away.

Impossible. His body reacted to this location as if Balen was already pressed up against him.

Zavrius had to fight the urge to peer around the corner and watch the other man slink towards him. He had to wait minutes for Balen to find his way here. His skin tickled. Several acts of betrayal were summoned from his mind, all of them heated thoughts, all of them involving Balen pressing close, mouth against Zavrius' neck, voice soft and sweet as his hands roamed— *Zavrius, control yourself.* He shifted, tried to shake the hot pull of desire that filled him. Zavrius buried the base of his palms against his eyes and breathed slowly.

"Are you ill?"

Zavrius jumped. Above him stood Balen, leaning with his arm stretched high over the prince's head. The flush on his cheeks was pink and blooming. Sweat had made his dark hair stringy, and he'd pushed it back in a way that opened up that beautiful face.

"How did you manage that?" Zavrius asked in wonderment. "Paladin armor is anything but stealthy."

Balen snorted. "I made no attempt to hide my approach. Which means you were distracted."

He stepped fully around the corner and didn't wait for Zavrius' response, which would have been *why, yes, I was.* He took the prince's lips with his own and breathed in so deeply that Zavrius felt part of his soul being sucked into Balen's lungs.

Zavrius could have conceivably kept quiet, and Balen would have continued kissing him like that, but he always loved words. He told Balen, "You were beautiful out there. Magnificent. You're doing so well. You looked—" he was breathless, flushed with desire, and Zavrius laughed at himself. "You looked so good you've made me a bumbling mess."

A low rumble emitted from Balen's chest. "Not nearly messy enough," he said. His armored thigh slipped between Zavrius' legs and pressed gently up.

He gave a sudden furtive look over Zavrius' shoulder, face draining of color. Zavrius spun, his body already icy with anticipatory fear.

A man and a woman clutched each other. Their eyes were buggy and large with alarm. Zavrius could barely see them through the blur of his own panic, but he knew they were nobility.

"You—can't," the woman squeaked. Her companion hastily shushed her, the grip on her forearm turning his brown knuckles ashy.

"F-forgive the interruption," he managed. He was afraid. Terrifically afraid. But not frightened enough to not share what they'd seen. Both bowed and dashed away, and Zavrius stared after them with his eyes straining, as if nothing bad would happen so long as he didn't blink. They'd come here for their own tryst, no doubt. Now, they were leaving rich with secrets that weren't their own—the best currency in court.

Above him, Balen was stiff. Zavrius craned to see the look in his eyes. Whole, undisturbed terror clouded those beautiful eyes. Zavrius hated his reaction, but he reached up and turned Balen's face towards him, hoping to dispel at least a fraction of that expression.

Balen stared at him and blinked rapidly. He tried to turn his head again, but Zavrius held him fast. "What can they do?" he chanced.

Zavrius didn't know. He squeezed his eyes shut and tried to think. What *could* they do? Spread the rumor?

What were rumors to a man like Zavrius?

"It's not my reputation I'm worried about," Zavrius whispered. "But if our relationship is public in this court, then. . ."

Balen had gone whiter. His expression twisted, eyes bulging as a vanguard of terrible possibility descended in his mind. He wheeled away from Zavrius. The loss hurt and the distance was suddenly insurmountable.

Don't, a voice said in Zavrius' mind, but the specifics weren't clear to him.

"Balen?"

"I have to. . ." he was backing away, staring back at the field. Balen cleared his throat. "I must go back to training. Can you. . .?"

He floundered. It was clear he didn't know what to ask for. Zavrius nodded. "I'll figure something out."

Zavrius even smiled then. He wanted Balen to be calm, if just to buy himself more time. But internally, fear poisoned his gut, and it pursued him even as he walked into the palace proper.

For the first day, it was fine. Then he heard the rumor whispered quickly beside him. Over the course of a week, he saw it take its toll. He watched Balen, watched how the man began to falter. Opponents he could usually best were now winning their matches quickly. And when Balen refused to see him one night to focus on his training, Zavrius understood that things had changed permanently.

The next morning, he watched Balen again, but the paladin spared not even a glance for Zavrius. Logic told Zavrius to breathe: Balen had never endured the ire of the court before. Not like this, not as an individual. More than that, he had to contend with the weight of rumors against Zavrius, too—everything rubbed off on his person. Zavrius could maintain grace for Balen in that context, couldn't he?

He left the training alone with his heart breaking.

What could he do? He knew better than any how quickly rumors spread in this place.

He could have gone to Petra, begged her to do something. But that woman collected information, and her form of quelling often involved death. So, in the end, there was only one place he could really go.

"What is it?"

Queen Arasne had admitted him immediately.

She had been feeling better and saw him in her study. After so long lying down, every time she left her room, she overdressed, and that day was no exception. She was in a gown of pressed black velvet, white ruffles showing at the skirt and the sleeves. The in-built corset pressed her torso into a flat, squarish shape. Her hair was pulled back out of her face, curls trapped in tight braids and wrapped in a crown-shape around her head. No servants were with her. They were entirely alone.

Perhaps that was why Zavrius felt safe enough to walk across the room and press himself into her arms.

She said nothing, hand fumbling over Zavrius' hair as he squeezed. When she returned the pressure, he released an appalling, pained noise that only made him bury his head miserably into the crook of his mother's neck.

"What's happened?"

He told her in sparing detail because it was far too late for embarrassment. When he was done, she was looking at him in a way that made him want to cry. Zavrius bit down on his tongue and blinked away his emotion.

"I've been a fool, haven't it?"

"You've had your fun," Arasne murmured. She retreated to her desk, where she lowered herself into the high-backed chair. Her voice was almost insolent—a strange word to describe a queen's manner, and yet Zavrius felt himself bristling.

"It is more than fun," he spat. "I love him."

Arasne glanced up at him. There was no anger in her eyes. "I know," she said. "That only makes it worse, though, in the end."

This wasn't what he'd wanted. Zavrius cast a desperate look back at the door. "Why are you doing this?"

Queen Arasne thought for a moment. "Because this isn't something you can wave away or ignore. Or if you do, then your paladin will have to learn to bear it, too. And all that comes with it."

"All that comes with it?"

The Queen cocked her head. "Surely you understand, Zavrius. Your brother won't. . .he won't accept a Prime with ties to you. That's what your paladin wants, isn't it? That's what you've said?"

Zavrius stared at her. He felt his body wither like her words had the power to undo him completely, make him deteriorate.

"I don't know why I came here," he lied, raising a hand to wipe at his nose. Something in him gave up.

His mother said nothing for a long while. She glanced up at the ceiling. "I won't tell you what to do. But you should ask your paladin what he wants more, and honor that choice."

These words skewered Zavrius through the heart. He wanted to say, *I know what he wants more*, wanted to stand there in his confidence that Balen would choose him. The truth curdled in his stomach, and he backed away clumsily to the door. "Yes. Yes, I'll ask."

He pushed out of the study, gasped for air, and clawed for relief as he pushed toward the exit to the Royal Apartments. Even outside them, the air felt too thick, too wet with his fear. Zavrius tried to conjure calm. The next thing he knew, he was standing in the gardens and breathing hard, each breath dragging in the sickly-sweet scent from the magnitude of florals surrounding him. He slumped back against the gedrok and let himself cry.

When he found he could think without bursting into tears, he wiped his cheeks and thought to himself. Here, he was expecting the worst, and perhaps Balen would change his mind and decide what they had was worth the same as a long-held childhood dream.

But Zavrius was smarter than that.

He got up. The hot sun had given way to a chilly afternoon, and when he squinted through the overgrown hedges, he saw the paladins were packing up. He thought about Theo. His brother would have heard by now. It didn't leave him much time.

He took himself and only himself—not with the crutch of an instrument in tow—and planted himself by the barracks. He needed to talk to Balen. They would figure it out together. Half an hour after this decision had been made, a sea of chatter wafted towards him, and he straightened. The first paladin who saw him bowed, and this action was mirrored by everyone who passed by him. "Prince Zavrius, Prince Zavrius." His name like a song. But at the end of the line, there was no Balen of Westgar.

Zavrius stiffened and stood up straighter. He saw one of the last paladins try to hide a pitying glance in his direction and flushed as he kicked off the wall. Zavrius walked aimlessly, undirected, trying to suppress the chill that ran through his body. For all his attempts at calm, his mind was a mess, now. Where was he? Where was Balen?

"Your brother called him away."

Zavrius spun back to the voice. The sheepish paladin bowed lower, responding to Zavrius' hard stare with greater deference. "My prince. I heard mention of the war room."

Zavrius hated how transparent he was; this paladin had seen through him, and found him to be a spongy, shivering mess of a man. "Thank you," he said, and he went.

He did not run even as his mind galloped ahead of him. Zavrius walked easily, with all the fear and concern in his body fading as a stony certainty filled up the fleshy cavity around his heart. The war room sat in the eastern wing of the palace, close to the barracks, and so it took only a few minutes for Zavrius to reach it. The door was distinguished from all others by being painted a dark blue-black, its handle marked out in gold. Zavrius pressed his ear to the wood, but no sound could pierce that thick door.

He'd never been in here. As far as he knew, it had been locked his whole life. Tentatively, he reached out and opened the door as quietly as he could. The hinges did not betray him. The door opened silently, and faint voices came to him. Zavrius slipped inside and closed the door behind him.

The war room was a windowless expanse sequestered centrally in the palace. Very little light burned in this room, which he was grateful for. The shadows fell like heavy rain and storm clouds, so the few lit candles could do little to drive them off. It allowed Zavrius to stand there without fear of being seen.

A large round table took up the front portion of the room. A map detailing Usleth, the Rezwyn Empire, and Western nations lay spread on it. Then, the room had been divided by a heavy velvet curtain that was pulled aside and tied off to an ornamental frame that delineated the space. There, in the back, stood two figures. The floor-to-ceiling bookshelves were packed with manuscripts, treaties, scrolls, letters on war and strategy, and various wartime correspondence.

The figures pored over a book together. Zavrius' heart wrenched.

A lounge lay by the door, and Sirellius had slept there often in the worst of times and before he left for that final fatal battle. Not knowing what to do with himself, Zavrius lowered himself onto the red velvet and stared across the room.

The light made things dreamlike. The fog of unreality fell upon the young prince as he stared. One figure turned, the bulk unmistakable, and the light cast from the candle exposed him with a prismatic rainbow sheen that faded a second later. Theo's voice sounded louder now. More confident than it had been when Zavrius first walked in.

"I am sorry to put you in this position."

"My prince, it is not your fault."

"You're very promising, you see. Very promising. Lestr says so. Hisud, too. And so I'd hate to see that talent go to waste. You could be a wonderful prime. There's no guarantee, naturally—you'd have to work hard. But I could see you winning the tournament when it comes down to it."

Balen said nothing. Zavrius waited with his breath held.

"Forgive me, my prince. I'm a paladin. My body is a lot stronger than my mind. I don't quite. . .understand what it is you're saying."

"I think you do know, young Balen," Theo murmured. For good measure, he cocked his head and lay a hand on Balen's shoulder. "I think you need to choose yourself. Which is more important to you? Your future, or. . ."

He didn't specify the second option. Zavrius had wanted him to—to define Zavrius either as his brother, as a hole for Balen to use, or as something else altogether. But that would have required a deeper understanding of Balen and Zavrius' relationship, and since Theo lacked that context, he'd opted to say nothing at all.

But couldn't Balen see that? The game was so obvious that Zavrius wanted to laugh. How easy it was to drive a wedge between what they'd had. He almost couldn't understand it.

"I don't know what I'm being offered," Balen said carefully.

"I could train you. Hisud, too. Personally."

Zavrius' stomach dropped. Theo only had an interest in Balen because of what he meant to Zavrius. Why? Or better yet, *how?* How could his brother hold this much hate in his heart for him? Zavrius clenched the swordbreaker at his side. He'd taken to wearing Balen's gift as a reminder of the other man's love. Now, he wanted to unsheathe it and stab the sharp tip into his brother's windpipe.

Zavrius stood up loudly. He had the satisfaction of watching them both startle. In perfect synchronicity, their silhouettes whipped around to face him.

"Zavrius?" they said together.

Zavrius felt like a comet as he walked towards them, his fire inevitable, and the crash fatal. Theo took three steps away to give him room to face Balen, but it was his brother Zavrius wanted to confront.

"Shall I walk you out?" he gestured with his head towards the door, and Theo followed graciously. Over his brother's shoulder, he saw Balen staring, grip on whatever book Theo had given him firm and unyielding.

"What are you doing?" he hissed to Theo.

"Giving him a choice. You backed him into a corner."

"*I* did?" Zavrius snapped.

"Zavrius. I need you to listen very carefully to me." His brother took him by the shoulders and Zavrius went rigid. His brother looked wretched up close. "You need to put this to bed. For the good of Usleth, you need to let him go."

"I don't understand why it matters." Zavrius' voice had gone embarrassingly high, and he glanced away before Theo could relish in it. His heart cracked; why couldn't he love Balen in peace? Why did it matter so much?

"Because you are a prince. You're a Dued Vuuthrik. And he is a paladin. Both of you have a duty; a duty to this country and to the Queen, and neither of you can fulfill that duty when you are distracted with the other."

"I'm not distra—"

"Look what happens to him when he has to spend half his energy combatting rumors. Look what happens to you—you've given up on your administrative tasks. I've heard letters are piling up on your desk unanswered. You don't get the luxury of avoiding this because you like what he can do to your body. There will be others."

He sounded so sincere. Zavrius found his resolve slipping. "Do you really believe that?" he asked, like Theo would suddenly decide to be truthful.

"I do."

"And you get no satisfaction in seeing me miserable?"

Zavrius chanced a look at him now. Theo's eyes were dark. Zavrius said, "He is fearful. He doesn't know you like I do. But I can smell what you're doing, Theo, I know you want me to suffer. I don't understand what I ever did to deserve your ire, but—"

A hand clasped around Zavrius' throat. He gasped as the air was choked out of him. Theo's eyes were burning and bright.

"If you want any chance of surviving one week past the death of our mother, you will learn to do as you are told."

Zavrius kicked weakly. His eyes began to strain in their sockets. He sent Balen a panicked look, but Theo had positioned them in a way Zavrius couldn't even see the paladin's shadow.

"Pl—ease," he gasped. He didn't know what he was begging for.

"I will not let my fucking country be tainted by your impropriety. I will not let you continue to sully our family name. Leave him. Or let him leave you. Then, you will focus on making yourself worthy. Do you understand me?"

Zavrius nodded and collapsed against his brother when Theo let go. A strangely comforting hand reached into his hair and pressed him close.

"There, there. That's it," Theo cooed as Zavrius caught his rasping breath. "Think on it, won't you?"

He slipped free of Zavrius and left, leaving Balen and Zavrius alone in the room.

Zavrius swayed on his feet. He could have said something to Balen. He could have cried out, announced what Theo had done. And what if Balen did nothing? What if Balen took one look at Zavrius and said, *I serve the throne. Theo will be king.*

Zavrius stayed silent. The brief burst of humiliation and fear gave way to a fruitless anger. He turned towards Balen, walking close. "What book did he give you?"

As Zavrius got closer, the light around Balen glowed. The paladin glanced down at the book in his hands, visibly swallowing as he did. "*The History of Prime Paladins*."

"Your name could be in that book," Zavrius surmised. "That's what he said?"

Balen didn't answer.

"You've been avoiding me. Like a coward."

"Yes." And then, "I'm sorry."

"Are you?" Zavrius wheezed a laugh. He opened his hands. "Then why listen to my brother? Unless you mean to follow through."

Balen looked at him unblinkingly. Zavrius lowered his arms. "Don't leave me."

Regret swamped him the instant those words left his mouth. Balen said again, "I'm sorry," with no further explanation.

"You're taking him up on his offer?" Zavrius asked, pressing him for details. His hand flexed at his side. How pathetic—how *dare* Balen do this to him.

"I have to. Zavrius, I love you." He put the book down, dropped it from his hands, and laid those bare palms on Zavrius' shoulders like Theo had. "I love you. I swear it. But I deserve the future I've wanted my whole life."

Could Zavrius fault him? Could he take away Balen's future? Could he live with himself if he tainted this perfect boy with all this courtly mess?

Balen was saying, "Maybe this doesn't have to be the end. Maybe in a few years, we could—"

"When Theo is king, I will be dead."

Balen's hands slipped. "Don't say that."

He thought Zavrius was being dramatic. The prince found he had no energy to correct Balen's misunderstanding. What he did have was anger, a multitude of it, a long stream of black energy circling in his veins. He didn't know what he was doing, but he drew the sword-breaker from its sheath and raised it, shaking in Balen's direction.

Balen looked at it, then back to him. He stepped back, hands hovering in the air. "Zav?"

"Don't call me that," Zavrius hissed. His hand shook. "I am Prince Zavrius Dued Vuuthrik, son of Queen Arasne. Never call me that stupid nickname again."

Balen nodded quietly. His eyes were wide. Quickly, Zavrius lost the shape of him to blurred vision—no. No, he wouldn't cry. He sniffled and raised both the dagger and his chin.

"I should give you this back," Zavrius said after a while. He must have looked a fool holding that dulled, serrated blade out like that. Quivering, he dropped his arm, but his grip on the hilt was vicelike. This had been a gift from Balen. It was his. Balen loved him. He didn't want to let that go.

He failed himself as one tear escaped his blockade. Shaking, he found himself saying, "Why?"

Why would you do this to me? Don't you understand what I gave you? More than my body, more than anything as simple as virginity: I gave you my trust. The great complex being of it, all the convoluted tendrils of my title, my responsibilities, my standing—let alone who I am beyond all that. I gave all of it to you; I wanted everything with you. I saw it all playing out, and I believed you. But Theo is first once again. Theo, who corrupts everything of mine. Only this time, you're the one who's chosen him.

Zavrius said none of it. Too much had been taken from him. He'd already been exposed in ways he'd never intended to be, and the great wounds left over from that vulnerability were still oozing blood. Another blow and he might crumble for good, so he couldn't give Balen another chance to hurt him.

Zavrius stepped back. He felt shuddering from the recesses of his mind a barrier, crashing down like a portcullis and sealing off this weak weeping part of him that had trusted a boy. He sheathed the sword breaker and breathed slow and deep.

"Balen," he whispered.

"Yes?" Balen said. Then, belatedly, the next words chased away the last strand of hope Zavrius had. "Prince Zavrius?"

"I think you'll make a wonderful Prime Paladin one day."

Epilogue

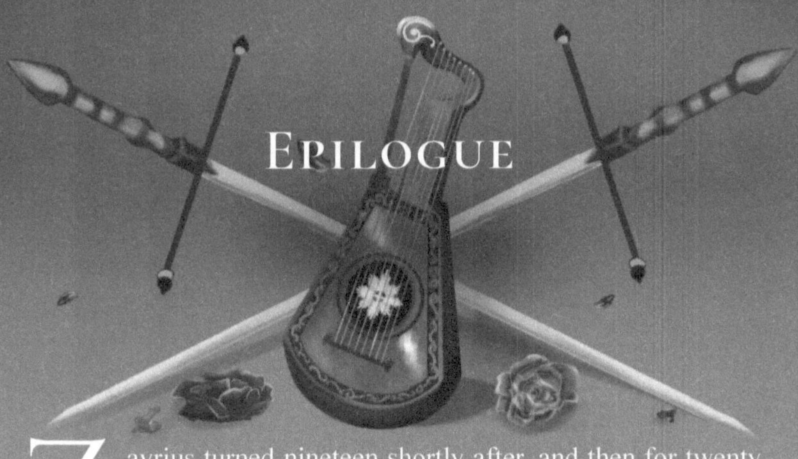

Zavrius turned nineteen shortly after, and then for twenty what seemed like mere weeks after that. By that age, all of this felt like a scabbed-over wound, but Zavrius never dared to test that theory by allowing himself to love another.

His focus went into his work. Into study. Into training with both lute-harp and dagger. Not, as Theo wanted, for the sake of Usleth, but for the sake of himself. It would not be enough to skirt by on nothing but his name. Zavrius Dued Vuuthrik needed to be brilliant. And it was easier this way, without his heart holding someone else.

But at night, on most nights, he would feel himself in free-fall, waiting to be caught—either by someone else or by the ground rushing up to meet him. Zavrius could feel it as certain as anything: a call to be more, a call to *allow* himself to be more. Sometimes, he would dream of soft nights and warm embraces, and his body would relax in the throes of nostalgia, and every waking moment was painful. But not always.

In truth, beneath the layers of distance and apathy, a pull like that of gedrok ichor lived inside him.

Zavrius' heart remained wanting. And Balen of Westgar remained beautiful to him.

ZAVRIUS AND BALEN'S STORY CONTINUES IN 'REFORGED'

END

Acknowledgments

Crucible wasn't supposed to happen.

I'd said—many times—that the *World of Reforged* series would end with *Reclaimed*. As far as I knew, that was true. But then I started thinking about young Zavrius and Balen, about the weight of their doomed love story—one that *Reforged* readers already knew could never last (else, how could there be a *Reforged*?).

So, I started writing *Crucible* in a serialized format, releasing a chapter a week to my Patreon backers. When the novel was complete, I saw an opportunity: Kickstarter. A chance to control a project from start to finish, to manage every creative aspect. Perhaps I even missed the chaos of video game production (though, mercifully, not middle management). I spent months planning, and I loved every second of it.

But I was anxious. Anxious about the project itself, and especially about the book's more intimate, lower-stakes focus—so different from the grand political machinations of later installments. Would my readers care? Would it resonate?

Clearly, I had forgotten who you all are.

Within an hour, *Crucible* was fully funded.

I've been published before, but watching in *real time* as my readership rallied behind this book was something else entirely—humbling, exhilarating, and deeply moving.

So, to those who made this possible:

To **Drew McBlain**, my editor, who endured my anxious ramblings about whether this book (or, in fact, everything I'd ever written) was terrible. Thank you for wading through my waffle and helping me carve out *Crucible*.

To my **early readers and Patrons**, thank you for catching typos, for your insightful questions, and for your ongoing support —your patronage made this book possible in the first place.

To my **friends**, thank you for tolerating my rising panic as the Kickstarter launch loomed. And thank you for laughing at me when it funded effortlessly. I deserved that.

To **Bronte-Marie Wesson**, for your time, your platforming, and your unwavering support. I'm so grateful we've been able to grow as authors together.

To my **partner, Beau**—for everything.

To **Maeve MacLysaght**, my agent, and **Nicole Kimberling**, editor and publisher of *Reforged*—thank you for blessing this endeavor and for jumping on calls to help me navigate logistics.

To the **manufacturers and artisans** who collaborated on this project—look at what we made! Thank you, eternally.

And finally, to **you, my readers**. Whether you grabbed this book through Kickstarter or picked it up later, I'm so lucky to have you. Enjoy Zavrius' pining.

Now, go forth and tell the world how much you *loved Crucible*. Or at least, lie convincingly.

With gratitude (and much caffeine),
Seth Haddon

About the Author

Seth Haddon is the queer Australian writer of Reforged, Reborn, and Reclaimed. His sci fi debut *Volatile Memory* releases 2025 with Tordotcom. He is a video game designer and producer, has a degree in ancient history, and previously worked with cats. Some of his previous adventures include exploring Pompeii with a famous archaeologist and being chased through a train station by a nun.

instagram.com/sethhaddon

patreon.com/authorsethhaddon

youtube.com/@SethHaddon

tiktok.com/@sethhaddon